EVERY SECRET THING

ANN TATLOCK

CENTER POINT PUBLISHING
THORNDIKE, MAINE

This Center Point Large Print edition
is published in the year 2008 by arrangement with
Bethany House, a division of Baker Publishing Group.

Brief quotations taken from: "The Highwayman" by Alfred Noyes; *Look Homeward Angel* by Thomas Wolfe; *To The Lighthouse* by Virginia Woolf; "The Love Song of J. Alfred Prufrock" by T. S. Eliot; *Vanity Fair* by William Makepeace Thackeray; *Our Town* by Thornton Wilder, © 1938, 1965 by the Wilder Family LLC; *Moments of Being* by Virginia Woolf, Jeanne Schulkind (ed.): Harcourt, Brace Jovanovich, New York and London, 1976.

The text of this Large Print edition is unabridged. In other aspects,
this book may vary from the original edition.
Printed in the United States of America.
Set in 16-point Times New Roman type.

ISBN: 978-1-60285-170-2

Library of Congress Cataloging-in-Publication Data

Tatlock, Ann.
Every secret thing / Ann Tatlock.--Center Point large print ed.
p. cm.
ISBN 978-1-60285-170-2 (lib. bdg. : alk. paper)
1. Women teachers--Fiction. 2. Preparatory school teachers--Fiction. 3. Christian fiction.
4. Large type books. I. Title.

PS3570.A85E84 2008
813'.54--dc22

2007049298

To
my English teacher at
Sanford School, Hockessin, Delaware
Bea Cope
because I think you too
have known those
moments of being.

PROLOGUE

The first thing I want you to know is that there really is a state called Delaware.

You see, when I left home to go away to college in the Midwest, I discovered I had spent my whole life in a place that most people were only vaguely aware of. "So where are you from?" I was asked time and again, and time and again when I replied, "I'm from Delaware," the response I got was, "What state is that in?"

No, no, no. You see, Delaware isn't *in* a state; it *is* a state. It was and is, in fact, the First State—so says the license plate of every car owned by every Delawarean. One of the thirteen original colonies, Delaware earned its rank as number one when, on December 7, 1787, it was the first state to approve the United States Constitution. Now, there's something to be said for that, isn't there? Delaware was a state before most other states were so much as a twinkle in the government's eye.

So, you might ask, if it led this country into nationhood, why is it we never hear anything about this state called Delaware? Good question. One I've often pondered myself. Did it accomplish this one historic act, and then sit back to rest on its laurels? I mean, let's face it. Delaware seldom makes the headlines, seldom makes the national news at all, save for those instances when a certain senator stirs up the waters in Washington with one biting partisan remark or another. But most people just ignore that kind of thing. I know I do.

When I was a child, a Bible passage I heard in Sunday school always made me think of Delaware. It was the story in the Gospel of John where Philip goes and finds Nathanael to tell him they've found the Messiah, the one Moses and the prophets wrote about. This should be good news for a couple of Jewish fellows, right? But oddly enough, the man is Jesus of Nazareth, son of Joseph. Instead of rejoicing because the Messiah has come, Nathanael is appalled to think he came from Nazareth, that haven for the Roman army, persecutors of the Jews. And so Nathanael cries out, "Can any good thing come out of Nazareth?"

Those words stuck with me until my impish mind tweaked the question, turning it around to become, "Can anything *at all* come out of *Delaware?*"

While growing up, my best friend Natalie and I dubbed our home state Dullaware. To us it was The Place Where Nothing Ever Happens. We did, however, think that people outside our state at least knew we existed. That crushing realization was saved for later.

It might be that Delaware is largely overlooked because of its size. In spite of the idealistic promotional slogan selling the state as a Small Wonder, the epithet nevertheless exposes Delaware for what it is: just a little slip of land, too pint-sized a place even to have its own commercial airport. To fly to Delaware you have to land in Philadelphia, or maybe Newark, New Jersey, or even Dulles Airport in Washington, but you don't land in Delaware proper unless you're in a private jet or a military plane. It might be said—only partly in jest, I suppose—that there is simply no place to put the runway. Consider the old joke of road travelers: "Delaware. If you blink, you miss it."

It's true that lengthwise, Delaware measures only eighty-five miles. And the width—well, the southern end of the state is the widest part and that's only thirty-five miles. Farther north, just below Wilmington where I grew up, the state is eight miles wide. Eight miles!

"Hey, want to hike across the state?"

"Sure. There's nothing better to do until supper."

I know, I know. It doesn't look promising. You just don't hear of people saving up for their dream vacation to Delaware or grabbing up land to retire there. You don't hear of people talking up its splendors in such a way that everyone longs to experience the place for himself.

When it comes to Delaware, you don't really hear much of anything.

But then, you have to consider, the state itself is not so different from most of us, is it? Think about it. You, me, that person down the street—we're all here, just as real as the next person, living out a life as real as any other life, and yet, unless you're as influential as New York or as big as Texas, very few people know that you exist, or that I exist, or that anyone exists beyond a vague knowing that there are "other people out there."

Can anything good come out of such a life?

In the same way Philip answered Nathanael's question about the good that can arise out of so doubtful a place, I can only invite you to come and see.

CHAPTER 1

I have lived in half a dozen states—in the Midwest, the South, along the Eastern Seaboard—but nowhere have I seen the evening light the way it appears on summer nights in Delaware. I struggle to tell you what it looks like, and chances are I won't succeed. That light is one of the few things I've come across that may actually be ineffable—that is, beyond the scope of human language. And that's because it doesn't appear to be light at all so much as it seems simply to be a sigh of contentment, as though the earth itself has let off a breath of satisfaction.

Wherever I went, wherever I lived over the years, I remembered that light. As a child, I let it cover me with its warmth, and in that light I first sensed the very real presence of the eternal.

Within the first week of my return to Delaware, that particular light showed up to welcome me. I was sitting at the dining room table in the faculty house called Pine Glen on the campus of Seaton Preparatory School. Books, index cards, loose papers, and piles of lesson plans covered the length of the table as I prepared for the classes that would begin in a few days. I had been teaching for years, and yet the mounds of paper in front of me appeared as insurmountable as a range of snowcapped mountains. Not only was I nearly overcome by feelings of inadequacy, but just being back at Seaton—now as a teacher rather than a student—flooded me with a confusing ambivalence. This was a place that I had once so loved and yet so hated, a place that had once so kindly nurtured me, yet filled me with an agonizing fear.

I was feeling some of that same fear—and it was leaning toward regret at having come back—when I lifted my face toward the breeze drifting in through the open window. That certain familiar twilight was circling the pine trees outside like a contented cat, and as had happened before, something broke in upon my dread, and I was comforted. For several minutes I didn't move because I didn't want that feeling to fade. I had not known it for a very long time.

When I was young, I called such instances my *moments of being*. I stole that expression from the novelist Virginia Woolf, and I admit that I did so without compunction. For one thing, no one knew about my moments of being, including Virginia Woolf herself, who was dead. And for another thing, and maybe more importantly, what she and I meant by moments of being were two entirely different things.

I lowered my head to the papers again. Before I could get back to work, though, my thoughts were interrupted by a car pulling up in front of the old clapboard house that was Pine Glen. I wasn't expecting company and couldn't imagine who might be stopping by past eight o'clock in the evening. I stepped uneasily to the window and peered out at a pale blue Honda Accord coming to a stop in the circular drive. The front door of the car eased open, and the driver emerged, and in the moment of recognition I felt as though I really had finally come home to Delaware. Walking up the pebbled path to my door was my lifelong friend Natalie Primrose. *No,* I thought, shaking my head, *it's Natalie Fraley, remember?* Twenty years since I was her bridesmaid, and would I still not remember to call her by her married name?

I met her at the door, arms wide, and we laughed as we greeted each other with a long and joyous hug.

"I can't believe you're here, Beth," she cried as she pulled back to look at me.

"I can hardly believe it myself," I said. "Come on in."

She stepped inside and looked around. "Imagine you living in Pine Glen. I can't believe it," she said again.

"Well, it's true. Believe it or not, here I am. Teaching English at Seaton Prep."

"Teaching? You look exactly the same as when you were a student here!"

I laughed out loud. "Except that I've got twelve fewer inches of hair and several dozen wrinkles that I didn't have then."

"No way, Beth. You look great—"

"So do you, Nat—"

"—and I like your hair shorter and wavy like that. How do you stay so thin? Look at me, carrying twenty pounds more than I should."

"Yeah, well, you've had three kids. I haven't."

"Still . . ." She shook her head. "How long has it been since I last saw you? Fifteen years?"

"Something like that. Maybe more. Way too long, that's all I know."

"I hope you don't mind my just dropping by. Maybe I should have called ahead—"

"Of course not!"

"—but I couldn't wait to see you. Figures we'd be out of town with the in-laws when you arrived—"

"When did you get back?"

"Just this afternoon. I told Ron and the kids they were on their own for the rest of the evening, and I jumped in the car and took off."

"I'm glad you did. Come on in and have a seat. Can I get you anything to drink? Coffee? Soda?"

"Nothing, thanks. I won't stay long. Hey, it looks like you've lived here for years. How'd you get unpacked so fast?"

"Well, I've been here for almost a week already. Still, you should see the upstairs. Boxes everywhere."

I motioned her into the living room, but before she had gone three steps, she stopped. "Wow," she said. I watched her eyes move across the bookcases that lined the walls of the room. "This isn't a house; it's a library. I've never seen so many books all in one place."

I shrugged. "Yeah, I guess I've picked up a few over the years. Once I have them, I can't seem to part with them."

"You always did like to read, I know, but . . ." She stopped and offered me a lopsided smile. "Well, books are probably more useful than my collection of ceramic cows. All they do is sit there looking silly. But I can't help it; I like them."

She took a seat in the wing chair by the fireplace and used the footstool to prop up one foot while the other foot stayed on the floor. I sat down on the couch across from her and tucked my feet beneath me.

"I have to say, Pine Glen looks a whole lot better than when the Buckleys lived here," she said. "Remember all that black suede furniture and those fuzzy psychedelic glow-in-the-dark posters they had on the walls? Talk about a lack of taste. And him an artist! This room looked like a cross between a funeral parlor and a really bad acid trip."

"How could I forget!" I laughed.

We were familiar with the Buckleys' décor because they had often hosted groups of students in their home on weekends. We all pitched in for pizza, then sat around talking about art and pop literature and the tunes of the Top 40 Countdown. Sometimes some of the kids brought their guitars, and we sat around singing songs by Cat Stevens and Jim Croce and Dan Fogelberg. Natalie and I came to these gatherings occasionally because her first love was art and Mr. Buckley was the upper school art teacher. His wife taught social studies and history in the middle school. Those were the daytime school-approved get-togethers at the Buckleys'. What the school authorities didn't know about were the late-night unauthorized get-togethers that Natalie and I only heard rumors of through the student grapevine. Apparently the Buckleys grew their own marijuana on a windowsill in one of the upstairs bedrooms, the yield of which they shared freely—if quietly—with certain members of the student body.

"But then, good grief," I went on, "it was the seventies! When you think about it, the Buckleys were really just a couple of hippies trying to make a living."

"Sure, I know. I liked them—I'm not saying I didn't—I just think, in hindsight, that Stan Buckley wouldn't have been my first choice for a high school art teacher. What were they thinking when they hired him? Talented or not, if any of my kids' teachers invited them over for late-night pot parties . . ." She finished the sentence by shaking her head.

"Yeah, pretty wild, I know. But the kids would have been smoking pot anyway, with or without the Buckleys' homegrown stash. There was plenty of that stuff around."

"No kidding. And somehow we missed it all and had a good time anyway."

I smiled at my old friend. "Not that we were perfect, of course."

"Goodness no."

"I mean, don't you remember—?" I stopped and looked at her. I had almost asked her if she didn't remember the two of us sneaking across campus at night, heading toward faculty Cabin 1, where some of our friends were already waiting for us. But, on second thought, I didn't want to bring it up.

"Remember what?"

“Oh, nothing.” I shrugged my shoulders and tried to pass it off with a small laugh.

“Well, anyway,” she said, “I’m just so glad you’re here.”

“I am too. So tell me, how’s life?”

“Good. Things are good. The kids are doing great, staying healthy. How about you?”

“I’m fine, I guess. A little nervous about school starting in a couple of days.”

Suddenly Natalie’s face collapsed into a picture of concern. I was about to assure her that I was always nervous at the start of a school year and that I’d soon get over it, but her mind was on something else.

“What about Nick?” she asked hesitantly.

Nick Watson. The man I had left behind in Maryland when I accepted the position here at Seaton.

“It’s over,” I said.

“There’s no hope at all?”

“No.” I tried to smile, but the best I could offer was an uncertain tremor at the corners of my mouth. “I couldn’t get him to commit. After three years, when I told him I wanted to move forward or break it off, he dawdled for a while and then just kind of drifted away.” I didn’t have to go into detail; Natalie knew most of the story already through e-mails and phone calls.

“I’m sorry, Beth,” she said quietly.

I waved a hand nonchalantly. “You know me. Unlucky in love.”

When she didn’t respond, an uneasy silence fell over

the room. I found myself groping for words to fill the void. "Hey, do you keep up with the old gang at all?" I finally asked, trying to sound cheerful.

"Umm, no. Not really. Last I heard, Janie was still up in Rochester working for some sort of chemical company. I don't know if you knew, but her husband left her a couple years back."

I nodded. "Yeah, she told me about it in a Christmas card."

"After almost twenty years together too." She clicked her tongue and sighed at the thought of Janie's failed marriage.

But I didn't want to talk about that. "What about the guys?" I asked.

She frowned in thought. "I've been really bad about keeping up with people. As far as I know, Ken's in Washington doing something or other with the government. I saw a notice in the alumni magazine about him once, saying he was married and had a couple of kids. At the time he was working as a lobbyist, I think—out there trying to persuade politicians to see things his way."

"Sounds like Ken."

"Yeah. And Ray—he's a doctor. I know that much for sure. He's over at Wilmington General, if I'm remembering right. I saw him briefly at the twentieth reunion but haven't seen him since."

"I remember hearing that he'd gone on to med school. I always knew he'd do well."

"Yeah, no question there."

"It's too bad we haven't kept in better touch. After the tenth reunion I never got back here again to visit, not even for homecoming. There didn't seem to be much reason to visit Delaware after Dad retired and the folks moved to North Carolina."

"Come back for homecoming?" Natalie said with a laugh. "I live right here in Hockessin, and I've hardly been to any of the reunions myself. Life just gets busy."

"That it does."

She was quiet a moment, then said, "Oh, and Artie! Apparently he's fallen off the face of the earth. The alumni office is trying to update its records, and no one can find him."

"Maybe he really did go off to the Belgian Congo to become a mercenary. Remember how he used to always talk about that?"

"He was one crazy kid."

"Yeah. But then, weren't we all?"

There were six of us in the old gang that hung out together in upper school. Three boys and three girls. The group congealed early in the eleventh grade when Mr. Fossett, the chemistry teacher, mysteriously failed to show up for class one morning. It was the period right before lunch, so with a couple of hours on our hands, five of us responded when Raymond Schmidt asked, "Anyone want to grab lunch at Burger King?" Ray drove a souped-up Camaro to school, and it was that car the six of us piled into, risking barn duty for the sake of Whoppers and fries. Ray had connections of sorts, since he was the great-nephew of the school's assistant headmaster, John Pettingill. Ray figured if we got caught leaving campus during school hours, we could go to his uncle and talk our way out of trouble. I wasn't so sure. Pettingill was known around campus as Commander because of his stint as a navy flyer during the Second World War. The product of military training in wartime, Commander generally ran a tight ship at Seaton and didn't put up with any nonsense. But I wasn't about to miss out on this midday adventure, even if it meant cleaning out the horse stalls later as punishment. So off we went to the strip of fast-food joints on Kirkwood Highway, returning right before fifth-period class without having piqued the suspicion of any of the staff. We pulled into campus high on sugar and saturated fat, laughing hysterically over the cardboard Burger King crowns we came back wearing. We were easily entertained in those days and found laughter in just about anything.

After that excursion it was understood that those of us who ventured out that day were a clan of sorts, bound to do everything together, as indivisible as a couple going steady, except we were six instead of two. We even gave our group a name, calling ourselves the Barbarians. As I remember, we chose the name after a history lecture in which Mr. Flint quoted someone as saying, "The future belongs to the barbarians." Surely that was us, wasn't it?

In addition, calling ourselves the Barbarians just seemed incredibly funny at the time. Most likely because no epithet could have been further from the truth.

We were a bunch of straight-laced kids, bookish, mostly clean-cut, out for the A, and all headed for college. We never got into any real trouble, never dabbled in drugs, knew nothing of sex beyond an occasional game of spin the bottle. We were the parents' dream in the ongoing nightmare of the sixties and seventies counterculture.

On graduation day, Raymond Schmidt and Jane Kidder shared the stage as class valedictorians. All of us were honored with awards—Ray and Janie for leadership and scholastic achievement, Arthur Sochs for his skills in mathematics, Ken Cunningham for his work on student government, Natalie Primrose for art and design, and me—I won the award I had long coveted, the Frank P. Milne Literary Award.

Oh, the future was ours, wasn't it?

But even on that day, in the midst of our accomplishment, in the midst of celebration, there was for four of us a certain melancholy that overshadowed all else. There was something left undone—no, something left unknown—and it gnawed at us like a cancer nibbling ever so slightly at someone's insides.

Now, all these years later, Natalie and I sat in the living room of Pine Glen, moving from vague memories of the past to talk of the present—her freelance artwork, her children, my new position as English teacher at Seaton Preparatory School. Before we knew it, night had settled in, and at ten o'clock she rose to leave. We stood, and in that moment I felt the old ambivalence come over me again, that distant but very real sense of dread.

As we walked across the room, I asked, as if on sudden impulse, "Do you ever think about Mr. Dutton?"

She gave me an incredulous look, as though I had asked the unthinkable. But then she laughed—actually laughed—and said, "Heavens no. Why on earth would I think about him?"

She hugged me then and dashed to her car, waving. She left with a toot of her horn and the spinning of tires on the gravel drive.

She must have made her peace with it, then. I never did. I had tried to forget, but I found myself unable to erase the memory. It lessened over the years, of course, becoming a dull and intermittent ache, but still I went on wondering. There seemed to be no clear answer to the mystery that was Theodore Dutton, with all the whys left dangling before me like fruit gone bad on the vine.

CHAPTER 2

I like to tell people I went to school in a barn—which is very nearly a true statement, though of course it must be qualified. What was known on campus as Heath Hall had originally been a barn until it was converted into a three-story classroom building in 1930. They brought in chalkboards and desks and chairs. They carpeted the stairs while leaving the classroom floors a bare hardwood. They slapped some steel fire escapes on either side of the structure to meet the safety codes of the time. Finally, they painted the whole thing white, and after that there was very little about the building that was barnlike, except that the silo had been left intact, and with flooring and plumbing added, it became the bathrooms.

It was a lovely place, really, this school that I attended and from which I graduated in 1977. Seaton Preparatory School was nestled on eighty-one acres of former farmland in Hockessin, Delaware. I'm not sure of all that the farm produced, but I do know there were apple orchards on the land because some of the trees survived, and between classes we would pick the ripest apples and eat them.

The original farmhouse was a large Victorian, and when the Seaton family purchased the farm with the idea of starting a school, the house was redone to suit that purpose. The first floor ultimately housed the school's main offices and cafeteria. Music was taught on the second floor, and for many years Mr. Barrister, the French teacher, lived alone in the small apartment on the third floor. Whenever the cooks grilled onions in the cafeteria, Mr. Barrister complained of his eyes watering.

From these first two original buildings, the school grew and expanded over the years to include numerous classroom buildings, dormitories, gymnasiums, faculty housing, athletic fields, tennis courts, a swimming pool, two stables and a riding ring, and down in the valley beyond the headmistress's house, a chapel named for one of Seaton's students killed in the Second World War.

I suppose you might think it was a school for children from wealthy families, but this wasn't necessarily so. True, I can think of at least one student from upstate New York who arrived on campus every semester in a chauffeured limousine. But once he was there, he was subject to dorm life and campus chores just like every other boarding student. I remember seeing him carrying trash and raking leaves, as part of Seaton's philosophy was not to pamper students but to teach them discipline and cooperation through helping to maintain the school grounds. Oddly enough, most of these chores were carried out on the weekends, making day students exempt and helping to create a schism between those who lived on campus and those who didn't. Not that friendships didn't form across that line, because they did. But it was no secret that boarders looked upon day students with a certain envy, wishing they too could go home at night to a house instead of a dorm, a family instead of a roommate.

Every year the dorms were filled with students from any number of states as well as from around the world. During the years I was there, I knew kids from Europe, Asia, the Caribbean, and the Middle East. In the 1970s we had quite an influx of boys from Iran trying to escape the draft. They had connections to America and enough money in the bank to get there. The student body was a “we are the world” mixture of whites, blacks, Orientals (as we called them then), Jews, Catholics, Protestants. You name it; we had it.

But I’m digressing. The point is that most of us who were students at Seaton came from ordinary middle-class families. Not a few, on scholarship, came straight from the working class. Seaton was not, by a long shot, the most prestigious school in Delaware, and it certainly was not the most expensive. The kids who really reeked of wealth attended Sterns Valley or Mencken Hill, and when we played their teams in field hockey or lacrosse, we knew we were considered inferior. But we didn’t care. Especially when we beat them.

I was myself from a middle-class family with a stay-at-home mom, a dad who worked as an engineer for DuPont, and two sisters who stood on either side of me in age. We lived two miles from Seaton, so I was a day student, driven to school by my father in the morning and picked up by my mother in the afternoon—an arrangement that lasted until I was old enough to drive myself my senior year.

Along with my sisters, I attended public school until I was twelve years old, but when I entered eighth grade, I was sent off on a different path and enrolled by my parents at Seaton. I credit this lucky happenstance to an earthworm. That may sound like another of my embellished statements, something along the lines of attending classes in a barn, but again, there is some truth to this.

To say I was a shy and quiet child would be an understatement. A skeletal, freckle-faced, red-haired kid who was afraid to so much as answer "Here" at roll call, I was a born target for class bullies. I attracted ridicule the way a citywide fire might attract a heat-seeking missile. By the time I was in seventh grade, I was crying myself to sleep every night while my parents paced the kitchen floor below, wondering what to do.

And then came the morning when some kid whose name I didn't even know got on the bus and threw an earthworm in my face. When my mother learned of this—because, of course, I told her—she threw up her hands and exclaimed to my dad, "Really, Ed, I think this is the final straw." The next thing I knew, I was touring Seaton as a prospective student while the middle school principal told my folks happily, "We know your daughter will do well here."

Sometimes I wonder how my life might have been different had it not been for that earthworm. Overall, I count my years at Seaton as a blessing, but still, a person can't help but wonder.

CHAPTER 3

The view from the window where I stood in Heath Hall was of the farmhouse—called Anderson Hall—and the Green where the amphitheater is. That's where we sat on the day we graduated, on that shady stage in our long white gowns and dark formal suits, ready to go out and conquer the world.

I went out and stayed out for a long time, but I did not conquer the world. And then I came back.

I was questioning the wisdom of that particular decision as I stood there looking out at the Green. The dread hanging over me was more than the ordinary anxiety of starting a new school year. This dread had more to do with the school, with Seaton itself. It was a feeling that floated upward like gossamer from some deep place, and I knew exactly where that place was. So I was thankful when my thoughts were interrupted by a friendly voice. "How goes it, Elizabeth?" I turned to see Joel Sexton, my fellow English teacher, standing in the doorway to my classroom.

"Just fine," I replied, hoping I sounded upbeat.

He nodded and smiled. "The campus hasn't changed much, has it, since—when did you say you graduated?"

"Seventy-seven."

"Hasn't changed much since then, has it?"

"Very little," I agreed, "except for the barns and the riding program." The stables had been torn down, and the pastureland on the north side of campus, once used for riding, had been sold for development. What sat there now was a neighborhood of cul-de-sacs and pompous houses. The sale had kept Seaton going during a bumpy financial time in the late 1980s and had been necessary for the survival of the school. But that neighborhood was what I saw from my bedroom window in Pine Glen, and I most often kept the shade drawn against the change that time had brought.

“So,” I asked, “what do we hang over the kids’ heads now that we can’t threaten them with barn duty?”

Joel laughed. He obviously remembered the punishment of raking the muck out of the stables and whitewashing the stalls. Joel was once a student at Seaton himself, a half dozen years behind me. He was still in middle school by the time I graduated, so our paths never crossed on campus. But he too was destined to become a veteran of morning assembly when upper school principal, Mildred Bidney, read the announcements for the day. She stood at the podium with a pad of ruled paper and a perfectly sharpened pencil, and as she read, she tapped the podium with first the tip of the pencil and then the eraser, and then the tip and then the eraser. I’d watch the pencil turning pinwheels while Mrs. Bidney droned on, finally reaching the last dreaded announcement of the morning. At that point the pencil was stilled, laid to rest on the ledge of the podium while Mrs. Bidney flipped the page on the ruled pad. The time had come to read the names of the students who had earned themselves barn duty.

Our principal obviously relished the opportunity to make public that list of perpetrators. Slowly she worked her way down the list, pausing for several nerve-wracking seconds after calling out each name. She peered out over the rim of her glasses, her eyes roaming the room. A hush as thick as a London fog settled over the assembly as those same eyes landed, hawklike, upon the unfortunate bearer of the name.

Only the most defiant student dared to meet that gaze without dropping his head in shame.

"Oh yeah, good old Mildew," Joel said now, for that was what we called the principal behind her back. Mildew or Old Biddy, which we thought uproariously funny. Joel laughed again as though he had returned briefly to adolescence and then shook his head as the laughter trailed off to a satisfied sigh. "But you don't have to worry," he added. "Jack has his own ways of keeping the kids in line."

Jack Farrell, upper school principal since 1997, had succeeded the principal who had succeeded Mildred Bidney. Mildew had retired sometime in the 1980s, right around the time the barns were torn down. I don't think there was any connection, but I can't be certain about that.

"So, Elizabeth," Joel said, "ready for classes to start?"

"Ready as I'll ever be," I said, resorting to clichés. "By the way, you can call me Beth. It's easier."

"All right then, Beth."

I had invited him to call me Beth a couple times before, but each time he had reverted back to my full name. There was a bit of the absentminded professor about him, but he had a charming smile and was genuinely friendly, and I counted myself fortunate to be teaching with him. Seaton's student body remained small, and Joel and I were the only two English teachers in the upper school. We each had our own classroom on the second floor of Heath Hall, but we shared an office that once belonged to Beatrice Mann and Tom Goss and later Theodore Dutton, the teachers under whom I fell in love with literature and poetry.

The phone rang in that office now, and Joel left to answer it. I took another look around my classroom and, feeling satisfied with the seating arrangement, joined Joel in the office. He was well settled in, having been there six years, so that his half of the room was a slipshod collection of books, papers, and cardboard boxes of who-knew-what. I didn't bother to ask. My half of the office, including my desk, was neatly arranged, with books and supplies carefully in place. I intended to keep it that way. I always felt better when I was organized.

I sat at my desk while Joel talked to the invisible someone at the other end of the line. As I waited, I thought I could smell the thousand cigarettes once smoked within these walls. Between classes both Mrs. Mann and Mr. Goss would retreat to their desks and light up, so entering the room, one would literally walk into a cloud of tobacco smoke. We thought nothing of it at the time. Now Seaton School was a tobacco-free campus, with no smoking at all, anywhere. That would not have gone over well in the 1970s among faculty and students alike.

When Joel hung up, he looked greatly in need of a cigarette himself, though as far as I knew he didn't smoke. "That was my wife," he said. "She's just been talking with the insurance adjuster. We had another car end up in the living room a couple nights ago."

For a stunned moment I couldn't speak. How could a car end up in their living room? Finally I muttered, "What do you mean?"

He laughed lightly, and it sounded forced. "Now I know why the property was such a steal. We've been in the house only a year, and twice already we've been awakened by cars crashing through the front wall."

"You're kidding."

"I wish I were."

"What happens?"

"We live over by Hoopes Reservoir, on one of those steep winding roads." He looked at me to see if I was tracking. I nodded and he went on. "Our house is right on a curve and set just off the road."

"Oh?"

"You know what Hoopes is famous for."

I did know. Kids drinking. All around the reservoir were secluded areas where kids could park their cars and work their way through a few bottles of anything from Boone's Farm Apple Wine to Mad Dog 20/20. At least that's what they drank back in my day. I knew about it because my older sister had been up there once or twice when she was supposed to be somewhere else.

"So nights can be dangerous in that part of town," Joel went on.

"You mean cars have actually crashed through your front wall?"

He nodded. "First a Mustang and now a Buick. Both came to rest just short of the entertainment center. At least the TV and stereo system were spared. We've had to replace two couches though. Both were pretty much totaled on impact."

I was aghast at the thought. "Has anyone been hurt?"

"Only my wallet. So far."

"My goodness, Joel! Maybe you ought to move."

"I can't afford to move right now. Besides"—one corner of his mouth went up in a playful smile—"my kids kind of enjoy coming downstairs to find the living room rearranged. Todd calls it the ultimate extreme makeover."

"But just being in that house is dangerous, don't you think?"

"Well, we don't spend a whole lot of time in the living room, especially on Saturday nights. Both times we've had these unexpected guests, it's been on a Saturday night. Or actually, very early Sunday morning."

"And it was young kids out drinking."

He nodded again. "Both times. Well," he paused and looked at his watch, "I'm going to head on home—or back to what's left of it. See you tomorrow morning at the faculty meeting?"

"Yes, I'll be there."

"All right, then. Have a good night and stay out of trouble."

"Yeah, and you—stay out of the living room."

Joel grabbed his briefcase and, laughing, headed for the door.

When he was gone I stayed at my desk for a while going over some paper work. Overhead, the ceiling squeaked and moaned under the weight of someone's footsteps, interrupting my thoughts and pulling my attention to the single window in the office. On the cobbled path below, Jack Farrell moved along at his usual fast clip, apparently headed for Pratt Lodge, longtime residence of the upper school principal. As he walked, he offered a slight bow and a playful salute to an unsmiling Harlan Quinn, headmaster of Seaton School for some half a dozen years now. The cold shell around Harlan Quinn deflected most attempts at the social niceties. Undeterred, Jack went on to wave a friendly hand at Delia Simpkins, who worked as administrative assistant in the office directly below my feet. She was getting into her car, probably heading out for the day. She offered Jack a small ripple of her fingers in return.

I was becoming well acquainted with the life of the school. After several days of faculty meetings and staff socials, I had learned the names of the people who ran the wheels and cogs of Seaton Prep. And now, ready or not, it was time to get this machine going. I only wished I felt a little more ready.

CHAPTER 4

"Good morning, everyone."

I paused to smile. In return, twelve adolescent faces settled into question marks.

"My name is Elizabeth Gunnar." I pointed toward the board where I'd written my name in yellow chalk.

"Miss Gunnar," I emphasized. "Welcome to English Composition."

"Whatever," someone said quietly.

I looked around the room. I didn't know who had spoken and wasn't even certain whether it was a boy or a girl. I decided to let it slide.

"As you know, I'm replacing Mrs. Erickson, who welcomed . . . let's see—" I put on my reading glasses and picked up a piece of paper from my desk—"David Jasper Erickson on August eighth, eight pounds two ounces, twenty-one inches long. Mother and baby are doing fine."

This announcement was greeted with nods, smiles, and a number of comments ranging from "That's cool" to "What kind of name is Jasper?" and was finally punctuated with another decidedly disinterested, "Whatever."

"Before we begin the lesson, I'd like to go through the roll so I can start putting names to faces. You guys have it easy. You only have to learn one new name," I said, pointing toward the chalkboard again to indicate that name was mine. "But I have a hundred and sixteen students in upper school that I hope to become acquainted with by the end of the week."

I smiled again. The students stared at me. Their stares were neither malicious nor dull. These kids were merely waiting, watching to see what I would do.

"So let's see." The reading glasses went back on. I looked at the roll book. "Steven Aldridge? Where's Steven?"

A hand flew up. He was a clean-cut, neatly dressed boy, studious looking. "All right, Steven. Thank you. Alexis Cunningham?"

Another hand went up to the accompaniment of jingling bangles and bracelets. "I go by Lexy," she corrected me.

"Okay, Lexy." I made a note of that in the book.

Working my way down the list, I arrived, near the bottom, at the name of Satchel Queen. When I wrote the names in the roll book a few days earlier, I expected Satchel to be an African-American boy, perhaps named after the baseball player Satchel Paige. There were in fact a couple of black students in the class, but neither one of them answered to the name of Satchel Queen.

And that was because Satchel Queen was not a boy at all, but a girl, a pale-skinned girl with straight dark hair, a gold-plated hoop in each ear, and an expression on her face that told me she was the one who muttered "Whatever" at the beginning of class. In response to her name she didn't raise her hand, but rather raised an eyebrow, as though she were calling out a silent bid.

With that, I realized, suddenly, where my challenge lay. There was always one in every class. In this particular section of English Composition, it would be the girl named Satchel.

I finished calling the roll, then turned and picked up a piece of chalk, lifting it to the dark surface of the board. I intended to begin speaking about some basic rules of grammar, but when the chalk tapped against the board, the present disappeared, and I saw distinctly the man who stood on this very spot a lifetime ago writing his name in a tight, left-leaning script. When he finished, he turned and smiled at us and said, "Good morning, class. My name is Theodore Dutton." And with that, every female student there, myself included, was a little bit in love.

The past came rushing back so completely that when the present returned, I didn't recognize the hand as my own, that hand suspended in the air, pressing the chalk against the board.

How old it looks, I thought, the knuckles enlarged, the skin beginning to fold in tiny wrinkles.

I was not old, only middle-aged, and yet I could well imagine how I looked to the fresh and scarcely blooming youths seated at the desks behind me. They saw the strands of gray among the reddish gold in my hair and the reading glasses on a chain around my neck, and they did not know that there was once a time when I sat where they sat now, young and full of hope. Anticipation was the dominant feeling of my adolescence, sometimes trumping even that other constant companion—fear. I expected good things of life; I thought fulfillment was tucked into the years that were yet to unfold. I was at a preparatory school being prepared for life and for success, and I believed that if I worked hard and did everything just right, I would be rewarded not so much with accomplishment but with love. Wasn't love, after all, the important thing, even far above whatever work we chose to do?

When I was twelve years old, I once saw the headmistress, Miss Margaret Seaton, strolling across the Green in her plaid wool coat and her sensible shoes, and because she was a spinster, I thought to myself, *Why, she has never even lived, and now she is old.*

To these children—for they too were still children, not yet eighteen—I was another Margaret Seaton. While I no longer thought that Miss Seaton had wasted her life, I couldn't help but wonder whether I had wasted mine. I felt myself beyond the hope of marriage, and certainly I was beyond all hope of having children, and I knew—I *knew*—that if I turned around I would see it in their faces like neon at midnight, the look that says, *Why, she has never even lived, and now she is old.*

The chalk made a single truncated line on the board. I had lost my train of thought.

Let's talk about words, I said to myself, because that's what Theodore Dutton said on that first day of school in September 1976. *"Let's talk about words and the power of words. . . ."*

CHAPTER 5

From the time I understood that certain shapes on a page were letters, and that letters could be strung together to form words, and words could be strung together to form sentences, and sentences could form paragraphs could form pages could form stories that took you beyond the ink itself into whole other worlds, I have always loved words. I think that was one reason

I liked Theodore Dutton so much, because he loved words too. Whenever he read aloud to us from the *Norton Anthology of English Literature*, it was like he was opening his hands toward us and casting pearls at our feet. I sat enraptured, and the sound of his voice went on echoing through my head long after class was over.

But that wasn't the initial reason I liked Theodore Dutton. I was, after all, an adolescent girl, prone to romantic notions. And as I said, on the first day of our senior year when he introduced himself to us, all the girls in the classroom let off a sigh of longing—first, because he was so attractive, and second, because he was so unattainable. He was not married. A quick glance at the ring finger of his left hand settled that question. But we supposed him to be somewhere around thirty years old, which meant him to be nearly twice our age. I myself was only sixteen and would not be seventeen until December.

Natalie sat beside me in that first class on that first morning of our senior year, and not five minutes into the lesson she was drawing hearts all over the otherwise blank pages of her notebook. I rolled my eyes at her, but she responded with a smile and scribbled a little note on the bottom of the page where I could see it: *Thank heavens Silly Goose left*. That was what we'd called Tom Goss, our English teacher the previous three years who had left to take a position at Trenton Academy in New Jersey. Theodore Dutton was hired as his replacement.

You would have had to be around in the seventies, but if you can picture a cross between Paul Michael Glaser of *Starsky and Hutch* and Erik Estrada of *CHiPs*, you'd have a good idea of what Theodore Dutton looked like. He was very tall and well proportioned, and his hair was a thick mesh of brown waves. I can't remember his eyes exactly, but they were probably brown, and they must have been just right, because there didn't seem to be much about him that wasn't perfect, according to the standards of the day. His chin was strong, and his cheeks were dimpled, and his hands were something you followed with your eyes just because they were so beautiful. More than that, he exuded a certain charm, and he seemed to be completely unaware of it, which made him all the more charming. While he commanded respect simply through his own self-confidence and his place of authority over us, we also knew intuitively from the outset that he was on our side, and unlike some teachers, he wanted to be our friend.

He scribbled two words on the chalkboard below his name and asked, "Who can tell me what we mean by reader response?"

A half dozen hands went up, including mine, and after casting a glance about the room, Mr. Dutton pointed at me with the piece of chalk, and I thought, *My goodness, he can see me*.

"Now don't forget," he said, "to begin by telling me your name. Just until I know who you all are."

A small wave of anxiety rolled through me then. I

didn't like to speak in class, but I wanted to answer the question. "Um, I'm Beth," I said, willing the telltale crimson flush to rise no higher than my chin. "Reader response is what a reader gets out of a certain text, what a reader thinks a writer is saying, even if the writer didn't mean to say that."

Theodore Dutton stared at me for a brief but unnerving moment. I wished then that he couldn't see me, as I felt the flush rise into my cheeks. At length he said, "Good start, Beth. Does anyone want to add to that?"

I think somebody added to it, but I can't be sure who it was or what he said. I was too busy catching my breath. In the next moment I realized that Ray Schmidt, on the other side of me from Natalie, was casting me a smile and a thumbs-up, and I smiled back at him because, you see, I liked him too.

Heath Hall did not have air-conditioning, so all the windows were thrown wide open and the final breath of summer filled the room. You could hear the birds outside, and I thought about how the skies would soon be filled with those thick black ribbons of birds flying south for the winter. I loved to put my head back and watch, wondering, *Where is the end of the ribbon?* Each one went on and on, a squawking undulating line against the blue. There was so much to wonder about. There was so much to anticipate.

That morning, when Mr. Dutton saw me and Ray Schmidt smiled at me, I thought, *This is going to be a very good year.*

CHAPTER 6

"Who can tell me," I said, "what I mean when I say reader response?"

I turned and found that the adolescent faces behind me had reverted yet again to question marks. But of course. This wasn't Senior Honors English, and the year wasn't 1976. This was Junior Composition, and we had all of us somehow slipped into the twenty-first century. I was now the teacher. What had become of my lesson plan?

Flustered, I glanced at the notes on my desk. "Never mind. We'll get to that later," I apologized, knowing full well we wouldn't get to that later. But I had to somehow pick up the pieces of this class and carry on.

"Let's open to page six of the grammar text. I want to begin by talking about the different types of words."

Surely I was safe with nouns and verbs, adjectives and adverbs. I knew them well, having spent my life among them. They were the last thing, of course, these students wanted to talk about, and frankly, at the moment, it was the last thing I wanted to talk about as well. But I stumbled ahead, my eye on the clock, willing this hour to be through, and then the next and the next.

As the seconds ticked off, I became more and more aware of a certain dissonance rising inside of me like nausea. I should not be standing up here as teacher; I should be there—a student, a child. I should not have come this far and still gotten nowhere.

Is this, I wondered, what they call a midlife crisis?

A warm wind blew in through the open windows and ruffled the papers on my desk. Heath Hall still didn't have air-conditioning, and the day was hot. There was talk of tearing this old building down and putting up a new one. Such a shame. Such a shame that nothing lasted, that we could not come to a moment of satisfaction and push a pause button and stay there. I would have pushed it long ago when I was young and living at home. I wanted to go home now, to the home where I had lived with my mother and my father and my sisters. But that wasn't possible. I could go to the house where I grew up just two miles down the road, but it was not my home. Everything about that life had sunk deeply into the past.

Through the milky haze my mind had become, I saw the minute hand on the clock had at long last reached the six. It was nine thirty, the end of the first class.

"Your homework assignment," I said, "is to finish reading this chapter and to answer the questions at the end."

The scraping of chair legs against wooden floor was a welcome sound as the students rose to go. I leaned against my desk, trying to connect, to offer a "See you tomorrow" or "Have a good day" to the students as they filed out.

Satchel Queen lingered. Or maybe it was simply her nature to move slowly. She dropped her grammar book into her backpack and slung the pack over one shoulder. When she rose from her chair, she lowered her eyes, avoiding my gaze. Her eyelids were painted an earthy shade of yellow, all the way up to her eyebrows. The eye shadow appeared to be the only makeup on her otherwise colorless skin. Her hair, so dark as to be almost black, was parted in the middle and held back with a couple of childish barrettes. Her large hoop earrings knocked against her slender neck as she moved. Narrow-faced and square-nosed, she was not a beautiful child, though I thought she might stand half a chance if she smiled.

She wanted to pass by me unseen, I was sure, yet I felt compelled to say something. "Satchel?"

She looked at me then with unconcealed suspicion. "Yeah?"

"Is this your first year at Seaton?"

She hesitated a moment. "Don't you know?"

"No, I'm afraid I don't."

"Yeah? I thought you guys had files on us, like permanent records or something."

"Well, yes, we do have files, but I can't remember everything I've read about each student."

"Uh-huh."

"So?"

"Yeah?"

"Is this your first year?"

"Yeah. Why?"

"I was just wondering. You're a boarding student?"

"Yeah." She nodded slightly, and shrugged the backpack up higher. She wasn't so much unfriendly as simply remote, like someone at the far end of a tunnel.

"Where are you from?"

"White Plains, I guess."

"You guess?"

"Yeah."

"You aren't sure?"

"Yeah, well, we just moved there this summer."

I offered her a smile. She remained expressionless. "I hope you'll like it here at Seaton."

"Uh, sure. Well, it's not exactly like I'm here because I want to be."

Generations of students had said the same thing, especially the boarders. I'd heard it a thousand times before in the years I was a student at Seaton. But when Satchel said it, I didn't know how to respond.

She must have sensed my predicament because she went on to explain. "See, like, my mom got married this summer and didn't need me around anymore. So she and Roger—that's her new husband—they decided to ship me off here."

"I see." Whether or not she was considered disposable by her mother, I didn't know. But obviously that was what Satchel believed. I frowned at the hurt she undoubtedly felt and the resentment she harbored toward the two people who had sent her here. I knew it would be superficial of me to say, *Oh, but I'm sure you must be wrong. I'm sure your mother loves you* when I wasn't sure of any such thing. So I simply said, "I was a student here once myself, you know. I think you'll find Seaton's not so bad. You may even find you like it here."

She looked at me a long moment, her eyes conveying her skepticism. Then she asked, "Is there anything else, Miss Gunnar? Because I really got to get to chemistry, you know?"

It was a long tunnel, and she was such a tiny figure at the far end. "No. Nothing else," I said. "Well, you have a good day, Satchel."

Her countenance remained amazingly blank. "Yeah, sure. Whatever."

CHAPTER 7

I somehow reached the end of that first day of teaching at Seaton. It was a tiresome journey, one that required all my reserves of energy. I had found myself navigating not only the byways of new faces and botched lesson plans, but also through the tumultuous emotions unearthed by my simply being there. As I walked the short distance from Heath Hall to Pine Glen in the late afternoon, I felt a weariness I had seldom known before.

Yes, I will admit that even in childhood, the first day of school generally had a negative effect on me. Certainly, on the one hand, there was the anticipation of being with old friends, making new friends, meeting new boys. That shiny surface life, that glowing patina of socializing was unquestionably alluring. I looked forward to parties and dances and football games and flirting and laughing and maybe even something like falling in love, because young people are naturally romantic and equipped with seemingly endless resources of hope.

But beneath all that was the ever present sense of dread. It was at times a subtle fear and alternately a gripping panic, and it was rooted in this one belief: School was a testing ground, and it was here that my worth as a person would be determined. If I did not do well at school, I would not do well at life, and then what would become of me?

You see, every time final exams came around and they set up those tables in the gym and had us solemnly file in with our blue books and sharpened pencils, I knew all this wasn't done simply to find out if I could diagram a sentence or work through an algebraic equation. I knew the real question at the heart of the matter was this: Are you good enough?

In my own heart of hearts I was never quite certain that I was. In fact, I was very nearly convinced that I wasn't. Life, I believed, was good, but I wasn't good enough for life.

Never mind the track record; never mind the fact that not once did I end up with a grade lower than a B, not even in chemistry, a subject which left me hopelessly confused. I was not for a moment appeased by the fact that each semester my name appeared on either the first or second honor roll posted outside Mrs. Bidney's door. That, oddly enough, meant little to me. My sights were set only on this: Every test, every class was simply a new opportunity to fail. It could happen yet.

What I remember most about those final exams was the little pool of sweat that gathered on the table beneath my right hand while I waited for the signal to turn the test over and begin. That small collection of liquid fear was large enough that it sometimes moistened the pages of my blue book and caused my pencil lead to smear. It's a wonder I could keep the pencil within my slippery grasp at all.

By the time exam week was over, I was exhausted and numb and prone to dreaming about running away and joining a hippie commune, where all a person had to do was tend a garden and prepare food in the communal kitchen and in the evenings sit around singing folk songs while a couple of bearded, unwashed guys strummed out-of-tune guitars. I could drop out of life and do that if it came down to it. As soon as I started to fail, this option, at least, was open to me.

Of course I never ran away. Somehow, I was able to outwit the world, and no one ever discovered what I really was inside. But it was like being Cinderella at the ball. I was all the time waiting for midnight to expose me as a pauper at a party where I didn't belong. Not knowing when the hour would come and the clock would strike twelve, I danced warily, with the hope that once I was out of school for good, I'd be home free. After that, I'd never have to prove myself again.

How young and naïve and wrong I was! I didn't know school was only the beginning, that the threat of being tested and found wanting would follow me all of my life.

When I reached Pine Glen at the end of that long first day of teaching, I was no different from the child I'd been years ago. I was just as afraid as ever that any second now the clock would strike midnight and flashes of imploding fairy dust would reveal me for what I was: Not good enough to be here, a chambermaid without an invitation to the ball.

CHAPTER 8

That night I turned to the first place I always turned for solace: my books. They were always there and never changing. They were completely dependable. Sometimes all I had to do was stand in front of a bookcase and read the spines all lined up neatly in a row, and I'd begin to feel better. But when I opened the pages—now, that was the real thing. With that, I was out of my own world and into the world I chose, where I could be another person, live another life. What could offer a better balm than that?

I was curled up with Dickens—who always made me smile—and my third cup of chamomile tea when the phone rang. I didn't want to be interrupted, but I reluctantly reached for the cordless on the side table by the couch.

"Hello?"

"So how'd it go?" It was Natalie.

"Well," I confessed, "I've had better days."

"So what happened?"

"Nothing, really. The classes went reasonably well, and there are some really great students here. It's just that . . . I don't know. I'm wrestling the old demons, I guess."

"That's because it was your first day in a new job. That's hard for anyone."

"I don't know, Natalie." I sighed heavily.

"Well, what then? Am I going to have to resume my role as cheerleader? Rah rah, go Beth; you can do it."

"Your enthusiasm overwhelms me."

"So I'm out of practice. Anyway, when are you going to realize you're both bright and competent?"

"At the rate I'm going, about three years after I'm dead."

Natalie laughed loudly. It was a beautiful sound. "Well, at least you've still got your sense of humor."

"Yeah, I guess. So how are you?"

"All right," she responded. "Same old, same old, really. Ron works too much, and the kids fight too much, and I'm drowning under piles of laundry, and I've got an impossible deadline to meet with this latest freelance job, and so, you know, the beat goes on."

"Sounds like a nice life to me."

"You're kidding, right?"

"No. No, I'm not."

"Sure, Beth. So let's switch places, just for a day."

"I would if I could."

"No, you wouldn't."

"Yes, I would."

She sighed. Or snorted. Anyway, it was some sort of sound of amused disgust coming from the other end of the line.

Then she said, "Listen, when's homecoming this year?"

"I'm not sure. First weekend of October, I think."

"Find out for sure. I want to put it on my calendar. We have to be there, just to see who comes back. You want to go, don't you?"

"It'll probably be expected of me. But yes, I want to go."

"Good. Maybe even Artie Sochs will come back from the Belgian Congo."

"Wouldn't that be something?"

"And Ray. He's local. He'll probably show up for some of the activities."

Raymond Schmidt. Natalie had spoken of him before, but tonight, at the mention of his name, I realized I would very much like to see him, to reconnect, to see how his life had turned out so far. He had always been the boy most likely to succeed, and I knew that, on some level at least, he had succeeded, and I wanted to know that he was happy.

"Okay, I'll find out when homecoming is, and we can plan on going together," I told Natalie.

We talked for a while then about comfortable things: a play she and Ron had seen at the Hotel du Pont, the stray dog her kids had brought home from the park, my thoughts about visiting my parents in Asheville over the Christmas break.

Finally, stifling a yawn, I was just about to tell her I needed to call it a night when she said, "Listen, I just have to ask you something because I'm curious."

She paused, seemingly needing my permission to go on. "Okay."

"Why did you ask me the other day if I ever thought about Dutton?"

I should have had a ready answer, but I didn't. "I don't really know," I said. "I've thought about him over the years but, boy, being here really brings it all back in living color."

"Yeah, no doubt. But don't let it bother you. I mean, you tend to dwell on things, you know? That's what you introverts are good at, isn't it—brooding on things."

"I suppose so."

"Take my advice and forget it. It was a terrible thing, but it was a long time ago. The man's been dead for ages—"

"But we really don't know that, do we?"

"Oh, come on, Beth. Don't tell me you think he survived. Ray was there; Ken too. They saw it with their own eyes."

"But why would Commander and the others have lied, then?"

"Who knows? They thought they were sparing us. They thought we were too young to handle the truth."

"I'm not so sure, Natalie."

"So Google him."

"What?"

"Type Theodore Dutton into Google and see what comes up."

I hadn't thought about that. "I guess I could. But I don't know if I'd be able to find out anything that way."

"Well, in this day and age, I should think you could find out just about anything about anyone, certainly about whether he's dead or alive."

Suddenly I wasn't so sure I wanted to know. I shut my eyes and tightened my grip around the receiver.

Natalie seemed to sense my fear. "Beth," she said quietly, "forget I suggested anything and just let it go. The man was crazy."

"No, he wasn't!"

"Well, you know what I mean. Back then we didn't know about things like posttraumatic stress syndrome and—"

"You think that's what caused it all?"

"Of course. He'd been in 'Nam, remember? And you know how he wouldn't talk about it, even when the guys asked him point-blank."

"That doesn't really explain it."

"I think it does. He looked like he had it all together, but he was just one more messed up vet."

We were quiet for a long moment. Then I said, "We should have done something."

"Like what? None of us knew he was ready to self-destruct."

And that was it, I suppose. That was the problem. Why did none of us have a clue? How could we have loved him and yet known so little about him?

"Don't let it eat at you, Beth. Just forget it."

I forced out a small laugh. "Easier said than done."

And then we said good-night and hung up the phone.

CHAPTER 9

Natalie didn't have much compassion left for a man she once called Teddy Bear. What started out as a scribbling of hearts in her notebook turned into a near obsession by the third week of our senior year. Natalie was thoroughly smitten with Theodore Dutton.

Of course, as her best friend, I was the only person who knew. I do imagine now, however, that Ken Cunningham had his suspicions. Ken had a crush on Natalie, but his pursuit of her—which had apparently been going well during our junior year—suddenly hit a snag somewhere early that fall of 1976. He and Natalie continued to date off and on, but Ken knew he had a rival somewhere.

"I want to marry Teddy," Natalie told me once.

"You're an idiot," I shot back.

"Why?" she asked, sounding genuinely pained.

"He's too old for you."

"Things like that don't matter. Older men and younger women get married all the time."

I decided to let her dream.

To tell you the truth, though, if I had been honest with Natalie, I would have admitted that that very thought had crossed my own mind. I just never fleshed it out with words the way Natalie did. Either my practical nature or my self-doubts dismissed the thought of marrying Theodore Dutton as readily as it appeared.

That year Ray Schmidt became a boarding student. His father had been transferred to Virginia, and rather than switching schools his senior year, Ray decided to board at Seaton and room with Ken. Ken had been a fixture in the dorms since ninth grade, when he came to the school to escape his parents' peripatetic lifestyle. His father was a military man, and by the time Ken was in the eighth grade, he'd been to thirteen schools around the States and overseas. He finally asked his parents to send him to a boarding school so he could stay in one place for more than a year.

Oddly enough, our friendship with Ray and Ken was what led Natalie and me to a more intimate relationship with Theodore Dutton.

It happened this way. I often spent the night at Natalie's house, which was in the West Hill neighborhood right next to Seaton. In fact, Natalie's yard backed up to the school. The two properties were naturally divided by a narrow strip of woods and a shallow rocky creek. Natalie walked to school, but she got there by walking to the end of her street and taking the path into Chapel Valley. That's what we called the valley where Seaton's chapel was. From there she walked the road that included a little arched bridge over the creek, then up the hill to the large circular drive at the center of the school.

This was the route we took that first night we ended

up at Mr. Dutton's cabin. It was a Friday night, and we had agreed to meet Ray and Ken on the Green at seven o'clock. We had no particular plans, and when we met the boys, we spent several minutes trying to decide what to do. They asked us what we wanted to do, and we said we didn't care, what did they want to do?

Ray said, "You guys want to go somewhere?" Even though he was a boarder, he still had his Camaro on campus.

I asked him, "Did you get permission?" because boarders were not to leave campus without prior permission.

He said, "No"—not that that really mattered to any of us. We'd gone off campus before without permission, and that was, as I mentioned, how we'd become the Barbarians.

But then Natalie said, "They're holding auditions for the play over in Hawthorne. Anyone want to go watch?" Hawthorne Gymnasium, the smaller of the two gyms on campus, housed the stage where all the productions were held.

"What are they doing this year?" Ray asked.

"I think it's *South Pacific*."

Ken shrugged. "Why not? Should be good for a few laughs."

So Ken put his arm around Natalie's shoulder, and Ray took my hand for the first time, and we headed across campus toward Hawthorne Gymnasium. But we never got there because as we came upon the two faculty cabins behind Cedar Hall, we saw Mr. Dutton standing in the open doorway of Cabin 1, just standing there leaning against the doorframe with his hands tucked deep into the pockets of his jeans.

"Mr. Dutton!" Ray called, and our English teacher raised a hand and beckoned us over.

"Ray, I've got that volume of Byron you wanted if you can hold on just a minute." He disappeared into the cabin.

I looked at Natalie, and she was beaming. When we reached the cabin, she poked her head through the open door, and I heard Mr. Dutton say, "Come on in, everyone. I know the book's here somewhere."

Students were allowed to visit in the faculty homes as long as we went in groups. We had frequented the gatherings at the Buckleys', but I had never been in either of the cabins. That was exactly what this was too—a rustic log structure of three small rooms with wooden floors and paneled walls. The cabins were generally assigned to the young unmarried male teachers like Theodore Dutton. Another bachelor and a science teacher in the middle school, Clarence Fosset, lived in Cabin 2.

Mr. Dutton waved toward a couple of worn couches and invited us to sit. As he went on searching for the elusive volume of Byron, he apologized for not being able to put his finger right on it. The problem was obvious, though. The room was full of books. Mr. Dutton's collection filled three large bookcases and spilled out onto the coffee table and even onto the floor. Across the room from the couches was an overstuffed chair where Mr. Dutton must have done his reading. Three or four books lay open and facedown on the footstool.

"Aha, here it is!" Mr. Dutton pulled a slim volume from one of the cases and whirled around to present it to Ray. "I think this will help you with your paper."

"Thanks, Mr. Dutton," Ray said as he thumbed through the pages.

"No problem. So what are you kids doing tonight?"

"We're heading over to Hawthorne to watch the auditions," Ken told him.

"But we're not in any hurry," Natalie added.

"Good, because I was just about to cut into a watermelon. Care to join me?"

Our enthusiastic response sent him scurrying to the kitchen. A banging of drawers and a rattle of dishes followed, and after a moment Mr. Dutton returned with a tray of thick slices of melon and a pile of paper plates and napkins. We all sat down on the floor and helped ourselves to one of the seeded half-moons of fruit. As we ate, the juice dripped down our chins and ran in sticky rivers down the insides of our arms, and soon the napkins were moist balls of crumpled paper scattered about the floor.

Mr. Dutton and Ray spoke briefly about the essay Ray was working on. Earlier that week Mr. Dutton had given us the assignment of analyzing a poem from the romantic period. I myself had chosen one by Keats. Natalie was attempting one by Coleridge, but at the moment that was the last thing on her mind.

"Where did you come from, Mr. Dutton?" she asked, and then to clarify she said, "I mean, where did you teach before you came here?"

"I spent a couple years teaching at a public school near Philadelphia. But I didn't like it. I wanted a change. So here I am." He smiled.

"And what about before that?" Ken asked.

"I was at the University of Pennsylvania earning my master's degree in English."

And then, as though it were a game, Ray asked, "And what about before that?"

Mr. Dutton looked at Ray a long time before he said, "Before that, I was drafted and spent a year in 'Nam."

A soldier in uniform! With that knowledge, our awe of the man gained even greater heights. Of course we had all been swayed by the climate of the times and counted ourselves among the war protesters—though, as children, we had never once actually gone out in public waving placards. But to think that Mr. Dutton had *been there* and fought for our country! What could be more romantic than that? I could almost feel the waves of admiration rolling off of Natalie, and even the boys were impressed.

Ray said excitedly, "Cool! Tell us about it."

But Theodore Dutton shook his head and dropped a piece of watermelon rind onto his plate. "No," he said. "I'm not going to tell you, because it's better for you not to know."

For about twenty awful seconds no one said anything at all. Ray looked embarrassed and chastised and as though he should apologize. Natalie and I exchanged a quick glance but otherwise didn't move. During that long silent interval Mr. Dutton didn't look at anyone, just down at the rind and the black seeds floating in the pink pool of juice on his plate.

Finally Natalie saved us all by saying, "Maybe I should try out for the part of Nellie in *South Pacific*. What do you think?"

Ken jumped in and said, "I think you'd be great if only you could sing."

While Natalie poked Ken with her elbow, Mr. Dutton looked up and smiled, and I knew he had rejoined us, coming back from wherever it was he had been.

We never did make it to the auditions that evening. We stayed with Mr. Dutton until long past nightfall, and he seemed to want us there as much as we wanted to be there. I don't remember all that we talked about that first night, but I do remember the way my best friend Natalie looked at Theodore Dutton, and I knew that she was dreaming of marrying him.

And I—because he was handsome and kind and brave and he loved books—I allowed myself to go so far as to dream: *I will marry someone just like him someday*.

I was absolutely certain it was possible, because that's the way adolescent girls think. And that's because they are too young yet to see the world as it is.

CHAPTER 10

My Home
by Satchel Queen

In the middle of my house is a very tall spiral staircase. I climb the stairs, going around and around and around until I reach my room on the top floor. Sometimes I try to count the number of steps as I go, but I always lose track. Once, I got to three hundred and I still wasn't at the top, so I know there are more than that.

You might think it isn't worthwhile to climb so many stairs just to get to my room, and sometimes I almost think so too, but that isn't the case once you get there. When I reach my room and look out one of the twenty-five windows, I know I'd climb those stairs all over again just to see what I can see from there. First there's the harbor and on the other side of that there's this peninsula that's like no other peninsula in the world. If the Native Americans who used to live on that land saw how the place looks now, they'd either drop dead of fright or they'd beat their drums and worship the Great Spirit, or maybe they'd just worship man, who most of the time thinks he's God anyway, because he can do things like build the buildings that make up the skyline of Manhattan.

If you pick out just one of those skyscrapers and

you think about the hours of manpower that went into building it, and you think about all the steel and concrete they used and consider the fact that hundreds of people can walk around inside and it doesn't fall over, it's pretty impressive. Now multiply that by the number of buildings in Manhattan, and you can hardly even wrap your mind around it. I can't anyway.

What's even more interesting is the ferry that travels from Manhattan to Staten Island. I can watch it for hours. I like the way it cuts through the water and leaves a V-shaped wake behind it. The wake always makes me think of a peacock's tail. I also like to watch the gulls circling behind the boat, squawking and swooping down for food. Sometimes the people on the ferry toss them popcorn or bread, and the gulls get all tangled up with each other just trying to get at it. All day long the ferry goes back and forth, back and forth, and I wonder who's on it and where they're going and whether they're coming back. And most of all I wonder, are they happy?

At noon, when the sun is highest over the water, there are about a million little lights flashing on the surface of the harbor. It's like the ferry is traveling through pixie dust or a field of diamonds or maybe the Milky Way. And I think, if all those people down there could see the way it looks from up here, if they could see themselves surrounded by all those dancing stars, they might like the trip across the harbor a little better. It might even make them happy—if they're not already. Just for a minute anyway.

I can see a lot from my room in my house. I wouldn't want to live anywhere else. Someday I'm not even going to leave here anymore. People can come up and see me if they want, but I'm going to stay right here, looking over the Manhattan skyline and watching the ferry sailing through the stars.

CHAPTER 11

"Satchel, do you know the difference between fact and fiction?"

The dark-haired girl standing by my desk nodded without changing expression. "Yeah."

When she didn't continue, I prodded, "Would you please tell me what it is?"

"Facts are true and fiction is made up."

"That's right." I picked her essay out of a pile of partly graded papers on my desk. "I asked you to write a brief essay describing your home, and you wrote about the view from the Statue of Liberty."

She looked at me just long enough to make me feel uneasy. I hoped her face would reveal a hint of either sudden understanding or sincere contrition, but neither look materialized.

Finally she muttered, "So?"

I didn't want to have to resort to my tough-teacher tone of voice. For one thing, I wasn't very good at it, and for another, I seriously doubted it would help. But I was beginning to feel annoyed. "Your essay is very creative, Satchel, but this isn't a creative writing class. You were simply to write a brief essay about your real home, the actual house in which you live."

She lifted her chin slightly. "So how can I do that?"

"What do you mean?"

"I mean, I'm homeless. How do you expect me to write about a home I don't have?"

For a moment I had visions of shopping carts and cardboard boxes and campfires for reheating food dug out of garbage cans. But that was hardly Satchel's situation. "Look," I said, "I know you live in the dorm and that makes you feel homeless, but can you work with me here and give me an essay about the house where your folks are—you know, the place you'll be going to for Thanksgiving break?"

"I don't think I can do that."

"Why not?"

"Well, like I told you before, Mom and I just moved to White Plains this summer when she married Roger. Roger already lived there, and we just moved into his house. Well, Mom did, anyway. I never lived there except for just a few weeks before coming here, but that doesn't make the place my home."

"Oh. Okay." I was beginning to see her predicament. "So where did you live before your mom got married and you moved to White Plains?"

"Brooklyn, mostly. But I was born in New Jersey.

Hoboken. I don't remember much about it. We moved to Brooklyn when I was three."

"I see." I looked at her paper in my hand, at the grade written in red ink at the top. "You know, when I said your paper was very creative, I meant it. You enjoy writing, don't you?"

She nodded tentatively.

"And I have an idea that you like to read."

"Yeah."

Her eyes narrowed, but in them I saw something like surprise. "I had a feeling you were a fellow bibliophile. Do you know what that is?"

"Someone who likes books?"

"Yes."

We looked at each other as though we had reached some sort of understanding. Then I said, "I gave you an F on this essay, Satchel, because you failed to fulfill the assignment. But I want to give you a chance to pull up your grade. I'm willing to forgive this F if you'd be willing to hand in a new essay by Friday."

"Yeah?"

I nodded.

"So what do you want me to write about?"

"Well . . ." I thought a moment. "Why don't you write about the home you'd *like* to live in?"

Her gaze dropped from my face down to the paper, then slowly moved back up again. "Like, that's what I already did, Miss Gunnar."

Tess Standefer, who'd been lingering in the hall since I called Satchel aside, now stood timidly in the doorway. Tess and Satchel were roommates and apparently had become friends as well.

"Excuse me, Miss Gunnar," Tess said, "but if Satchel and I don't get going, we're going to be late for Mr. Wadino's class again. We already got our second tardy from him yesterday."

They'd been late twice already? After only two weeks of school?

"All right," I said. I looked at Satchel. "We'll talk about this more later."

I expected her to toss out her usual response of "Whatever." But she left without saying anything at all.

CHAPTER 12

I was sitting at the dining room table reading student essays around ten o'clock that night when I heard a knock at the front door. Or I thought I did. The sound was so faint I couldn't be sure.

But when I went to the door and opened it, there was Satchel Queen standing on the wooden stoop, looking small and pale under the dim outside light.

"Satchel, do you know what time it is? What are you doing out of the dorm?"

She shrugged without pulling her hands out of the pockets of her jeans. "I thought you wanted to talk some more about my paper."

"Now?"

She shrugged again.

"Who's your dorm parent?" I asked.

"Miss Wilson."

"Does she know you're here?"

"I don't think so."

"You just walked out of the dorm without telling her?"

"Not exactly. I climbed out the window." The shoulders went up again. "No big deal; my room's on the ground floor."

"But you're not supposed to leave the dorm after nine."

"Listen, Miss Gunnar, if you don't want to talk—" She moved backward one step.

"No, it's all right," I blurted, suddenly wanting her to stay. "Since you're here, why don't you come on in?"

She looked at me a moment as though to determine whether I meant it. When I opened the screen door and stepped aside to let her in, she entered slowly and stood in the front hall. Her eyes moved left then right, taking in the dining room and the living room.

"So this is where you live," she said mildly.

I shut the door. "Yes, this is it."

I flipped on the overhead light in the living room and motioned for Satchel to sit. Before she did, though, she stood in the middle of the room and turned a full circle, taking in a 360-degree view of my bookcases.

"Whoa," she said. "You really are one of those book-lover people, aren't you?"

"Yes, I guess I am. They become kind of like friends, if you know what I mean."

She nodded. Then she looked at me straight on, and her face opened into something like a smile.

"Would you like something to drink?" I asked. "Bottled water? A soda?"

"No thanks."

"I just bought some ice cream. How about a bowl?"

"No," she said. "I don't eat ice cream anymore. But do you have any dried mango?"

"No. I'm afraid I don't."

"That's okay."

"You sure there's nothing else you'd like?"

"I'm sure."

"Well, let's sit down, all right?"

She sat in the wing chair by the fireplace and propped her feet up on the footstool like she owned the place. I settled myself on the couch.

Her eyes continued to scan the room until they came to rest on me. "I don't want to flunk your class, Miss Gunnar," she said.

"I don't think you're going to flunk my class."

"I pretty much have an F average so far, don't I?"

I thought of the F I'd given her on her composition. "Well, like I said, I'm willing to let you rewrite your paper. I know you can get a higher grade."

Her eyes were wandering again. She seemed captivated by my collection of books. I watched her carefully, glad to find a student who enjoyed reading. "I don't like math," she remarked abruptly, her eyes alighting on me once again. "I'm not good at math."

I didn't know why we were suddenly speaking of math, but I said, "All right."

"And I don't like science. It's a bore."

"Okay."

"But I like to read. I even kind of like to write."

I nodded. "That's good. I'm glad you do."

"Not poetry, though. I mean, I know people my age are always spilling their guts writing poetry, but I don't do that. I just like to read it. Like Emily Dickinson, you know? I like Emily Dickinson."

I was beginning to warm to Satchel Queen. "Really?"

"Yeah, because she's real. You read her and you think, this lady knows what time it is. You know what I mean?"

Again I nodded. "I do know what you mean, Satchel. She seemed to understand the human condition, didn't she?" I thought I would take a chance by adding, "She knew what it was to be alone."

This time Satchel nodded, very slightly. "Yeah."

"Do you have brothers and sisters, Satchel?"

"Naw. It's just my mom and me. And now Roger."

"Do you like Roger?"

"He's all right. He's got a lot of money."

"Uh-huh. Enough to send you here to Seaton."

"Yeah."

"I'm sure you'd rather be at home with them."

"Naw. Not really. My mom—" she shook her head—"she was always dating these jerks. It was like she was a magnet for losers. So they'd dump her, and she'd come crying to me, and I had to make everything better, you know—like *I* was the mother and *she* was the kid. I got tired of it."

How sad, I thought. Aloud I said, "Yes, I guess you would."

"So she finally met a decent guy who was willing to marry her, and I don't know, I guess after that she didn't need me anymore."

Once again I didn't know how to respond to Satchel Queen. I was surprised at her willingness to tell me about herself. At the same time I was stunned by her mother's weaknesses and seeming indifference toward her own child.

At length I asked, "Have you ever actually been in the Statue of Liberty?"

She lifted her chin and let it drop. "Yeah. My dad took me up there once, all the way up to the crown. That was when you could still go up there. I was really little, but I remember it. He lifted me up on his shoulders so I could see out the windows. I thought it must be what it's like to fly in an airplane and look down at everything."

I wanted to ask about her dad, but instead I asked, "You've never flown?"

She shook her head. "Naw. I've never been anywhere, really."

"Maybe that's something you can do when you're grown up."

"Uh-huh. I'd like to travel around the world, just to see what it's like. You ever been anywhere?"

"Yes. Europe and parts of Asia and South America."

"Wow, you're lucky."

"Well, I never married and had children, so I've had the freedom to travel."

She nodded knowingly. "Yeah, I'm never going to get married either."

I gave a little laugh. "Well, you're only—what? Sixteen?"

"Seventeen."

"You're too young to say you'll never get married."

"It never works out, even if you do."

"You don't think so?"

"Naw. It's a huge crock. It's no use thinking someone will love you all your life."

She is too young yet to know that, I thought, and the instinct to protect her rose in my chest. "I know some people who are happily married," I replied.

"Yeah? Well I don't."

"Not even your mother and Roger?"

"I guess they're happy right now, since they're still practically on their honeymoon. But who knows how long it'll last."

"You shouldn't be so negative, Satchel."

"Why not?"

Why not indeed? What had she seen all her life but her mother's failed relationships?

"Just a minute, all right?" I rose from the couch and went to the dining room to find her essay among the piles on the table. Satchel stared at me quizzically when I returned. "Here's what I'm going to do, Satchel," I said. "I'm going to raise your grade on this paper to a B. Now, say the Statue of Liberty was your house. The assignment still was to write about your house, not the view from the window. If you'd written more about the statue itself, I'd have given you an A."

Satchel stood and took the paper I was offering her. Once she saw for herself that I had crossed out the F and changed the grade to a B, she smiled briefly. "Thanks, Miss Gunnar."

"But next time be sure to stick to the subject."

"What's it going to be? I mean, what are you going to ask us to write about? Maybe I can start thinking about it now."

"I'm going to ask you to write about a particular event that's been significant to you. It can be something you've lived through personally, or it can be something that happened in history. It doesn't matter, so long as you describe the event accurately."

"Okay."

I offered what I hoped was a smile of encouragement. "I'm glad you came tonight, Satchel."

"Yeah."

"But you'd better get back before Miss Wilson does room check at eleven. If you're not there, we're both in trouble."

"Don't worry, Miss Gunnar. She'd never notice if I weren't there."

"Oh yeah?" I laughed. "What makes you think that? You're not invisible, you know."

She looked at me askance, as though she couldn't understand what I had said. And then we headed for the door. I turned the knob and pulled back the barrier to the warm darkness and the night songs of the cicadas.

"You're not, you know," I pressed.
"Not what?"
"Invisible."
She hesitated, her intense eyes searching my face. And then she said, almost in a whisper, "I guess not."
Then she stepped onto the stoop and disappeared into the night.

CHAPTER 13

The child thought of herself as invisible, which I understood only too well. That was how I myself had felt for much of my own childhood. I really don't know whether that was because I tried so hard not to be seen, or because I actually believed my insignificance rendered me unseeable.
I was twelve years old and new to Seaton when I first came to think of myself as invisible. Our class was practicing for a Reader's Theatre performance of "The Highwayman" for middle school assembly when our teacher made the unfortunate decision to give me a solo part.
The tragic poem by Alfred Noyes, when read aloud, has a galloping cadence, echoing the horse's hooves pounding the road toward a lonesome inn. In that faraway place somewhere in old England, "the wind was a torrent of darkness among the gusty trees, the moon was a ghostly galleon tossed upon cloudy seas," and "the road was a ribbon of moonlight over the purple moor" when "the highwayman came riding, riding,

riding up to the old inn door." When "he whistled a tune to the window, who should be waiting there, but the landlord's black-eyed daughter, Bess, the landlord's daughter, plaiting a dark red love-knot into her long black hair."

On the night of the poem's events, though, Bess was not at the window braiding her hair as she had been a hundred times before. On this night the inn had been overtaken by Red Coats, and the landlord's daughter was dragged to her room and tied up with a musket beneath her breast. From the window she could see the road her lover would ride to the inn, and she knew when he arrived, King George's soldiers would kill him. She knew she must warn him. She struggled against the rope that bound her hands until one finger touched the trigger. And then . . . "her finger moved in the moonlight, her musket shattered the moonlight, shattered her breast in the moonlight and warned him—with her death."

The poem was hauntingly beautiful, and as our class read it in unison, I found myself lost in it. But then Mr. Echols said, "Okay, when we get to the part where she shoots herself, I want everyone to be quiet while one person announces her death."

That one person was me, and those final three words were my solo part. It shouldn't have been difficult. It should have, in fact, been rather dramatic. The class fell into the rhythm of the poem, galloping toward the fatal shot, building up to the crescendo of the young lover's sacrificial act, then suddenly falling silent for the announcement that I had been chosen to deliver.

I said the words. I really did. I felt those three words—"with her death"—pass through my throat and out my mouth. But they were greeted with a stunned silence. Then a snicker. And then the question, "Did someone say something?" followed finally by outright laughter.

Mr. Echols didn't give up on me right away. I think it wasn't until the next rehearsal that he gave the part to someone else.

Still, that was when I knew I wasn't able to do something because, in a very real sense, I simply wasn't there.

CHAPTER 14

Several days after Satchel came to see me at Pine Glen, my phone rang early in the morning. I reached for the extension in my bedroom.

"Hello?" I was leery. I didn't like early morning phone calls.

"Beth, it's me."

"Oh, hi, Natalie."

"You awake?"

"I'm getting dressed for class. Why? What's up?"

"There's been an accident."

"What—"

"It's on the local news right now. A bunch of kids went off the road over by Hoopes."

"Who?"

"I don't know. They haven't released names."

"Then what—"

"They're Seaton kids, Beth. Boarding students."

"How do you know?"

"One of the kids in the car told the police. But that's all the info the media has released."

"Was anyone hurt?"

"All of them."

"How badly?"

"At least one is critical."

A wave of anxiety slammed against my ribs. "I've got to go, Nat."

I hung up and dialed Joel Sexton's home phone number.

"Sexton."

"Joel, it's Beth. Listen, did a car crash into your living room last night?"

He breathed out what sounded like a laugh. "Yeah, and good morning to you too, Beth."

"No, I mean it, Joel. There's been an accident."

"Where?"

"Out your way. Somewhere over by Hoopes."

"Well, it wasn't here. I'm sitting in my living room right now drinking a cup of coffee."

"It was Seaton kids."

He responded with an oath, and I heard a crashing sound, like a coffee mug coming down hard on a table.

"Who?" he asked.

"I don't know. Names haven't been released."

"Oh my—"

"I've got to go, Joel."

In another minute I was down the stairs and out the front door. I scarcely knew what I was doing as I climbed the grassy hill to Leeds Hall, the girls' dorm. I knew only that I had to see for myself whether Satchel was there.

The front door was unlocked at six thirty each morning so the kids could start going to breakfast. Just inside the door and to the left was Miss Wilson's apartment. I knocked rapidly, hoping she wasn't showering or otherwise couldn't hear me.

In the next moment the door flew open, and Miss Wilson started to say something less than welcoming. But she stopped abruptly when she saw that the person pounding on her door was an adult.

"Good morning, Miss—"

"Which room is Satchel Queen's?"

"What?"

"Satchel. Which room is hers?"

She cocked her head and frowned. "Room 106—last one on the right at the end of the hall. Why? Is she in—"

I didn't wait for her to finish. I rushed down the hall in long strides and, without knocking, flung open the door to room 106. The shades were drawn, and the room was dark, but I could see a slumbering figure in one of the beds. The other bed was empty. I didn't know which bed belonged to Satchel and which belonged to Tess.

I found myself calling out her name. "Satchel!"

The shadowy figure sat up in bed and rubbed her

eyes. She turned on the lamp on the nightstand next to her bed.

"Miss Gunnar? What are you doing here?" It was Satchel, and she was frowning at me.

I was so relieved I wanted to go to the bed and throw my arms around the young girl. Instead, I asked, "Where's Tess?"

Satchel shrugged. "I heard her get up a few minutes ago. She must have gone to the bathroom. Why?"

I couldn't respond. I couldn't get the words unstuck from my throat.

"Miss Gunnar?"

I nodded.

"What happened to your shoes?"

I looked down at my bare feet, wet with morning dew and crisscrossed with blades of freshly mown grass. I wanted to laugh. But even in the midst of my relief, I realized someone had been hurt, students from Seaton, and I didn't know who.

"There's been an accident, Satchel."

"What happened?"

I thought a moment. "I'm sure Mr. Farrell will tell us what he knows during morning assembly."

She was quiet a minute before saying, "Okay."

Tess entered the room then, yawning. "Oh, hi, Miss Gunnar."

"Good morning, Tess."

She padded over to her closet and pulled out a shirt and a pair of jeans. "Come on, Satchel," she said. "Let's go get breakfast. I'm starving."

It didn't seem to surprise her that I was there, and I thought that might be the best moment to make my exit.

"See you girls in assembly."

"Yeah." Tess lifted a hand sleepily and waved me off.

Satchel said nothing. She continued to stare at me through perplexed and narrowed eyes, as though my unexpected appearance in her room was the strangest event imaginable.

Maybe to her it was.

By the end of the day everyone knew the names of the students whose night out in a beer-laden Mitsubishi had ended abruptly after an encounter with a tree. While all four of them—two boys and two girls—remained hospitalized, chances of recovery looked good. The driver, who had at first been critical, was upgraded to serious.

I was in the office talking with Joel shortly before five o'clock when Satchel appeared in the doorway.

"Miss Gunnar?"

I smiled. "Yes, Satchel?"

She must have gone out of her way to find me. The day students had long before headed home, and the boarding students were beginning to meander to the cafeteria for supper.

Satchel pulled back a corner of her mouth as her eyes moved to Joel. He took the cue.

"Well," he said, "I'm going to drop these papers off at the front office and then go home. See you tomorrow, Beth. Take it easy, Satchel."

"Sure, Mr. Sexton."

She took a step farther into the room but didn't sit down. "Are the kids who were in the accident going to be all right?" she asked.

"Yes, I think so."

"What's going to happen to them?"

"What do you mean?"

"Like, is Seaton going to kick them out?"

I sighed. "First, they'll simply be allowed to recover. After that they'll probably be suspended for a week or two. I'm not sure, but that's my best guess."

Satchel nodded. She was wearing her backpack, and yet she clutched a pile of books tightly against her chest. I had a feeling those books were a breastplate in a suit of armor.

"Miss Gunnar?" she said again.

"Yes, Satchel?"

"You thought it was me, didn't you? I mean, you thought I'd gone out drinking and got in that accident."

I pressed my lips together in thought. "I'm sorry, Satchel. Yes, I was afraid it was you. I should never have assumed you'd go out drinking like that. I'm sorry," I said again.

"No," she said quickly. Then she stopped and frowned. "I mean, you came up the hill in your bare feet and all just to see if I was okay."

For a moment neither of us said anything more. We simply looked at each other. Then I said, "Yes, of course. I had to know whether you were all right."

The perplexed gaze remained, but she nodded

slightly. As she did, she took one step backward. Her lips were a thin line. She turned halfway toward the door. "I'll see you tomorrow, Miss Gunnar."

"Okay, Satchel."

"And, um, thanks, Miss Gunnar."

I smiled, though I'm not sure she saw, because even as she spoke the final word she was disappearing out the door.

CHAPTER 15

I wanted to do for Satchel Queen what Theodore Dutton did for me. At least what he did for me before the tragedy happened.

Those months that he was with us, Theodore Dutton didn't let me be invisible. He simply wouldn't allow it. He'd call on me in class even when I didn't raise my hand. He'd read portions of my essays aloud if he thought they were particularly good. He asked me to be his senior assistant for his two freshman English classes, which meant helping him grade grammar tests and giving feedback on student writing assignments.

I was honored beyond all words that he would put such faith in me, and for the first time I felt something at the core of my being that I understood to be confidence. Theodore Dutton believed I was capable, and I could only accept his faith in me as a gift. Each time I went to the English office to sit at his desk and work on the pile of papers he had left for me, I was deeply satisfied in a way I'd never been before.

"I've decided I'm going to be an English teacher," I announced to him one day.

"But of course you are," he responded simply, and my future was sealed.

Natalie was understandably jealous of the attention Mr. Dutton gave me. It almost brought us to blows, until I finally convinced her that the extra time I spent with him had nothing at all to do with the man and everything to do with English. I was a lover of literature the way she was a lover of art.

And while we both loved Theodore Dutton, I would scarcely admit it even to myself, much less to her.

The best times were those when we gathered at Mr. Dutton's cabin, Ray and Ken and Natalie and me. Sometimes Janie and Artie joined us, but since they both lived more than ten miles from school, it was hard for them to get back to campus in the evening. They had to plan ahead to finagle the car keys from their parents, which the other four of us didn't have to do. I just had to spend the night at Natalie's, and from there the two of us met the boys outside the cabin at the designated time.

We got in the habit of going there every Friday night and sometimes during the week as well. There were only a few times Mr. Dutton wasn't there and our knock on the door went unanswered. Once or twice we suspected he was inside, but he didn't come to the door. We thought perhaps he was napping, and we didn't want to wake him.

It never occurred to us that he might have a life outside of Seaton, that there might be other people he wanted to see, other things he wanted to do. We were the center of our own world, and we thought we were the center of his.

I suppose that was because when we were with him, he engaged us so completely. He listened, he laughed, he led us on amazing adventures through stories and poems and ideas until we felt we had traveled the world, though we'd never even left the cabin. If Ken brought along his guitar and played a piece he'd been working on, Mr. Dutton would rest his hands behind his head and stare up at the ceiling, listening with as much enjoyment as if he were at Carnegie Hall.

"Hey," he said one night, "my nephew is coming next weekend, and he's a really good guitarist. Why don't you guys come on over, and he and Ken can do some jamming?"

So we did. The rest of us sat around eating popcorn and drinking Cokes while Ken and this kid named Lennon Dutton strummed songs by Dan Fogelberg and Cat Stevens and Lynyrd Skynyrd. We nodded our heads and tapped our feet, and sometimes we sang along, and when the two of them played "Free Bird," I thought I'd just about died and gone to heaven.

Mr. Dutton's nephew was a shy skinny kid with bangs that fell over his eyes and a complexion marred by acne. But he had an attractive smile that made dimples in his cheeks and a laugh that was like a shot of adrenaline straight to your spine. In between songs we laughed until our sides ached, and most of the time I don't think we even knew what we were laughing about.

It was just that good to be alive.

Before we left that night, I asked Lennon Dutton if his parents had been Beatles fans.

"No," he said. "Why?"

"I thought maybe they'd named you after John Lennon."

"Nope," he answered. "I don't think so."

"If I know my brother," Mr. Dutton interjected, "they probably named Len after the Lennon sisters."

I thought of the buxom girls who shot to fame on *The Lawrence Welk Show*, and Lennon Dutton must have been picturing them too because he rolled his eyes and laughed his infectious laugh. "Yeah, over Mom's dead body," he said.

After that night we saw Lennon Dutton a few more times when he came from Pennsylvania to visit his uncle. But mostly we spent our time at the cabin just talking among ourselves or listening to Mr. Dutton read aloud.

I was never invisible at those times. I was fully there and fully seen. And like I said, it was so good to be alive you could feel the ache of it in your bones. That little cabin was my corner of Eden, the place where life was first breathed into my soul.

CHAPTER 16

"Miss Gunnar?"

"Yes, Satchel?"

"Do you think you're either a saint or a poet?"

"Excuse me?"

"A saint or a poet. Do you think you're one of those?"

I was getting used to Satchel showing up at my house in the evenings, sometimes early, sometimes late. She often came with questions about the essay she was working on for my class or the latest book she had checked out of the library. She sometimes came and looked over my bookshelves, then sat silently reading while I worked at the dining room table grading papers. She seemed simply to want to be there, even if there was no particular reason. I liked having her there.

We sat in the living room now on a chilly September night. She pulled a copy of Thornton Wilder's *Our Town* out of her backpack. It was the play the upper school was producing this year; auditions had already been held, and rehearsals were under way. Satchel, a self-described behind-the-scenes person, had joined the stage crew.

"You know this play, right?" She held the book up for me to see.

"Of course. It's one of my favorites."

"So you know how Emily comes back from the dead and she's allowed to relive one day of her life, and so she lives an ordinary day from her childhood, right?"

I nodded, indicating she should go on.

"It's when she comes back from the dead that she realizes life is really wonderful. And it isn't the big things—it's the small things that she thinks are, like, so incredibly beautiful." Satchel opened to a page marked with a Post-it note. "So she's heading back to the grave, but then she breaks down crying and she has to stop a few minutes and look at everything again and say good-bye. And she starts saying good-bye to all the things she realizes she loved in life, like her home and her family, but also the little things like, like—" Satchel paused and looked down at the book—"like clocks ticking and sunflowers and new ironed dresses and hot baths. And she turns to the stage manager, and she asks, 'Do any human beings ever realize life while they live it?—every, every minute?' And the stage manager says, 'No.' But then after a minute he says, 'The saints and poets, maybe—they do some.' "

Satchel let the book fall to her lap as she raised her eyes to me. She seemed to think I had an answer for her, but I didn't, because I wasn't quite sure what she was asking.

Finally, I said, "And that's how you want to live?"

"I don't know if I can," she answered. "I don't know if anybody can, really."

"Why not?"

Instead of answering my question, she asked another. "Do you have to believe in God to be a poet or a saint?"

"I'm not sure Emily did, beyond the conventions of the time."

"Do you?"

"Believe in God?" I asked.

She nodded.

"Yes," I said.

She thought about my response, then said, "I don't know. I mean, how can anybody know something like that?"

The question disturbed me so that I stood and walked to the front window. A dark and starless night pressed up against the pane, and briefly I thought of the poet Sylvia Plath's image of a fatherless heaven. It made me shiver, and I hugged my sweater more tightly around me. From the time I first read Sylvia's poems, that image had nettled me, and I wanted to grab the poet and argue, *You cannot have a heaven without a Father*. But I couldn't argue with her because she was dead. Like Virginia Woolf, she had killed herself, laying her head upon an oven door and turning on the gas.

I turned from the window and looked at Satchel. "I think we can know that God is there."

"Yeah?"

"Yeah, I do."

"So, like . . ." She looked pensive a moment. "Where do you have to go to find Him? Tibet or something?"

"No," I offered tentatively. "No, I don't think we have to go anywhere, not even to church."

Her largely expressionless eyes, which had been making the rounds of the room, came to rest on me. I thought I saw in them a flicker of something like curiosity, or maybe it was simply doubt.

"Really. I don't think we have to go anywhere," I repeated. "I think He comes to us."

CHAPTER 17

I told Satchel then of the day I heard the bells in the basilica. I had heard them many times before, but this time it was different.

For about a year I lived and worked in Minneapolis, teaching remedial reading at a community college on the edge of downtown. During breaks between classes, when the weather allowed, I walked around the lake in the public park next to the college. Also nearby—just across the street—was a large Catholic basilica whose bells called out the hour with deep echoing rings.

On this particular autumn day I walked through the park with my eyes downcast, looking at the crisp colored leaves on the path at my feet. I was terribly unhappy, wanting desperately to be visible but instead was lost, like the wind-grieved ghost of which Thomas Wolfe spoke. I felt the warmth of the sun and heard the rustle of the wind-tossed leaves, but they were far less real to me than my own inner emptiness. "Which one of us is not forever a stranger and alone?" Wolfe asked. And in anguish and in isolation I knew that he was right. "O waste of loss, in the hot mazes, lost, among bright stars on this most weary unbright cinder, lost! Remembering speechlessly we seek the great forgotten language, the lost lane-end into heaven, a stone, a leaf, an unfound door . . .”

I could not find the way out of the aloneness. And I thought that it would consume me before I ever found the way.

Following the path around the lake, I heard the bells in the basilica strike three o’clock. And that was when it happened. When those notes rang out and drifted down from the sky soft and rich as scattered rose petals, I heard the forgotten language, and in that instant, I understood.

It was a voice, unmistakable, saying, *I’m here, and I love you.*

The language is sometimes forgotten but not lost, because I had heard and understood it before. The first time it came, I was walking beneath the tall pines on the road leading into Seaton. There, amid the pine needles and the resinous scent of the trees, I heard it saying, *I’m here, and it’s all right. Everything will be all right.*

Just as God had come to me on the road into Seaton, it was God who broke in when, walking through the park, I could find no slit in the veil, no hint of light in the dark and wordless isolation.

But that wasn’t the end of the story. As lovely as the bells were that rang three times, I wanted to hear them chime the hour at noon. I wanted to hear not just three times but twelve times that He loved me.

The next day I returned to the park and sat on a bench across from the basilica. It was shortly before twelve. In another moment the bells began to chime. Slowly and heavily they tolled, calling out the hour. I counted along. One, two, three, four . . . I was satisfied at twelve, but the bells didn't stop there. They rang once more, and then again, and on and on. For a full three minutes they rang like laughter over the park, over the city, over me.

I knew then what I hadn't known before: How great is the love of the One who made us.

What I didn't tell Satchel was that I had long forgotten about the bells until that night when she asked me about God. I hadn't thought about the bells in the basilica for years. I didn't tell Satchel that a person can go on believing in God without giving so much as a passing thought to His love, which in the end completely misses the point of believing and leaves one as helpless as a cloud in a fatherless heaven.

CHAPTER 18

"So maybe they were just working on the bells," Satchel suggested. "Testing them or something. Or maybe they got stuck."

"Probably," I agreed. Then I added, "But it's the timing that's interesting, don't you think? It happened when I needed it to happen."

"I guess so." She sounded unconvinced.

I drew in a deep breath, buying some time to try to read her thoughts. Then I said, "But I didn't answer your question about the poets and the saints, did I?"

She shrugged. "That's all right. It doesn't really

matter. I'm not a poet, and I'll sure never be a saint." She offered me a small dry laugh.

"But you *are* a poet, Satchel."

"Naw." She shook her head. "Remember? I don't write poetry."

"No, but I mean, you have the eye of a poet anyway. I think you notice things, the way Emily did when she came back from the dead."

She was quiet a long time then. I let her think.

Finally she said, "You know what I really like, Miss Gunnar?"

"What, Satchel?"

"The smell of dead fish and gasoline."

I thought she might be joking and that perhaps I was supposed to laugh. But I took my cue from her expressionless face and only cocked my head to ask her to explain.

"Really," she said. "I can't smell fish and gasoline without thinking of the best summers of my life. Okay, so see, when I was little, my grandma—my dad's mom—owned a cottage on Lake Conesus in upstate New York. We used to go up there for a week or two in the summer—my mom, my dad, and me. And my dad, he'd always rent a motorboat so we could go out on the lake. He'd wake me up early, and we'd go out on the water just as the sun was coming up. Well, the shore of the lake usually had dead fish on it, you know? Like, they'd die and wash up there on the rocks and start to rot. So there'd be that fishy smell, and then Dad and I would walk out on the dock and get into the boat and tie our life jackets on. And then when he started the motor, there was the smell of gasoline, and then we'd push off from the dock, and we'd be flying over the water. . . ." She paused and shut her eyes. "And I'd sit there in the front of the boat holding my arms out, and I'd feel like I was flying. That's the only time I've really felt like I was—I don't know—alive, I guess." She opened her eyes and looked at me.

"It sounds wonderful, Satchel," I said.

"It was. There were so many things, like—well, sometimes we'd build a fire on the shore at night and roast marshmallows. Or Dad and I, we'd walk along the edge of the water and collect rocks and put them in a bucket. And sometimes"—her eyes grew brighter—"sometimes Grandma watered her grass with a sprinkler, the kind that looks like a huge fan waving back and forth. You know what I mean?"

I nodded.

"And if you looked at the sprinkler from just the right angle, you'd see rainbows in the water because of the way the sun was shining on it. I remember running through the sprinkler even with my clothes on and jumping around saying, 'Look at me, Daddy! I'm jumping through rainbows!' "

She stopped then, her smile lingering while her eyes misted over. But she didn't cry. She pulled the tears back into herself and said, "I wish I could do it again. But my grandma died and the cottage got sold, so we never went there again."

I asked, tentatively, "Where is your father now?"

Her lips became a taut line at the center of her face. She dropped the copy of *Our Town* into her backpack and pushed herself up from the wing chair. "I gotta go, Miss Gunnar," she said. "I promised Tess I'd study for the French test with her."

As I watched her turn to go, I understood that I wasn't going to hear about her father tonight. "Is the test tomorrow?" I asked.

"Yeah. But I'm not worried. Mrs. Connelly's tests are pretty easy because, to tell you the truth, I don't think she's fluent in French herself."

"Oh!" I frowned. "Well, that's not good."

Satchel shrugged. "So who needs to speak French when anywhere you go in the world, they speak English?"

We had made our way to the door, where Satchel stood with her hand on the doorknob. "Well, thanks for telling me about the bells and all that, Miss Gunnar. Maybe there's something to it."

For the first time I dared to touch Satchel by putting my hand on her shoulder. She didn't flinch, but instead seemed to lean into my touch. "And thank you for telling me about the rainbows, Satchel. I think Emily in *Our Town* would have put jumping through rainbows right up there with clocks ticking and new ironed dresses."

"You think so?"

"Yeah, I do."

She smiled. "Well, good night, Miss Gunnar."

"Good night, Satchel."

CHAPTER 19

Sometime in the fall of 1976 we started reading Virginia Woolf for Theodore Dutton's class. I neither enjoyed nor fully understood her novels, and why Mr. Dutton required us to read three of them in as many weeks was beyond me, except—as I supposed at the time—that was simply what one did in Honors English. We spent more time on Woolf than any other writer, and I think now it was because Mr. Dutton favored her works. I think she spoke to him.

To me, her only intelligible utterances were of sorrow and doom. Think of poor Mrs. Ramsey in *To the Lighthouse*, annoyed with herself for having said, "We are in the hands of the Lord."

"How could any Lord have made this world? she asked. With her mind she had always seized the fact that there is no reason, order, justice: but suffering, death, the poor. There was no treachery too base for the world to commit; she knew that. No happiness lasted; she knew that."

Virginia Woolf was not a cheery person. I pictured her as Mrs. Ramsey sailing toward the lighthouse, proclaiming stoically, "We perished, each alone."

Yet, when at last we read her essay "A Sketch of the Past," it was then I became intrigued by her. She wrote about what she called her moments of being. These moments, she explained, were embedded in the many more moments of life's nonbeing. She described the moments of being as a sudden shock, a welcome shock, in which she sensed something beyond the visible, or, as she wrote, the shock "is or will become a revelation of some order; it is a token of some real thing behind appearances."

When I read that, my sixteen-year-old self whispered, "It's God, of course." But Virginia Woolf was a brilliant woman, and she did not believe in God. "Certainly and emphatically there is no God," she wrote, so how to explain the moments of being?

Because Mr. Dutton mentioned Woolf's published diaries in class, I went on to read parts of them on my own. The copy I read was from the public library, but even so I underlined these words in pencil: "I have some restless searcher in me. Why is there not a discovery in life? I have questioned. Something one can lay hands on and say 'This is it'? I'm looking: but that's not it, that's not it. What is it? And shall I die before I find it?"

I was haunted by that question. "Shall I die before I find it?" I wanted to tell her, "It's so simple, don't you see . . . ?" But I knew that Virginia Woolf had filled her pockets with stones and drowned herself in the River Ouse in 1941.

I wrote an essay for Mr. Dutton's class explaining my theory that Virginia Woolf's moments of being were actually those instances in which God was revealing himself to her.

It was no secret at Seaton that I was a churchgoing believer. I suppose it wasn't so much the way I acted—

a person could be a good kid making good grades without being a Christian. No, I think the real give-away was the bumper sticker on my car that said in two-inch, no-nonsense type: *Jesus is Lord.* By my senior year I finally had my license, and because I was able to drive myself to school, my father bought a new car for my mother and gave me the red and white 1960 Pontiac station wagon Mom had been driving since I was born. With my classmates behind the wheels of Camaros, Mustangs, and Falcons, I wanted neither that rattletrap with fins nor the bumper sticker that came with it. It was either that, though, or walk to school, my parents being understandably reluctant to haul me around any longer. I considered at least scraping off the bumper sticker, but in the end decided that was tanta-mount to Peter's betrayal in the garden, and I simply couldn't do it. So every morning I drove to campus in an antiquated evangelistic station wagon and parked it amid the jacked-up newer models sporting various rock group decals and racing strips. My strategy was to act as though there was nothing at all different about my car, that it was something that any high school senior would be proud to drive. Apparently my strategy worked, as very little was ever said about that old Pontiac. Now I have to wonder whether it was simply expected of someone like me to drive some-thing like that, making it all a nonissue in the first place.

Anyway, there I was, the campus Jesus Freak writing this English paper about divine revelation and turning it in to be graded by a man who, I assumed, believed in God.

But I was wrong. Theodore Dutton was like Virginia Woolf in that regard. In both their worlds, certainly and emphatically there was no God.

I found that out on one of the nights that the gang went to visit him at his cabin. We were all there, all six of the Barbarians, including Janie and Artie. We were lounging about the room drinking a watery hot chocolate and talking about the Bloomsbury Group of which Virginia Woolf was a member. I was feeling rather smug and proud of myself for writing what I thought was an exceptionally good essay, and I hoped Mr. Dutton might mention it during the course of the evening.

I sat on one of the couches beside Ray that night, leaning against him with my cheek on his shoulder. I was just about to say something about Woolf's diaries when Artie spoke up and the conversation turned toward agnosticism, one of his favorite subjects, right up there with his fascination for the French Foreign Legion.

Artie Sochs was, like the members of the Bloomsbury Group, a skeptic. According to Artie, the basic principles of empiricism didn't allow for belief in something that couldn't be experienced. Artie was heavy into math and science; he liked the conclusive experiments and irrefutable answers these disciplines offered. He had no patience with philosophical speculation.

"Stephen was right," he said, speaking of Virginia Woolf's father. "When he gave up the faith, he said it was like giving up a huge burden. That's all it is, you know. Belief in God just slows down human progress."

I heard Ray sigh. "Yeah, sure, Artie. We know the drill. You can't see God, so he isn't there. But that's not necessarily so. There are lots of things we can't see, but that doesn't mean they don't exist."

"Like what?"

Ray thought a moment. "Well, like anger, for one. I mean, think about it. Put a little bit of the pure stuff of anger right here in my hand, will you?"

He held his hand out toward Artie. Artie shrugged it off. "Yeah, well, we know anger's there because we see the effects of it. That's obvious."

"And we don't see the effects of God?"

The room fell silent. Artie cast me a look that was a direct challenge to my bumper sticker. He and I had discussed all this before and had reached an impasse, neither of us willing to budge. I looked helplessly at Mr. Dutton.

Our teacher sat backward in a ladder-back chair brought in from the kitchen, his forearms resting on the top rail. He frowned while scratching absently at one sleeve. "We're all entitled to our individual beliefs," he said, "whatever they may be."

"Yeah, so," said Ken Cunningham, lying on the floor with his hands beneath his head, "what do you believe, Mr. Dutton? Do you think God exists?"

Mr. Dutton seemed to hesitate ever so slightly. Then he said, "No, I don't. But I would never try to convince another person to believe—or not believe—the way I do."

"Still, you'd call yourself an atheist. Right?" Artie asked.

"I don't like labels, but if I have to have one, I guess that'd be it."

Artie looked triumphant. My own cheeks burned, and I was glad the lighting in the room was dim.

We went on then to speak of other things as though this one issue had been settled and we were reluctant to bring it up again. The sage had spoken; the students were silenced. I had let myself be silenced, melting into my cloak of invisibility.

Mr. Dutton handed back our papers later that week. He gave me an A, along with the comment, "Well written. Interesting premise."

But I didn't want the A. I wasn't interested in premises. I wanted what I had written to be true, not just for me but for Theodore Dutton. That it wasn't true for him rattled me more than I cared to admit, and it cast a shadow into my personal corner of Eden.

CHAPTER 20

"So this is where you grew up, huh?" Satchel asked.

"This is it."

We stood in front of a two-story fieldstone house on Heritage Drive in a neighborhood called Westminster.

I had told Satchel I grew up right here in Wilmington, and she asked to see the house. We drove out from Seaton on a Sunday afternoon and parked on the street where my family and I once lived.

"Who lives in the house now?" she asked.

I shrugged. "I have no idea."

"Want to ring the doorbell and find out?"

"No, I don't think so. I wouldn't want to bother them."

"You could tell them you used to live here."

I felt as though I should live there still, as though I should be able to walk in through the front door and find my mother and my father and my sisters at home. Dad should be reading the paper in his easy chair, his feet propped up on the footstool, our dog curled up on the floor beside him. My sisters should be upstairs listening to the Top 40 Countdown while curling their hair in front of the bathroom mirror, and Mom should be in the kitchen cooking a pot roast and kneading dough for homemade bread. That's how it should be and would be if time hadn't changed all that, wiped it away like chalk off a blackboard. That was probably why I hadn't come to see the house since returning to Delaware. This place that still housed so much of my heart—how could it not belong to me?

"See the upstairs middle window?" I asked, pointing.

"Uh-huh."

"That was my bedroom."

She looked up, squinting against the sun. "Well," she

said finally, "it looks like it was a pretty nice place to grow up."

"It was," I said, nodding, "though I didn't know it at the time."

"What do you mean?"

"Well—" I stopped and thought about her question. "I just took everything for granted. And I thought Delaware was boring. My friend Natalie and I called it Dullaware, as in D-u-l-l."

She didn't respond for a while. Then she said, "You mean, you went to school, and you came home and your mom was there, and then your dad came home from work, and you all sat around the kitchen table eating supper?"

I laughed lightly. "Yes, that's how it was. Every day."

She looked at me, then looked away, but not before I saw the way her eyes narrowed and two lines formed between her brows.

"So, do you want to walk around the neighborhood?" I asked.

"Sure."

The center of the neighborhood was a lopsided circle of intersecting streets, exactly one mile around, with other streets like tendrils leading off the main loop. I knew every foot of it by heart.

"Are your parents still alive?" Satchel asked as we started out.

"Yes, they are."

"You're lucky."

I nodded.

"Where do they live now?"

"Asheville, North Carolina. They retired there. My dad always wanted to live in the mountains."

"That's cool."

We walked to where Heritage Drive meets up with Ambleside Drive. Turning right, we came upon the covered bridge that passed over the little creek running through the neighborhood.

"This is where I waited for the bus when I went to public school."

"Yeah? Under a covered bridge? That's cool," she said again. "So how come you ended up going to Seaton?"

"Well, I was a quiet kid, very shy. My parents thought I'd do better in a smaller classroom."

"I get it. You were one of the kids all the other kids ragged on."

I smiled. "I guess you could put it that way."

"But it was better at Seaton?"

"Oh yes. For the most part. As I've mentioned before, I made some good friends. I was happy there."

It was a long gradual climb up Ambleside, then down again toward Cheltenham. We took a right turn and went up again toward the crest of Cheltenham, the best hill in the neighborhood to sail down on a bike or a sled. All these years later I could still feel the wind in my face, the sensation of weightlessness, of flying without wings.

"I think I would have liked living here," Satchel said. "And if I'd had your life, I think I would have known I was lucky."

"I suspect you might have, Satchel."

"I don't think your childhood was boring. I think it was more, like, innocent. I mean, the way a childhood is supposed to be, you know?"

"Um-hmm." I nodded. We started the trek down Cheltenham. "That reminds me of something Edna St. Vincent Millay once said."

"Yeah? No offense, Miss Gunnar, but everything reminds you of something some writer once said."

I laughed. "I suppose you're right."

We kept walking, our feet slapping against the pavement as we descended the steep grade.

"So what'd she say?" Satchel asked.

I stole a moment to catch my breath. The hill I ran up as a child now left me winded going down. "She said that childhood is the kingdom where nobody dies." Then I added, as Millay had, "Nobody that matters, that is."

We walked the length of Cheltenham, over the concrete bridge arching the creek on this side of the neighborhood, then turned back onto Heritage Drive. "She was right, you know," I went on. "When you're a kid, you're so full of life, you don't have time to think about anything else."

We reached my car, parked along the curb in front of my former home. Satchel began to open the passenger side door when she stopped and looked up at the house.

"Well," she said, lifting her shoulders in a small dispirited shrug, "I guess by that definition, I never even *had* a childhood, not even a boring one."

On the two-mile drive back to Seaton, Satchel turned on the radio and fiddled with the dial, finding just the right music to fill the void where otherwise words might have been.

CHAPTER 21

September receded and October rolled in, and still I knew nothing about Satchel's father. I suspected he was no longer living, but I didn't ask, and she didn't tell. I would simply have to wait until the time was right for me to know.

Natalie reminded me that I'd promised to go to homecoming with her that first weekend of the month. I wanted to go to the Saturday night reception, but starting early in the morning I had a pounding headache that wouldn't let go, and by early afternoon I called Natalie to tell her I might not make it. She retorted that if I didn't come of my own accord, she'd show up at Pine Glen and drag me there herself, as she had no intention of going without me. I took a couple more aspirin and slept the afternoon away and was feeling well enough by evening to get dressed and head over to the larger of the two gymnasiums, Kennemac Gym.

"You're late," Natalie said when I found her holding a plate of hors d'oeuvres just inside the main doors. "People have been mingling for an hour."

"You're lucky I'm here," I said groggily, "and I just

hope you appreciate the sacrifice I'm making for you."

"Yeah, right. You know you wouldn't miss this night for anything."

We both laughed, friends long enough to engage in some harmless bantering.

"You'll never guess who else is here," she said.

"Who? Artie Sochs, home from the Belgian Congo?"

"Better than that. It's Ray."

"Ray Schmidt?"

"Who else?"

Of course Ray Schmidt. I'd been wondering whether he'd show up. In fact, I'd been thinking about him that morning when the headache settled in. "Did you talk with him?" I asked.

"Not yet. He's only just arrived. Must have come in while I was in the ladies' room. See, he's over there."

"Where?"

"There."

I tried to follow the nod of her head, but the gym was large and the crowd was thick, and I couldn't see anyone who looked like the Ray I remembered.

"He's got his back to us."

"Oh." I pretended I didn't care. Turning back to Natalie, I asked, "So did the hubby come with you?"

"No." She bit into a cheese-laden cracker and shook her head. "Jason had a game, so Ron took him to that. Believe me, he'd rather watch softball than come to a high school reunion with me."

"Yeah, I suppose so. Well, anyone else here we know?"

"Ken Cunningham's around here somewhere. I haven't spoken with him yet, but I saw him."

"Really? It's practically a Barbarian reunion."

Natalie laughed. "Yeah, except for Janie and Artie. Other than that, there are a few here from our class but not many."

I nodded. "Well, I'm going to get something to eat."

"Don't you want to see Ray?"

I did. And I didn't.

"Let me get something to drink first."

"The punch isn't spiked, if that's what you mean."

"That wasn't what I meant." Though if I'd been a drinking woman, that's exactly what I'd have meant.

We moved together to the serving tables piled high with various finger foods, chocolates, and cakes. Someone was dipping out cups of punch and offered me one. I took it and clutched the cup nervously.

"Hey, listen." Natalie cocked an ear and pointed off toward nothing in particular. "Remember how we used to call the radio station and request this song?"

Listening, I recognized the tune as one that was popular when we were in school. It drifted over from a far corner of the gym where a three-piece band sat nestled under a dubious spotlight. The space in front of them served as a dance floor where a few brave souls were trying to revive their long-forgotten disco moves.

"Yeah," I said, "and now it's a golden oldie."

For the next half hour or so Natalie and I mingled within the swirling mix of music and conversation and laughter. I sought out familiar faces with an increasing sense of disappointment, resorting finally to looking at name tags and realizing that many of the alumni were far younger than I. No wonder so few people were attempting to dance. Seventies music wouldn't mean much to a nineties audience. The anachronistic band played on, though, trying valiantly to coax down memory lane a crowd of people who simply couldn't go back that far.

At some point Ken Cunningham approached us, greeting us each with an awkward hug we could only half return without spilling punch down his back. He had thickened, becoming chinless and jowled, and his hair was prematurely gray, an unflattering crown that aged him beyond his years. He introduced us to his wife, a rather nondescript woman who looked so unhappy to be there that I considered yelling "Fire!" so we could all clear the gym and go home.

"You girls look great," Ken gushed, looking from Natalie to me and back to Natalie again. "You both look more beautiful today than you did in high school."

His obvious flattery only served to shrink his wife even further. He sounded tipsy and unctuous, and I wondered what had happened to him in the years since we'd been in school. He'd spent too much time among politicians, I thought, and I suddenly had no real desire to speak to him. But I asked him anyway, "So how've you been, Ken?"

"Great!" he responded loudly. "Doing great. How about the two of you?"

"Good, Ken. Good," Natalie answered. "You still in D.C.?"

"Oh sure. I mean, where can you go from there? It's addictive, you know?"

"I bet." That was me, growing more despondent by the second.

"Yeah, I'm thinking of running for office."

"Oh yeah?" Natalie asked. "What, specifically?"

"President," he said.

Natalie's brows flew up. "President of the United States?"

"What else?" He finished off his punch in one long gulp. "On the Democratic ticket, of course. I want to out-Clinton Clinton, especially when it comes to the interns, you know?" He gave a raucous laugh, fueled with alcohol.

I looked at his wife. She was studying the floor and didn't meet my gaze.

Turning to Natalie, I said, "I thought you said the punch wasn't spiked."

"What's that?" Ken asked.

"Nothing," Natalie said, casting me a sideways glance meant to shut me up.

Ken's wife looked up from the floor. "Will you excuse me a moment?"

"Sure, hon'," Ken said. "It's through those doors and down the stairs."

He waved her off to the ladies' room, not noticing that she headed toward the front door of the gym instead. He didn't notice because he was too busy paying attention to Natalie. “Hey listen, Nat, they’re playing our song. Wanna dance?”

To my surprise, she did. Natalie was thoroughly committed to her husband, I knew, but I was less certain of Ken’s commitment to his wife. Obviously I didn’t know who Ken was anymore.

Left alone, I decided it was time to seek out Raymond Schmidt. I’d get it over with and then go home.

Until that moment I’d put off seeing Ray out of fear. It was the memory of who we’d been to each other our senior year: steady dates, confidants, the one with whom we’d shared goals and fears and dreams. I was afraid to see the person I’d considered my first love.

Too, I was afraid simply because he had been there. He had lived through senior year with us, including the final dreadful months.

But when Natalie and Ken moved off toward the dance floor, I turned and scanned the room, then tentatively wandered through the crowd until I found him. He was by himself too, looking at some photographs taped to the far wall, a history of Seaton in a series of black-and-white moments. I touched his elbow. When he turned to see who it was and I could look at him straight on, I saw that the years had been kind to him. He appeared older and more mature, but at the same time more refined. He looked strong and self-assured, and he looked pleased to see me.

“Beth,” he said, and my name sounded like delighted laughter in his mouth.

We hugged, not awkwardly, but as though we were

used to falling into each other's embrace. "Hello, Ray. Or I guess it's Dr. Schmidt now, right?"

He smiled. "It's been Dr. Schmidt for a long time—almost too long," he said with a laugh. "You look great, Beth, really great."

Coming from him, the words sounded sincere.

He added, "I was hoping you'd be here."

"You were?" I asked, but he didn't hear me, and he went on to ask me how I was. "Good. I've been good," I replied. "And you?"

"Not bad. Hey, I hear you're teaching here now."

"That's right. I'm part of Seaton's faculty, if you can imagine that."

"You like it?"

"I do. It's strange being here as a teacher instead of a student."

"Yeah, I guess it would be. You'll have to—whoa!" A small child with tousled hair sideswiped him. "Slow down, buddy. Wait a minute." Ray laid a hand on top of the child's head to stop him. "Let me introduce you to my old friend, Mrs.—"

He stopped then and looked at me.

"Gunnar," I said. "It hasn't changed."

For a moment Ray looked unsure. Then he said to the boy, "Ben, this is an old friend of mine, Miss Gunnar. Can you say hello?"

The boy looked up at me with his father's eyes. Obediently, he said, "Hello."

"This is my youngest," Ray explained. "Ben."

"I'm happy to meet you, Ben."

Ray's hand remained settled on top of the boy's blond curls. His wedding band glinted in the artificial light of the gym's fluorescent lamps.

In the next moment a woman was there beside us, a very young woman, blonde like Ben and beautiful. She was far younger than Ray and I, and I thought, *She must be his second wife*. But that was speculation. She and I exchanged a tentative smile, and Ray started to say something when suddenly he stopped and, reaching into his breast pocket, pulled out a cell phone.

"Excuse me a minute," he said. "I've got a call." He moved to an open door and stepped outside.

The child ran off then, and the woman smiled apologetically at me as if to say, *You know what children are like,* and then she took off after him, and I was once again alone. But only for a moment.

When Ray came back, his whole face a frown, he said, "I'm sorry, Beth. There's an emergency. I have to go."

"Oh! I understand—" I began.

He cut me off by saying once more, "I'm sorry. We'll have to talk another time." And then he looked about the room to find his wife and son and, spying them, gave my shoulder a quick squeeze and then was gone.

I was disappointed. I would have liked to ask him about his life, his family, his work. But I decided that in those few moments I had learned as much as I needed to know. He was a busy doctor with a beautiful wife and an adorable young son and presumably one or more older children too. He looked trim and successful and happy. What more did I need to know? He had done well for himself, and above all else, I was happy for my old friend.

Left with that impression, I found it rather odd when a few days later Raymond Schmidt called Pine Glen and invited me to dinner.

CHAPTER 22

"Do you mean," I asked, "have dinner with you and your family?"

"Well, no," he said. Then he rushed to add, "Of course I'd like you to meet the kids sometime, but for now I was thinking just the two of us could grab something to eat over at the Lincolnshire. You remember the place, don't you?"

I did, and it was no fast-food restaurant where people grabbed something to eat. It was a place where patrons dined leisurely at tables arrayed with silverware and crystal and delicate china on stiff white tablecloths.

It was startlingly inappropriate for a married man and a single woman, even those simply sharing a meal as old friends.

"Yes, I know the Lincolnshire, but I'm afraid, well, I'm afraid I can't do that, Ray."

"If you're busy this Saturday, we could make it the following week."

"No, it's not that. It's—" I stopped. I couldn't believe the conversation we were having. I felt silly saying what should have been perfectly obvious to Ray, *would* have been obvious to the Ray I'd known in high school. I tried to laugh, but that only made me sound nervous, which I was. Finally I blurted, "What on earth would your wife think?"

"My wife? What's she—" Ray stopped. Then he said, "Oh, wait a minute, you think—"

"I know we're old friends but—"

"No, no, no. Hold on a minute. I was just assuming you knew."

"Knew what?"

"Well, that I'm not married."

Not married? The towheaded boy? The dazzling blonde? The wedding ring?

Once more I fumbled for words. "But, the woman at homecoming—"

"Oh, now I understand! That was Ingrid. I forgot I didn't—I had to leave before I could introduce you to her. Ingrid is my au pair. From Sweden. She helps take care of Ben and Lisa. Not that Lisa's incapable of taking care of herself, since she's a senior this year. But I need someone around the house. . . ."

And on he went about the child care, the housework, all that he couldn't do because of the hours he spent at the hospital. When he finished, I wanted to ask again about the wedding ring, which he hadn't explained, but I decided by that point I would be going beyond what I needed to know and risking an attitude of peevishness. After all, if he wanted to wear a wedding ring even though he wasn't married, what was that to me?

I made a mental note to ask him about it later.

"So would you like to have dinner with me Saturday night?"

What could I say? There was nothing in the world to keep me from saying yes.

CHAPTER 23

My Dad
by Satchel Queen

People say you can't remember anything from when you were a baby, but I think they might be wrong. I have a memory in my head, and I must have been a baby or maybe a toddler because I'm lying in my crib looking up at my dad's face. He's smiling and making funny noises that might have been words, but I don't know because I didn't know yet what words are. But I knew my dad was happy, and it seemed to have something to do with me.

When I was born my father was twenty years old and my mother was nineteen and I was what people call a surprise. My mom and dad weren't married and even though I came along they never got married. The three of us lived together, though—mostly.

For Dad, I was something good, like a surprise party. I was something to celebrate. For Mom, I guess it wasn't what you'd call a party having me. It was one of those unexpected things that catches you off guard and you wish life wouldn't bring you.

Dad was a good-looking man and very big. At least he seemed really big to me because I was a baby. Even when I got bigger, he was still big. If I shut my eyes today I can feel what it was like when he picked me up and carried me against his shoulder. It was warm and safe and it smelled good there because of the aftershave he wore. It was a cheap aftershave because we never had much money, but I didn't know that at the time.

Dad was an artist, but he worked for the sanitation department in Brooklyn. He said that artists are meant to create beauty, and that by collecting garbage and getting rid of it, he was helping the world to be more beautiful.

Mom didn't like Dad being a garbage man. I know because I used to hear them fight about it late at night when they thought I was asleep. I was *asleep, until their yelling woke me up. Sometimes our neighbor in the next apartment woke up too because I could hear him banging on the wall, telling Mom and Dad to pipe down. Well, he didn't put it that way but I won't write what our neighbor really said.*

Dad was always happy anyway. Except for our neighbor and maybe my mom sometimes, everybody liked him. He had about a thousand friends, I guess, because everybody wanted to be around Daniel Queen. He'd take me to the corner bar on Friday nights—the owner was Dad's friend and let me in even though I was a kid—and everybody said, "Danny Queen, tell us a story!" And he would. Dad could tell a story like no one else. When he got done the place was so full of laughter I could feel the floor shaking.

When he wasn't working, Dad took me all over the city. We went to the Statue of Liberty and Central Park and Grand Central Station and Lincoln Center, when it was all decorated for Christmas. He took me to the top of the Empire State Building and up to the top of the World Trade Center too, back when the towers were still there. If you've ever seen the city from the top of buildings like that, you never forget it.

One summer day when I was eight years old, Dad took me to the beach at Coney Island. Like most times when we went somewhere, it was just the two of us. We went to Coney Island pretty often because we both liked the ocean. We liked to walk along the shore right at the spot where the waves come in and go back out. I was always fascinated by the little shells and pebbles that did somersaults over the wet sand as the water went back out. Dad and I would collect some and put them in our pockets.

Anyway, this one summer day was different than the others. We bought ice cream cones, and we sat on a bench on the boardwalk to eat them. Dad got butter pecan and I got plain chocolate. The wind kept blowing my hair into the ice cream until Dad took off his baseball cap and stuck it on my head backward.

"That better?" he asked.

I nodded. He always took care of everything.

We kept on licking our ice cream and watching the seagulls flying around and listening to the waves coming in. There were lots of people walking on the boardwalk and lying on the beach. I loved to be there because it made me feel like I was part of something good.

I heard people laughing and there was music coming from somewhere, and I asked Dad if he had enough money for me to ride the merry-go-round. He said he did and we'd go there as soon as we finished our cones.

And then he said, "Satchel, you'll never forget your old dad, will you?"

I didn't know what he meant but I thought maybe it had to do with Father's Day that was coming up, so I said, "Don't worry, Dad, I won't forget," because I had already made him a card with hearts all over it.

He said, "That's good, Satchel," and he put his arm around me and squeezed my shoulder and said, "I'll always love you."

I said, "I'll always love you too, Dad."

Then I rode the merry-go-round, and every time I passed Dad he raised his hand and waved at me, and I had no idea he was waving good-bye.

The first time I read the poem called "Richard Cory" by Edwin Arlington Robinson when I was about fourteen, I had the creepy feeling that this

Robinson guy knew Daniel Queen. My dad wasn't rich, but everyone admired him and watched for him to come and were happy if he so much as said, "Good morning." And then, like Richard Cory, one calm summer night Daniel Queen went home and put a bullet through his head.

He didn't need to worry. Even if I live to be a hundred years old, I will never forget my dad.

CHAPTER 24

Just as I reached the final paragraph of her essay, Satchel appeared on the hillside sloping down from the dorm. It was almost as though she knew I was reading her story and she was coming to weigh my reaction. Hurriedly I pushed back from the table and stepped to the bathroom, where I dried my eyes and tried to steady my breath.

Then I met Satchel at the door.

"Can I come in a minute, Miss Gunnar?"

"Of course."

The chill of autumn had settled in, and Satchel wore a denim jacket and a pair of jeans. Both were tattered and faded and right in style. She sat down in the wing chair, kicked off her shoes, and tucked her legs beneath her.

"So what are you doing?" she asked.

"I've just been grading essays."

"Don't you ever do anything, you know, just for fun?"

I thought a moment. "Well, I'm going out to dinner tonight, if that counts."

"With a man?"

"Yes."

"So it's a date?"

"No. He's an old friend. We were classmates here at Seaton. We thought we'd get together and just catch up."

She gave me a look that said she didn't believe me. "So what's this guy do?"

"He's a doctor."

"Oh yeah? Mr. Moneybags, huh?"

I laughed. "I don't know. I suppose he does all right."

Satchel nodded. "Yeah, so if you marry him, maybe you can stop teaching and spending all your time reading boring essays."

"Good grief, Satchel, I don't intend to marry the guy, and I don't want to stop teaching. I happen to like what I do. Besides, I don't think the essays are boring at all. In fact . . ." I paused a moment, then said, "I just finished reading yours."

She fidgeted in the chair. "Yeah?"

"Yes. And I want you to know that I'm sorry."

"For what?"

"About your father. I didn't know."

She shrugged. "How could you know? It's probably not part of my permanent record or anything, is it?"

I looked at her until she dropped her eyes. I said, "The suicide of a parent is a terrible thing for a child to live through. It's something you never get over. I know you must miss your father terribly."

Keeping her gaze on her lap, she nodded. "You want to know what's really rotten, Miss Gunnar?"

"What's that, Satchel?"

"When he died, I think my mom was just relieved. I mean, I never saw her cry. Not once."

I struggled to find something to say. "Well, maybe she did cry, when she was alone. Maybe she didn't want you to see her cry."

"Why not? I saw her cry plenty of times later when this boyfriend dumped her or that boyfriend cheated on her."

I shook my head and sighed heavily. "I don't know, Satchel. Some people are hard to understand. I'm sure your mother's not a bad person—"

"Yeah, right. You can say that because you don't know her."

I flinched, then ceded the argument to her. "You've got a point. I don't know her."

This child was an orphan, with an indifferent mother and a father who had loved her, although not enough to stay alive for her.

"I'm glad you shared your story with me, Satchel," I said. "Thank you for that."

"Yeah sure. Like, I just thought you ought to know."

"I appreciate that." Then I added, "After . . . this happened, did you ever talk with anyone?"

Satchel's eyes narrowed. "You mean, like a head doctor or something?"

I nodded in reply.

"Naw," she said. "Why should I? Talking isn't going to bring my dad back."

"No. But sometimes it helps."

"Helps with what?"

"Well, with the grief. It can help you find closure."

"No offense, Miss Gunnar," she said with a roll of her eyes, "but I hate that word *closure*. It's a stupid word."

"Yeah," I agreed. "You're right."

"I don't want anything closed, and I don't want any help. I just wanted you to know what happened."

"All right."

She leaned against the arm of the chair, her chin in one hand, staring absently at the empty fireplace. Finally she said, "So tell me something good, Miss Gunnar."

With those words Satchel declared her father's suicide a mute topic. She had said all she wanted to say, and now we were done. I would honor that and follow her lead in this conversation. "Something good?" I repeated.

"A story. Like the story of the bells."

"Oh. Well . . ."

The room was quiet while my mind tossed about anxiously, trying to find something to say, something appropriate. What, I wondered, would Satchel consider good?

Thankfully she helped me out by asking, "This guy you're having dinner with tonight—what's his name?"

"Raymond Schmidt. Ray."

"So tell me what it was like when you and Ray were kids."

I smiled then. "We had fun. We were part of this group—there were six of us, three guys and three girls. We called ourselves the Barbarians."

Satchel looked at me doubtfully. "No offense, Miss Gunnar, but I don't think the name works. I mean, I don't really see you as a barbarian, you know?"

I laughed. "No. The truth is, we were anything but barbaric. I guess that's why we thought it was funny."

She shrugged. "Okay. Whatever works."

"The six of us hung out together and did—I don't know—lots of crazy things."

"Like what?"

"Well, things that would probably sound pretty tame to kids today."

"So tell me."

"We'd sneak off campus to go to Burger King, or we'd climb up the fire escape on Heath Hall after dark and sit around telling stories and drinking sodas."

She sat motionless for a moment as though waiting for more. When I didn't go on, she said, "That's not only tame, Miss Gunnar. That's pretty lame."

I couldn't help laughing. "I guess so. But being part of that group is one of the best memories I have."

She nodded as if she understood, but I was fairly sure she didn't.

Then she said, "I bet you and Ray had a thing going, didn't you?"

"We dated for a while," I confessed. "Nothing serious."

"And now you're having dinner tonight?"

"Yes."

"He never married?"

"He's divorced."

"Everyone is. Except you."

"Well, not quite everyone."

She turned her gaze back to the fireplace. "So you liked it here when you were a student?"

"For the most part, yes."

"What'd you like about it?"

"Lots of things."

"So name one."

"My friends."

"And?"

"You said one."

"So name another."

I thought a moment. "I liked the campus. I liked the valley where the chapel is. We called it Chapel Valley. Have you been there?"

She nodded.

"In the spring the valley is filled with daisies. It's really beautiful."

"Yeah?" She sounded unconvinced.

"Sometimes we had picnics there on the weekends—the six of us. We'd grab some fast food and take a couple of blankets out there and eat lunch in the shade of the chapel."

"Sounds like a crowd. You should have gone with just Ray."

"I did once."

"Yeah? What happened?"

"Nothing, really. Though I do remember picking a daisy and pulling off the petals and asking it if Ray loved me. You know the old custom, 'He loves me, he loves me not. . . .' "

"Yeah, well, that's rigged. It always ends up with 'he loves me.' "

"This time it didn't. When I pulled off the last petal, it was 'he loves me not.' "

"Really? So what did Ray say?"

"Nothing. At least nothing I remember."

"He didn't say he loved you?"

"No. I'm sure he didn't say that."

"The creep."

I shrugged. "By then it didn't matter. We were only days away from graduation, and we knew we were going our separate ways. Different colleges and all that."

"You didn't love him?"

I shook my head. "We were kids."

"Kids can love each other."

"Well . . ."

"So what *didn't* you like about Seaton?"

I didn't have to think long to find an answer. "I didn't like being afraid all the time."

"Afraid of what?"

"Of failure, mostly."

Her face grew small as she frowned. "You'd never fail, Miss Gunnar. You're too smart."

"Maybe. But I always thought I might."

"That's crazy."

"That's exactly what my friend Natalie used to say."

"Yeah? And she was right."

But I didn't want to talk about that, so I asked, "And what about you? What do you like about Seaton?"

"I like your class."

I smiled. "And what else?"

She shrugged. "Not much."

"Really?"

She shook her head.

"That's too bad, Satchel. I wish you were happy here."

"I'm not exactly *un*happy."

"No?"

"No. Anyway, there's one good thing."

"What's that?"

"I'd rather be here than with Mom and Roger."

How does one respond to something like that? We simply looked at each other because there were no appropriate words to fill the gap.

She rose then, wiggled her feet back into her shoes, and stuck her hands in the pockets of her jacket. "I guess I better go get lunch before the cafeteria closes. Grilled cheese sandwiches today. Lucky me, huh?"

I stood too, but neither of us made a move for the door. I sensed she had more to say.

After a moment she said, "It's okay, isn't it? Me writing about my dad and all? I mean, that was the topic, wasn't it, to write about someone we know?"

"Of course it's okay. You did a wonderful job. The essay is excellent."

"I just didn't want to mess up like I did on the first one."

"No, you didn't mess up. All of your essays have been very good."

"Okay. Thanks."

Still she stood there, unwilling to leave. "Miss Gunnar?"

"Yes?"

"Have you ever known anyone who killed himself?"

I thought of Theodore Dutton. "I don't know, Satchel."

"You don't know?"

"No. I knew a man once who—" I stopped and shook my head. "I think—"

"Well, you'd know if he killed himself," she interrupted, "because like you said, it's something you never get over, you know? Like, you live with it every day of your life after something like that happens."

"Yes, Satchel. I know you do."

After she left, I went back to the pile of essays in the dining room and reread Satchel's story. And then I put my head down on the table, my forehead pressed against her words, and took up where I had left off earlier, with nothing now to stop the tears.

CHAPTER 25

The daisy had told me that Raymond Schmidt loved me not. Then we went our separate ways.

Now two middle-aged people sat across from each other over white linen and candlelight, one of them feeling giddy as a schoolgirl.

How I hated that feeling. Despised it. To be giddy was to be high on hope, and hope was a bumpy ride, no matter where it took you in the end. Only too often I'd crashed. The night I went with Ray to the Lincolnshire Restaurant, I was well aware of the risk. How many calamitous journeys in my life had started at a table for two just like this one?

Ray's left hand was bare, the wedding ring left behind on a dresser or bathroom counter somewhere. Of course I noticed that. I noticed it while his hands were still on the steering wheel of the car; I noted it with silent satisfaction as the two of us moved down the road on the wings of small talk. I assumed it was a purposeful decision on his part to take off the wedding ring. Best not to accompany a woman to dinner while wearing the trappings of a former relationship.

Now, as we waited for our food to arrive, Ray folded those same bare hands on the table, leaned forward slightly, and said, "So . . ."

Upon such a small word, such a slim foundation, relationships have been built, people have been born, deals have been closed, corporations have merged, empires have been built, treaties have been signed, wars have ceased, dreams have come true, and hearts have been irretrievably broken.

"So, Beth, tell me how you've been all these years."

I inhaled deeply. "Good, Ray. I've been good," I said, which was almost as good as saying nothing at all. "And you?" I asked.

He nodded, as though he were agreeing instead of answering a question. "Fair to middling," he quipped, offering me the same boyish smile he had offered me a thousand times in high school. "It's strange to think you're teaching at Seaton. You say you like it?"

"Yes. I really do. I'm glad I came back."

"I am too, Beth. That is, I'm glad you have work you enjoy."

"Don't you?" I asked. "Don't you enjoy your work?"

"Sometimes. And sometimes I'd rather be almost anywhere than at the hospital."

"Well, that's an honest answer."

He smiled, lifted his shoulders. "When I was in med school, I studied diseases. I learned the names, the causes, the symptoms. I was so busy learning about diseases I almost forgot medicine had anything to do with people. But when you start to practice, that's when you hear the stories. No, that's not it. The thing is, you become part of the stories. You're the one who delivers the bad news. You're the one who can't cure the disease, can't save the life, can't keep families together." He looked down at his hands and shrugged again. "After a while there are just too many stories."

I absorbed his words, trying to understand. "But surely you see a lot of stories with happy endings. I mean, people do get better; you help them get better."

"Yes," he agreed. "And that's what I try to dwell on. It's just hard to forget the others."

"I'm sure it is, Ray," I offered quietly.

The waiter arrived then, bearing a tray with two large platters of seafood fettuccini, a basket of warm bread, a side dish scooped full of real butter. I hadn't had food prepared like this in ages.

"It smells delicious."

Ray picked up a fork. "Well, dig in."

A certain sadness clung to him the way the scent of tobacco settles into the woven fabric of a smoking jacket. I could see that now. He didn't want me to see it, I'm sure, because he smiled valiantly, the practiced smile of one with a polished bedside manner. But I knew Ray, knew who he had been, saw who he was now, and detected the subtle nuances between the carefree boy and the careworn man.

We began to eat, and after a bite or two, Ray said, "You never married, Beth?"

The bread I was swallowing became a lump in my throat. I washed it down with water and shook my head.

"May I ask why not?" His voice was gentle, as though he were probing a wound with gloved hands.

"I simply never met the right one."

"Well . . ." He paused and broke another piece off the loaf of bread. "Maybe that's better than thinking you've found the right one, only to discover years later that you were wrong."

I was about to spear a scallop with the prongs of my fork, but I stopped and lifted my eyes to Ray's face. "Is that what happened to you, Ray?"

For a long moment neither of us moved. We both seemed to be waiting for something, though I couldn't imagine what it was.

At last Ray said, "To tell you the truth, Beth, I'm still not really sure what happened."

"What do you mean?"

He shook his head. "Well, it's just that one day Brenda—my wife—was there, and quite literally the next, she was gone. Ben was a newborn, not two weeks old, when she woke up one morning and said she'd had enough. She left and didn't come back."

"You never heard from her again?"

"Only from her lawyer."

I sucked in air, held it in my lungs. I wanted to say, *That's terrible, terrible. . . . What kind of woman would leave her baby, her family, just walk out and never come back?*

Instead, I only murmured, "I'm so sorry."

He shook his head again, as though to say I shouldn't be sorry. Then he added, "Actually, that's not quite true. I've spoken with her a few times on the phone when she's called to talk with the kids. Or she tries to talk with them. They're not real interested. But anyway, she took off a long time ago, and I eventually got over it. Ben's six now. Best little guy in the world." He smiled; this time it was genuine.

"He's adorable," I agreed, remembering the little blond boy at homecoming. "And you have other children as well?"

"Yes. Josh is nineteen, in his second year at Penn State—"

"Premed?"

"No. Business, thank heavens. Maybe he'll be able to work reasonable hours, unlike his old man. Or, unlike his old man before he sold his practice and became a hospitalist a couple of years ago."

"A hospitalist?"

"I had my own practice as an internist for years, but I sold it. Now I work at the hospital and pretty much choose my own hours. Pretty nice. Plus, it helps when it comes to parenting. Which brings me to Lisa, my daughter. She's seventeen and a senior in high school this year. Smart as a whip. Seems to be interested in international marketing. I think she wants a job that will allow her to see the world."

"Nothing wrong with that."

"Not a thing. I predict she'll do well and have fun doing it."

I thought of this young girl with her whole life ahead of her. The clean slate appeared enviable, and I wished her well. I hoped all the lines would fall to her in pleasant places. *That happens sometimes, doesn't it?* I wondered.

"And then of course there's Ben," Ray went on. "A bit of a surprise but the apple of my eye."

And quite possibly the reason for Ray's divorce, though of course I'd never say as much. "You're a lucky man, with children like yours."

"Yes, I am. They're three great kids. You'll have to meet my older two someday."

"I'd like that."

We smiled at each other.

Then, as we ate, we spoke of other things—of old times, old friends, memories unearthed by this sudden intersecting of our lives. I wondered whether after this night I would ever see Ray again, let alone meet his children. People get busy and forget. Sometimes people think twice and choose to stay away. One candlelight dinner does not necessarily lead to a second. White linen is not necessarily an open door.

This may be my only chance, I thought. I wanted to know everything there was to know about Raymond Schmidt. And when that topic was exhausted, I wanted to ask him one more thing. What did he see that April night in 1977? What did he see the final time he was in the cabin where Theodore Dutton lived? He had told me before, but I wanted him to tell me again. I wanted to know if he could shed any light at all on that vague dark image that had haunted me for too many years.

But, in the end, I didn't ask. Because if I was to have just this one night with Ray, it simply seemed like too sad a place to go.

CHAPTER 26

We had made plans to meet at Theodore Dutton's cabin at midnight on that Friday in April 1977. Mr. Dutton didn't know we were coming. It was the first of the month, April Fool's day, and Ray and Ken came up with the idea of pulling a sort of practical joke on our teacher.

Earlier in the week a convict serving a life sentence for murder had escaped from the men's prison in Smyrna, about thirty-five miles south of us in central Delaware. This provided the boys fodder for their joke. Exactly what they intended to do, Natalie and I didn't know. We were simply to show up at the appointed time.

We were late. I was spending the night at Natalie's, and we wanted to exit the house no later than 11:45, but Mr. and Mrs. Primrose chose that night to stay up drinking bottomless cups of decaf in the kitchen. Their voices reached us in low murmurs, like mourners at a wake.

"They're probably talking about Tony." Natalie sounded irritated at the thought of her younger brother. "He and Brian were caught smoking pot by Brian's dad earlier this week. They lit up right in the basement, the idiots. What'd they expect?"

"I didn't know Tony smoked pot."

"I didn't either, till now."

"What are your mom and dad going to do?"

Natalie shrugged. “I don’t know, but I wish they’d hurry up and decide so we can get out of here.”

She wanted nothing to stand in her way when she was ready to visit Theodore Dutton.

Moments later we heard muted footsteps on the carpeted stairs, husband and wife ascending in soft-soled slippers. Natalie and I scrambled into bed fully clothed, pulling the covers up to our chins. Sure enough, the silhouette of Mrs. Primrose stopped briefly in the doorway before moving on. It was exactly what my own mother would have done, in spite of my age. And I liked it, in spite of my age. I always felt warm in such moments of maternal care.

We heard a door close, a toilet flush, a light switch swatted. We lay still, breathing in measured breaths, waiting for the slow descending of sleep, not upon ourselves but upon Natalie’s parents. Outside we heard the night songs rising up from the grass and then, shrilly, a siren slicing the night somewhere in the distance.

“Oh great,” Natalie whispered. “Rotten timing.”

It came closer, alarmingly close, then stopped. Whatever it was—ambulance, fire truck, police—it must have turned down one of the country roads just beyond Seaton and disappeared.

The quiet settled over us again. Finally, after what seemed a very long time—in reality it was only a few minutes—Mr. Primrose’s snores signaled the all clear.

“Do you think your mom’s asleep too?” I asked.

“Yeah. She’s always out cold as soon as her head hits the pillow.”

"What if she's not, and she catches us?"

Natalie threw back the covers and sat up. "Don't worry. Let's just go," she said.

I followed her. Down the stairs, out the side door, along the street to the valley where the daisies would soon be in bloom. As yet, though by the calendar it was spring, we were still riding the coattail of winter, and the chill in the air was enough to turn our breath to fog. We zipped up the jackets we had grabbed on the way out and thrust our hands deep into the pockets as we hurried through the valley and up to the center of campus.

The night was lighted by a dazzling array of stars and a thick slice of moon. I hung my head back as I walked and drank in the beauty of it. And I shivered, not so much against the cold as with the thrill of being somewhere I wasn't supposed to be, seeing something I wasn't supposed to see, which made it all the more enchanting.

I must have stopped a moment because the next thing I realized Natalie was pulling on my sleeve and pointing toward a twirling light coming from the parking lot beyond Cedar Hall.

"What in the world—" she began, and then the light moved down the drive, a siren jolted our flesh, and the ambulance we thought had disappeared somewhere in rural Delaware was right there ahead of us. Its taillights cut a blurry red line through campus, then finally disappeared at the curve in front of Pine Glen. We heard the ambulance turn out onto the highway, becoming nothing but a siren tearing down Route 41 toward Wilmington.

Natalie and I looked at each other and started to run. We didn't know why we were running or what we would come to at the end, but we ran toward Mr. Dutton's cabin because we knew the boys would be there. And they were. We spotted them outside on the strip of grass between the cabin and the path, fidgeting amidst a murmuring crowd of cops and faculty members. Someone must have summoned Mildred Bidney, who lived across campus in Pratt Lodge, because she stood there with a scarf on her head that scarcely concealed the sponge rollers underneath. She wore a long wool coat that wasn't quite as long as the nightgown it covered and a pair of rubber-soled house shoes. Stan Buckley was there also, presumably awakened when the ambulance passed Pine Glen on its way into campus. He and Clarence Fosset of Cabin 2 both stood shivering in slacks and V-necked undershirts; Mr. Fosset lit a cigarette and, holding it between his lips, momentarily curled his palms around the burning tip for warmth.

Cabin 1 was dimly lighted, but we could see people moving around inside. Every once in a while there was a small burst of light, like the flash of a camera. As Natalie and I approached the scene, the grown-ups greeted us with expressions of shock and surprise. The thought of being punished might have crossed our minds, but our fear and curiosity overrode it.

"Girls, what are you doing here?" Mrs. Bidney asked angrily.

Natalie responded with another question. "What happened?" The panic in her voice was palpable.

No one answered. Mrs. Bidney and the cops exchanged glances.

Ken's face was ashen; I could see that, even in the dim glow cast from the policemen's flashlights. He clutched his stomach as though he were ill. Ray, to my astonishment, was crying. Not huge sobs, just quiet tears that he brushed away with the back of one hand. My heart stopped in my chest, and I couldn't get my lungs to take in air. I didn't yet know what had happened, but I knew it had to do with Theodore Dutton, and that it was something terrible.

At long last Stan Buckley broke the silence. "Mr. Dutton has been taken to the hospital, girls."

"But why?" Natalie's voice was shrill now and demanding. She turned to Ken. "Tell me what happened."

"Girls, you'll have to step aside." The policeman who spoke had a deep and lilting voice, full of authority. "We're taking the boys to the station for questioning."

"Are they under arrest?"

I thought of their practical joke, of the escaped murderer, of their intent to scare Mr. Dutton, and I wondered, *What on earth have they done?*

Mrs. Bidney looked at us with wild eyes. She was

obviously afraid of what was unfolding here. "Natalie, Beth, do your parents know where you are?"

"She's staying with me," Natalie answered dumbly.

"You shouldn't be out here. We'll need to contact your parents—"

"I'll take care of the girls," Mr. Buckley interrupted. "Let's just let these officers finish their business."

Mrs. Bidney looked sharply at Mr. Buckley, then back at Natalie and me. She took a step toward us, peering at us through her glasses. "Mr. Dutton is ill. He's been taken to the hospital. Do you understand?"

Not understanding at all, we both nodded. I gazed at Ray then, my face surely rife with terror and questions, but he only shook his head as if to say, *Don't ask.*

Ken, though, sent a hand signal to Natalie which I easily intercepted. He made a knife of one index finger and sliced it back and forth over the opposite wrist.

Natalie gasped loudly. I wanted to reach out and grab Ken by the collar and demand, *What are you saying? What do you mean?* but I discovered that my bones were locked and my muscles frozen. More than that, I sensed that if I did move, it would be into a world that I wanted desperately not to enter. In the next moment I became aware that the policemen and the boys were walking away toward a tangle of squad cars parked pell-mell in the lot, Mildred Bidney was stepping across campus with Mr. Fosset, and Mr. Buckley was still there with Natalie and me, saying something absurd, something like, "Don't worry, girls. He's going to be all right. I suggest you run on home now." But I couldn't hear him anymore because Natalie was screaming, and then her knees buckled and she slumped to the damp ground. She rolled up into a tight ball with her forehead pressed to the grass, and when I knelt and put my arms around her, I could feel each relentless shiver as she wept.

That was the instant when life as I knew it came to an end. The stars seemed to tumble right out of the sky and my childhood shattered like glass, and something inside of me crept off on wounded feet to a small dark place, a crevice sealed over like a tomb.

CHAPTER 27

Commander Pettingill got up at Monday morning assembly and told us Mr. Dutton had suffered a heart attack. "But he's receiving the best possible care at Wilmington General, and we're sure he'll recuperate in due time," Commander said. "We plan to keep you updated as we receive more news ourselves."

Until that moment I would never have believed that adults might actually lie to you. As Commander stood at the podium smiling down his assurances upon us, Raymond Schmidt, Ken Cunningham, Natalie Primrose, and I sat with lips pressed firmly into taut lines. We had been expecting this announcement, but I'd been hoping against hope that we'd be told the truth. Now I knew that wasn't going to happen.

The fact was that Theodore Dutton was a suicide.

I knew that because the people who knew the truth

had told me so. The previous afternoon, on Sunday, Natalie and I met Ray and Ken in the valley.

"Dutton killed himself," Ken said flatly, his hands hanging over his knees like deflated balloons. A chilly breeze blew over the steps of the chapel where we'd agreed to meet, and where we now sat.

"Are you sure he's dead?" I asked. "I mean, completely sure?"

Ray nodded. "No one can lose that much blood and not be dead."

Natalie started to weep, and Ken put an arm around her shoulder. I sat motionless a moment, trying to take it in. I'd been trying to take it in for the better part of two days, but it was too big to fit into my heart all at once, so I was taking it in piece by little piece. Theodore Dutton had sliced his wrist open. Theodore Dutton was dead. Theodore Dutton was not coming back.

I began to cry silently, tears spilling over and running down my cheeks. Ray took my hand in his, squeezing it firmly. I asked in a near whisper, "What happened Friday night before we got there?"

They had snuck up quietly on the cabin, Ray told us. It was dark inside. They peered in all the windows but couldn't see much. It looked like maybe Dutton was under a pile of blankets on the bed, but he didn't wake up when they tapped on the window. "Let's try the front door," Ken had said. So they did. It was unlocked. This was going to be good. They were going to scare the pants off Mr. Dutton.

They entered the cabin smiling, trying not to laugh out loud. Served him right not to lock his door when there was a murderer on the loose. It took them only a moment to find him. But he wasn't where they thought he was. He wasn't in the bed. He was on the bathroom floor, curled up in a circle of blood. His left wrist was sliced open like a piece of fruit. His right hand still clung loosely to a razor blade. There was more blood on the floor than would fill the empty Jack Daniels bottle at Mr. Dutton's feet.

"No way he could have survived that," Ray concluded.

"Did you feel for a pulse?" I asked.

Ray shook his head. "We didn't touch him. We just called the police."

"Could you tell if he was breathing?"

He looked down at the ground. "I didn't wait long enough to notice. I ran for the phone. After that, I didn't go back into the bathroom."

I turned to Ken.

"Did you, Ken?"

"Did I what?"

"Did you go back in and notice if he was breathing?"

He shook his head, dropped his eyes just as Ray had done. "Naw, I couldn't. I—"

Ken tightened his grip on Natalie, who was crying into the sleeves of her jacket.

No one spoke for a long time.

Then Ray said, "Listen, we can never tell anybody any of this."

"Not even our parents?" I asked.

"No."

Natalie lifted her head, wiped her eyes on her sleeve. "What about Janie and Artie?"

"Not even them."

"Why not?"

Ray looked at me, then away. Referring to his great uncle, Commander Pettingill, he said, "Uncle John is going to tell everyone on Monday that Mr. Dutton had a heart attack."

"How do you know that?" I demanded.

"Just a minute. There's more," Ray said. "They're going to tell everyone he's still alive."

"What?" I was dumbstruck.

Ray and Ken exchanged a glance then. Ken nodded. Ray sighed.

"Uncle John picked us up at the police station Friday night," he explained. "Well, by then it was pretty much Saturday morning. Apparently Bidney called him and told him what was going on. So he picked us up and drove us back to campus. We'd already spent half the night telling a bunch of cops what we saw in Dutton's cabin. We had to keep telling the same story over and over till we felt like we were about to go crazy. So then Uncle John comes and gets us, and he takes us back to the dorm and tells us to get a few hours' sleep because at ten o'clock he wanted us to meet him in his office. So by ten o'clock we were up, and we went to his office. Bidney was there and some other people—Buckley and Fosset and some bigwigs on the board of directors for the school. The first thing they told us was that if we hadn't stumbled across Dutton when we did, he'd be dead."

"But he is dead!" I interrupted.

Ken said, "Yeah, but they don't want anybody to know that."

"Why not?"

"Well, obviously, Beth," Ray answered, "they don't want anyone to know Dutton committed suicide."

"But why not?" I asked again.

Ray shook his head and took a deep breath. "I don't know. I don't know." The words were almost a moan. "Maybe they want to protect his family—"

"Come on, Ray," Ken said, "you know the real reason. They don't want a suicide on campus becoming public news. I mean, think of how it would make the school look. Right? If parents learn a teacher killed himself, they're going to start getting bad feelings about Seaton. They might start pulling their kids out—"

"I can't believe that," I interrupted.

"Think about it, Beth," Ken went on. "Seaton's always been holding on by a shoestring. We don't get to dip into public funds, remember? The school is at the mercy of parents willing to shell out tuition money. Something like a suicide might make parents panic. . . ." He seemed to want to say more, but he stopped and shook his head.

I felt my jaw tighten. "So how are they going to hide it? How are they going to keep it out of the papers?"

Ray said, "Think of who's on the board of directors for the school, Beth. Do you think they don't have all sorts of connections?"

I knew who he was talking about. Members of wealthy Delaware families who had practically built the state's economy with their own hands. People with clout. People who could pull strings and watch other people dance.

No one was ever going to know that Theodore Dutton had committed suicide on the campus of Seaton Preparatory School.

Both Natalie and I had stopped crying. We were angry now and mystified. Natalie asked, "Doesn't Bidney know—doesn't anyone know that Beth and I know what happened?"

Ray shook his head. "They think you don't know. Even though you were there—well, Mr. Dutton was already gone by then. You didn't see him yourself, and nobody told you. And . . ." Ray paused. His mouth became a small tight line.

"What, Ray?" I asked.

"The second thing they told us Saturday morning is that we were never to tell anyone that Dutton slit his wrist. They let us know it would be in our own best interest to stay quiet."

"And you agreed?"

Ray dropped his eyes to the ground and nodded. "If they knew we were talking to you right now, we'd be expelled for sure."

"I can't believe it," I whispered.

Ken looked at me with resentment in his eyes. "Believe it," he said.

"So Monday morning Uncle John is going to tell everyone Mr. Dutton had a heart attack and that he's okay. And the four of us, we have to keep our mouths shut."

"You think we should never tell anyone the truth?" I asked warily.

"From this point on," Ray said, "I think we should just stay out of it."

"It doesn't seem right."

"You've got to promise, Beth."

"Maybe Commander will change his mind. Maybe tomorrow he'll decide to tell what really happened."

But he didn't. As the upper school students filed out of assembly on Monday morning, we listened to the murmurs of the other kids talking about the heart attack. Several girls cried. Someone cracked a joke, saying working in a prison camp like Seaton had done Mr. Dutton in.

Ray grabbed my arm and pulled me down the side hall. Ken and Natalie followed. We were awkwardly quiet as a kid pushed passed us on his way to the bathroom in the silo. When the bathroom door eased shut, Ray looked at the three of us.

He opened his mouth, shut it again. He looked at the floor then back at us. Finally he said, "Another couple months and we're out of here. We just have to keep our mouths shut for a couple of months, and then we never have to think about any of this again."

He was right about one thing. We'd be graduating in a couple of months. But as for the part about never having to think about Theodore Dutton again, he was dead wrong.

CHAPTER 28

At the end of that school day I drove myself home in my 1960 Pontiac station wagon with the fins and the *Jesus is Lord* bumper sticker, just like always. And just like always, Mom was there in the kitchen already peeling potatoes for supper.

"Hi, honey," she called when I came in the door. "How was your day?"

I dropped my books in the den and stopped to pet Shadow, our rat terrier who went nuts with joy whenever anybody came home. Then I met Mom at the kitchen sink, where I kissed her cheek.

"What's for supper?" I asked, ignoring the question she had asked of me.

"Hash and eggs. Want to use the grinder for me?"

"Sure."

She made her own hash by dropping cubes of cooked beef and chunks of raw potato into the meat grinder. Turning the handle of that grinder had always been one of the coveted chores among my sisters and me, ever since we were small kids. We liked to watch the meat and potatoes come out the other end a blended mess.

I stood at the kitchen table, where the grinder was

screwed temporarily onto the edge, and began dropping the ingredients in as I cranked the handle.

Mom washed her hands and wiped them dry on her apron. Then she started unloading clean dishes from the dishwasher. "Don't forget, you and Carrie have Youth Club at church tonight," she remarked absently.

"I know."

"You'll want to get your homework done before you go."

"All right."

She started to hum as she lifted the dishes from the washer and into the cupboards. I recognized the song as a hymn.

"Oh, hey," she said suddenly, interrupting herself. "We got a letter from Marla today."

Marla was my older sister, in her sophomore year at Gettysburg College. "Yeah? How's she doing?"

"She got a date for the spring banquet, so I guess you could say she's doing pretty well!" Mom said cheerfully.

"Anyone we know?"

She shook her head. "A Dave Something-or-other. She says she's known him awhile, but this is the first time he's asked her out."

"That's good." I went on turning the crank.

Just then the public school bus squealed to a stop at the corner, and I knew it was dropping off my younger sister. After a moment we heard the front door open.

"Mom?"

"In the kitchen, honey."

Shadow yelped and ran to meet Carrie, then, leaping and wagging her tail, she walked with my sister down the hall to the kitchen. When Carrie saw me cranking the grinder, she said "Hey, can I finish doing that?"

I stepped away from the table. "Go ahead if you want."

In another hour Dad came home. Shadow went wild again, doing her special Daddy's Home dance on the footstool in the den. Still clutching his briefcase, Dad paused long enough to scratch Shadow's head and tell her she was a good dog. He came into the kitchen and gave Mom a kiss and patted my shoulder as I sat at the table doing homework. Then he changed his clothes and read the paper for an hour while eating a snack of crackers and cheese.

At five thirty, just like always, we sat down to dinner. Dad said grace. Mom dished out the hash and the fried eggs. Dad asked what was new, and Carrie piped up about cutting two seconds off her time at track practice, and Mom said she was probably going to break some school records before she graduated.

I didn't say anything. Shadow nudged my leg under the table, and I slipped her a little hash on the end of my finger.

"Beth's feeding Shadow again!" Carrie squealed.

Mom frowned. "Not at the table, Beth."

Dad asked for the pepper, and Mom picked up the shaker to pass it to him. Suddenly that hand-painted porcelain shaker stopped in midair, almost directly in front of my face. Mom turned to me and said, "Oh dear, Beth, how could I have forgotten?" Dad reached for the pepper, and Mom let her empty hand fall back to the table. “Darla Primrose called today and told me your English teacher had a heart attack over the weekend. She said he’s over at Wilmington General. He’s an awfully young fellow to have a heart attack, isn’t he?”

The room fell silent. Of course I knew they would hear the news eventually. Soon everyone would know the story about Mr. Dutton. I just wasn’t ready to talk about it. I stared at my plate, at the hash and eggs with the red ketchup poured out over it in neat red stripes, and I began to feel the tears press heavily against the back of my eyes. Slowly I lifted my gaze to my mother’s face.

When she saw my tears, she smiled kindly and laid her hand across my forearm. “Oh, honey,” she said, “don’t cry. I know how you like your English teacher so well, but—don’t worry. Mrs. Primrose said he’s going to be fine. She said she called Commander Pettingill as soon as she heard, and Commander told her he’d just hung up from talking with Mr. Dutton himself. Apparently he was doing much better and resting comfortably.”

Liar, I thought. *He’s lying.*

The tears escaped and slid down my face. I glanced at Carrie, who rolled her eyes at me.

“Good grief, Beth, you’d cry if a leaf fell off the willow tree in the backyard.”

“That’s enough, Carrie,” Dad said. “Your sister is understandably upset.”

Oh no, I thought. *No, you don't understand at all.*

I looked at Dad, then back at Mom. How I loved those two people, trusted them, needed them. "But Mr. Dutton . . ." I started, "it was . . . he . . ."

It was all there, the whole story right at the back of my tongue, but I swallowed it. I had always told my parents everything, but not this time.

"Can I be excused?" I whispered.

Mom glanced over at Dad. He nodded. "You go on, honey. And you don't have to go to church tonight if you don't feel up to it. But listen, Beth, a lot of people recover from heart attacks and do just fine. Try not to worry too much."

They had always treated me gently because I was the "sensitive one." I took things harder than most people, they said. I was born with "a thin skin over deep feelings" was how they put it. My sisters had another name for it. They said I was a crybaby. My sisters' assessment may have been more accurate, but this time I felt I had a right to my tears. I just didn't have the right to explain.

I left the table and went to my room. For the first time in my life, I wished my heart was made of stone.

CHAPTER 29

"Mr. Dutton was kind of young to have a heart attack, wasn't he, Commander?"

"Yes." Commander Pettingill cleared his throat. "It's unusual, but these things happen."

I sat in a stiff wooden chair in Commander's office

on the first floor of Heath Hall. Three days had passed since his announcement about Theodore Dutton. The previous night I'd worked up the courage to call Wilmington General to see if they had a patient by that name. The person who answered the phone sounded rushed and harried and hung up directly after telling me they didn't.

So I worked up my courage again to confront Commander. I'd asked Natalie to come with me, but she refused, saying Mr. Dutton was dead and the school wasn't going to change its story, so what was the use of talking with Commander?

For whatever reason, I thought I might be able to back him into a corner, catch him in his lie, make him confess—if only to me. But after I made the comment about Mr. Dutton being too young to have a heart attack, I had no idea what else to say. Commander agreed with me, putting that topic to rest, and after that there was really nowhere else to go. I could hardly come right out and tell him I knew he was lying. He was, after all, the assistant headmaster of Seaton Preparatory School, and I, only a student. I felt weak with fear and gripped the arms of the chair to steady myself.

Commander Pettingill must have mistaken my fear for concern because he leaned forward with his hands on his desk and smiled at me kindly. "Don't worry, Beth," he said. "We're staying in touch with the doctors. Mr. Dutton is coming along nicely."

Commander had no idea at all that I was there to confront him. He thought I had come to him seeking reassurance! How to back him into that corner?

"Do you think," I began, but the words were so small I had to start over. "Do you think I could visit him in the hospital then?"

"Oh no, no." He leaned back in the large leather chair that rocked against his weight. "I'm afraid that's not possible. You see, he's been moved. He's been taken to a hospital in Pennsylvania, closer to his family."

"Oh?" What a tangled web we weave. "Do you know the name of it? The hospital?"

"Let's see." He formed a tent with his hands and laid them against his lips. He did an admirable job of frowning, as though deep in thought. "St. John's? No, that's not it. It's on the tip of my tongue but . . . hmm. Goodness, what's become of my memory?"

I waited. His memory refused to cooperate.

After a moment, the old man shrugged. "Well, it'll come to me. Is there anything else, dear?"

I managed to hold his gaze momentarily before shaking my head and rising from the chair. "No. I guess that's it."

"Well," he said, rising as well, "I know this unfortunate event has come as a shock to you, but try not to let it interfere with your schoolwork." He gave me a small obsequious smile.

I had always liked Commander Pettingill, had always had the greatest respect for him. Until now.

I didn't say good-bye. I walked toward the door, stone-faced.

When I had almost reached the threshold, Commander said, “Oh, Beth?”

Turning back, I lifted my chin slightly, defiantly.

“Perhaps you’d like to send Mr. Dutton a card at his parents’ address? You know, a little get-well card or something?”

What was he saying? I waited, trying to comprehend as he went on. “I have the address here somewhere. What did I do with it?” Shuffling some papers on his desk, he came up at last with a small scrap bearing an address. “Yes, here it is. Let me copy it for you.” He did and handed me the paper. “I’m sure he’d enjoy hearing from you.”

I felt my eyes narrow almost to slits. “This is his parents’ address?”

“Yes. I’m sure they’ll get your letter to him if you’d care to write. At any rate, he should be out of the hospital soon and recuperating at his parents’ home.”

I looked at the address scribbled on the paper, and for one brief instant wondered whether it was a real place or a spontaneous fabrication on the part of Commander Pettingill. By now I wouldn’t put it past him.

I moved my gaze to Commander’s face again. “Okay,” I said, feeling as though I was accepting some sort of challenge. “I’ll write to him. Thanks.”

That afternoon I drove to Eckerd’s drugstore and picked out a get-well card. I told Mr. Dutton we all missed him and hoped he’d be better soon. I asked him to please write and let us know how he was, and I put my address inside the card as well as on the outside of the envelope.

The card went out in the next day's mail.

For a week or so I actually entertained the idea that I might hear back from Theodore Dutton. But I suppose that was only a morbid sort of wishful thinking, and in the end I wasn't too surprised that I never got a response.

CHAPTER 30

And so we moved forward with our lives, simply because there was nothing else to be done. I left Delaware, went to college, immersed myself in my career, and sometimes, for long stretches, I was able to forget. But never completely. It always came back, often as sorrow, other times as guilt or regret or anger. The ghost that haunted me took many forms, but I always knew where it came from.

When Jack Farrell called me in the spring of 2003 and offered me the teaching job at Seaton, I thanked him and asked him for a few days to think it over. But I knew right away I would accept it. I was ready for a change, ready to leave Maryland, and perhaps most of all, ready to make a clean break with my unwilling-to-commit boyfriend, Nick Watson. Returning to my hometown, my own alma mater, to teach was an opportunity that came out of nowhere just when I needed to go somewhere other than where I was.

By mid-October I was certain I had made the right

decision. If not completely happy, I was at least content. I enjoyed the students, loved living in Pine Glen, was glad to have rekindled my friendship with Natalie after so many years apart. She and I talked on the phone, exchanged e-mails, and sometimes she'd come over to sit and chat or walk around the campus.

On the Sunday after I had dinner with Ray, Natalie and I found ourselves strolling over the hills of Seaton and through the patches of apple trees, past Heath Hall and Anderson Hall and the headmaster's house and Webb Hall, where the lower school met, down and around the chapel in the valley and back again. The day was warm with sunshine and autumn colors both, one of those Indian summer days that never fails to call you outdoors.

As we circled around the chapel and back toward the footbridge, Natalie got around to asking what I knew was on her mind. "So Ray took you to the Lincolnshire last night, huh?"

"Yes, believe it or not."

"Pretty fancy."

"Yeah, and he drives a Lexus too."

She looked at me sideways. "I don't mean wealthy fancy. I mean romantic fancy."

"Oh." I shrugged. "Well, it wasn't like that. I mean, it wasn't a date really."

"Oh? Then what would you call it?"

"Just a couple of old friends catching up on their lives."

"Right, Beth. And I'm Secretary of State Condoleezza Rice."

"Come on, Natalie. You know it's not like that."

"Are you kidding? It's perfect. You come back, run into your old high school sweetheart at homecoming, he happens to be divorced, you get back together, and live happily ever after."

I laughed out loud, hoping it sounded sincere. "I don't think so, Natalie."

"Why not? Don't you want to get married?"

"Well, yes, I suppose—"

"So there you go. Who better than Ray?"

"Ray?"

"Of course! He wouldn't have asked you out if he weren't interested."

"I don't know—"

"Listen. You two have known each other all your lives, you were crazy about each other in high school, he needs a wife, and you want a husband. It's a fairy tale in the making."

"You always were a dreamer, Nat."

She stopped and looked at me. "You never dreamed enough, Beth. Why don't you try to think a little positively here, like maybe it *could* happen? Or what? Don't you like him?"

"Sure, I like him." I shrugged nonchalantly as we walked together up the hill toward the circular drive at the center of campus. "He's a great guy. But that doesn't mean we're meant to be together."

Natalie sighed. "Honestly, Beth. If I didn't know better, I'd say you're still single because you never really wanted to get married."

"That's not true," I countered, but even as I said it, something flinched inside of me. "I've always wanted to get married. I just never found the right one."

"Uh-huh."

Her tone told me she wasn't convinced.

"So if he asks you out again, will you go?"

"Sure. Why not?"

"Why do you try so hard to pretend like you're not thrilled?"

"I'm not a kid anymore, Nat. As the saying goes, I've been around the block a few times."

"Yeah, and now you're back here where you belong, so maybe things will finally work out for you."

"Maybe."

"Oh, Beth." Another huge sigh.

We walked past Cedar Hall, and I followed Natalie's lead when she turned up the path toward the spot where the faculty cabins had been. I was surprised when she stopped in front of Cabin 1. No longer used for faculty housing, it was now a storage shed for the middle school's gardening tools. Cabin 2 had been demolished somewhere along the way, the land turned into a vegetable garden that the students planted and tended each spring as part of the middle school curriculum.

I hadn't been this close to Cabin 1 since returning to Seaton two months earlier. I had purposely avoided it. Now Natalie said, "You know, I've been thinking about Theodore Dutton since you mentioned him."

"You have?"

She nodded.

"I thought you told me to just forget about him."

"I did. But then I became curious. Did you ever Google him?"

"No."

"Well, I did."

I froze. "What'd you find out?"

She was looking at the cabin rather than at me. She frowned when she said, "Not much. Nothing, really. There are some Duttons out there, but nobody that matches our Theodore."

No. Of course not. Because he wasn't out there to be found, was he? I said, "Well, I guess it doesn't really matter."

"No, it really doesn't. He's been dead a long time. What else is there to know?"

My gaze followed Natalie's toward the cabin. I almost shivered in spite of the sun. "I've sometimes wondered whether he might have survived the suicide attempt. I mean, Commander and the others were so adamant that he was alive."

"Of course they were. To protect the school. Ray and Ken saw the man, and he was dead." She lifted her shoulders, let them drop. "Hard to discount the testimony of eyewitnesses."

I nodded. "But it was dark, you know. And they never touched him to see if he was breathing or had a pulse."

"They said no one could survive after losing as much blood as he did."

"I know. I remember."

"But—" she turned to me and offered a sad smile—"what would you do, anyway, if you found out he was alive?"

I didn't have to think about that for long. "I'd ask him why he did it."

"As if he would tell you," she said. "And anyway, I can't see you asking him. It'd take a lot of nerve, you know, asking somebody a question like that."

"But haven't you ever wondered why?"

"Sure. I wondered for a long time."

"How did you stop?"

She took a breath, thinking. "It wasn't any conscious thing. I got married, had kids. I ran out of time for pondering mysteries like some guy we once knew who tried to kill himself. Who *did* kill himself."

"Yeah, I suppose." I paused a moment. "You know, he didn't care what it might do to us."

"No." She looked at me sharply then and shook her head. "No, he didn't. And maybe that was part of it too, for me. He didn't care about us, so I stopped caring about him."

We started to walk away then, back down the path running beside Cedar Hall. "Did you ever tell anyone? That it was actually suicide, I mean?"

"No. Did you?"

"No."

She shook her head again. "I can still remember Commander getting up at assembly that morning and telling everyone it was a heart attack."

"I'll never forget it."

"It was a rotten thing to do to a bunch of kids, all the way around."

"Yes, it really was."

"But you know what?"

"What?" I asked.

"Welcome to the world, baby Jane."

I nodded, letting out a small laugh. "Yeah. And you wonder why I'm not more of a dreamer."

We exchanged a rueful smile, then walked in silence back to Pine Glen.

CHAPTER 31

"Ray, there's something I've been meaning to ask you."

Ray lifted his eyes at me over the rim of the Starbucks cup. He drank slowly before lowering the mocha latte.

Though we had talked on the phone several times, I hadn't seen Ray since we'd gone to the Lincolnshire almost two weeks earlier. So when he called me from the hospital that evening and asked me to meet him for coffee at the Starbucks on Kirkwood Highway, I willingly left my students' essays behind and hopped in the car.

The thought of spilling what was on my mind was somewhat unnerving. For one thing, it felt as though I was entering territory I had no right to enter. For another thing, Ray looked tired and didn't appear as though he would want to go there either. But it had been gnawing on me for these last couple of weeks, and it was gnawing on me right now. And so, whether the hour was right or wrong, I blurted it out.

"I'm just wondering why you wear a wedding ring if you're not married."

Ray looked at the ring with eyebrows raised, as though he was surprised to find it circling his finger. Then he smiled. "I mostly wear it at work. I don't want to appear to my patients to be the eligible doctor, if you know what I mean. It just makes life easier."

Oh. So that was all. The ring wasn't pasted to his finger with sentimental attachment.

Then Ray added. "The staff knows, of course, that I'm divorced. But wearing a ring around the hospital isn't all that uncommon. I'm not the only single doctor who wears one."

As I nodded, I found I had another question, which I couldn't help asking. "Do you miss her, Ray?"

"Brenda?"

I nodded again.

"For a long time I did. But I don't anymore."

"Do you know where she is?"

"Richmond, I think. She moves around a lot."

"She's remarried?"

"Not that I know of. Last I heard she wasn't."

"Does she ever see the kids?"

A pained expression settled over Ray's face. "No. I think I mentioned before that she calls them sometimes. On their birthdays. Occasionally at Christmas.

They don't really want to talk to her. Ben, of course, doesn't even know who she is. It just confuses him when she calls." He took a sip of coffee and waved a hand. "But enough about her. What about you? How's life at Seaton?"

"Good," I said. "We have a bunch of smart kids there; they keep me on my toes."

He smiled. "No troublemakers sneaking off campus to eat at Burger King, are there?"

I chuckled. "Not that I know of." Then I remembered, somberly, the foursome who had left campus shortly after the start of the school year. "Last month, though, we had four students go out drinking and driving over by Hoopes. They ended up going off the road and running into a tree."

"Anyone killed?" Ray asked.

"No, thankfully. They were all injured, the driver pretty badly, but they're on the mend now. They were expelled from Seaton even though one of the boys had been a student there since first grade. I thought they might just be suspended, but the principal is being tough about it. I think he wants to let the students know the school isn't going to tolerate drinking."

Ray shook his head slowly from side to side. "He's doing the right thing. I've seen too many times what drinking and driving can do."

"I'm sure you have."

"Kids think they're immortal."

"Yes, they do. Unfortunately."

"When we were kids, at least I knew better than to get behind the wheel when I'd been drinking."

I tried to laugh, but it came out sounding like a gasp. "What are you talking about, Ray? We never drank when we were kids."

He hid behind the coffee cup a moment, then lowered it and looked up at me. "Well, *you* never did."

I frowned and shook my head. Maybe I shouldn't have been surprised, but I was. Never once had I seen Ray Schmidt take a drink of anything stronger than Dr. Pepper.

"You mean in college, right?"

"No, I mean in high school."

"Ray, I had no idea you ever drank in high school."

"I didn't very often. Never until senior year, in fact, when I lived in the dorm."

The boarding students had always had a reputation for dabbling in anything off-limits. Pot, beer, even acid wasn't hard to find in the dorms. But Ray?

"Well," I conceded, "I guess it's kind of hard to avoid it when it's going on all around you. I know the dorms could be pretty wild."

Ray shook his head. "It wasn't the guys in the dorms I drank with, Beth. No—" he laughed lightly—"it wasn't them."

"Well, who then, Ray?"

"You really can't guess?"

"No."

"It was Dutton. Remember him?"

"Dutton?"

"Yeah. The guy was crazy."

"Mr. Dutton? Our English teacher?"

Ray laughed again, a small derisive laugh. "Yeah. Good role model, huh? It's pretty unbelievable, when you think about it now. First this guy has Ken and me drinking with him in his cabin, and then, two months before school's out, he kills himself right there on campus. Here we all thought he was such a great guy, and it turns out he was nothing but some crazy jerk."

I didn't know how to respond. Not only could I scarcely believe we were talking about Theodore Dutton, but I certainly couldn't imagine Ray throwing back beers in Cabin 1. I must have been sitting there slack-jawed because Ray looked at me and said, "Well, you don't have to look quite so surprised."

"I *am* surprised," I confessed. "I never saw you drinking with Mr. Dutton."

"That's because we never drank in front of you. I—well, face it, Beth, you were about as straitlaced as they come. Not that there was anything wrong with that. I mean, I liked that about you. And I did like you, Beth. I was crazy about you. You know that."

He looked at me long and hard. I dropped my eyes, suddenly uneasy.

"I knew you wouldn't approve of my drinking," he went on. "So Dutton, Ken, and I—we passed the beer around only when you girls weren't there."

"He gave you beer?"

"Sure, unless he had already moved on to something stronger by the time we got to the cabin. Jim Beam.

Jack Daniels. Whatever. Listen, at first I almost took a pass, but—" he stopped and shrugged his shoulders—"I thought, why not join them? I liked Dutton and I wanted him to like me. You know how it is when you're a kid. And Ken—he could already drink like a fish."

My mind flashed back to homecoming. Natalie had fled the dance floor after only a couple of dances because Ken, she said, was DUI—Dancing Under the Influence. *"It was not a pretty sight"* was how she put it. But I wasn't interested in talking about Ken right now.

"So did you go to Dutton's cabin often?" I asked. "I mean, without Natalie and me?"

"I guess. Ken and I were right there on campus, you know, living in the dorm. When study hall was over at nine o'clock, we'd just mosey on over there, and Dutton would be glad to see us. He wasn't a man who liked to drink alone. But listen, Beth, it's not as bad as you think. We primarily went there to visit with the guy. I mean, we liked him. We liked talking with him. We didn't always end up drinking. And if we did have something to drink, it was one or two beers, and that was it. Only a couple of times did Ken and I get really plastered."

"And what about Dutton?"

"Well, of course he could drink us under the table. I'm talking sometimes hand over fist. Yeah, he was probably already an alcoholic."

"I had no idea."

"No, probably not. But don't you remember him coming to class with a hangover?"

"No. I don't remember anything like that at all."

"You know, his eyes all bloodshot and his face unshaved and a look that told you he had a pounding headache."

"I don't remember," I said again.

Ray laughed. How he could think any of this was funny, I couldn't imagine. "Yeah, well, you and Natalie were so infatuated with the guy, he could do no wrong in your eyes."

"I wasn't infatuated with Mr. Dutton."

"No?" He looked amused.

"No."

"Listen, Beth. I could tell. . . . I always knew. With Dutton there, I couldn't compete. None of us guys had a chance."

"Ray, that isn't true!"

He raised his coffee to his lips, took a long drink, lowered the cup. He said nothing.

I looked at the drink in my hands. It was only half gone, but my stomach was turning. I asked quietly, "So he was an alcoholic?"

"That's my best guess now, though I never thought about it at the time."

"Maybe he was dealing with something like post-traumatic stress syndrome, since he'd been in Vietnam."

"Yeah, probably that too."

"Well, then, don't you think maybe you should have told somebody? About his drinking?"

"What? Get Dutton fired while at the same time getting Ken and myself in deep trouble?"

"But didn't it seem to you like Dutton needed help?"

Ray shrugged. "I was seventeen, eighteen years old. I sure didn't know then what I know now. I figured he was pretty much like any other guy who liked to drink, which was most every guy I knew. He occasionally came to class with a hangover—so what? You remember Mr. Keaton and his wife, the dorm parents? Where do you think the guys in my dorm got their booze?"

"From the Keatons?"

Ray nodded. "Just the same way they got their pot from the Buckleys, who grew their own stuff."

"I knew that about the Buckleys, but I had no idea about the Keatons. I can't believe it, Ray."

"Believe it. It was a whole different world when you were living in the dorms. As a day student, you missed all that stuff. At least it was a whole lot easier for you to steer clear of it. I won't say you wore rose-colored glasses, but you lived in . . . well, you lived in such a pretty world, Beth."

I felt suddenly defensive. "Was that my fault?"

"Your fault?" He smiled kindly, shook his head. "Not at all. You were lucky."

"But if it wasn't real . . ."

"Your world? Oh no. It was real. You were just sheltered from some of the uglier things."

"You're saying I was naïve."

He shrugged. "We were all naïve to one extent or

another. And that's exactly how it should be. Listen, I wish my kids were growing up the way you and I did, in a good home with both a father and a mother. I mean, I do the best I can, and I think they have a good home, but a series of au pairs can't substitute for a mother. I know it's affected my kids. So there's nothing wrong with being sheltered at first, having a taste of what's really good before life starts dishing out the bad. That'll come soon enough."

"Yes." I sighed heavily. "And you know, Ray, I think Dutton's suicide was the first really bad thing ever to happen to me."

He nodded. "We were blindsided. Believe me, if I'd suspected the guy was suicidal, I'd have done something. But how could I have known? Ken and I—we were his drinking buddies, not his confidants. And drinking made Dutton happy, not maudlin. We did it for the laughs. I never thought he'd try to do himself in. Never."

We sat in silence for a time while the coffee shop bustled with people coming and going. My nausea increased, and I longed for fresh air, but I didn't move. At length I said, "Well, I don't know what to say."

"What's to say?" Ray shrugged. "It's all water under the bridge. I don't even know why I started talking about all that. I sure didn't ask you to meet me here so we could talk about some loser we once knew. Actually, I wanted to ask you if you might come with me to a fund-raiser at the hospital Saturday night. These events are a real bore, but it'd be nice to have you there. Think you can come?"

Still stunned by Ray's revelation, I nevertheless managed to smile and nod my acceptance of Ray's invitation.

CHAPTER 32

There was that time in mid-October of 1976 when Theodore Dutton said it was simply too glorious a day to be inside, so he led us like the Pied Piper from Heath Hall to Chapel Valley where we found a bit of shade and laid ourselves down in the grass. Mr. Dutton gave no lecture, asked no questions, expected no response. He simply tucked his hands beneath his head and allowed one poem and then another to roll easily off his tongue until I felt that this unimaginable moment was itself a poem, a snatch of living verse. The images were those of blue sky, warm sun, birdsong, the earthy smell of dirt and clover, and our teacher's strong and reassuring voice.

"Now, I want you to consider this, friends," he said at length. "I want you to consider the improbability of your being here. I mean, think of the centuries of accidents and coincidences that led to your being born. Just the right people had to meet and mate and give rise to other people who gave rise to you. Go back just one generation and consider what would have happened if your parents hadn't met, if they'd married someone else or hadn't married at all. Just one misstep in centuries of generations, and everything would be different. That's enough to make you realize you're lucky to be alive. You made it into the world, every one of you, and that means you're a winner. I hope you savor every minute of your lives while you're here. Now breathe in. Do you feel the air in your lungs? Do you feel that? You're alive, and the world is beautiful, and it all belongs to you."

After dazzling us with his philosophizing, Mr. Dutton fell silent, and no one dared to move. There we were, all of us lying in the field, simply feeling what it was to be alive upon the earth. We didn't have to prove ourselves good enough to be there; we simply had to *be*, and that in itself was enough. To my adolescent soul, it was almost achingly beautiful.

I thought that if Virginia Woolf could have somehow been there with us, she would have exclaimed, *Oh, this is it! This is what I have been looking for,* because I felt myself to be held not by the world at all but by God. I was resting in the palm of God's hand, and Theodore Dutton was the priest who brought me there.

I think that's why I loved him. He was the first person to understand and share my appreciation for beauty. He was himself aware of the sacredness of everyday life. Even though he didn't believe in God, I still thought of him as one who could lead us to the altar of truth.

I was a child and unaware of the danger of lesser gods.

When Ray told me who Theodore Dutton really was,

even then it was hard to let go of the image of the man lying in the valley, his hands beneath his head, his face to the sun. He was the one who made us believe that life was good, that *we ourselves* were good. He was the one who made me feel unafraid and satisfied in who I was. He seemed at the time to be the one with all the answers. Whoever would have thought he would leave me with so many questions?

CHAPTER 33

The last evening of October 2003 I wasn't really expecting any trick-or-treaters to stop by Pine Glen, but I had a bowl of Hershey miniatures ready just in case. Halloween happened to fall on a Friday this year, and the upper school students were enjoying a costume party in Hawthorne Gymnasium. Pizza and punch, dancing and games, plenty of chaperones. It was scheduled to go on no later than eleven o'clock, at which time day students would have to clear off campus and boarders would be required to return to their dorms.

When my doorbell rang at five minutes after nine, I figured a few stray students had come around looking for a handout. I carried the candy bowl to the door, ready to treat whoever was there. But standing on the stoop was one lone student, dressed in her signature denim jacket and jeans.

"So who are you supposed to be?" I asked.

"Satchel Queen."

"Well, that's creative."

She shrugged. "Once I dressed up like Marilyn Monroe for Halloween. I figured someday some kid might dress up like me. I just beat her to it."

"You've got a point. Want some chocolate?" I held out the bowl to her.

"No, thanks," Satchel said. "You don't have any dried mango, do you?"

"Sorry, I don't." I knew Satchel liked dried mango, but I kept forgetting to buy some when I went to the store.

"Can I come in for a while?"

"Sure. But wouldn't you rather be at the party?"

"Not really."

"Well, come on in then."

We went to the living room and took our usual places. She leaned back into the cushions of the wing chair and propped her feet up on the footstool. I sat across from her on the couch and settled the candy bowl on the side table.

"So you weren't having a good time at the party?" I asked.

"It was lame."

Satchel was a girl who didn't enjoy socializing, I'd begun to realize. She was a loner, though I wasn't sure whether her reclusive tendency was an inborn need for solitude or a learned survival mechanism. Her only real pleasure seemed to come from books and, oddly enough, from visiting me.

"That's too bad," I said. "It sounded like it'd be fun."

"Well, the pizza was a nice change of pace from cafeteria food. But the band . . ." She smirked and shook her head. "And the only person who would talk to me was Tess, and that was only in between dances. Then again, I'm not exactly Miss Popularity, you know."

"Hmm . . . So where's Tess now?"

"Still dancing with Marty, probably."

"Marty?"

"Marty Higgins. They've got a thing going, you know?"

"They're dating?"

"Yeah, I guess you could put it that way."

"Oh, I didn't know."

"Yeah, well, it just happened tonight. He came as Elvis and she came as Dolly Parton, and bingo—next thing you know they're singing the blues together."

I laughed out loud.

Satchel didn't join me.

After a moment she said sullenly, "It seems to be going around, doesn't it?"

"What do you mean?"

"I mean, this pairing up thing."

"Oh?"

"Yeah, I saw you leave campus last Saturday with that dude in the Lexus."

I nodded. "That was Ray," I said. "I told you about him. Remember?"

"Yeah, I remember."

Silence.

"So?" I asked.

"So are you dating him?"

"It seems you asked me that before."

"Yeah, and you said you weren't. You said you were just going out to catch up on the news. But then you went out again. So what? You didn't have enough time to catch up the first time?"

It was an odd question, and I didn't know how to respond. On top of that I suddenly felt as though I were being interrogated, and I wasn't sure why Satchel thought I owed her an explanation for something I had done.

"Is this something you've been brooding about all week?" I asked.

"Sort of."

"Why didn't you ask me earlier?"

"I don't know."

"Because if you had," I said, "I would have told you that I went with Ray to a fund-raiser at the hospital where he works." I shrugged nonchalantly, then added, "He warned me it would be a bore, and it was. He had to spend most of the evening talking up the hospital to the men with the wallets. I don't suppose he and I exchanged a dozen words. There was a great buffet line, though. And half a dozen desserts to die for." I smiled and waited, hoping for some sort of positive response from Satchel. But there was none. She sat staring into the fireplace.

After an awkward moment I asked, "Is something bothering you, Satchel?"

"Yeah." She glanced at me, then looked away again. "I guess you could say that."

"Anything I can help with?"

"I don't think so."

I had to steal a moment to think, to figure out where she was coming from. I looked beyond Satchel to the front windows. In the glow of the porch light the pine trees waved their long boughs in the wind. It would be a blustery night for trick-or-treating, I thought, much like the nights my sisters and I tramped around our neighborhood in costume.

"Did you ever go trick-or-treating, Satchel?"

"Sure. My dad used to take me out when I was a kid. But I stopped doing that kind of stuff after he died. My mom never had time to take me."

I nodded, but she didn't notice. "You know, Satchel," I said, "I'll always have time for you. You don't need to worry about that."

She narrowed her eyes and looked directly at me. "That's not what I'm worried about."

"Then what is it?"

"I'm worried about you."

"Me?"

"Yeah. You know, I don't want you to fall in love or anything."

I was taken aback and momentarily speechless. Then I muttered, "But why not?"

"Because you do, then you got something to lose."

She looked angry when she said it, angry and sad and afraid. I knew exactly how she felt, and I knew that she was right, but I didn't want to tell her so. Leaning forward, I laced my fingers together over my knees. "But that's the risk we take, isn't it, Satchel?"

"It's not worth it, Miss Gunnar."

"No?"

"No."

It was Daniel Queen who taught her that, the father's final lesson, given to his daughter in the moment of his death. Actions speak louder than words; the self-inflicted deathblow outshouts life every time. In one irredeemable moment you negate every positive word you ever said.

"Do you think, then, that it's better to always be alone?" I asked.

She fidgeted, then looked at me squarely again. "Tell you the truth, Miss Gunnar, most of the time I don't know what to think."

"Well—" I took a deep breath and leaned back again. "I appreciate your concern, but you really don't need to waste any time worrying about me. I like my life the way it is right now. I'm not planning on falling in love with Ray, or anyone else, for that matter."

She gave me as skeptical a look as she had ever given me. "Yeah," she said, "well, we really don't have any say about that, do we? When you fall in love, it just happens. So let me just give you one thing to think about."

I blinked. I lifted my shoulders in baffled acquiescence. "Well, okay."

"If you don't want to get burned, don't play with fire."

As her English teacher, I almost told her that was a cliché, but then I thought better of it. There was a reason those words had become ingrained in American culture, and that was because they were good advice.

CHAPTER 34

"Beth?"

"Oh—hi, Mom!" I settled on the couch and pulled the afghan over my legs.

"For a minute it didn't sound like you."

"Sorry about that. I'm a little hoarse—just a bit of a cold. How are you?"

"I'm fine, dear. Am I interrupting anything?"

"Yes. I was cleaning the kitchen, so I'm glad you called." I heard her laugh.

"Well, I was just sitting here thinking about you, and I thought I'd get you on the phone."

"Thanks, Mom. I'm glad you did."

"Are you doing all right, other than the cold?"

"I'm doing just fine. I had lunch with Natalie yesterday."

"Oh? And how is she?"

"Fine. She's fine."

"Do her folks still live over in West Hill?"

"Oh no. They moved ages ago. I told you. Remember? They're in Florida now."

"That's right. I don't know why I forgot about that."

"Anything new with Marla and Carrie? I really owe

them both a phone call. I don't know where the time goes."

"They're busy too, dear. When you're raising kids and working like they're both doing, you don't have time for much else."

"I suppose not."

We were quiet a moment, and then she got to the real reason for her call.

"How's Ray?" she asked. "Have you seen him lately?"

I sighed quietly. "Well, you know, we talk on the phone and get together for a cup of coffee occasionally."

"He's such a nice boy, Beth."

"He's hardly a boy anymore, Mom. He grew up just like I did. Remember?" I laughed, but it fell flat.

"Well, do you think the two of you might get serious?"

"You were never one to mince words, were you, Mom?"

"I just want you to be happy, Beth."

"I know, Mom. I *am* happy."

"You know what I mean."

"I know."

"I'm not trying to be pushy, dear."

"I know, Mom. You just want me to be happily married."

When she didn't respond, I said, "Tell you the truth, I don't think it's entirely out of the question. I mean, that Ray and I should end up together. I would be interested—"

"Really, dear?"

"Well, we're not serious *yet,* of course. We don't have any kind of understanding. I guess I don't really know how Ray feels—"

"Oh, I'm sure he's interested, dear."

I sighed again. "Well, time will tell, won't it?"

"I do think it's about time you settled down, sweetheart. Why you've never accepted a man's proposal when you've had so many—"

"I haven't had so many proposals, Mom!"

"There've been plenty of men who wanted to marry you. Certainly Nick did—"

"Wait a minute, Mom. Nick was the one who wouldn't commit."

"That's not what he said."

"You talked to Nick?"

"Well, it's been some time ago now—"

"Mom!"

In the background I heard my father say, "Joan, are you getting on Beth's case again?"

"No, we're just talking about—"

"I heard what you said, Joan. Listen, give me the phone a minute. Let me talk to Beth. Beth, you still there?"

"Hi, Dad. Yes, I'm here."

"Listen, how are you, honey?"

"I'm fine, Dad."

"I know you are. And I know we don't have to worry about you. You've made a good life for yourself. I'm proud of you. You know that, don't you, honey?"

"Thanks, Dad."

"Don't let your mother bother you with talk about getting married. She just wants what's best for you, like I do."

"I know, Dad. And I appreciate that."

"Listen, you're coming to see us over Christmas, aren't you? Your sisters and their families are all coming, and we sure would like for you to join us."

"I'm planning to be there."

"Well, that's good, then. I'll be looking forward to seeing you, honey."

"I can't wait to see you too, Dad."

"Hey, is work going all right? Is everyone there treating you all right?"

"It's great, Dad. I'm really happy here."

"That's my girl. Listen, I'll put your mother back on, but tell her I said you can only talk about the weather and the price of gasoline; that's all."

I laughed. "I love you, Dad."

"I love you too, sweetheart."

"And Dad?"

"Yes, sweetie?"

"Thanks for understanding."

I sensed him smiling as he handed the phone back to Mom.

CHAPTER 35

Dusk came early on those leaden and leafless autumn afternoons, making for long chilly evenings. I sometimes stayed in the office till well past six o'clock talking with Joel Sexton, who had lately been looking for any excuse to linger at work a little longer. It seems his wife was after him to sell the house and move, and Joel's reluctance brought a certain tension into the marriage.

"Yeah," he said by way of explanation, "she says she wants to get out while the house is back in one piece. She told me in no uncertain terms that if she wakes up to one more car in our living room, she's packing up, taking the kids, and going back to her folks. And she doesn't want me following her there either."

"But it's not your fault cars drive off the road and into the house."

"No. But Glenda says we should have known the house was susceptible to drunks before we ever bought it."

"How on earth could you have known that?"

Joel shrugged. "You got me. And now I'm supposed to pawn the house off on some other poor Joe without telling him the place is a death trap. I just can't do that with a clear conscience."

"No, I suppose not." I thought a moment. "It seems like there ought to be some sort of guardrail at the curve to keep cars from going over."

"You'd think so, wouldn't you? I contacted the state about that possibility and ended up being gagged by a mile of bureaucratic red tape."

"Our tax dollars at work, huh?"

"Exactly." He scratched at his jaw before adding, "I think what I ought to do is burn the place down, make it look like an accident and collect on the insurance."

I feigned shock and dismay. "And that you can do with a clear conscience?"

We looked at each other and burst out laughing, true belly laughter that petered out to sighs.

"You know, Joel," I suggested, "maybe you should apply for faculty housing next year. Then you could rent out your house. That way you'd actually make a little income from it."

"Hey, that's not a bad idea. You're not looking to rent, are you?"

"No, afraid not."

"I didn't think so. Besides, you already know about the house's little drawback. You wouldn't want to be rear-ended while watching late night television."

"I'd rather not."

"Well, back to the old drawing board."

"I don't know, Joel. Seriously, think about campus housing for a year or two. At least it will get you out of the death trap and back onto good terms with your wife."

Joel nodded while giving me a crooked smile. "You were smart to never marry," he mumbled.

"Well, that's two against."

"Two against what?"

"Two votes I've gotten against marriage recently."

"Yeah? Anybody for it?"

I nodded. "My mother and my best friend."

"Wow, two people who are supposed to love you."

I laughed again and shook my head. "Yeah, can you believe it? I—" Before I could finish my thought, Satchel appeared in the doorway of our office and gave me a look of distress.

"Miss Gunnar, I'm glad I found you. Can I talk to you?"

"Sure." I glanced over at Joel. I knew he had an exam he wanted to finish composing before heading home, so I said to Satchel, "I'm just about to walk home. Want to walk with me?"

She nodded tearfully and stepped back into the hall to wait. A moment later we were out the door and moving against a brisk wind that slapped at our cheeks and made pinwheels of our hair. "What's the matter, Satchel?" I asked.

"I just talked to my mom."

She stopped, so I asked, "What'd she say?"

"She and Roger are leaving tomorrow for Europe, and they won't be back till close to Christmas. I told her I couldn't stay here over Thanksgiving break because they close down the dorm, and she said I can't stay in her and Roger's house alone. So I said, so what am I supposed to do? And she said I have to talk to the headmaster and see if he can find me someplace to stay. But I don't want to talk to Quinn. Tell you the truth, I'd rather spend Thanksgiving under a bridge or in a culvert or something rather than talk to that old creep. So I don't know. I guess I could talk to Farrell about it, but—"

I finally interrupted Satchel with a wave of my hand. "You don't have to talk to anyone," I said. "You can stay with me over the holiday."

"You're not going out of town?"

"Not for Thanksgiving."

"You mean I can stay at Pine Glen with you?"

"Of course. I'd be happy to have your company. We can even cook a turkey and make a pumpkin pie and enjoy a regular Thanksgiving meal together."

"Wow! Thanks, Miss Gunnar!" She looked happy and relieved and excited, and she went on looking that way until about an hour later. Satchel was still at Pine Glen when Ray called and invited me to have Thanksgiving dinner with him and his family.

"That would be wonderful, Ray! But, I wonder, well . . . one of my students will be staying with me over the break," I explained. "It's Satchel. I think I've mentioned her."

"So bring her along. The more the merrier."

And yet Satchel looked anything but merry when I told her our plans had changed, and we'd now be having turkey with the Schmidts.

CHAPTER 36

It seemed Satchel began to change her mind, though, when we arrived at the Schmidts' spacious home and were greeted at the door by Ray's nineteen-year-old son, Josh. By the time we sat down to eat, I believe she was thoroughly in favor of being there.

"More turkey, Miss Gunnar?" Josh smiled at me and passed the platter piled high with meat. He was a cordial, good-natured young man who looked startlingly like the Ray I'd known in high school. Home from Penn State for the holiday, he had prepared the entire Thanksgiving meal almost single-handedly.

I smiled in return and took the platter. "Thank you, Josh. You're a wonderful cook! Everything's delicious."

"Thanks, Miss Gunnar. I kind of enjoy it."

Josh glanced at Satchel then, and unlike the guarded teen I was used to, she dropped her eyes demurely.

"We'd have starved to death if Josh hadn't taken over in the kitchen after Mom left," Lisa said. "Dad's hopeless when it comes to cooking."

I glanced at Ray to see how he'd react to the mention of the children's mother, but he only gave Lisa an apologetic smile. "So I have one drawback as a parent. You can't be perfect at everything, you know."

"Daddy's like Mary Poppins!" Ben exclaimed. "Practically perfect in every way!"

Ray winked at Ben. "Thanks, son."

"Yeah, you got him trained just right, Dad," Lisa said.

Lisa was the same age as Satchel but a year ahead of her in school. She was as fair as Satchel was dark, as soft as Satchel was hard, yet the girls had taken easily to each other while setting the table for dinner. I hoped they might forge a friendship that would last beyond the day.

"So, like, who cooks when Josh isn't here?" Satchel asked.

"Ingrid. She's the au pair." Lisa glanced at Satchel as she ladled some gravy over a mound of potatoes. "She's here to take care of Ben, not me. But I like that she does the cooking."

Satchel looked around. "So where is she now?"

"New York," Ray said. "She's visiting with a friend over the holiday. Seems someone she knows from Sweden has a job as an au pair in Brooklyn."

"Yeah? That's where I'm from."

"Really?" Lisa asked excitedly. "What's it like? I always thought it'd be so cool to live in New York City."

"Yeah? It's all right, I guess. I don't live in Brooklyn anymore, though. Mom and Roger—that's my stepdad—they live in White Plains. They're in Europe right now, though. That's how come I'm staying with Miss Gunnar over the Thanksgiving break."

"Wow, Europe! I always wanted to go to Europe."

"You always wanted to go anywhere, Lisa," Josh chided. "Anywhere that isn't Delaware."

"Yeah." Lisa sighed. "Someday I'm going to travel around the world. What about you, Satchel? Do you want to travel?"

"Maybe." Satchel shrugged. "I guess I'd like to see some other places. But then I'm going to find a home and just stay put." She looked around the table, then picked up a bowl that was close to her right hand. "Hey, doesn't anyone want any mango?"

Her personal contribution to the dinner had been a bag of dried mango. She passed the bowl around the table, and everyone accepted an obligatory piece. Eating dried mango was an acquired taste, but it was growing on me, now that we had a supply of it in the kitchen at Pine Glen.

"So, Josh, you think Penn State is a good place to study business?" Satchel asked.

Josh had a mouthful of food, but he talked around it. "Sure. It's all right. I like it." He washed the food down with a long drink of water. "You thinking about going into business?"

"Yeah, I think I might."

"Business?" I asked.

Satchel looked at me and nodded. "Sure, why not?"

"I didn't know you were interested in business. How long have you been thinking about that?"

"About an hour now."

She and Josh exchanged a smile while Ray and I swapped a quizzical look. Your son and my . . . my what? I realized I felt possessive of Satchel in a way I had never felt with any other student. We had spent the morning at Pine Glen baking pies and preparing a cranberry salad, and for the first time I could remember, Satchel Queen and genuine laughter occupied the same space. Not that anything was funny; I think she was simply happy. And so was I. Happy to be in a warm kitchen on a chilly morning making pies. While we rolled out the dough and prepared the pumpkin filling, my mind kept drifting back to when my own mother and I kneaded bread dough side by side on the kitchen counter.

Ben piped up then, snapping me out of my reverie. "I'm going to be a doctor like Dad," he said proudly.

"You have plenty of time to think about that," his father responded.

"Yeah, and you have plenty of time to talk him out of it," Josh said. "Just like you did with me."

"I never talked you out of medicine, Josh," Ray countered. "You were never interested in it."

"Not after the hours he saw you working," Lisa agreed. "Who'd want a job that never let you come home?"

For a moment Ray looked uncomfortable. But then he smiled. "Well, that's all changed now, isn't it? I've finally got a schedule that allows me to be home at a reasonable hour."

"Fat lot of good it did me," Josh said.

I looked at him to gauge the emotions behind the words. Where he might have been angry, he was smiling.

"Dad sells his practice just in time for me to fly the

coop," he went on. "But at least it's good for Ben." He looked at Ben and winked. "Right, squirt?"

Ben nodded enthusiastically. Then he added, "But I wish you didn't have to work tomorrow, Dad."

"Me too, Ben. It's just for a few hours, though. I'll be home earlier than usual, I promise."

I began to imagine what life must have been like for this family when Brenda left. Too, what it must have been like for them before Brenda left. It seems it had become motherless after years of being as good as fatherless. But I didn't want to think about that right now. It had nothing to do with now, which was far removed from all that. Now was good and worth enjoying without dredging up the past.

We finished the meal with fat slivers of pie and declared ourselves full. Lisa, Satchel, and I then cleaned the kitchen while Ray built a fire in the fireplace. Josh set up a card table in front of the hearth where the kids later played Monopoly. Ray and I watched the game from a nearby couch, sipping hot chocolate and listening to the chatter and laughter of the kids. Ray's arm was draped casually around the back of the couch, and occasionally his hand touched my shoulder.

I felt as though I had come to rest after a long struggle. Something in my head kept telling me that this was where I was supposed to be, that I had finally made it. At midnight Ray picked up a slumbering Ben from the floor in front of the fireplace. I walked with Ray to Ben's room, where I turned down the covers on the bed. Together we tucked him in. Through it all, he didn't stir.

I thought, *I am completely satisfied. I don't have to look backward or forward anymore. I can just be.*

It was a feeling that didn't last very long.

Early the next afternoon, Satchel and I were watching a video at Pine Glen when Ray called.

"Beth, are you sitting down?"

"Yes. Why?" Had something happened to one of his children?

"Well, I'm not really sure, but . . ." His voice trailed off. In the background I heard traffic, the sound of horns honking, someone hollering.

"Ray, where are you?"

"I'm outside the hospital. I stepped outside to call you. Listen, it could mean my job if anyone knew I was doing this."

"Doing what?"

My question was met with silence. Then, "It's about a patient, Beth."

"All right. So please just tell me what it is."

"I'm not sure," he said again, "but—you know Dutton? Our English teacher?"

In spite of Ray's warning to sit down, I jumped up abruptly from the couch. I felt something dreadful shiver through me. "Yes. Why? What is it?"

"We have a Theodore Dutton here at the hospital. I think it might be him."

CHAPTER 37

The reason for Ray's uncertainty was apparent. The ailing man in the hospital bed was hardly the robust Theodore Dutton we had known.

This man was heavyset, with a full face and thinning gray hair. His bulbous nose and cheeks were webbed with tiny red veins, and his jawline settled into a double chin. I could find little physical connection between this man and our high school teacher other than an overall vague and questionable resemblance.

"I suppose," I said, "there could be any number of people named Theodore Dutton."

Ray continued to look intently at the patient's face. "I think it's him."

"Why?"

"The age is right. And—"

"And what?"

Ray answered by gently lifting the man's left arm high enough for me to see the protruding pink scar along the wrist. Then Ray settled his eyes on me.

I nodded. So here he was, all these years later. I didn't even have to go looking for him. Life had caught him and spit him out on shore like the lost cargo of some sunken ship, washing him right up to where I'd stumble over him in the sand.

"So what's wrong with him?" I asked.

"He's in a diabetic coma. His wife discovered him unresponsive when she went to bed around midnight last night. He'd gone to bed earlier, not feeling well. She called an ambulance, and here he is. He obviously hasn't taken care of himself, and yesterday being Thanksgiving—well . . ." He stopped and shrugged.

"Will he come out of it?"

"I don't know."

"You mean he could die?"

"There's always that chance."

We fell silent a moment. A familiar angry squall started brewing somewhere deep inside of me. "Well, that would be pretty ironic, wouldn't it?"

"What do you mean?"

"To find him now, only to have him die like this."

Ray looked at the IV machine that dripped something into Dutton's arm. Before he could turn back to me, we heard Ray's name paged over the PA system, calling him to another room.

"I've got to go."

"I know."

But he didn't move. "There's a cardinal rule around here about patient confidentiality, you know."

I nodded, pressing my lips into a tight line.

Ray went on, "I probably shouldn't have called you, but I thought you'd want to know about this, Beth."

"Of course I do." Then I added, "I appreciate your letting me know, Ray."

He nodded. "I'll call you after I get off work, all right?"

"Yes. I'll be home."

He started to head toward the door but stopped and

turned back. "Listen, I'll come by tonight. I'll bring the kids and something to eat. Maybe we'll find a little time to talk."

"All right, Ray. That would be good."

He nodded and smiled briefly, and then he left me alone with Theodore Dutton.

I shivered in the presence of this stranger. The storm inside of me kicked up a myriad of feelings and blew them into a strange whirling mix of wonder, anger, amazement, and fear. I was left reeling, both light-headed and befuddled. The ghost had put on flesh, and here he was, resurrected in the form of an aging and ailing man, someone who both was and wasn't the teacher I had loved.

I don't know how long I went on standing there before a woman entered the room. When she saw me, she looked surprised, almost taken aback. "Can I help you?" she asked.

"No. I mean, I'm just . . . visiting."

"Do I know you?"

"No, I don't think so. Are you—are you family of Mr. Dutton?"

"I'm his wife."

"Oh. I'm—I was his student once. At Seaton. When Mr. Dutton taught at Seaton school."

"Oh?" She seemed to be trying to place the name. "In Hockessin, right?"

"Yes, that's right."

"I see." She hesitantly extended a hand. "I'm Isabel Dutton. And you are . . . ?"

"Beth." I took her hand. Her clasp was firm and warm. "Beth Gunnar."

"Well, it's nice to meet you, Beth." She offered me a flustered smile. "Won't you . . . ?" She let go of my hand and waved toward a black vinyl chair. "Won't you have a seat?"

"Thank you. I'll only stay a minute."

She was a plain woman with short white hair and keen blue eyes. She had an intelligent yet affable face, untouched by makeup. Even her clothes were simple—jeans and a sweater, a pair of loafers. Her only jewelry was her wedding ring. She stood shorter than I by several inches, yet she seemed taller, larger somehow, because of an almost palpable inner strength.

She settled herself on the foot of her husband's bed and leaned her weight against one locked arm. "How did you know Ted was here?"

"Oh!" How to explain without getting Ray in serious trouble? For a moment, I felt the urge to lie, to make up a story about walking down the hall and seeing Theodore Dutton's name outside the door, as though by chance. But I wasn't good at lying, not even to protect someone.

"Somebody on staff here was also a student of your husband's," I began, resolving to take the brunt of the fallout should this woman explode over the breach of confidentiality. I would never reveal the name of the staff member, even if this woman carried a complaint to the hospital administration. "I hope you can understand. He knew I would be concerned and so he called me. . . .”

My words trailed off as I noted the woman’s bewildered gaze. Why would someone call me about a man we hadn’t seen in decades? I rushed to explain, “You see, your husband was a great inspiration to me. I decided I wanted to teach English too, just like he did. So I am—I mean, I’ve been an English teacher for many years, thanks to your husband. I teach at Seaton now.”

The woman didn’t move as she seemingly allowed my words to sink in. Then she smiled. “I see. I’m happy to hear that. I think Ted has been a great inspiration to many young people.”

I took a deep breath, and the anxiety that had been ballooning in my chest deflated as I exhaled. Apparently Mrs. Dutton didn’t intend to make an issue out of the illicit phone call. Maybe she didn’t even realize it went against hospital protocol. “Oh yes,” I quickly agreed. “He was wonderful—a wonderful teacher.”

Isabel Dutton gazed at her husband and smiled sadly. “He never was good about taking care of himself, though. Whenever I reminded him about diet or medication, he waved me off. He said I was only interfering.”

“Oh? I’m sorry. I hope he’ll be all right.”

“So do I.” She sighed then and turned her gaze to me. She waited. Apparently, it was my turn to say something.

"Does Mr. Dutton still teach?" I asked.

"No, not any longer. Actually, we've owned a secondhand bookstore for four—no, five years now. Bel's Book Nook?"

She said the name of the store in such a way that I knew she was asking if I'd heard of it. I had to shake my head no.

"Well, it hasn't made us rich," she went on, offering up this fact with a laugh. "But we both love books; we love what we do."

"Where is your store?"

"Here in Wilmington. On Lancaster Pike."

"You're kidding."

"No. Why?"

"You live right here in Wilmington?"

"Yes. Since buying the store. Though actually we spent most of our married life in New York. Ted has a nephew who attended Cornell and then afterward got a job teaching at a small liberal arts college not far from Ithaca. We went there to be near him. Ted ended up teaching in a private high school there."

When she mentioned the nephew, a vague memory rose in my mind of a boy with a guitar and an infectious laugh whom we occasionally found visiting at Cabin 1. "His nephew," I said. "Would that be—what was his name? Lennon, right? Was that Lennon who went to Cornell?"

She looked surprised. "Do you know him?"

"Not really." I shook my head. "I met him a couple of times when Mr. Dutton was teaching at Seaton."

She nodded. "Len is more like a son to Ted than a nephew, especially since Ted and I never had children. It was hard to leave him, but we finally decided we needed to get away from the harsh New York winters. And Delaware is my home. I missed it. I wanted to come back. So we bought the store and moved down here. It was a good move, I think." She smiled again, then asked, "What about you? Have you always taught at Seaton?"

"Oh no. This is my first year there. I left Delaware right after graduating in 1977. I've lived all over the place, mostly in the Midwest; although before I moved here this past summer, I was living in Maryland on the Eastern Shore."

I wasn't sure she was listening. Her gaze was on her husband; she seemed to be watching intently as his chest rose and fell, then rose and fell again. I thought perhaps it was a strain to talk with a stranger while your husband lay suspended somewhere between life and death.

I stood to go. "Well, I won't keep you any longer."

She didn't try to dissuade me. She held out her hand again. "Thank you for stopping by. I'll tell Ted you came to see him."

"Please do," I said. "I hope he remembers me."

"Oh, he will. He's got an amazing memory. So far, it's still intact." Another small smile.

"And I hope that he's better soon."

"Thank you."

I started to go but stopped and turned back. "If

there's anything I can do, please let me know. Really, I—well, just a minute."

I reached into my purse for pen and paper and scribbled my phone number for her. She accepted it uncertainly, without glancing at it. "Thank you."

"Don't hesitate to call."

"All right. Thank you," she said again.

She was unfailingly polite, and I was sure that under different circumstances, she and I might have been friends. I was sorry to leave her to her solitary vigil, especially since I was just as anxious as she was for Theodore Dutton to wake up.

CHAPTER 38

Ray showed up around seven o'clock that evening with Josh, Lisa, and Ben, as well as three large pizzas and four one-liter bottles of soda. After we ate, the kids, including Satchel, bundled up in winter garb and headed out for a walk around the largely deserted campus.

Ray and I watched them from the front windows, four swaddled figures moving from lamplight to lamplight through a shimmering Milky Way of falling snow. Satchel held on to little Ben's hand; he'd pressed his mitten against her glove as soon as they walked out the door. Lisa, on the other side, locked arms with Satchel so that the three of them marched up the hill, pressed close together in a line. Josh walked a couple steps ahead, as though on point.

Earlier that afternoon when I got home from the hospital, Satchel had asked, "So who's this guy you went to see?"

I was reluctant to talk about Theodore Dutton but I could hardly avoid it. "He was an English teacher here at Seaton," I said. "Ray and I were both in his class senior year."

"You know, you don't look so hot, Miss Gunnar. Are you all right?"

"Yes. Yes, I'm fine."

She eyed me doubtfully. "So how is he? Your teacher—like, is he going to be okay?"

"Yes. Well, I don't know, really. I think so."

"What's wrong with him?"

"He's in a diabetic coma."

"A diabetic coma? That doesn't sound so good. I guess you're worried about him, huh?"

I nodded while I hung up my coat in the hall closet. I was moving slowly, as though I were pushing against something heavy and viscous.

"Listen, Miss Gunnar, can I get you something to drink? Some water or something?"

"No. Thank you, though, Satchel. Actually, I'm really tired. I think I'll go stretch out on my bed for a while, take a little nap."

"Sure, okay. I think you could use the rest."

"Oh, and Ray's coming tonight with Josh and the kids. He's bringing supper."

"Yeah?" All concern for me vanished as her face lit up. I couldn't help but smile.

Now, as I watched the little band of hikers walking through the snow, I smiled again. It was good to see Satchel enjoying herself as part of a group.

I might have stood there a long time enjoying the moment, but Ray's words pulled me inevitably into the past.

"It's been a long time," he said, "since we walked this campus ourselves at night."

"Yes, it sure has." And those were the days we needed to revisit, because they nagged at us, demanding our attention. I stepped away from the window. "I imagine the coffee's ready."

A pot of decaf was brewing in the kitchen. Ray followed me and sat at the small round table while I poured each of us a mug.

"Black, right?"

"Yeah, that's fine."

I set the mug in front of him and sat down. I stirred some cream into my own coffee and set the dripping spoon on a white paper napkin. Ray and I both watched as a brown halo blossomed around the bowl of the spoon.

There was so much to be said, and I didn't know where to begin.

Finally Ray broke the silence. "I would have bet my right arm the man was dead."

I raised my eyes to him. "Commander told us he was alive."

"I thought he was lying. Didn't you?"

"Yes."

“I just don’t get it.”

Commander Pettingill was himself long dead; so was Mildred Bidney. Other faculty members who might have known something about that night had left Seaton years before.

I clutched the mug with both hands and stole a few moments to think by sipping slowly. “Commander was your mom’s uncle, right?”

“Uh-huh.”

“So maybe he told your parents something.”

“Nope. No such luck.”

“It wouldn’t hurt to ask.”

“I already did. I called them before I came over here tonight.”

“You did?”

He nodded.

“And they don’t know why we were told it was a heart attack?”

“They’re as much in the dark as we are,” he said.

“Oh.” I sipped the coffee. “But then again, it isn’t *that* so much that I want to know anyway.”

“Then what do you want to know?”

“Why he did it.”

“Why Dutton tried to kill himself?”

“Yes.”

Ray shrugged. “Now that, I’m afraid, is none of our business.”

I set the mug down on the table. My heart was suddenly thumping, and I had to struggle to keep the anger out of my voice. “You know, Ray, we admired Mr.

Dutton. We looked up to him. And we were just kids. It was terrible what he did to us."

Ray looked amused, as though swallowing laughter. "What he did to him*self* was terrible. It's got nothing to do with us."

"What do you mean? Are you saying he thought he could just destroy himself and it wouldn't affect us?"

"Listen, Beth. I don't think he was thinking about us at all. I mean, come on. By the time someone puts the blade to his wrist or the gun to his head or whatever he chooses to do, he's not thinking about anything but himself and his own despair."

"But that's just it. Why the despair? And why did we never suspect anything?"

Ray sighed heavily. "People are complicated creatures, Beth. Sometimes, when it comes to what we do, the choices people make, there's just no explanation that anyone can understand. The person himself may not even fully understand his own mind."

"But, Ray," I asked, exasperated, "don't you want to know? Haven't you ever wondered why Dutton did what he did?"

He lifted the mug to his lips, changed his mind, and set it down again. "Not after we graduated, no. I was too busy with life."

"But you were the one who found him, you and Ken—"

"Yeah. So?"

"So how could you just forget about him?"

He shrugged, almost nonchalantly. "What else could

I have done? No one was going to give us any straight answers. As far as I knew, the guy was dead, and that was that. End of story."

"But you see, *now* maybe—now that we know he's alive—maybe we can finally get some answers."

He frowned, his whole face folding into a look of distaste. "Listen, Beth, why are you so obsessed with this?"

"I'm not obsessed. I just want to know what happened."

He gazed at me for a long moment. "And just what are you going to do? Ask him when he wakes up? *If* he wakes up. 'So, Mr. Dutton, haven't seen you in a while, not since you tried to kill yourself. And by the way, I was wondering—' "

I held up a hand and shook my head. "I'd be tactful about it."

"And you know what he's going to tell you?"

"What?"

"That it's none of your business."

"But it *is* my business."

"Why?"

Frustration rose full-blown in my chest as I struggled to put the words together. "Because for months he told us that life was good and beautiful and worth living, and I believed him. And then he goes and kills himself—or we thought he did—and that kind of cancels out everything he ever said, doesn't it? It never made any sense."

When I finished, we were both quiet. Ray pushed his

mug aside and put one hand over mine on the tabletop. "The man still doesn't owe you an explanation, Beth. So just forget it."

I wanted to tell Ray that I disagreed, that in my opinion Mr. Dutton did owe me—us—an explanation. And I wanted to tell him that I couldn't forget it, even if I wanted to. But before I could say as much, the front door burst open, and the children spilled in, bringing with them a gust of cold air mixed with chatter and laughter. That put an end to our conversation about Theodore Dutton. For now.

CHAPTER 39

Classes resumed the Monday after Thanksgiving. Satchel reluctantly moved back to the dorm. Ray went back to work after having Saturday and Sunday off. Ray's son Josh exchanged addresses with Satchel and drove back to Penn State. And sometime toward the middle of that week Theodore Dutton was released from the hospital and sent home.

He wasn't Ray's patient, and Ray didn't see him again after the day Dutton was admitted. Ray made a point of not following our former teacher's progress and finally learned of Dutton's discharge only when someone mentioned it in passing. He told me about it that night, adding, "So listen, Beth, he's home and he's all right. You don't have to worry about him anymore."

Natalie was incredulous when I called to tell her Theodore Dutton was alive. She was out of town with her family over Thanksgiving, and by the time I carved out a moment to call her, Dutton was already home.

I spilled the news as soon as Natalie picked up the phone, and after a suspended period of silence, she said, "I don't believe it."

"It's true."

"Are you sure?"

"I saw him at the hospital."

"And you're sure it was *our* Theodore Dutton?"

I thought of the scar on his wrist. "Yes."

"Did you talk with him?"

"He wasn't conscious, but I spoke with his wife. She was aware he had taught at Seaton."

"So what in the world is he doing now?"

"They own a bookstore on Lancaster Pike."

"No way!"

"Yeah. It's called Bel's Book Nook. Ever heard of it?"

"No." Another pause. Then Natalie said, "Well, if this doesn't beat all. Commander was telling the truth when he said Dutton was alive."

"Yes, at least part of what he told us was true."

"Well, what do you know? I can't believe it," she said again. After a moment, she added, "And you say he's been right here in Wilmington all this time?"

"Oh no. Apparently he spent a good number of years teaching at a school in upstate New York. His wife said they moved back down here four or five years ago."

"So the old guy got married, huh? What's his wife like?"

"We only spoke for a few minutes, but she seems very nice."

"They have kids?"

"No, she mentioned they don't. But she also said Dutton has always been particularly close to his nephew Lennon. Remember him?"

A long pause, then, "No. Should I?"

"We met him a few times when he was visiting Dutton. You know, long hair, guitar, he used to jam with Ken."

"Oh yeah! I do remember him. Vaguely." She gave a small laugh and said, "Well, whoever would have thought Dutton was alive? At least that answers your question, doesn't it?"

"Part of it anyway."

"What do you mean?"

"I mean, yes, I've wondered whether he was alive, and now I know he is. But what I still don't know is why he did it."

"Why he tried to kill himself?"

"Yeah."

"Forget it, Beth. It happened so long ago it doesn't matter anymore."

Was I the only one who wanted to know? "You sound just like Ray," I retorted.

"Why? What did Ray say?"

"That whatever the reason was, it's none of my business."

"I hate to say it, Beth, but I'm with Ray on that one."

I sighed heavily into the phone. "Come on, Natalie.

Don't you want to know what happened to the man you once called Teddy Bear?"

She had to think about that. I heard her breathing on the other end of the line. "I don't know," she confessed. Then she added more firmly, "No, I don't. Like I told you before, I stopped caring about all of this a long time ago, and I'm not about to go dredging the whole mess up again at this point in my life. Forget about it, Beth. Let sleeping dogs lie. Don't beat a dead horse. It's water under the bridge . . . and . . . and every other cliché I can throw at you to convince you to just put it all behind you."

When she finished, I didn't respond. Finally I said, "So I guess that means you don't want to go confront him with me?"

She laughed out loud. So did I.

Forgetting did seem to be the only reasonable option, and I tried. As those first days of December slipped by, I tried to push Theodore Dutton to the back of my mind, someplace dark and preferably bottomless. But the thought of him kept rising up like fog seeping in under the crack of a door. I found myself wondering about him even when I determined to fix my mind on something else. I could not let him go.

Still, I wouldn't seek him out. No, Ray and Natalie had a point. If I sought him out, how would I ever put him behind me?

Ultimately, though, it didn't seem to be up to me. Life caught him up again and rolled him into my path as though he were a bit of unfinished business that I simply had to attend to. I was broadsided, practically knocked windless, when one wintry night not long before Christmas, Isabel Dutton called and said her husband would be pleased if I would come visit them.

CHAPTER 40

The anxiety in the pit of my stomach felt sickly familiar. It was the sensation of going to school on the first day of a new year and wondering what lay ahead.

I took several deep breaths of icy air as I moved up the walkway toward the Duttons' modest clapboard house. The windows glowed with the muted light of electric Christmas candles, and a wreath of fragrant pine boughs hung on the door. The house itself was warm and welcoming, and yet the barbed tangle of nerves kept tumbling around inside of me, leaving me weak and shaky.

I couldn't find a doorbell, but the large wreath circled a brass knocker, which I tapped tentatively. I heard footsteps, heard a lock being unlatched, and then I was face-to-face with Isabel Dutton.

She was smiling. "Hello, Beth. So nice of you to come. Won't you come in?"

I could see at once the woman's touch inside the house. The place was tastefully decorated with an assortment of antique furniture and bric-a-brac. Persian rugs adorned the hardwood floors, and chintz curtains hung in the windows. Paintings, not just prints, filled the walls. All that remained of that little cabin on campus was the books. But now they were neatly arrayed on shelves rather than tumbling all over the tables and floor.

"How is Mr. Dutton?" I asked, handing my coat to Isabel.

"Much better, thanks." She hung up the coat, then said, "He's anxious to see you." She nodded her head slightly toward the back of the house. "He's in the den."

I followed her down a narrow hall to a room that was unmistakably Theodore Dutton's. All was in disarray, with books everywhere. In the midst of it, in an easy chair with his feet propped up, sat Mr. Dutton himself. His eyes were shut.

"Ted," his wife said softly. "Beth is here."

The figure roused himself then and, blinking a pair of eyes made large by his glasses, looked up at me. He squinted and frowned, as though he couldn't see or couldn't remember who I was.

Then he held out a hand. I stepped across the room and took it. "Beth Gunnar," he said. He held my hand in a firm grip. "I'm so glad you came."

"Hello, Mr. Dutton. It's good to see you. How are you?"

The eyes that searched my face were cloudy and uncertain. "I can't—" he dropped his hand, waved toward a small sofa to his left. "I can't see very well anymore. Did Bel tell you?"

"No." I let my purse slide to the floor and sat down on the couch.

"It's the diabetes. Nasty disease."

"I'm sorry."

He waved his hand again, as though to wave away my sympathy.

"I'll bring us some tea," his wife said.

"All right, dear," Mr. Dutton said. Then he added, "And do we have a little cake to go with it?"

"You know we don't, Ted. Don't even try that with me."

He grinned playfully. Isabel Dutton left the room, and there I sat with Theodore Dutton, the dead man come to life. I clasped my hands together in my lap to keep them from trembling.

"Beth Gunnar." When he said my name, it sounded like a sigh. "I was delighted to hear you came by while I was in the hospital. And I understand one of the doctors there was also a student of mine?"

"Yes. That's right."

I had promised myself I wouldn't reveal the name, but Theodore Dutton was smiling at me eagerly. "And who was that?" he asked.

I hesitated a moment, then said reluctantly, "Well, you may not remember him. Ray Schmidt?"

"Ray—oh my, yes! Of course I remember him. Wonderful boy, top-flight student. I thought he might pursue the arts, but he opted for medicine, did he?"

"Yes, it seems he did."

"Wise move on his part, I suppose. Not much money in the arts." Mr. Dutton's head moved slowly from side to side. "Still, I'm having trouble picturing that young boy as a doctor."

"Well, he's not a young boy anymore. In fact, he has a son who is older than Ray was when you knew us at Seaton."

The head continued moving like a metronome. "Oh dear. Where has the time gone?"

"I wish I knew." I smiled wistfully.

The metronome stopped counting out the lost years, and Mr. Dutton settled his wide-eyed gaze at me. "Bel tells me you're teaching English at Seaton."

"Yes. I just started this year."

He gave a satisfied nod. "I always knew you would do well. I was hoping you might pursue teaching. We used to talk about that, didn't we?"

"Yes, we did. You were the one who encouraged me. And now the room where I teach is the room where you taught in Heath Hall."

"Well now, what do you know about that. Funny how things work out, isn't it?"

"Yes, I guess it is."

Isabel returned with three teacups on a tray, along with a creamer and sugar bowl. All were of a hand-painted china. Somehow I wouldn't have expected anything less from her.

I accepted the tea, declining the cream and sugar. Wisps of steam rose from the cup, so I waited for it to cool. I was afraid to lift it to my lips in case the cup itself should shudder, revealing my nervousness.

Dutton sipped his at once. He seemed to relish the warmth of the tea, taking it in as if to stave off the cold of the room, though he wore a heavy cardigan and had a wool plaid blanket covering his lap.

He pressed his lips together, nodded. "Thank you, Bel," he said. "That's just what I needed."

His wife cast him an unspoken word of acknowledgment when he settled the cup in the saucer. Then, as though he were finished with the pleasantries, his face took on a stern expression. "Beth," he said, "I owe you an apology."

At last! I thought. *At last we will talk about that night, get it out in the open, come to some sort of understanding.*

But I feigned surprise. "Oh?"

"Yes. You wrote to me after I left Seaton, and I never responded."

I cocked my head. He wanted to talk about my get-well card? "You remember that?" I asked.

"Oh yes," Bel jumped in. "As I think I told you, his memory is amazing. He's not doing so well in other ways, but there's nothing wrong with his mind." She smiled broadly, amused by her husband's retrospection.

I attempted to return her smile, then turned what must have been a dubious gaze upon Theodore Dutton. I thought it might be a good thing if he couldn't quite see my face.

"Yes, it was nice of you to write to me, Beth, while I was recuperating. I really should have acknowledged the card you sent, but, you see, my recovery from the heart attack was rather lengthy and . . ."

He went on, but I didn't hear what he said. My mind

had ground to a halt at the words *heart attack*. The room seemed to tilt a moment and then right itself. I set my teacup down on a nearby coffee table and gripped the arm of the couch tightly with one hand.

So Theodore Dutton too was willing to take part in this charade? He too believed the student body had been duped into believing he'd had a heart attack?

Most had, yes. Most of our graduating class left Seaton thinking Dutton's heart had somehow gone haywire. Even the substitute teacher they brought in to replace him thought Dutton would be coming back, "once he's recovered from his unfortunate illness."

But what Theodore Dutton didn't know was that a few of us knew better. Obviously no one ever told him who had found him, who had been there. But, of course not. All of that too would be edited out of the revised version of that night's story.

An hour passed, during which time I reconnected with the conversation. We spoke of Seaton and of my work there, we spoke of their store and of the book Bel was reading to him because he could no longer read for himself. And all the while I thought of the poem by T. S. Eliot, the one I first read in Dutton's class. I heard, from somewhere in my brain, the lines mocking me, *"Should I, after tea and cakes and ices / Have the strength to force the moment to its crisis?"* And I knew that no, no, all was small talk. We walked the surface while the past lay buried just beneath our feet, and I wouldn't speak of it because, like J. Alfred Prufrock, I was afraid.

I would measure out my life in coffee spoons, speaking of small and meaningless things, never daring to ask questions of any consequence. I was Prufrock, listening to my own self-recrimination:

> And would it have been worth it, after all,
> After the cups, the marmalade, the tea,
> Among the porcelain, among some talk of you and me,
> Would it have been worth while,
> To have bitten off the matter with a smile,
> To have squeezed the universe into a ball
> To roll it toward some overwhelming question,
> To say: "I am Lazarus, come from the dead,
> Come back to tell you all, I shall tell you all"—
> If one, settling a pillow by her head,
> Should say: "That is not what I meant at all.
> That is not it, at all."

At the end of the hour the fear was gone, replaced with an unyielding sadness and a withering resignation. I rose to go.

"I'm so delighted you came, Beth."

"It was good to see you, Mr. Dutton."

"You must stop by the store sometime," Isabel added. "We closed it temporarily, but we'll reopen next week."

"I'll try to do that."

"And give our greetings to Ray," Theodore Dutton said.

"Of course."
"Tell him we should like to see him sometime."
"I have heard the mermaids singing, each to each. I do not think that they will sing to me. . . ."

CHAPTER 41

My Favorite Thing to Do
by Satchel Queen

Ever since I was a little kid, I've liked to look at the old photographs in history books. I like to look at the pictures of men in bowler hats and women carrying parasols and little girls dressed up in pinafores. I like to imagine what it would be like to ride in a horse-drawn buggy or in a Model-T Ford. The old days are totally fascinating to me, because they are a time I will never experience myself.

Sometimes I wish I could step into a photo the way Mary Poppins and her friend Bert and the Banks children stepped into the chalk drawing and it became real. I thought that was the greatest thing in the world when I saw that movie with my dad. Imagine stepping into an old photo and all of a sudden everything is real and people are talking and cars are moving and clocks are ticking, and for a little while you can see what it was like to live in another time. There are so many times and places I would like to see. We don't get to choose the place and time we're born into, and I suppose we should be satisfied where we are, but I can't help thinking that maybe there's a place and time I might like more than here and now. I wish that I could look around and see, and I wish, if I could find such a place, I could stay there.

Another thing I like to do when I look at an old photograph of a group of people is pick out just one person and imagine what their life was like. Sometimes I might pick one young woman and think, What was her name? Who did she marry? Did she have children? Was she happy? The funny thing is, I always imagine happy things for these people, even though I know everyone has problems in their lives. But when I look at an old picture I don't think about the bad things. It's almost as though a story comes into my head, and it's a good story with a happy ending.

It would be interesting to meet these people in heaven, if there is a heaven, and ask them what their life was like and see how far off I was. But maybe some of them really were happy. I hope so anyway. I'd like to think that somebody somewhere is happy.

Then I wonder whether someday my own face might be in a history book, not because I'm famous but because I just happened to be in a photograph that was used in the book. And I wonder whether someone a hundred years from now might look at my picture and ask themselves, Who was she and what did she do and was she happy?

And then sometimes when I start to think about it

too hard I get a little scared, even though looking at old pictures is one of my favorite things. I get scared because from one face in one place at one time, the picture starts to expand, and I begin to think about all the other places and all the other times. I might think about a soldier who fought in Vietnam or in the Second World War or in the Civil War. Then from there I'll jump over to think about a slave who worked on a plantation in Mississippi before slavery was abolished. Or an Indian who lived on the land before the white men came. Or a sailor who sailed with Christopher Columbus. Or a handmaiden who waited on Queen Isabella. Or a noblewoman who went to the guillotine during the French Revolution, a Chinaman who helped build the Great Wall of China, a slave who hauled stones to the Egyptian pyramids, a shepherdess who drew water from a well in the deserts of Saudi Arabia, a child sitting in a grass hut in Africa. And after a while I don't see them by themselves anymore, but I start to see them altogether, and that's when it gets to be too big. I'm sitting here in the present and I look all the way back to when those first human beings stood on two feet under the same sun shining on me today, and even though there is a finite number of people who have ever lived, it looks to me to be as infinite as the universe. It just seems like an endless procession of people.

When you think about all the people who have ever lived and all the people who are alive now and all the people who are going to live but just haven't been born yet, you have to stop and wonder, with all those people and all those lives, how can anyone see me? And can even God see me in a crowd like this?

If I'm not careful, my favorite thing to do leaves me feeling small and sad. If I think about everyone at once, I'm totally lost, like I'm drowning. So I go back to a photograph and look at just one person and try to imagine that her life was good and meaningful and maybe even happy, even if she's dead now, and even if hardly anyone knew she was alive when she really was alive. I hope someday someone will do the same for me.

CHAPTER 42

The picture window in my parents' living room looks out over a sea of mountains, each wave solid in its crest, motionless, neither rolling nor waning. Thousands of years ago the earth stopped heaving and laid itself to rest. Now nothing disturbs its sleep. The hills may shiver now and again, as though yawning and stretching. But it would take one huge quake to change the lay of the land, and such a catastrophe isn't likely in western North Carolina. The only things that change in the mountains are the colors, which are as predictable as clockwork. You can stand at the window and say, *Oh, there's Mt. Pisgah,* or *There's the mountain that looks like a man sleeping,* and whether the mountains are in winter or summer or autumn garb, you will be right.

Three days after Christmas the scene was of dark and leafless trees, arms lifted toward an overcast sky the color of a frozen pond. Slowly the ridge of the mountains began to glow as though backlit with fire until the snow on the peaks captured the morning light, tossing it back heavenward in a glimmering volley.

It was a lovely scene, and yet a person feels inescapably small and mortal in the face of the eternal landscape. You say to yourself knowingly, *The mountains were here a long time before I was, and they'll still be here long after I'm gone. They keep going while I'm the one who disappears.*

I thought of Satchel. She turned in her final essay for the semester three days before Christmas break. It was two days late. I told her I would have to deduct half a grade. She said she could accept the lower grade; what she couldn't do was turn the essay in until she had it right.

When I read it, I knew she had it right. When a person considers her place in this wide world, she begins to drown.

I stood at the picture window, feeling the cold seep in through the pane. Even my heavy terry-cloth robe and the mug of hot coffee in my hands couldn't keep me from shivering.

"You're up early, sweetheart." My mother, also in robe and slippers, came and joined me at the window. She too clutched a mug of steaming coffee.

"I thought I'd enjoy the sunrise."

She nodded. "Beautiful, isn't it?"

"It sure is."

"I don't enjoy this view near enough. That's what happens, isn't it? You begin to take the beautiful things for granted until you hardly even see them anymore."

"I'm afraid so, Mom. I wonder why that is?"

"A lack of gratitude, I suppose."

She settled herself on the couch then and sipped pensively at her coffee. After a moment she said, "Well, now that the house is quiet, we can talk."

Both of my sisters and their families had left the previous day, moving on to celebrate the New Year with their respective in-laws. I would be staying with my parents a couple more days before heading back to Delaware.

When Mom said she wanted to talk, I sat down in the recliner across from her.

"Is Dad up yet?" I asked.

"He's never out of bed before nine anymore if he can help it."

"Nice to be retired."

"Hmm." She nodded. "So what about you, dear? What's bothering you?"

"Why do you think anything's bothering me?"

"I'm your mother. I know."

"Uh-huh." I smiled at her. "Well, Mom, there are a couple of things, I guess."

"Like what?"

I stole a moment by taking a long sip of the coffee. "It's the strangest thing, really. Do you remember the English teacher I had senior year, Mr. Dutton?"

"Mr. Dutton?" She looked toward the window, then back at me. "Vaguely."

"The one who had a heart attack."

"Oh yes. I remember that now."

"Well, it wasn't a heart attack."

"It wasn't? What was it, then?"

For the first time I told her the whole story, from the night of April 1, 1977, right up to my visit with the Duttons at their home only days before. When I finished, the sun was considerably higher, the coffee in my mug had grown cold, and Mom's face had passed from rosy to fiery to ashen.

A few silent moments went by before she said, "Why did you never tell me any of this?"

"Well, like I said, Mom, I wanted to, but we had made a promise to Ray and Ken—"

"But you were just children, Beth. You never should have kept all this to yourself."

I shrugged. "What's done is done."

"So all these years you thought he was dead, that he'd killed himself?"

I nodded.

"And now you've found him again, and he's alive."

"Strange, isn't it?"

"Oh, Beth." She leaned forward toward me. "I don't know what to say. I'm sorry. I'm sorry for how this must have affected you. I only wish I'd known."

"You couldn't know, Mom. That's the thing—it was all so quickly swept under the rug."

"But I knew Commander. I knew what kind of person he was. I can't believe he lied about what happened."

"He did what he thought was right at the time. And anyway, it wasn't just Commander. There were others involved. It was just . . . unfortunate. The whole thing was just unfortunate."

"I'm so sorry, sweetheart," Mom said again. "What are you going to do now?"

"Nothing. I mean, what can I do?"

"Will you be able to put it behind you now that you know the man's alive?"

I had to think about that. "Not exactly."

"What do you mean?"

"Bel, his wife, is very busy with the store right now, and she asked me to find a student who might be willing to read to Mr. Dutton on Saturdays. His sight is so bad because of the diabetes that it's hard for him to read anymore. Anyway, I volunteered Satchel, and she's willing to do it."

"Satchel? That little girl who called you here?"

"Yeah."

Satchel had indeed called me at my parents' home on Christmas Day. I'd given her the number right before she left for White Plains. When she called, she said she just wanted to wish me a merry Christmas, but the constant sniffling on the other end of the line told me she was crying. She tried to pass it off as simply a cold, but when I pressed her, she admitted to the tears. "They don't even know I'm here," she'd wailed. She didn't want to be with her mother and Roger; she just wanted to get back to school. I sympathized with her and told her to find some good books to read. It would help to pass the time. I promised her dinner at Pine Glen as soon as we got back. I promised to have plenty of dried mango on hand that we could eat before or after or during dinner, or all three. That seemed to cheer her up.

"She must be very fond of you, this Satchel," Mom said.

I nodded. "We have kind of a special relationship. She spends a lot of time with me at Pine Glen."

"She no doubt sees you as a substitute mother, judging from what she told you about her own mother when she called."

"I think she does. And that's all right. I like it. I like having her around."

"I'm glad, then. But what else are you worried about? Is it something to do with Satchel?"

"No, not really. I worry about her, but—"

"It's Ray then, isn't it?"

"You can read me like a book, Mom."

"I just know you, honey." She smiled gently.

I sighed. "His former wife, Brenda, is in Delaware visiting the kids for Christmas."

"She is? I thought she was completely out of the picture."

"So did I. Apparently she decided it was time to

reconnect. She called Ray and told him she'd be staying at a hotel in Newport and asked if he could arrange for her to see the children."

"That's a pretty bold move on her part. Did Ray agree to it?"

"He talked to the kids, and they said they were willing to meet with her." I shrugged, trying to sound nonchalant.

"And what does Ray think about all this?"

"Well, that's the thing. I don't know. I'm just not sure he ever really got over her. He says he did, but I don't know. . . ."

My voice trailed off. Mom nodded. "So you're worried about the two of them seeing each other again."

"I guess I am. I probably shouldn't be. You know how I've always had to worry about everything."

"Yes." She smiled and nodded. "Of the three, you were always my best worrier. And I understand how you feel, Beth. I really do. But I think you should put it in God's hands and leave it there. He'll know what to do."

"You've always said that, Mom."

"Um-hmm. And I've always believed it too."

"You don't think Ray and Brenda might consider getting back together?"

She shook her head. "I imagine there's very little chance of that."

I wished I had her faith.

"Sounds like your dad is up and puttering around the kitchen," Mom said. "How about some breakfast?

Everything looks better when you have a little food on your stomach."

"Sounds good. Maybe we can talk Dad into making his famous chocolate chip pancakes."

"I don't think it'll be too hard to persuade him." She smiled, and we walked together toward the kitchen.

CHAPTER 43

Pine Glen was tucked beneath a three-inch blanket of snow that first Saturday night of the New Year. The usually draughty house was warmed by crackling flames in the fireplace. I wondered briefly why I hadn't bothered to build a fire earlier in the winter, but then, I hadn't built this one either. Ray had hauled some logs from his place, and Josh had opened the flue and arranged the wood and newspaper over the grate. A couple of matches later the kids were roasting marshmallows to make s'mores for our evening dessert.

We had eaten large portions of spaghetti and garlic bread and salad with Italian dressing, the meal I'd promised Satchel we would have as soon as we got home. I hadn't intended to invite Ray and his family—in fact, I didn't invite them at all. Satchel had done it, calling Lisa as soon as she dropped her suitcase in her dorm room and sped down the hall to the pay phone. Ray later called me to verify the invitation, and I, knowing nothing about it, said of course Satchel and I were planning for them to come.

So there we were, looking very much like a contented family gathered around the hearth on a snowy night. And all the while my heart was constricting with a fearful curiosity as to what had happened with Ray's former wife, Brenda.

"Who wants a s'more? You want it, Miss Gunnar?"

"Sure, Josh. Thanks." I didn't much care for s'mores but didn't want to turn it down since Josh had, as he said, "painstakingly roasted the marshmallow to perfection." I took small bites of the gooey graham cracker sandwich. Warm chocolate always tasted bitter to me, like something spoiled. Josh made another for his father, who sat in the wing chair, unusually quiet.

The evening slid by on small talk among the kids, talk about Christmas gifts and New Year's resolutions and the classes Josh would be taking when he returned to Penn State. Satchel hung enthusiastically on every word Josh spoke, and I wondered whether he noticed the longing on her face or the giddiness in her laughter. She was not the same girl who, two months earlier, told me not to play with fire by falling in love.

I glanced at Ray, sensing he was not really there in the room with us, that while he was in the chair only feet from me, his mind was somewhere else.

Ben sat on the floor at Ray's feet, wrapped in the afghan that normally covered the back of the couch. He took large bites of his third s'more, then licked his sticky fingers and dried them on his shirt.

"My mommy showed us how to make these. Aren't they good?" Ben looked at me when he spoke, so I assumed it was from me that he expected an answer.

"They're delicious, Ben," I offered, feigning enthusiasm.

So there she was, right among us. And when Brenda showed up, Ray returned, moving his eyes around the room and settling them on his young son. I couldn't read his face. It was blank and smooth as a communion wafer.

"So, Ben," I ventured, "how was your visit with your mom?"

The child shrugged. "Good, I guess."

"I thought it was weird," Lisa interjected. "I mean, she leaves us and we don't see her for years, and all of a sudden she wants to do Christmas together like nothing ever happened? I don't think so."

"Yeah, well, it probably soothed her conscience or something, coming to see us and giving us a bunch of gifts. Like it would make up for lost time." Josh stretched out on the floor, crossed one foot over the other, and slipped his hands beneath his head.

"She was looking for closure, kids," Ray said quietly. Finally saying something. Finally joining us.

Josh laughed. "Sure, Dad. First of all, that word is only so much psychobabble. And second, I highly doubt that she's really interested in us. She's only interested in you. Or, I should say, your money. After years of trying to make it on her own, she realizes what she had wasn't so bad."

"That's not fair, Josh, and you know it."

"I agree with Josh, Dad," Lisa said. "She's tired of having to make it on her own. She figures she had a pretty good deal before, so why not try again?"

Ray glanced at me, then away. "Let's drop it, kids."

"At least I'm out of here in a few more days," Josh said. "Just in time not to have to deal with her when she comes back."

"Lucky you," Lisa said.

"She's coming back?" It was Satchel who asked what I was afraid to ask.

Josh nodded. "She's moving back to Wilmington. Says she's got some sort of receptionist job with DuPont. She's already signed a lease on an apartment somewhere."

I felt myself stiffen, muscles pulling taut against the news. I looked at Ray. He stared at the fire.

Satchel, meanwhile, was watching me. I knew she was; I could feel her gaze. And I knew what she was thinking. It was the same thing I was thinking. I glanced at her, tried to smile, glanced away.

In spite of the heat of the snapping fire, I felt chilled to the bone.

CHAPTER 44

"Ted, your company's here." Bel laid a gentle hand on her husband's shoulder. At her touch he drew in a breath, lifted his head from the back of the chair, and blinked several times. Then he smiled.

"I must have drifted off," he explained unnecessarily. He elbowed his way out of a slump and straightened the buttons of his cardigan. "This chair is worse than a sleeping pill, Bel. We ought to just get rid of it. Well, Beth, so good of you to come and to bring, um . . ."

"Satchel," I reminded him. "Satchel Queen. A lover of literature and one of my best students."

Satchel smiled shyly, pleased at my introduction. She took Theodore Dutton's outstretched hand and squeezed it self-consciously before pulling away.

We were in the back room of Bel's Book Nook, a spacious but windowless room with a concrete floor painted gray and a variety of built-in bookshelves that weren't painted at all. Up against one wall was a small kitchen area: sink, counter, cabinets, refrigerator, microwave, coffeepot, and hot plate, as well as a small Formica-topped table and chairs. Mr. Dutton's over-stuffed chair sat a few feet from the kitchen in the center of an area rug the color of red clay. All in all, the place put me in mind of Mole's underground dwelling in *The Wind in the Willows*, that "lowly little house with its spirit of divine discontent and longing."

Bel dragged a couple of the chairs away from the table and waved us into them. "I don't mean to be impolite," she said, "but with Selma out sick today, I've got to stay out front. We really need to hire one more person." She paused a moment and laughed lightly. "As soon as our ship comes in."

"I'm sure that'll be any day now, dear," Mr. Dutton said.

I had a feeling I'd just been privy to a standing joke between them.

"Selma's been a godsend," Bel went on. "Selma

Rainbo. She's been with us from the get-go, and I couldn't manage without her. You'll meet her next time you're here, Satchel."

"Her last name's Rainbow, like a rainbow?" Satchel drew an arch in the air with one index finger.

"No *w* on the end," Bel explained.

"No lie? Selma Rainbo? That's cool." Satchel nodded.

Bel smiled. Turning to me, she said, "There are some cold drinks in the fridge. Just help yourselves. And holler if you need anything. I'm not far away."

Bel left and Satchel wandered to the refrigerator where she pulled out a can of Coke. "You want anything, Miss Gunnar?" she asked.

"No thanks, Satchel. What about you, Mr. Dutton? Would you like something to drink?"

Dutton frowned a moment. "Is there any coffee in the pot?"

Satchel looked at the coffeepot. "Yup, a little."

"Still hot?"

She felt the pot with the back of her hand. "Yup. You want some?"

"Half a cup, please. Just black. There are some mugs in the cabinet right above the pot."

Satchel returned with the Coke and the mug of coffee, which Mr. Dutton accepted gratefully.

"I can use a shot of caffeine right about now," he said.

Satchel sat and squirmed a moment, searching for a comfortable spot in the rigid, upright chair. Finally, she pulled the tab on the can of Coke. After a long sip she said, "You don't have any dried mango, do you, Mr. Dutton?"

I couldn't help laughing at the look of bewilderment on Mr. Dutton's face. To Satchel, I said, "I don't think he has any mango, but you can have some later at my place."

"Dried mango?" Dutton asked. "Am I missing something?"

"It's Satchel's favorite food. She'd practically live on it if she could."

"Well, then, Satchel, next time you come, I'll be sure to have some on hand."

"Hey, thanks. That'd be cool."

With the pleasantries completed, Satchel looked expectantly at the ailing man cushioned in the cradle of the overstuffed chair. He returned her gaze, his eyes oversized marbles behind the thick lenses of his glasses. Now I remembered how blue his eyes were.

"Tell me, Satchel," he asked, "who are your favorite authors?"

Satchel shrugged nonchalantly, though her voice held an air of confidence. "I have a lot of favorites. Thornton Wilder, Charles Dickens, Willa Cather. People like that."

"Really?" Mr. Dutton was wide awake now, and I guessed it had more to do with delight than caffeine.

"Sure. And that Irish guy—what's-his-name. The one that wrote *Angela's Ashes*. I really liked that book."

Theodore Dutton smiled broadly. "You can tell a lot about a person from the books they read. Did you know that?"

Satchel shrugged again. "I guess so." She lifted the aluminum can to her lips, tilted her head back slightly, and took another drink. One corner of her mouth was visible to me, and it was curled up in a tiny amused smile.

"I understand you're willing to spend some time reading to me."

Satchel nodded.

"My eyes—" He waved a hand toward his face. "The diabetes has done a number on them."

"Yeah. Miss Gunnar told me."

"It saddens me. For one thing, I'm not much use around the store anymore. And for another thing, I'm hardly able to read to myself. I have to have a lot of light and use a rather large magnifying glass, and it all gets rather cumbersome. But I don't want to stop reading."

Satchel looked around the room. The many shelves were brimming with used books. More books grew up like stalagmite from the floor, forming stacks that seemed precariously high. One false move and I could well imagine the domino effect of volumes tumbling all over one another from one end of the room to the other. This was obviously where Bel and Selma sorted the inventory before placing the books out in the store to be sold. And here Theodore Dutton sat comfortably in the midst of them in an overstuffed chair next to a table that was itself covered with books.

"If you stopped reading, you might as well be dead, huh?" Satchel asked.

Mr. Dutton laughed loudly. "I think we're going to get along very well, Satchel. We understand each other already."

Satchel smiled, then momentarily hid again behind the Coke. I could tell she was starting to enjoy herself.

"Do you like Thackeray?" Mr. Dutton asked.

"Don't think I've read him."

He exchanged his coffee mug for a thick volume from the pile beside his chair. "*Vanity Fair*?"

"Nope." Satchel shook her head. "I've heard of it, but I never read it."

"Delightful story," Dutton exclaimed. "Bel's been reading it to me for some time now, and we've almost reached the final chapters. Of course, having read it several times already, I know how it ends. So you and I, Satchel, can either pick up where Bel left off, or we can start with something new. Whatever you like."

Satchel's shoulders went up again. "It doesn't matter to me what we read. You're the one who has to listen."

"Well, then, why don't we go on with *Vanity Fair*. Next time you come, that is. For now, let's just talk some more, get better acquainted. Do you have any questions for me?" Dutton put the book aside and laced his fingers together over his waist.

Satchel thought a moment. She looked around the room again, then back at Dutton. "Just one," she said.

Dutton smiled placidly, a smile that invited her to ask what was on her mind.

She pointed toward the ceiling. "What's that?"

Not sure Dutton could see as far as the ceiling, I scrambled to help out. "It looks like the entrance to an attic. You know, Satchel, you pull on that rope, and the stairs come down."

"Ah yes." Mr. Dutton nodded. "That's just the attic. We use it for storage."

Satchel shot another glance at the attic door. "Don't tell me. The place is full of books."

Another booming laugh. "Delightful girl," Mr. Dutton exclaimed, looking at me. Then to Satchel, "Guilty as charged, I'm afraid. I've spent my life collecting books, and now I'm drowning in them."

"Yeah." Satchel nodded knowingly. "It's the only way to go."

Mr. Dutton screwed up his eyes and nodded enthusiastically. "Yes, you and I are going to get along just fine, Satchel. I knew Beth wouldn't disappoint me when we asked her to pick out her best student for us."

My student and my former teacher exchanged a smile then, obviously pleased with each other. I sat on the periphery watching—and hoping I hadn't made a mistake.

CHAPTER 45

"Penny for your thoughts."

Joel Sexton's voice pulled me out of the bewildering maze my mind was wandering and brought me back to our office in Heath Hall. I looked over at Joel and tried to offer him a smile.

"I'm not sure they're worth that much."

"I don't know, Beth. You spend an awful lot of time gazing out the window. You must be pondering something big."

I shook my head. "No. I just like to watch the snow fall."

"But it's not even snowing."

I glanced at the window again. He was right. The afternoon sun shone unimpeded across an open sky. The temperature had risen enough to melt the snow and ice that had covered the fire escape the day before.

"Listen, Beth," Joel said gently, "if something's bothering you, I'd like to help."

I closed the grammar book I'd been pretending to read and pushed some papers aside on my desk. "Thanks, Joel. I appreciate it. Really. But I'm fine."

He gave me a look that told me he didn't believe me. "You're not happy here at Seaton, are you?"

"No," I protested. "I mean, I am. I'm happy here. It's just—"

I stopped and looked at Joel. He raised his eyebrows to flag me on.

"Well, okay. I'm not sure I should have accepted this job. I'm not sure I'm right for it."

"Not right for it? Are you kidding? You're a fabulous teacher, Beth."

"Well—"

"You're great with the kids. You really know your stuff, and on top of that, you make it interesting for a bunch of teenagers who basically couldn't care less about reading or writing."

"Well, thank you, but I'm not so sure about all that."

"Just look at Satchel. You've taken her under your wing, and she's thriving. She really seems happy."

I nodded. "Yeah, you're right about that. But I'm afraid I can't take all the credit for her happiness. Satchel happens to be infatuated with a certain young man, for one thing, and—"

"Really? Someone here at school?"

"No, he's a student at Penn State."

"Ah, an older man, is it?"

I laughed lightly. "They're not exactly dating, but—I think she wishes they were. So you've got the endorphin effect going on there, and you know a little of that goes a long way. And then she's really enjoying her work with Theodore Dutton."

Joel cocked his head. "Name sounds familiar, but I can't place him."

"He was an English teacher here when I was in upper school."

"Really? I never had him for English."

"He wasn't here very long. He had to leave suddenly near the end of my senior year."

"Oh? What happened?"

I looked at Joel, then out the window. "Heart attack," I said.

"Bummer. And he never came back?"

"No. But he and his wife own a secondhand bookstore over on Lancaster Pike now. Bel's Book Nook. Ever heard of it?"

"Don't think so."

"Satchel's working there part-time. She's been there about three weeks now. She was supposed to spend a couple hours on Saturdays reading to Mr. Dutton, but Bel needed help in the store, and Satchel just kind of ended up filling in."

"And she likes it?"

"Loves it. And, you know, one of the best things about it is the Duttons trust her. She's allowed to help customers find what they're looking for, and then she rings up the sales at the cash register. They've even given her a key to the store. She's the first one there every Saturday morning, running the vacuum cleaner before they open up the shop."

"How's she get there? Her folks give her a car?"

"No. She catches the bus right at the south entrance to school. Tuesdays and Thursdays too. She catches one of the afternoon buses and goes in to work for a few hours. She had to get special permission from school to leave campus on weekdays, but Farrell gave it to her, thankfully. I think for the first time, she really feels . . . I don't know . . . grown-up, important. Needed. And wanted too. They like her and they want her there, and she knows that."

"That's great, Beth. And she gets paid for this, right?"

I nodded. "A little bit of cash and a whole lot of dried mango."

"Dried mango?"

"Her favorite food."

"Oh. Okay." Joel shrugged. "Well, anyway, it sounds like a good deal for Satchel. You arrange this job for her?"

"Sort of. The Duttons were looking for someone, and I recommended Satchel."

"And to think at the beginning of the year I had Satchel pegged as a troublemaker."

"So did I."

"She might have been if you hadn't taken an interest in her."

I thought a moment. "Maybe."

"Maybe, nothing. It's true. So you see, you're needed around here."

"I hope so."

Joel scratched the back of his head, then looked at his watch. "Ho, boy, time for my favorite class. Freshman English."

"Do I detect a note of sarcasm in that?"

"Is the Pope Catholic?"

"Do you teach the freshmen what a cliché is?"

Laughing, Joel pushed his chair back from the desk

and stood. He gathered up the books and papers he would need for the class and headed for the door. "So listen, Beth," he said, turning back a moment, "are you sure that's all that's bothering you? Just insecurities about the job?"

"Yeah." I shrugged. "I guess that's it."

"You got nothing to worry about," Joel offered. "In my opinion, you're right where you should be, doing exactly what you should be doing. And next year I'm going to give you the opportunity to teach the freshmen classes. That should provide ample opportunity for challenge and reward."

"Thanks, Joel. I appreciate that."

CHAPTER 46

Throughout the long gray month of January, Ray and I saw each other from time to time. We met for coffee after he got off work. He stopped by Pine Glen briefly once or twice. We talked on the phone. But just as on that first Saturday night after Christmas break, he wasn't really there, and our conversations were stilted and awkward. Every time we were together, he grew more and more translucent, until at length I could scarcely see him anymore. Finally he no longer met my gaze or held my hand or kissed my cheek goodnight.

Satchel said that when you love someone, you have something to lose. She was right about that.

I didn't want to love Ray Schmidt. I really didn't.

But like Satchel also said, we don't have any choice when it comes to whom we love. It's something that happens to us, like getting a door prize or getting a jury summons or getting cancer. Good or bad, there it is, and we can't help it.

While I had denied to my friends and my family—and even to myself—that there was anything other than friendship between Ray and me, my heart knew otherwise. I have to wonder how the mind and the heart can live out two different stories at one time. Yet they can and do.

I allowed myself to realize what I felt for Ray only as I watched him growing distant. It may have been his backing off that opened the channel between my heart and mind so that the message could get through, and I could comprehend what I was feeling. I knew I loved him because there was so much pain involved in watching him fade away like some sort of apparition vanishing at dawn.

On the first of February, a Sunday afternoon, the phone rang at Pine Glen. "We need to talk," Ray said, and I thought, *No, I really don't think we do. The not talking was enough.*

But he came over anyway and sat in the chair that Satchel always sat in when she was there, and he looked as though he hadn't slept since sometime before Christmas, which may have been very close to the truth.

"I don't know how to begin," he said.

I wished he wouldn't begin at all, because I didn't

want to hear it. "It's all right, Ray," I told him. "I know what you want to say."

"But I want to explain."

I nodded. "All right."

He looked stricken. My heart pounded. "Brenda and I have been . . . talking. She's—I don't know how to describe it, but . . . she's changed. She really has. I know that sounds trite, but it's true."

His eyes pleaded with me to believe him. He waited for me to respond. I said nothing.

"I care about you, Beth," he went on. "I thought maybe you and I . . . that maybe this time we could—"

He stopped. He seemed not to know how to go on.

And so I finished for him. "But Brenda's coming back changes everything," I said.

"I guess so."

"Do you still love her?"

The question appeared to startle him. "No. I don't know. She was my wife."

"She deserted you. And your children."

"Yes." His knuckles turned white and taut as he squeezed his hands together. "I hated her for a long time. But I hated her, you see, because I loved her. Does that make sense?"

I felt myself turning to stone. "Yes, I understand."

"She wants me to forgive her."

"Can you?"

"I don't know. But I believe I ought to try. I want to try."

Silence. Then I asked, "And she wants to reconcile?"

He shook his head firmly. “We haven’t talked of that.”

But they will, I thought. *They’ll talk of it.*

“I need some time,” Ray said.

I nodded, a small stiff nod.

“I don’t want to lose your friendship, Beth. And I’m not saying . . .”

Not saying what? Oddly, he got that far and then didn’t say anything more. He just looked at me with such a pained expression that I very nearly felt sorry for him.

“I just need some time,” he repeated.

I told him I understood. What else was there to say? She was, after all, his wife. She had claimed him long ago, made a marriage with him, had children. If they should be reconciled, who was I to interfere? Doesn’t a wife have first rights, even a former one, and even if it meant that, once again, your own dream was coming true for someone else?

At the door he took my hand and said quietly, “I’m sorry, Beth.”

The air outside was cold and full of snow. When Ray was gone, I shut the door. I would not cry this time. I was too old and tired for all that. Young women cried and railed and cursed, calling life unfair. I wouldn’t do that anymore; the years had taught me better.

I went back to the living room—empty now except for my friends. My faithful, ever present, unchanging friends. Rows upon rows of them, all in a line, welcoming me.

We're the one thing that will never leave you, they said.

I lifted my hand to touch them. Jane Austen. Charles Dickens. Thomas Wolfe. Dostoyevsky. Tolstoy. Solzhenitsyn. Oh, and the poets! T. S. Eliot. Butler. Yeats. Keats. Emily Dickinson.

We're all here. Everything you know of truth and beauty and even of love lies in us.

I pulled them from the shelves, one book and then another and another until my arms were full. I thought of the words, the passages, the verses I had known all my life. Still here, unchanged, more alive to me than any living soul. I took them to the couch where I sat and opened one. I began to read. I didn't know and didn't care which book it was; all I wanted was the words. Like a lush, I drank them in, drinking until I drifted into that place of forgetful sleep.

CHAPTER 47

My Dream Job
by Satchel Queen

Before I write about my dream job, I have to tell you a true story. It was a conversation with Mr. Theodore Dutton that got me thinking about what I'd like to do with my life, if I could.

For several Saturdays now I've been reading to Mr. Ted from the book Vanity Fair *by William Makepeace Thackeray. Finally last weekend we finished the book. Well, the book ends with these words: "Ah!* Vanita Vanitatum!*" (That's Latin for vanity of vanities.) "Which of us is happy in this world? Which of us has his desire? Or having it, is satisfied?"*

When I read that, Mr. Ted and I just kind of sat there without saying much. I guess we were both thinking about those words.

Finally I said, "Do you think he's saying that no one's happy in this world?"

Mr. Ted shook his head. "That seems to be what he's saying, doesn't it?"

"Do you think it's true?"

Mr. Ted took such a long time to answer I thought maybe he didn't hear me. But finally he said, "What do you think, Satchel? Are you happy?"

I had to think about that before I could answer. Then I said, "Sometimes I am. What about you, Mr. Ted? Are you happy?"

Mr. Ted smiled a little. But it was kind of a sad smile. "Sometimes," he said.

"I wish everyone could be happy all the time," I said.

"I think that's what we all wish, Satchel."

"Do you think it will ever be like that?"

"No, I'm afraid not. Not in this world anyway."

That's when I decided if I could do anything I wanted to do, I'd build a machine that would suck all the sadness out of people and replace it with happiness. It would work the same way a dialysis machine works. See, one of my mother's boyfriends, before she married Roger, was a man named Evan, and Evan had a problem with his kidneys and he had to go to dialysis three times a week. I asked him once what happened when he went for his treatment and he said the nurses hooked him up to a machine that took the blood out of him, washed all the poisons out of it, and then put the clean blood back into his veins. It was the machine that kept him healthy and alive.

When you consider the word "sanguine" you realize there is something important about our blood. The dictionary gives three definitions for sanguine:

1. of the color of blood; ruddy; said esp. of complexions

2. in medieval physiology, having the warm, passionate, cheerful temperament and the healthy, ruddy complexion of one in whom the blood is the predominant humor of the four

3. cheerful and confident; optimistic; hopeful.

It makes a person wonder whether happiness is flowing through our veins just like red blood cells and platelets. And maybe somehow sadness gets in there like a sickness and starts to crowd out all the hope. So I'd like to build a machine that can separate the happy blood from the sad poisons and siphon off the bad part while putting the good part back into the human body.

Only with my machine, unlike with dialysis,

you'd only have to have your blood washed one time. Only once, and then you're set for life. I'd also let everyone have it done for free so even people without health insurance can get the sadness taken out of them. Imagine what the world would be like if everyone everywhere were happy and satisfied.

P.S. Miss Gunnar, you said to use our imaginations and write about anything, even if it's something we don't think we'll really end up doing. So that's what I did. I'd like to make everyone happy, the way I feel when I'm with you or Mr. Ted or when I get a letter from Josh. That's my dream job. I hope I didn't botch this assignment. Sincerely, your friend, Satchel Queen.

CHAPTER 48

There truly must be some correlation between blood and emotions, because as I sat in the back room of the bookstore reading Satchel's essay aloud to Theodore Dutton, I suddenly understood the expression, "It made my blood boil." I was angry with Dutton, though I was trying hard not to show it.

When I finished reading, Dutton said happily, "That child does have quite an imagination, doesn't she? Whoever would have thought of something like that—a machine to wash our blood of sorrow. Leave it to Satchel." He shook his head while offering me an amused smile.

"She *is* just a child, Mr. Dutton," I said with strained politeness. "I certainly don't think you should tell her that no one is ever happy in this world."

He looked at me a long moment through those disarmingly thick glasses, the lenses like two magnifying glasses enlarging his eyes. Then he said, "First of all, I really do think you should call me Ted. Our relationship isn't one of teacher and pupil anymore, now is it? We can simply be friends, I hope."

I wasn't interested in being his friend. My allegiance lay with Satchel; I had an almost maternal desire to protect her. "I know we can't shield children from all the hard things in life," I went on, "and I also know that the present generation is especially worldly wise as well as cynical, but I still think one of our duties as adults is to at least offer them some sort of hope."

"Oh, I couldn't agree with you more, Beth, I—"

"To prepare them for the world is one thing, but to purposely discourage them is something else altogether. I mean, when you were a teacher . . ." I couldn't go on. I didn't want to think about what he had done to his students when he was a teacher.

He leaned forward in his chair. He seemed to be studying my face.

"When I was a teacher, what, Beth?"

Silence. Then, "Nothing. Nothing, really. It's just that I recommended Satchel for this position thinking it would be good for her."

"And she seems very content to be here."

"But you're only feeding into her cynicism when you tell her no one is happy. She trusts you, and she's going to soak up everything you say and do like . . . like . . ."

My breath caught in my throat, leaving me speechless. We sat there without moving, an old-fashioned tableau, a scene depicting—what? Two bewildered people unable to bridge the gap with words?

"Beth," Dutton said quietly, "what is it that's really bothering you?"

I couldn't say. I could only choke out one whispered sentence: "Please don't hurt her."

Dutton leaned back in the chair, obviously dumbfounded. "I have no intention of hurting Satchel. I don't understand what you're getting at. She comes and reads to me, she works around the store, she sits and eats her dried mango quite happily. We laugh together. I believe she enjoys being here."

"Her father committed suicide."

The words jumped from my mouth, seemingly of themselves, hitting Dutton hard like a punch between the eyes. He looked startled, and the color drained from his face. "When?" he asked. "You mean, it's just happened?"

"No. When Satchel was eight or so."

"I'm sorry to hear that. I didn't know." He put a hand to the side of his head, as though he was in sudden pain. He rubbed circles into a small spot above his right temple while his eyes roamed the room. "But that has been some time now, hasn't it? She seems to have adjusted well. What does that have to do with today or with this essay?" He looked up at my face then. "Or with me?"

I folded Satchel's essay and tucked it into my purse, then rose to go. "All I ask is that you let her have what's left of her childhood."

"Of course, Beth. Listen, I think you misunderstand. Satchel didn't write about our whole conversation in that essay. She didn't write the half of it. Why don't you sit back down and let me explain?"

"Well, I—"

"Uncle Ted, do you happen to know where—oh, excuse me. I didn't know anyone was with you."

Turning toward the voice, I saw a man who looked eerily like the Theodore Dutton I'd known in high school, except a little older. He wore jeans and a flannel shirt over his tall and lanky frame, and his dark hair was disheveled, as if he'd tumbled out of bed only moments ago. He had a rugged look about him, but his eyes were intelligent and his smile engaging.

"Len, come on back. I'd like you to meet Beth Gunnar. She's Satchel's teacher, the one Satchel talks about. Beth, this is my nephew, Len. He's just back from Europe. He's been on sabbatical from Quentin College in upstate New York, and he decided to come here and spend some time with Bel and me before he returns to teaching. Wonderful, isn't it?"

The man stepped toward me, hand extended. "Very nice to meet you, Beth."

Lennon Dutton. The long-haired boy with the guitar. But that was long ago, and in the intervening years he seemed to have left all that behind and grown into the image of his uncle. I started to tell him we had already met, years ago in Cabin 1, but I suspected he wouldn't remember. "Nice to meet you too," I replied, accepting his outstretched hand.

"So you're the Miss Gunnar that Satchel goes on about," he said, pumping my arm enthusiastically.

"Does she?"

"Oh my, yes," Theodore Dutton laughed. "Miss Gunnar this and Miss Gunnar that. She adores you, you know."

"Does she?" I asked again.

Mr. Dutton waved a hand, and his nephew seemed not to hear my question. Len said, "So you teach where Uncle Ted used to teach, right? Over at Seaton?"

"Yes. Yes, English. Over at Seaton." I was flustered, seeing Lennon Dutton unexpectedly after so many years, flustered by the family resemblance. I reclaimed my hand and pushed my sweaty palm into a pocket of my slacks. "And you're teaching at a college?"

He nodded. "I'm taking a break from all that, though. I've been doing some research in Europe, like Uncle Ted said, and now I'm going to spend some time here helping out around the store. Actually, I've been wanting to do this for a long time—just come down here and work among the books. Academia can be a bit stuffy, even at a small private school like Quentin, and . . . well, this comes as a welcome break."

"Do you teach English?"

A shake of the head. "History," he said. "Medieval

history is my primary interest. That's what I've been doing in Europe, studying the church in the Middle Ages and the effect the Protestant Revolution had on—well, never mind. I won't go into all that."

"Oh no, really. I'd like to hear about it sometime. It sounds very—"

"Well, what's going on back here? Having a party and you didn't invite me?" Bel entered the room, laughing. "Beth, I trust Ted introduced you to our nephew, Len."

"Of course. Len was just telling her about his time in Europe," Mr. Dutton replied.

"Wonderful, isn't it? London, Brussels, Frankfurt—imagine! Then last Saturday he took a flight from Frankfurt to Philadelphia, and here he is. He called us from the airport and said he'd come to help."

Len smiled sheepishly. "I'll be more help around here once I'm past the jet lag."

"The price one pays for traveling the world." Mr. Dutton laughed and looked up at us from his chair.

"Beth, can you stay and have lunch with us?" Bel asked. "I've just stocked up the fridge, now that Len's here."

"You didn't have to do that for me, Aunt Bel."

"Oh yes I did. Look at you, skin and bones. Did you forget to eat while you were in Europe? Well, never mind. You won't be going hungry as long as you're staying with us. I can't do much cooking here at the store with only a microwave, but there's plenty of fresh fruit and frozen dinners, and I'll be bringing in leftovers from home. Speaking of which, I've got last night's chili for lunch today. Can you join us, Beth?"

"Thanks, Bel, but I've got a one o'clock class. I'm afraid I've got to go."

"That's too bad. Well, come back another time, and we'll all have lunch together."

"All right. Yes, that would be fine."

"By the way, Satchel's coming in tomorrow, isn't she?"

"Let's see, tomorrow's Tuesday. As far as I know, she's planning to be here."

"Do you suppose she could stay until closing? Usually Selma's here, but her husband is having hernia surgery, and she's asked for a couple days off."

"I think that should be fine. I'll talk with the principal about getting her permission to stay late. You close at nine, right?"

"Yes, nine o'clock."

"All right. I'll come pick Satchel up so she doesn't have to take the bus back to campus."

By the time I said good-bye to the three of them, I had almost forgotten why I'd come. But as I reached into my purse for my car key, I felt Satchel's essay tucked in there beside my wallet. Then I remembered.

I looked at Theodore Dutton and found that he was already looking at me, his face a picture of entreaty. He seemed to have suddenly realized, as I did, that something had been left unsaid, that we had been interrupted before we had reached an understanding. But it was too late now. Bel had laced her arm through mine and was walking me toward the door, away from her husband and whatever it was he had wanted to say to me.

CHAPTER 49

The next evening I drove back to Bel's Book Nook to pick up Satchel. The night was clear and unusually mild for February, and the black bowl of space overhead was brimming with stars. When I pulled into the small lot in front of the store, I could see Lennon Dutton through the plate-glass window, going over some receipts at the register.

The bell tinkled quaintly when I opened the door, and I was greeted with the musty odor of aging books. Len looked up at me and smiled. "Hello, Beth. How are you tonight?"

"Fine, thanks. And you? A little more rested?"

Still smiling, he shrugged and gathered the receipts into a pile on the counter. "I suspect I'll be on Europe time for a few more days. But that's all right. I'll adjust."

"Where's Satchel? In the back room?"

He shook his head. "No, she's taken Uncle Ted out for a walk."

"They're out walking? It's cold out there."

"It's not so bad. Besides, they're all bundled up. I insisted they go because Uncle Ted needs the exercise. He and Aunt Bel intend to fatten me up, and I intend to slim Ted down. It gives us something to work toward while I'm here." He laughed an amused little laugh, then picked up an armload of books and stepped out from behind the counter. "They're just going down the street a short ways. They should be back any minute, and then you might as well take Satchel home. It's been a quiet evening; it won't take us long to close up."

I looked around the store. It was empty of customers. "Is Bel here?" I asked.

He nodded toward the back room. "She's puttering around back there. We got a lot of books in today on exchange, so she wanted to start going through them." He dropped the load he was carrying onto a cart, which he then pushed slowly down one of the aisles while his eyes scanned the shelves. "Go on back if you'd like. I know she's got a pot of decaf brewing."

"All right," I said. But I didn't go. I randomly pulled a book from the shelf and pretended to look at it. After a moment I said, "Len, you know we met before, don't you? Years ago."

He stopped pushing the cart and turned back to look at me. "Did we?" he asked.

"I don't expect you to remember. It was when your uncle was teaching at Seaton. Sometimes you'd visit him, and there'd be a group of students there in his cabin. . . ."

My voice trailed off. He seemed to be trying to remember, and I wanted to give him a minute to think. I reshelved the book and waited.

"Hmm . . ." he said finally, shaking his head.

"You used to bring your guitar and play with a boy

named Ken. I was there and my friend Natalie and our friend Ray."

"Yeah?" He frowned. "I haven't picked up a guitar in years. I used to really enjoy it, though."

He didn't remember. That was all right. "It was a long time ago."

"Well, now that you mention it, I do remember that cabin on campus where Uncle Ted lived. I guess I visited him there a few times. That was back when he was batching it, before he met Bel, right?"

I nodded. "He wasn't married yet. They usually stuck bachelors in those cabins back then, and your uncle was one of the few unmarried teachers at school that year."

"Yeah? I guess I'm not surprised. We Dutton men aren't known for marrying young." He pushed the cart a foot or two, stopped again, shelved a book where he decided it belonged. "So how long was Uncle Ted at Seaton?"

"Not long. He had to leave before the year was over."

"Oh yeah. That's when he had the heart attack, wasn't it?"

I almost believed that story myself now. A widespread lie eventually takes on the sheen of truth. "Yes," I said. "In April of our senior year."

His eyebrows rose in surprise. "You have a good memory. I had almost forgotten Uncle Ted was at Seaton when he had the heart attack."

"Well, we were all very fond of Ted." The last word sounded strange as it dropped from my tongue. I had so far avoided calling him Ted, as it was too familiar; I simply couldn't think of him that way. "He was a favorite teacher for many of us. It came as a shock when he had to leave."

Len nodded. "He's been a remarkable teacher all his life. Well, just a great person, really. He's the one who encouraged me to study history when my own dad said I'd never make a decent living with a degree like that. Dad wanted me to follow in his footsteps and become a dentist." Len laughed loudly. "The last thing I wanted was to spend my days poking around in people's mouths. Nope, fighting tooth decay just didn't do it for me, you know? So I'm glad I listened to Uncle Ted when he told me to pursue my interests. My dad and Uncle Ted are brothers, but they're as different as night and day. Kind of funny how that happens, isn't it?"

Before I could respond, the bell over the door tinkled, and Satchel and Dutton slipped in on a gust of laughter.

"It's cold out there!" Dutton cried merrily. "Len, you're going to be the death of me."

"Don't listen to him, Len," Satchel said. "It's just fab out there! Oh, hi, Miss Gunnar. Hey, you know what? You could see about a billion stars in the sky. Mr. Ted showed me Orion's Belt. You know, those three stars lined up in a row. I never saw it before. It's so cool!"

"There you two are," Bel said as she approached from the back room. "Did you manage to stay warm?"

She started unwrapping the scarf from around her husband's neck as Dutton said, "We survived, dear.

But if the temperature drops any lower than it is right now, Satchel and I will have to become mall walkers."

"All right!" Satchel exclaimed, her eyes widening. "I'll do the mall with you anytime you want, Mr. Ted."

"A little cold isn't going to hurt you, Uncle," Len said. "It gets the circulation going."

"Says you." Mr. Dutton smiled playfully. "Meanwhile you stay indoors where it's warm."

"Len's right, dear," Bel insisted. "You haven't been getting the exercise you need. Remember what the doctor told you last time we saw him?"

Mr. Dutton ignored her. "So, Beth, you've come to take Satchel away from us, have you?"

"I'm afraid so. We both have early classes in the morning."

"Well, then, we reluctantly surrender her to you, though we always hate to see her go."

"I'll be back Thursday, Mr. Ted. Don't worry about that. Maybe we can get another walk in."

"And maybe Mother Nature will be kind enough to send a blizzard so we can all stay indoors."

"Now Ted, quit complaining and come warm up with a nice cup of hot coffee." Bel linked arms with her husband and started to lead him off but turned back long enough to say good-night to me and Satchel.

"Ready to go?" I asked Satchel.

"Just a minute. I'll be right back." She rushed off toward the back of the store.

Len smiled after her. "Uncle Ted is really enjoying her company."

I had to agree. "He seems to be good for her too."

"Yes. Well, I guess they're good for each other. Maybe she can inspire him to take better care of himself. I worry about him, with the diabetes and all. That's really why I'm here. I decided I'd come when I heard he was in a coma."

"But they have that under control now, don't they?"

"If you mean that Bel is watching his diet and making sure he takes his insulin, yes. But when your health is as frail as his, you never know."

"Hmm." I nodded. "Let's hope he lives to be old."

Len smiled. "I suppose he's got enough stubbornness in him to keep him alive a good long while yet."

Satchel reappeared chewing on a piece of mango. She carried several more pieces in a plastic bag. "Okay," she said, "I guess this'll last me till we get back to campus. I'm ready to go."

CHAPTER 50

"Happy Valentine's Day."

"Thanks, Natalie. Same to you."

I had hoped, when I picked up the phone, that it might be Ray. When I heard Natalie's voice, I was disappointed but not surprised.

"So what's up?" she asked.

"Not much, other than the usual Saturday morning chores. I just finished washing and waxing the kitchen floor."

"Why?"

"Why what?"

"Why were you washing and waxing the kitchen floor?"

"Um, because it was dirty?"

"You know I've always said that a clean house is the sign of a life misspent."

"So I should be doing something else?"

"Yes. Anything else but that."

"You're a liberated woman, Nat."

"I just know how to use my time wisely, and washing and waxing are not on my to-do list."

"Okay, well, so what are you and Ron doing for Valentine's Day?"

"We've decided we're actually going to treat ourselves to dinner out tonight."

"Nice."

"But we're taking the kids too."

"Better yet."

"That's what you think."

"Listen, consider yourself lucky. I'd love to be going on a family outing."

Silence. Then Natalie said, "I guess that's why I called, Beth. I hate to think of you alone on Valentine's Day."

"No big deal," I said. "I'm staying busy."

"There's got to be something better to do than clean the house."

I laughed a little for her sake. "Nat, you're a good friend, but you don't need to worry about me."

"Listen, why don't you come to dinner with us tonight?"

"What?"

"I mean it. Come with us."

"Oh sure. Ron would love that."

"He'd be fine with it. Like I said, we've already got the kids tagging along."

"Thanks, but no. Anyway, there's a Valentine's dance here on campus tonight, and I've volunteered to help chaperone."

Another silence. Then tentatively, "Have you talked to Ray recently?"

"He called a few nights ago."

"What did he have to say?"

"Not much after he said hello."

I heard her sigh through the telephone line. "I'm sorry, Beth. I was really hoping—"

"Never mind, Nat. It's all right. Oh hey, you'll never believe who I ran into at the bookstore this week."

"Yeah? Who?"

"Lennon Dutton. Remember him?"

After a long pause Natalie said, "No. Should I?"

"He's Mr. Dutton's nephew. We'd see him sometimes when he stayed with Dutton in the cabin."

"Yeah?"

"You know, kind of a shy kid with long hair."

"We knew about a thousand shy kids with long hair when we were in high school, Beth."

"Yeah, I guess we did. Well, anyway, he ended up a history professor at some school in New York. He's on sabbatical, and he's helping out at the store."

"Oh? I wish I could remember him, but it doesn't ring a bell."

"Never mind, then. It's not important."

"So how's our friend Ted doing these days?"

"You could find out for yourself if you'd ever come to the bookstore with me."

"No, thanks."

"I can't believe you don't want to see Theodore Dutton."

"You should believe it by now, since I've already turned you down a dozen times."

"But why don't you want to see him?"

"Because I don't believe in dredging up the past. There's only one way I'm going to look, and that's forward."

"Well, you're probably right, Nat."

"I know I'm right. Besides, I liked Dutton better when he was dead. I didn't have to think about him. If I saw him now, I'd probably strangle him for what he did."

I laughed out loud. "I know how you feel. I really do."

"You mean you feel like you want to strangle him sometimes?"

"Yeah, I do."

"So why are you bothering with him? Why don't you just distance yourself from the guy?"

"For one thing, he's good with Satchel. Both he and Bel have been good to her."

"And? Anything else?"

I thought a moment. "I guess that's kind of like asking the question, why does someone climb a mountain?"

"And now I'm supposed to say, 'Because it's there,' right?"

"That's right."

"Well, the Atlantic Ocean's there too, but you won't find me swimming across it. Face it, Beth, you're still hankering to find out why Dutton attempted suicide, as if he's ever going to tell you."

"I can't just bury the past the way you do."

"It's called minding my own business, moving on with my own life, which I did a long time ago, thank heavens. You know what happens to most people who climb mountains just because they're there?"

"What?"

"They fall off. The body may or may not ever be recovered."

"Okay, so maybe the mountain thing was a bad analogy."

"I don't know, Beth. I'm just saying, you do what you want, but I have no desire to see Theodore Dutton. I don't trust him, and why you ever allowed your student to get involved with him is beyond me."

I was stunned. "Really, Nat? You really think I've done the wrong thing?"

She sighed deeply. "I don't know. I hope not. You say she's happy working for him, so maybe it's all right.

Does she know what happened our senior year, what Dutton did?"

"No, I never told her."

"That's just as well, I imagine. Let her think he's some nice old man who's half blind and needs to be read to."

"But that's exactly what he is, Natalie."

"Yeah, right. According to what you told me yourself, he had no qualms about handing out the beer and getting smashed with Ray and Ken when they showed up at his cabin. And let's not forget that bit of insanity the night the boys found him on the bathroom floor."

"That was a long time ago. People change."

"Are you sure Dutton's changed?"

"Yes," I answered tentatively. Then I added, "He's hardly the hard-drinking bachelor he was when we knew him. I mean, no . . . no, he's not like that at all. If you saw him, you'd see what I mean. He's just a harmless old guy now who can't really do all that much for himself, and—" I stopped then and took a deep breath. "Okay, Natalie, it's true I've had my doubts. I've thought maybe I should never have introduced Satchel to Dutton. But it's too late now. You might say they've bonded."

"Well, listen, Beth," Natalie said, "my personal dislike for the guy doesn't really count for much. For all we know, he's been resurrected a better person and only good can come of Satchel knowing him. Let's hope so. But anyway, I didn't call you to talk about

Dutton. I just wanted to wish you a happy Valentine's Day."

"Thanks, Nat. I appreciate that."

"Sure you won't join us for dinner?"

"I'm sure. But thanks."

That night I went to Hawthorne Gymnasium to help chaperone the Valentine's Day dance. Satchel wasn't there. She had called from the bookstore and asked me to see if the principal would allow her to stay at work until closing. Because she was holding down a responsible job, Mr. Farrell had no problem granting her permission. I had hoped she would come to the dance, where I could see her. But these days she was spending far more time with the Duttons than she was with me.

CHAPTER 51

A month later the Duttons invited Satchel to stay with them during spring break, but her parents insisted she spend the week with them in White Plains. I flew to North Carolina to visit my folks and to watch the warmer season ease in over the mountains. When I got there, spring was already arriving in hints, with shades of green slowly uncoiling over the dark landscape and tentative blossoms breaking up through the brown earth around the yard where my mother had planted tulips and crocuses.

In my suitcase I'd smuggled a half dozen companions for the trip—books I'd been wanting to read for months but hadn't yet found time for. I knew I wouldn't read them all in the span of seven days, but I wanted them with me anyway. Three novels, two biographies, and one slim volume of poetry, the latter an aging hardcover collection of nineteenth century verse written by American women. Theodore Dutton gave it to me just before I left town.

"When somebody brought this in on exchange, I put it aside for you," he said. "I remember how you used to enjoy poetry whenever we read it in class."

I accepted the gift gratefully. "I can't believe you remembered, Mr. Dutton."

He laughed. "In all my years of teaching, only a handful of students have really appreciated poetry the way you did. It's a little hard to forget something like that."

I stacked the books on the table beside the guest bed. Every morning I took the volume of poetry to the living room and read it by the picture window while sipping a cup of coffee. The verses brought a sense of quiet to that first hour of dawn, setting the tone for the day. It was a restful week, refreshing in the solitude it offered and in the chance it gave me to separate myself from Seaton and teaching and the Duttons and, most of all, from Ray.

On my final morning in Asheville I sought out, as usual, the recliner in the living room but was surprised to find my father already in it. He wore a plaid bathrobe over a pair of pajama pants and a T-shirt. His feet, in fur-lined slippers, were propped up on the recliner's footrest. His hair was disheveled from sleep, and his face was dotted with whiskers, and he was reading through a pair of dark-framed glasses that badly needed cleaning.

"What are you doing up so early, Dad?" I asked, settling on the couch across from him.

He shrugged. "I couldn't sleep, so I decided to go ahead and get up."

"Anything wrong?"

"No, not really. I just get a bit of insomnia now and again. I don't like lying around in bed when that happens, so whenever I can't sleep, I get up and get busy."

I glanced at the open book on Dad's lap. "Reading through the Bible again?"

He nodded. "Genesis straight through to Revelation. No matter how many times I go through it, I'm always amazed at what I learn with each new reading. It seems to be completely inexhaustible."

"I suppose it must be," I agreed. I had read the Bible through myself, years before. Now I couldn't remember the last time I had opened one. "So where are you now?"

"The book of Hosea." He tapped the Bible with an index finger. "This one has always baffled and comforted me at the same time."

"How so?"

"You remember the story of Hosea and Gomer, don't you?"

"Yeah, I think so," I lied.

"You know, she was a prostitute. Here's Hosea, a prophet, a man of God, and what does God tell him to do? Marry a prostitute!" Dad shook his head and gazed briefly out the picture window. The corners of his mouth turned back in a smile of bemusement.

"That does seem strange," I said. "You'd think God would want him to marry someone a little more . . . well, pure, I guess."

"You'd think so, wouldn't you? I always kind of felt sorry for Hosea. Here's this poor guy just trying to be obedient, and for that he's saddled with a cheating wife. She didn't suddenly decide to become monogamous when she married him, you know. She went on carrying out her profession as if Hosea wasn't even there. So when the children came along, Hosea didn't know whether half of them were his or somebody else's. He just kept taking old Gomer back, though. Sometimes he even went out looking for her and brought her home."

I drank from my mug of coffee, then wrapped both hands around it again for the warmth. "It all seems out of character for God, doesn't it?"

"Well, yes and no," Dad said. "You have to consider the fact that God is always trying to say something."

"What do you mean?"

"It's all symbolic, of course, this marriage between Hosea and Gomer."

"Is it?"

"Well, yes. It's the picture of God and His people. God is Hosea, and the rest of us, well, we're Gomer, I'm afraid. We leave, we drift away, we turn our attention to other things. We *love* other things to the point of more or less ignoring God. But in spite of all that, God always takes us back. Comes after us, even. That's what's comforting."

I inhaled deeply. Dear Dad. I was beginning to see what he was getting at. We hadn't mentioned it all week, and he wanted to talk about it before I went home again. I smiled gently and said, "You're trying to talk to me about Ray and Brenda, aren't you?"

He looked at me with eyebrows raised. "Am I?"

"Well, sure. You know, Brenda left him and went out to play the field, or whatever it was she did, and now she's shown up again, and he's forgiving her and he's willing to take her back. So it's like Hosea and Gomer, right? Thanks, Dad, but don't worry. I already know Ray's doing the right thing. I don't like it, but I accept it."

Dad closed the Bible and laid it aside. He looked genuinely perplexed. After a moment, though, his face opened up, and he said, "I really hadn't thought of that before, but Ray and Brenda would be kind of a modern day Hosea and Gomer, wouldn't they? At least in the fact that she strayed and he took her back. But that didn't occur to me until you mentioned it just now."

"Really?"

"Really." He shrugged. "So no, I wasn't trying to talk to you about Ray. I see you as capable of handling that yourself. I will say, though, that I think you've handled the situation with grace, and I'm proud of you."

"I don't know about that, Dad, but thanks. I know Mom is disappointed. Again."

"Don't worry about your mother. She'll get over it."

"Poor Mom. I bet she's got a hope chest stashed away for me somewhere, and she's still adding to it."

Dad laughed loudly. Then he said, "All she really wants is for you to be happy. You can't fault a mother for that."

He pushed the handle on the side of the recliner that dropped the footrest. "I think I'll get some more coffee," he said, picking up the empty mug. "By the way, what book have you got there? A book of Psalms?"

I held it up so he could see the cover. "No. Poetry. Mr. Dutton gave it to me. I often read poetry in the morning because it—I don't know—centers me or something."

"Centers you? What does that mean?"

"You know, makes me feel peaceful, helps me transcend the world and all its problems for a little while."

I smiled at Dad and thought he might smile in return, but he didn't. Something like concern flashed across his face, but before I could ask him what was wrong, he said, "The Psalms are beautiful poetry too."

I blinked and shook my head. "I know, Dad. Sure, the Psalms are beautiful."

"Well, then—" he looked at the mug in his hand—"can I get you some more coffee?"

"No, thanks. I'm fine."

He leaned over and kissed my forehead. "I love you, Beth."

"Love you too, Dad."

Then he smiled and went to the kitchen to replenish his drink.

CHAPTER 52

I sat at my desk in my classroom in Heath Hall, watching the students trickle in after morning assembly. It was our first day back from spring break as well as the start of a new semester, the final stretch of the school year. My first class of the morning was a one-semester course called Drama as Literature. Eight students had signed up for the class. When the ritual claiming of the desks was completed and a quiet had settled over the room, seven students sat facing me.

"Where's Satchel?" I asked. "Has anyone seen her?"

A girl who lived in the dorm raised her hand. "Tess told me at breakfast this morning that she didn't come back."

For a moment I couldn't respond. I held the girl's gaze as though daring her to defend herself. Then very quietly I asked, "Are you sure?"

"Well, yeah," she retorted. "That's what Tess told me, and she should know. She has to room with her."

"Did Tess say why Satchel didn't come back?"

The girl shrugged complacently. "No. She said she didn't even hear anything from her. Satchel just didn't show up yesterday when the rest of us came back."

"All right." I glanced out the window at the metallic March sky, trying to process what this student had just told me. "She might have gotten sick or something and just couldn't get back yesterday. But maybe she'll show up today. Let's hope so anyway."

As I scanned the vacant faces before me, I knew I was talking to myself. It didn't matter to them where Satchel was or whether she was coming back. It mattered only to me.

I pushed my chair back from the desk and walked to the blackboard. I had to will my feet not to go any farther, not to go out the door and down the stairs to the office to see what the secretary could tell me about Satchel. I had a class to teach.

I wrote the name Thornton Wilder on the board. "How many of you were in the fall production of *Our Town*?"

The hour dragged by on leaden feet. I found myself repeatedly glancing at the clock. More than once I had to ask a student to repeat a question or comment because my mind was somewhere else. My mind was with Satchel. Wherever that was.

When at last the clock's minute hand moved far enough to release us, the students jumped up from their chairs and fled the room. I was close behind. Descending the musty staircase, I almost tripped over the long adolescent legs of boys and girls reclining on the steps between classes. "The staircase isn't a lounge, you know," I huffed. But I didn't stop to shoo them elsewhere; I was too intent on reaching the administrative offices on the first floor.

Delia Simpkins was just hanging up the phone when I reached her desk. "Do you have any word on Satchel Queen?" I asked her.

She pointed at the phone. "I was just talking to her father."

"Stepfather," I corrected.

"Whatever. They're withdrawing her from school."

"What? Why?"

"They need her at home."

"They can't do that."

Delia Simpkins looked at me askance. "Yes, they can. Any parent has the right to—"

"But why? What did he say? What does he mean, they need her at home?"

The secretary picked up a pencil and starting turning it over on the desk the way Mildred Bidney used to do just before she read the barn duty list in morning assembly. "Apparently," she said, "the mother is pregnant and not feeling well. They want Satchel at home to help her around the house."

"But they can't do that."

This time she didn't bother to respond. She simply looked at me while the pencil turned point to eraser and back again.

Finally I said, "So they can pull her out of school this late into the school year?"

"Sure. They're enrolling her today in the public school there."

"But they can't do that," I said one more time.

The pencil stopped. Delia Simpkins looked up at me with something like confusion and something like concern. "Listen, Beth. I don't know what planet you woke up on this morning, but around here it works this way: She's their kid. Her parents can do whatever they want, and like it or not, we can't do anything about it."

CHAPTER 53

Night after night as I worked at the dining room table, I'd lift my head toward the window, expecting any minute to see Satchel strolling down the hill from the dorm. She'd be coming to talk about what we were discussing in class or to chat about life in general. Or maybe she wouldn't want to talk at all, but rather sit quietly in her usual spot by the fireplace, an open book in her hands.

Then I'd remember. Satchel was gone, yanked out of school to fulfill a role her parents required of her. They had made their plans believing that the school was a faceless institution. They didn't know that I was here, yearning to talk with the child. I hadn't even had the chance to say good-bye.

I thought of the Duttons and how they had shared my distress over Satchel when I stopped by Bel's Book Nook to tell them the news.

"How can they do this?" Bel had exclaimed, slapping the counter with an open hand. "That isn't what's best for Satchel. Don't they know—"

"Are you sure, Beth?" Mr. Dutton interrupted. He sat behind the counter on a stool, looking up at me with muddled eyes. "Are you sure she won't be coming back?"

"I'm sure. The secrctary has already started the paper work—"

"They're keeping her home," Bel said, "to play

nursemaid to her pregnant mother?"

"Apparently the mother has always been somewhat dependent on Satchel, and—"

"Then why did they send her to Seaton in the first place?"

"I'm not sure, exactly, except that Satchel's mother and stepfather were only recently married and—"

"Yes, yes. We know all that. Satchel told us all about them. And frankly, I'm not impressed."

"Can we call them?" Mr. Dutton asked. "Do you suppose we could try to reason with them, see if they won't allow her to at least finish out the school year?"

The three of us fell silent, studying each other, hoping one or the other of us would come up with an answer. Mr. Dutton's pale skin turned crimson as he waited. Bel dabbed with a tissue at eyes that threatened to spill over.

At length I said, "No, we can't call them. It's no use."

"But—"

"I asked the same question of our principal. He said no. It's the parents' right to take a child out of school, and there's nothing we can do about it."

Lennon Dutton entered the shop while I was speaking. He met us at the counter and, after looking pensively at each of our faces, asked, "What's wrong?"

"Satchel's gone," Bel said.

"What do you mean?"

I explained, and as the four of us talked about Satchel, the air became heavy with a palpable sadness. Len said in the end, "I think the three of you were really her family. More of a family to her than her own parents anyway."

He was right. Satchel Queen was a child of my heart.

After a dozen days and nights of gazing out the dining room window, watching for her to appear on the crest of the hill, I pulled the drapes.

CHAPTER 54

Dear Miss Gunnar,

I've been thinking about calling you, but I decided I better not. If I did, the call would show up on the phone bill, and Mom would have one huge hissy fit about me spending too much money, and Roger would give me the lecture about having to work to learn the value of a dollar. As if he's not Mr. Moneybags and they didn't spend last fall tramping all over Europe at hundreds of dollars a day. I thought about calling you collect but—no offense—I know you don't make a whole lot of money doing what you do, so I didn't feel right reversing the charges. So I finally decided I'd write to you because Mom and Roger don't have to know, and I can afford a stamp on my own.

I just want to say I really miss you, Miss Gunnar, and I miss the Duttons, and I even miss Seaton. When Mom and Roger told me they were pulling me out, I couldn't believe it. First they sent me to boarding school when I didn't want to go, and then when I was finally happy there, they pulled me out.

That night when they told me, we had a huge fight about it, with Mom and Roger and me all screaming, and I just kept telling them I hated them because I thought maybe then they'd want to get rid of me again and send me back to Seaton. But no such luck.

They're keeping me home because Mom's got morning sickness real bad. The doctor says maybe she's having twins. Mom says that's okay as long as it's twin boys. And I keep thinking, yeah, because you were never happy with the girl you had. Only Dad was happy about that.

So anyway, they have this housekeeper that comes in every day but only part-time. She takes care of everything while Mom lies around in bed watching TV or shopping online on her laptop. I think she's using this morning sickness business as an excuse to lie around all day. When I get home from school, the housekeeper leaves and I take over. I guess I'm needed, but I'm not wanted, and I sure would rather be wanted. Roger doesn't do anything to help around the house. I think he figures he brings home the bacon and that's enough. I think he's happy about the baby (or the babies) because he doesn't have any other kids, but who knows for sure. It's not like we're all touchy feely around here and having heart-to-heart talks all the time. If Roger tells me he liked the tuna casserole I made for dinner, that's a red-letter day. Yeah, I'm the cook around here, if you can believe it.

I've been at the public school for a little more

than a week now, and I hate it. It's pretty much made up of Goths, drug addicts, and a whole bunch of other slime bags, and that includes the teachers. My English teacher must have been hired off the street just because nobody else would take the job. He doesn't know one thing about poetry or literature. Remember that poem by Christina Rossetti you and I talked about once called "The Dirge"? Well, I mentioned that in this guy's class the other day, and he thought I was talking about some song written by The Grateful Dead. Sheesh. I mean, how am I going to learn anything from him? He's just not like you at all, Miss Gunnar.

Have you seen Mr. Ted and Miss Bel and Mr. Len? I guess they know by now what happened. Please tell them that it wasn't my choice, though. I really liked working for them. Tell them when I get out of high school, I'll come back and work for them again. I'll be eighteen then, and I can do what I want. It's really not that far away, is it, even though it seems like a million years. When I think about all of you, I start to cry. I've been crying a lot these days.

Another rotten thing is that Josh and I aren't really talking anymore. I guess I'm not too surprised. I kind of expected it. But still, it hurts. He's dating someone at Penn State now. Did you know that? Maybe not, because I know you don't talk to Dr. Schmidt that much anymore, so there wouldn't be any way for you to get the news. I think about all of us when we were toasting marshmallows at your house, remember? And it all just seems like a really good dream, and then you wake up into real life and suddenly everything stinks. I wonder why real life can never be as good as dreams.

I know you've told me about a million times you think Dr. Schmidt is doing the right thing, and I guess I have to accept the fact that that's how a grown-up might look at it. But for myself, I still think he ought to be with you instead of trying to make it up with someone who dumped him. But you know, really, I'm finding out that more and more of life just doesn't make sense.

I guess that's it for now. I'll write again and I hope you'll write me. I know I'll see you again someday because, like I said, eighteen isn't all that far away. I'm not going to stay in this house one minute past high school graduation.

Sincerely, your friend forever,
Satchel Queen

CHAPTER 55

I wrote to Satchel at the return address on the envelope, but I don't believe my letter ever reached her. The day after I dropped the letter in the mailbox, Jack Farrell called me into his office.

"Have a seat, Beth," he said. The somber look on his face told me he was about to tell me something I didn't want to hear.

He waved me into one of the wing chairs situated by the window; he sat across from me in the other. He fidgeted a moment and ran an index finger across his lips before he began to speak.

"Harlan Quinn got a call from the White Plains police this morning," he said. "He routed the call to me."

The place that was my heart immediately became a well of fear. Why would the White Plains police be calling our headmaster? "It's Satchel, isn't it?" I asked. "Is she all right?"

Jack sighed heavily as he leaned forward in the chair. "She's run away, Beth."

"What?"

"Her parents reported her missing yesterday morning. Her mother's car was missing too. Apparently Satchel found the key and just drove off."

"Have the police put out a bulletin on the car?"

"Yes, and it was found last night—"

"And Satchel?"

Jack Farrell opened his hands and turned his palms toward me. "The car had been abandoned by the side of the interstate in Jersey, just south of Newark. It was out of gas."

"So Satchel probably took off from there on foot?"

"Presumably so. She may not have had the cash to fill up the tank."

"Does anyone have any idea where she might be headed?"

"Yes. That's why the police called Harlan. Her parents feel certain she's headed here. She was driving south on 95, and that's a straight shot into Wilmington."

"But the car ran out of gas."

"Yes."

"And now she's out there by herself. How can she walk all the way—"

"She'll most likely try to hitch a ride, don't you think?"

"But that's the worst thing she can do."

Jack leaned back again in the chair and frowned. "Beth, we have to hope she shows up here. And when she does, the minute she does, you'll have to let me know."

"You think she'll come to me?"

"I think that's exactly what she'll do. When she does, don't let her out of your sight. Call me, anytime, day or night. You have my cell number, right?"

"Yes."

"Good." He looked at me intently a moment, his dark eyes questioning. "You will call me, won't you, Beth?"

"Of course."

"We've got to do everything we can to get that child home to her family."

"Of course," I said again. Reluctantly.

"Well." He stood, signaling the end of our conversation.

Following suit, I got up from the chair. "Thank you for letting me know, Jack."

He nodded. "It's a sad situation, but let's hope it gets resolved quickly and easily."

"Yes, I hope so."

He walked me to the door of his office. More gently now he said, "Try not to worry too much, Beth."

I nodded. But it was advice I couldn't take. "Do you know what happens to young girls when they run away from home?"

Jack Farrell laid an unfamiliar but comforting hand on my shoulder. "For now, we're going to assume that Satchel is heading straight for you."

I ascended the stairs to my classroom, only half aware of my surroundings. My mind wanted to be with Satchel, to will her to keep coming, to help her reach me before anything might happen to her. But as I entered my classroom I was greeted by the questioning glances and barely concealed disappointment of a dozen sophomores. Had I been gone five minutes more, they could have, by school rules, left the room and considered Sophomore English canceled for the day. But, too late. Here I was. I told them to open their textbooks to chapter 10.

Satchel would have to find her way to me on her own.

CHAPTER 56

"I hope you don't mind my just stopping by."

"No. Of course not, Ray. Come on in. The house is a mess, but—" I shrugged and stepped aside to let Ray enter the front hall. "Actually, I was just making myself some chamomile tea. I thought it might help me sleep. Come on back to the kitchen."

"I won't stay long. I know it's getting late."

He followed me to the kitchen where a glance at the clock told me it was almost nine thirty. I'd planned to spend some time reading and drinking tea and was, in fact, just heading upstairs to put on my pajamas when the doorbell rang.

When the tea was done steeping I poured two cups. As I poured, I watched the teapot shiver from the tremble in my hand. Though we'd spoken on the phone, I hadn't seen Ray for many weeks.

"So are you just getting off work?" I asked as I set the teacup before him on the kitchen table.

"No." He pulled the cup toward him but didn't drink. "I was putting Ben to bed when I decided I had to come and see you. I'm sorry. I should have called ahead."

"It's all right. You're always welcome to stop by." I laughed a little, but it sounded unconvincing.

"I was worried about you, Beth, because I heard about Satchel."

"You heard she was pulled from school?"

"Yes, and that she has since run away." He sipped the tea, then looked at me sheepishly. "Natalie called to tell me. She said she thought I might like to know. She was right."

I nodded. I'd called Natalie early that evening to tell her about Satchel. She must have called Ray as soon as we hung up. I stirred my tea with a spoon to cool it down. The spoon made small rippling circles in the tea as it clinked against the sides of the porcelain cup. "Thank you for being concerned, Ray."

For a moment neither of us said anything. I almost wished that the radio was playing or that the phone would ring—anything to fill the void.

Finally Ray said, "Have you gotten any word from the police?"

"Nothing since the call to Harlan this morning."

"And how long has she been gone?"

"Two days." I looked up at the clock again. I could actually hear it ticking. "They think she's making her way back to Delaware. Without the car, of course."

"So I understand."

"They're guessing that she wants to make her way back to me."

"That's probably a good guess."

"I'm not so sure. She might try to contact the Duttons instead."

"Let's hope she contacts someone."

"Yes," I agreed. "But if and when she does, we'll just have to turn her in. I hate to think of sending her back to her mother and stepfather."

"Are they abusive? Is there something social services should know?"

I shook my head. "No, it's not what you'd call an abusive situation. There's just . . . I don't know. A lack of love. I guess that's the best way to describe it."

"But she's safe there?"

"Oh yes. I think so. Just not happy."

"Then you have to notify the police if she shows up here. What else can you do?"

"I know." I finally stopped stirring the tea. But I didn't trust my hands to carry the cup the brief distance to my lips. "There isn't anything else I can do."

While my eyes were on my hands, I heard Ray sigh. "Are you doing all right, Beth?"

I didn't want to cry. I took a deep breath. "I'm worried. I wonder where Satchel is, where she's sleeping, whether she's cold . . ."

Ray nodded as I spoke. "I know. I'm worried too."

"You don't suppose," I said, looking up at Ray, "she'd try to go to Josh instead?"

Ray considered that for a moment, his face tightening into a frown. "No, I don't think so. There's really nothing between Josh and Satchel. Josh says they've always been just friends."

"I suppose you're right," I said. "She'd have no reason to go there. I just hope she shows up *somewhere*. I don't care who finds her, as long as somebody finds her."

"I know, Beth. I hope so too."

He finished his tea, and I offered him more but he declined. Again, the room was heavy with silence, a silence weighted with words that neither of us seemed able to speak. I expected any second to hear him say he had to go, but the clock ticked on, and he remained.

"So how are you doing, Ray?" I asked reluctantly.

"I'm doing well." He rubbed an index finger along the rim of the saucer. He didn't look at me.

"And the kids?"

"Doing great. Yeah, doing great."

I thought I might attempt to lift the teacup to my lips but decided against it. Not now. Certainly not right now. Fortifying myself with a deep breath, I asked, "And Brenda?"

His eyes came up, met mine, went back down. He seemed to have to think about his answer for a while. "We're, um, we're seeing each other. You know, getting reacquainted."

I watched his finger caressing the saucer. "That's good, Ray."

"Yeah." It was more of a sigh than a word.

"So maybe it'll work out again?"

"Maybe."

I swallowed, moistened my lips. I startled even myself by saying, "I think you still love her, Ray."

He looked up at me then and held my gaze. How, I wondered, could anyone look so infinitely sad and so marvelously happy at one and the same time?

"I don't think I ever really stopped loving her, Beth."

All the air escaped my lungs in one long sigh. "You can forgive her, then?"

"Yes. Yes, I think I can."

"That's good, Ray, really—"

"I'm just sorry, Beth—I never meant to hurt you—"

I cut him off. "Stop, Ray. Don't apologize. I'm happy for you. I really am."

The sadness that I had seen clinging to him for months seemed to slip away then. A small and tentative smile settled on his face. "Did anyone ever tell you that you are one rare lady?"

I nodded slowly, as though in thought. "I think you did once, many years ago."

"Well, if I did, I was right."

"Thanks."

He smiled fully then and nodded. He pushed his chair back from the table and rose to go. At the door he said, "I almost forgot to tell you. When I put Ben to bed tonight, he prayed for Satchel, that she'd be safe."

"Tell Ben I thank him for that. And tell him to keep it up."

"I will. And we will. We'll both keep praying for her."

When I shut the door behind Ray, I went to the dining room and pulled open the drapes. I watched the taillights of Ray's car disappear out of campus. When all I could see was my own reflection in the dark window, I realized with shame that I had myself not prayed one prayer for Satchel's safe return. I wanted to now. I wanted to put her into the hands of a loving God, but as I tried to gather up my thoughts and fashion them into a prayer, I discovered that the words were rusted and wouldn't break apart into meaningful sentences. How long had it been since I had prayed about anything at all? What had happened to the God I had known, the one who had come to me in those moments of being?

I turned from the window and walked to the living room. My eyes roamed the shelves, seeking out the all-familiar books. I scanned the spines; I read the titles. I lifted a hand to take a volume from the shelf, but then I stopped, letting my hand fall to my side. Because I suddenly knew what I hadn't known before.

Not every altar in this world is made of wood and stone.

CHAPTER 57

That night I dreamed I was in the eighth grade again. Our class had gathered in the assembly hall to practice for our Reader's Theatre performance of "The Highwayman." My part was coming up, those three little words, "with her death." I was ready for it this time. I could say those words and be heard. The highwayman was galloping toward the inn as the class recited in unison: "Then her finger moved in the moonlight, / Her musket shattered the moonlight, / Shattered her breast in the moonlight and warned him—"

Stop. Silence. That was my cue. "With her death." That was all I had to say. It was so simple.

But the words weren't there, because *I* wasn't there. I could not be seen, and neither could I speak.

As I moved about the school from there unseen, I felt on the one hand a great sense of relief. I could float freely, watching. I could simply observe without participating. I didn't have to prove myself. I didn't have to be good enough. No sitting down to sweaty palms at final exams. No running on the hockey field and bungling a goal. No passing through the smoking lounge on my way to my locker and hearing the occasional snicker that followed me. Nothing.

On the other hand I felt an almost sickening sense of isolation. I had no name, no face, no identity. The vacuum in which I moved was enormous, a black hole from which I couldn't escape. I could not step out of the hole and into a place in the world. I was invisible. I existed only to the point of knowing that I didn't exist. I wanted to scream, but I had no voice; I couldn't make a sound. The black hole pulled me farther in, sucking me up and sending me tumbling through lightless space, an endless free fall through an empty universe.

I awoke suddenly in a dark room. It was morning but not yet daybreak. I lay in the bed staring up at the ceiling, feeling my heart knocking up against my rib cage. I listened to myself breathe. I became aware of the soft weight of the linens against my skin. Slowly the terror passed. The bed felt warm and comforting. The room was there with everything in its place—the chest of drawers, the rocking chair, my desk. The familiarity cradled me.

This was my home. Outside the window was the campus of Seaton School. This place rested on the soil of a state called Delaware. The First State. The first state of a new nation, one nation under God.

I smiled, remembering the question from my childhood. *Could anything at all come out of Delaware?*

How did that Bible story go? Philip told Nathanael

they'd found the one the prophets wrote about. It was Jesus of Nazareth, the son of Joseph. And Nathanael said, "Can any good thing come out of Nazareth?" Philip invited him to come and see.

So Nathanael went. And even before he had quite arrived, Jesus saw him coming and called out to him.

Nathanael didn't understand. "How do you know me?" he asked.

Jesus answered like it was commonplace, like everyone could see people who weren't even there. While Nathanael was out of sight, while he was still standing under the fig tree where anyone with human eyes wouldn't have seen him for the distance, Jesus claimed to have seen him anyway. That's what He told Nathanael: "I saw you."

I remembered that now, the words coming to me the way the morning sun tapped at my bedroom windows. As a child, I had known those words, had known that story by heart. In my moments of being I had felt those same benevolent eyes on me, confirming my created presence within His sacred presence, affirming His love for even me. But I had forgotten. Not all at once, but through slow distraction and inattentiveness I lost the ability to know the one real thing beyond appearances. I could not see, because I thought I could not be seen.

Dear God, I thought. *God of the moments, God of the bells, God who sees me and comes to me, could it be that you too know what it is to love and not to be loved in return?*

"Forgive me," I whispered.

Two small and barely audible words, but I knew they had been heard.

The day was waiting; I had classes to teach, students to see, papers to grade. I got up and slipped on my robe, wiggled my feet into my slippers, headed for the stairs. Those words, "I saw you," and those same gentle eyes followed me down.

At the bottom, in the hallway, instead of turning right to go to the kitchen as I usually did, I turned left, inexplicably, into the living room. I took only one step, then stopped short.

There on the couch, wrapped up like a gift in the knitted afghan, lay Satchel, fast asleep.

CHAPTER 58

I kept one eye on the clock as Satchel pounced hungrily on the plate of scrambled eggs and toast I'd placed before her. In another few minutes I'd call the office in Heath Hall and ask Joel to dismiss my eight-thirty class. I wasn't ready yet to call Jack Farrell. I wanted to talk to Satchel first.

After she cleaned the plate, she finished off a glass of orange juice in a couple of swallows. She settled the empty glass on the table and wiped her mouth with a paper napkin.

"You were hungry," I said.

She nodded. Pushing her chair away from the table, she got up and carried the dirty dishes to the sink.

There, she stood with her back to me looking out the kitchen window.

"Where have you been the last couple of days?" I asked.

She turned around slowly, sighing. "Trying to get here."

"They found your mother's car."

"I figured they would. Little hard to miss a car on the side of 95. I ran out of gas."

"I know. What did you do then? Walk?"

"Some. Then I finally hitched a ride."

"That was dangerous, Satchel."

She shrugged. "I made it, didn't I?"

"Thank God, you did."

She looked at me, saying nothing.

"How'd you get into the house?"

"Easy. You really should get locks on your windows."

"You just crawled in through a window?"

"Yeah, that big one in the living room."

The thought unnerved me a little. "All right, I'll get locks." Then I added, "But I'm glad you got in."

She leaned back against the counter and crossed her arms. Two dark crescents hung beneath her eyes like shaded moons, while her eyes themselves looked large and luminous against her colorless skin. Her unkempt hair was loose and stringy on one side, matted from sleep on the other. She wore a dark knitted sweater over a button-down shirt, the tails of which hung out over the belt loops of her tattered jeans. After just a few days the look of the streets had rubbed off on her.

"I don't want to go back," she said firmly.

"I know you don't."

"Let them hire a maid. That's all they want me around for anyway."

"I know, Satchel," I said again.

"I want to stay here."

I glanced at the clock. "Listen," I said, "let me call Mr. Sexton and have him cancel my first class. Then we can go into the living room and talk."

"You're not going to tell him I'm here, are you?"

"No."

She looked at me warily.

"Honest, Satchel. I just want to ask him to cancel the class. Can you hand me the cordless?"

She did, and I made the call without giving Joel a reason for my being late.

In the living room Satchel and I sat down beside each other on the couch. She pulled the afghan around her, holding the front closed like a cloak. She inhaled deeply, as though she were pulling the warmth into her lungs. For several days she had been cold and hungry—that much I knew.

"I'm glad you're all right, Satchel. I was worried sick," I said.

"Really?" She seemed surprised, and pleased.

"Of course. What do you think? That you might be lost out there and I simply wouldn't care?"

She looked at me sheepishly then. "I'm sorry I worried you."

"Oh, Satchel." I sighed heavily. "It was wrong to run away. Everyone was worried—the Duttons, the people here at school, your parents—"

"Mom and Roger don't care about me."

"Of course they do."

An expression of anger crossed her face but only briefly. As soon as it passed, Satchel said quietly, "Can I stay here with you, Miss Gunnar?"

I wanted to say yes, of course she could stay with me. Instead, I shook my head. "No, Satchel. You can't. Your parents have taken you out of Seaton, and it's not up to me to keep you here."

"So you'd make me go back?"

"I don't have any choice. *You* don't have any choice. Where you go—well, it's your parents' call."

"But . . ." She gazed at me a long moment with wide eyes. "Being here with you and the Duttons, this is the only place I've ever really been happy since Dad . . ."

She covered her face with the afghan then and began to weep. I put an arm around her and pulled her close. "I'm sorry, Satchel," I said. "I really am. If it were up to me, I'd let you stay here. I want you here. But it simply isn't up to me."

"But you could talk to them," Satchel wailed, her words muffled by the afghan. "You could talk to Mom and Roger and see if they'd let me finish out the year here. Maybe if you tell them you want me here . . ."

"I don't think it would be much use. They've already made up their minds."

She lifted her head and looked at me accusingly. "You don't want me either, do you?"

"Oh, Satchel. That isn't it at all. I wish you could stay here. I wish you were my own child—"

I stopped. Satchel and I looked at each other.

"Won't you talk to them, Miss Gunnar?" she asked finally.

I sighed heavily once again.

"Bring me the phone," I said.

CHAPTER 59

Satchel punched in the numbers herself, then handed the cordless back to me. As I listened to the ringing on the other end, I was keenly, almost shamefully, aware that I shouldn't be doing this, that I should be calling Jack Farrell instead. After half a dozen rings I began to feel confident that no one would answer. With relief I moved an index finger to the Off button. But too late. In the next moment I heard a click and a woman's weary voice saying, "Hello?"

"Mrs.—" I stopped, unable to remember Satchel's mother's name.

"Leeson," Satchel whispered.

"Leeson?" I repeated.

From the other end of the line: "Yes?"

I cleared my throat and tried again. "Mrs. Leeson, this is Beth Gunnar, Satchel's English teacher at Seaton School."

A long pause. Then another uncertain, "Yes?"

“Well, I’m calling because Satchel’s here, and—”

“Satchel’s there?”

“Yes, she showed up—”

The woman cried out, then said away from the phone, “Roger! Roger, it’s Satchel! She’s showed up.” Then back into the mouthpiece, “Put Satchel on the line, will you? Let me talk to her.”

Satchel, able to hear her mother through the phone, drew back and shook her head.

“Well,” I said, “first I’d like to talk with you about—”

“I said, let me talk to Satchel!”

“She doesn’t want—”

“Please put my daughter on the line.”

Satchel, frowning, took the phone and said, “Mom, I’m here at Miss Gunnar’s house. I want—”

“How could you do what you did, Satchel? How could you just take my car like that and run away?” Like Satchel a moment ago, I had no trouble hearing the woman’s voice as it came through the phone line.

“I told you I wouldn’t stay. I told you—”

“You’re coming home as soon as—”

Satchel narrowed her eyes and angrily tossed the phone down on the couch. I picked it up. Mrs. Leeson was still talking.

“—and Roger can get down there and—”

“Mrs. Leeson. Mrs. Leeson, it’s Beth Gunnar again.”

“What? Where’s Satchel?”

“I called to talk with you about—”

"What is it, Judy?" The voice in the background belonged to a man, presumably Roger. "Who are you talking to?"

"It's Satchel's teacher at Seaton."

"Let me have the phone."

"No, Roger, I'm—"

"Judy, give me the phone."

"But I'm—ow, that hurt my hand—"

"Hello? Who is this?" asked a Brooklyn accent.

"This is Beth Gunnar, Satchel's English teacher," I said again.

"Oh yeah. How are you, Miss Gunnar?"

"Um, I'm fine. I'm calling because—"

"Is Satchel all right?"

"Yes, she's fine. She's here with me, at my home."

"Thank God," he said, sounding genuinely relieved.

"Yes. Yes, well—she asked me to call and talk with you. If it's at all possible, she'd like to finish out the school year here—"

"That's out of the question," Satchel's mother interrupted.

"Judy, hang up the extension. Let me handle this."

"No, Roger, she's my daughter, and I want her here."

"Judy, hang up the phone."

A long pause followed. Then I heard the sound of a phone being hung up.

"So," Mr. Leeson said, "Satchel thinks she wants to stay at Seaton for the year?"

"Yes, she'd at least like to finish out this year. There are only a couple of months left."

"Yeah? The school here in White Plains isn't good enough for her?"

"I don't know about that, Mr. Leeson, I just know—"

"Let me talk to Satchel."

One thing I could say about Satchel's parents—they weren't very good at holding a conversation. I handed the phone to Satchel.

"Yeah?"

"So, kid, you all right?"

"Yeah, I'm all right."

"What's the matter? You don't like it here in White Plains?"

"It isn't that, Roger, it's more like—"

"Your mother—she thinks she needs you right now, you know? You don't want to be around to help her out?"

"No. I mean, yeah, but—"

"But you'd rather be down there."

Satchel nodded. "Yeah."

Another long pause. Satchel looked up at me, her eyes two pools of anxiety.

"Tell you what," her stepfather said. "Put your teacher back on the line, will you?"

Satchel handed me the phone. "Yes, Mr. Leeson?"

"Listen, I've got nothing against the kid finishing out the year there—"

"Roger!" From somewhere in the background.

"Let me finish, Judy." Then back to me: "Tell you what," he said again, "Judy and I, we'll come down there and talk this thing through, all right?"

"Sure. All right."

"Roger, I—"

"Be quiet, Judy." To me: "All right, then. I can't make it down there today because I've got to be in the office. In fact, I should be there right now. But tomorrow I'll take the day off, and we'll come down. You arrange a meeting with the principal and yourself and the two of us, all right?"

"Yes, I'll do that."

"We'll see if we can't talk this thing through."

I smiled up at Satchel. "Great, Mr. Leeson. Yes, that'll be great."

"In the meantime, can Satchel stay with you?"

"Absolutely."

"Don't let her out of your sight."

"No, I won't. I promise."

"All right, then, we'll be there sometime tomorrow afternoon. Judy, she's not doing so good in the morning, but she's better by afternoon. I'll call from the road, let you know how we're doing time wise."

"Good, good. I'll call Mr. Farrell right now and arrange the meeting."

"Thank you, Miss Gunnar. And I'm sorry for any imposition."

"Not at all. Don't worry."

After we disconnected, I stared at the receiver for a minute. Then I said, "I think maybe you've got Roger on your side."

Satchel smiled, but the relief was short-lived. "Now all we have to do is convince Mom to let me stay," she said. "And that's not going to be easy."

CHAPTER 60

Jack Farrell called in a substitute to cover my classes while I stayed home with Satchel. She slept a good deal, and when she was awake, she ate a good deal. In the late afternoon she showered and changed into a pair of loose-fitting jeans and a sweater that I let her pick out of my closet. She had packed a suitcase when she ran away but left it in the trunk of her mother's Infiniti G Coupe when the gas gauge hit empty and the car sputtered to a stop. The only thing she carried on the road with her was a backpack with a few dollars, a hairbrush, a pair of sunglasses, a leather key ring with her keys to the dorm and to Bel's Book Nook, a bag of dried mango, and a paperback copy of George Eliot's *The Mill on the Floss*. Theodore Dutton had given her the book shortly before spring break.

We spent the entire day at Pine Glen. I thought we might call the Duttons to tell them she was here, but she wanted to wait until after the meeting with her parents. She was hoping, after the whole thing was settled, to go to the Duttons and tell them the good news in person.

I hoped that would be the case as well, that somehow Roger would persuade Satchel's mother to let her finish the year. While Satchel appeared calm about the meeting, I felt like a defendant awaiting a verdict. I wanted Satchel to stay, for her sake and for my own. I steeled myself against the thought that she might be carried back to White Plains no later than the next afternoon.

When an early dusk settled in, I realized Satchel needed a more comfortable place to sleep than the couch in the living room. I rummaged through the linen closet in the upstairs hall, then carried a couple of pillows and clean sheets to the second bedroom, a spacious sunny room that might have made a nice guest room or an office if I weren't using it for storage. It had come furnished with a daybed and a chest of drawers, something left over from one of the previous occupants of Pine Glen. Since my move, though, the room was cluttered with odds and ends normally relegated to the basement or garage, neither of which I had. A stationary bike, a couple of unused floor lamps, boxes of kitchen items and knickknacks and memorabilia I intended to sort through but hadn't so far. And books. Mostly books. Some shelved, some in piles on the floor, some still in unopened boxes left over from the move. I had too many books. Clearly, it was time to get rid of some of them, not because I didn't love them, but because I loved them too much.

I would do that soon, I resolved, but first take care of Satchel. I put the clean sheets and a comforter on the bed for her and even fluffed up the pillows. Then I headed to the kitchen, where I roasted a chicken for dinner and made mashed potatoes while Satchel cut up vegetables for a tossed salad. We ate, we watched the news, she read in the wing chair with her feet propped up while I sat on the couch going over my lesson plans for the next day. Once when I looked up, I noticed that the book was in Satchel's lap and her eyes were closed. I smiled and went back to my papers.

A few minutes later I looked up again and said, "Satchel, why don't you go on up to bed? You're falling asleep."

She shook her head but didn't open her eyes. "I'm not asleep."

"Then what are you doing?"

"I'm asking God to let me stay."

"You are?"

She nodded. She opened her eyes and looked at me. "I think He wants me here."

"You do?" I was afraid she was projecting her own desires onto God and would be severely disappointed if her parents took her back to White Plains. "Why do you think that?"

"Well," she said, drawing her legs up into the chair and tucking them beneath her. "Do you remember that story about the bells in the church you told me about?"

"Yes, I remember."

"It's something like that, I guess."

I waited for her to go on, but she appeared deep in thought. "What do you mean?" I prodded.

She came back then from wherever she had been and said, "I hated being in White Plains. I hated every minute of it. I was so mad." She shook her head slowly. "I told God I hated Him for giving me such a lousy life."

"So what happened?"

"I cried a lot. I got mad a lot. I got in trouble in school for fighting with other kids." Her eyes darted toward me as she rushed to add, "Not fistfights. Just yelling, screaming—that kind of thing. I couldn't seem to help it. I just had to yell at somebody."

I nodded. "That's understandable."

"Then one morning I woke up and I didn't feel angry anymore. I didn't feel anything—but in a good way, I mean. It felt good not to feel mad. So I was lying there in bed, and I turned toward the window, and there was the most beautiful pattern of frost on the glass. I couldn't believe it. I got out of bed and went to the window so I could look at it closer. And you know, if you looked real close, every little speck of frost was shaped like a snowflake, like there were a zillion little tiny snowflakes that had formed a pattern on the window. My dad used to tell me that Jack Frost came around in the winter to paint the windows, but I knew this wasn't the work of any Jack Frost. And then while I was kneeling there looking at it, the sun started coming up, and when it hit that frost on the window, it just about blinded me. It was like a star exploding or something. And it was like God telling me everything was going to be all right. That's when I decided to come back here. The next day I ran away."

I hesitated to respond. Finally I said, "I thought you weren't sure you believed in God."

"I do now."

"Because you saw the frost?"

Satchel shook her head. "It wasn't so much seeing

something as knowing something. Like when you heard the bells, and you knew God was there."

I nodded, unsure of how to respond.

"It's not the frost or the bells or anything like that," Satchel said. "The way Mr. Ted put it was . . . well, he had a name for it. Something Latin. *Sensus divinus,* or something."

"Sensus divinitatis?" I asked.

Satchel's eyes widened. "I think that's it. It means people can sense the divine."

"And Mr. Dutton told you this?"

"Yeah." Satchel nodded. "We were talking about it before spring break. Before that too, I guess. We kind of talked about it a lot."

"You did? What did he say?"

"Um, well . . ." She put a hand to her head and rubbed her temple with an open palm, as though to loosen the thoughts at the back of her mind, to bring them up to the light where she could see them. "He said a lot of people have written about it. You know, a lot of the poets and the saints." She paused and smiled. "Because it's a universal thing, you know? Though some people see it as one thing, and some people see it as another, and some people just don't see it at all, even though it's, like, something we're born with."

"I'm not sure I'm following you, Satchel."

Two lines formed between her eyes as she frowned. "Mr. Ted said Virginia Woolf wrote about it, even though she didn't know what it was."

"Virginia Woolf?"

"Yeah. He said she wrote about those times when she sensed something, and she really felt like she was alive or like she was connected to something, or something like that. I think he said she called it her 'moments of being.' Mr. Ted said he had a student once who wrote a paper about it, who said, you know, that those moments of being were when God came to Virginia Woolf, and she sensed him, but she just couldn't figure out what it was."

I scarcely breathed. With some difficulty I asked, "Did Mr. Dutton tell you who that student was?"

"No." She shook her head. "Why?"

"Nothing. I was just wondering."

"Oh. So anyway, Mr. Ted said it took him a long time to realize maybe there was something to that. I mean, something to the idea of God coming to people. He said he believes it now, though."

"He does?"

"Yeah." She sounded far away and dreamy. "Yeah, he does. And I think he's right, because to me, Mr. Ted's a poet and, you know, I think he may even be a saint."

"A saint?" I whispered.

"He understands things, like you do, Miss Gunnar. He's a lot like you, or maybe you're a lot like him because he was your teacher. I don't know. But anyway, that's what I like about you and Mr. Ted. You understand things. Not like my mom and Roger. They're like, well . . . they're like cardboard or something, like they're just made out of cardboard. My mother thinks beauty is a perm and a wax job, you know? I don't think she's ever read a poem in her life. And Roger—he's nothing like what my dad was like, which is probably why Mom's crazy about him. I mean, to him, everything's about money, you know? He's checking out the stock market before he even has his first cup of coffee in the morning. Know what I mean? And . . ."

Satchel went on and I listened, though barely, catching only fragments of what she said. I was preoccupied with the pendulum of my emotions swinging rashly between awe and anger. Theodore Dutton seemed to me an ever-deepening enigma, a riddle without an answer, and I didn't like being left dangling and frustrated. I didn't like it at all.

CHAPTER 61

Judy Leeson, Satchel's mother, was a petite woman who looked scarcely out of high school, though she must have been in her late thirties. She had bottle-blond hair and painted acrylic fingernails, and she wore a stylish maternity pantsuit that downplayed her newly swollen belly. Her husband was an older man, graying but distinguished, his smooth skin tanned in spite of the season, his Gucci suit murmuring wealth.

At first glance they appeared a pleasant enough couple though somewhat reserved, maybe a bit standoffish. Roger Leeson managed a smile and a respectable handshake when I met him in Jack Farrell's office. Judy Leeson offered a hand as lifeless as a sock monkey and half as warm. I knew I was in trouble when she met my gaze with a brief reluctant glance.

Neither hugged Satchel, who entered the office on my heels and stood silently while Jack introduced me to the Leesons. After the introductions, Mrs. Leeson looked at her daughter as though the girl seemed vaguely familiar, but she couldn't quite place her. Again, it was Roger Leeson who smiled and made an attempt to greet Satchel, though his "Hello, kid" was met with a grunt as Satchel dropped her eyes to her shoes.

Jack Farrell invited us to sit. We settled ourselves into the chairs placed around his office, then bounced awkward glances off one another for several unnerving seconds. Finally Jack cleared his throat and said, "Our headmaster—ah, here he is now."

Harlan Quinn rushed stiffly into the room, his aging limbs like rusty pistons reluctant to work. "You must excuse me for being late," he said breathlessly. "I can't seem to make a simple trek across campus without being waylaid by questions. As though I'm the only one with any answers around here—"

"You're not late at all, sir," Jack interrupted. "We were just getting started."

"Ah, good, good. That's fine, then."

"I'd like to introduce you to the Leesons."

Roger Leeson rose quickly and shook the old man's hand. Judy Leeson remained seated and lifted her limp hand, briefly allowing her painted fingertips to touch the old man's weathered skin. Her marriage to Roger had lifted her from poverty to plenty, and she wore the arrogance of the *nouveau riche* very well. These few minutes were enough for me to understand why Satchel didn't care to return to White Plains.

"So," said Harlan Quinn, settling himself in the last available chair in the room. "We're here to discuss the matter of . . ." He glanced around, apparently looking for someone to finish his sentence.

Jack stepped up quickly to fill in the blank. "Our former student, Satchel Queen. The Leesons are her parents. They've withdrawn her from Seaton, though Satchel would like to finish out the year."

"Ah yes."

I watched the old man's head bob in reply, and I wished he would do us all a favor and retire.

"Satchel ran away from home," I volunteered, "but she has in a very real sense turned herself in. She's willing to talk with her parents and see if they can't compromise somehow."

"I see." The head bobbed again. "Yes, I remember." He turned his gaze to Roger Leeson and asked, "You prefer to have the child at home?"

"Well, you see—" Roger began, but his wife cut him off, saying, "Of course we do. What kind of question is that?"

"Now, Judy, we agreed that I would do the talking—"

"You decided that, Roger. I didn't agree to anything—"

"Mr. and Mrs.—" Harlan began.

"—she is my daughter, after all, and if I want her home, she should be home—"

"Mr. and Mrs. Leeson," Harlan tried again. "If I may interrupt . . ."

Surprisingly, the Leesons quieted, turning in unison to face the headmaster.

"Now then. You sent the child to us in September, asking us to provide her with a quality education. I wonder, has there been a problem in that regard?"

"Oh no, Mr. Quinn," Roger rushed in to say. "No, it isn't that at all. Seaton is a fine school, top-notch. It's just that Judy here is expecting and could use some help around—"

"I just want my daughter with me," Judy interrupted. "Is that too much to ask?"

Beside me, Satchel said under her breath, "Yeah, right."

Harlan said, "Perfectly understandable, Mrs. Leeson. Of course you do. Your daughter should be with you. But perhaps you would be willing to wait just a couple of months—"

"But I need her—I want her home now."

"Judy, you said you'd be willing to think about—"

"Don't put words in my mouth, Roger."

"On the way down, dear, you said you'd consider—"

Satchel jumped up. "She just wants me around to wait on her hand and foot!"

"That's not true!" her mother protested.

"Yes it is, and you know it."

"Satchel, darling—"

"Darling? Oh, that's good, Mom. Put on your best show for these people."

I tugged at Satchel's sleeve. "Satchel, this isn't helping," I pleaded.

She yanked her arm away without looking at me. "If Dad were here, he'd let me stay, because he'd know that was best for me."

Judy blanched while Roger shifted in his seat, crossing and uncrossing his legs. An electrified hush passed through the room, shocking us all. But it took Satchel's mother only a moment to snap back, and when she did, she was calm and cold. "Well, your father isn't here, is he?" she said evenly. "So it's up to me to decide what's best for you."

Satchel narrowed her eyes. "Yeah, right," she said defiantly, the words drawn out.

I tugged on her arm again. She sat.

Roger Leeson sucked in air and said, "It seems your mother has made up her mind—"

"So what about you, Roger? You'd let me stay, wouldn't you?"

Her stepfather looked at Satchel with amazingly apologetic eyes. For a moment I almost felt sorry for him.

"Satchel, listen, I think it's best—"

Satchel exhaled loudly, shook her head, and dropped her gaze to her shoes again. In doing so, she conceded defeat.

Jack, who'd been quiet up till now, said awkwardly, "I think I speak for Headmaster Quinn, Miss Gunnar, and myself when I say we're sorry to lose Satchel. She was an excellent student and an asset to Seaton. But of course we defer to the family in these rare situations when—"

Satchel interrupted Jack's soliloquy by leaping up and dashing from the office. I looked across the room at Roger and Judy Leeson, trying to gauge their reaction. They sat ashen, wide-eyed and silent, as though too stunned even to move. Mumbling some words of excuse, I ran after Satchel, catching up with her at the crest of the hill leading to Pine Glen. I pulled the child into my arms and held her as she sobbed into my blouse.

"It's going to be all right, Satchel," I said helplessly, not believing it myself.

"No it isn't, Miss Gunnar. It isn't." Her words were muffled, and her head rocked on my shoulder as she spoke. "I know I'm supposed to be here, and they just don't understand."

"Maybe they'll change their minds over the summer. Maybe they'll let you come back next year."

"But I'm supposed to be here now. Why can't they just let me stay?"

Twenty minutes later I watched Satchel climb into her stepfather's BMW, her backpack slung over her shoulder. I blew her a kiss as the car pulled away, but she didn't respond—not a wave, not a smile, nothing. She looked as though she had turned to stone.

Late that night I got the call from Jack Farrell. When the Leesons had stopped for gas somewhere in the middle of New Jersey, Satchel headed for the ladies' room at the station and didn't come back. For whatever reason, her parents had trusted her out of their sight, and when they weren't looking, she ran. This time no one assumed she was making her way back to Seaton.

CHAPTER 62

Theodore Dutton, for all his love of words, couldn't seem to find a single one with which to respond after I told him about Satchel, how she had been found, and how she was lost again. He tried once, twice, and then again to grab at something floating through his mind, but it must have been as fragile as gossamer, because when he opened his mouth, there was nothing there.

Finally Len Dutton spoke. "Does anyone have any idea at all where she might be headed?"

"None," I said.

We sat around the small table in the back room at Bel's Book Nook. It was just the three of us, as Bel had left to run errands an hour before I arrived. Selma Rainbo was out front manning the cash register.

"And you say this happened yesterday?"

"Yes. They were driving back to New York late yesterday afternoon when Satchel ran off."

"This wouldn't have happened at all if her parents had simply let her finish out the year," Len said.

I nodded. "It's really all so senseless. And unnecessary. Her stepfather might have let her stay, but her mother refused."

Mr. Dutton clenched his hands together on the table. He squeezed until his knuckles turned pasty, and then he released the grip like a sigh. He looked older than I had ever seen him. I knew there was something he wanted to say, and so I waited. Len sat quietly too, his fingers a tent over his lips.

At last Mr. Dutton said, "We can only do one thing." His voice was raspy and faraway, like a scratchy record on an old Victrola.

"What's that, Uncle Ted?" Len dropped his hands and leaned forward.

"Pray." He nodded slowly as his lips grew taut and his eyes moistened.

I looked at him fully, and he met my gaze. "You speak of prayer, Mr. Dutton, as though you think it might help."

"It's the only thing, Beth, that can help. It's all we can do for Satchel now."

"You told her . . . about my essay. Virginia Woolf . . ."

"The moments of being."

"Then you know?"

"Yes, now I know."

"What happened?"

"I finally listened." He leaned forward, bringing his face closer to mine, as though to make sure he could see me. "I had always sensed it, you see—what person doesn't? But for a long time I didn't understand. That thing beyond the appearances that Woolf wrote about—we give it so many names, or we say it is nothing at all, choosing to live as though it isn't there.

But it is insistent, so maddeningly insistent, and I finally listened. . . .”

Bel’s sudden appearance in the doorway interrupted him. “Beth, Selma said you were here. Have you had word about Satchel?”

“She has, Aunt Bel,” Len said. “Come on, have a seat and we’ll fill you in.”

She joined us at the table, and I repeated the events of the previous day. By the time I finished, Bel was weeping quietly.

“Dear Satchel,” she said, “I’m so afraid for her.”

“Listen, Aunt Bel, why don’t you and Uncle Ted go on home for the day. Get some rest. I’ll stay here with Selma, and she and I can close up shop tonight. As it is, you’re not going to be good for much around here.”

Bel nodded and wiped her eyes with a paper napkin from the pile on the table. “I think you’re right, Len. Thank you . . . thank you for staying and taking care of things.”

“That’s what I’m here for,” Len said. “Go get some rest, and I’ll see you at home tonight.”

Obediently, Bel and Dutton pushed their chairs back from the table. As Dutton stood, he faltered, as though his legs were weak. Bel caught his arm on one side; I caught his hand on the other. For a long moment Theodore Dutton held on to my hand. He looked at me, and something passed between us, a communion of sorts, an understanding.

“I believe she got it wrong, you know,” he said.

"Virginia Woolf?"

"Yes. In the end she thought it all came down to us. 'We are the words,' she said. 'We are the music; we are the thing itself.'" He shook his head slowly. "But it isn't that at all."

"It's God, of course," I whispered.

A small smile formed at the corners of his mouth. "It can be nothing else."

"Thank you," I said, "for praying for Satchel."

He squeezed my hand gently. "Thank you," he said, "for . . . everything."

Bel looked at us quizzically but said nothing. She helped her husband put on his jacket, then took his arm and led him to the door. I watched them leave, the two of them walking slowly, like people bent over by grief. I thought of how Satchel had wanted to come herself to tell them the news that she was back. Instead, I had come with the news that she was gone.

Turning back to Len, I was struck again by how much he looked like the Theodore Dutton I had once known. He more closely resembled my former English teacher than the elderly man who just left the room.

Len met my gaze. "You know," he said, "they almost came to think of Satchel as a daughter."

"I feel the same way," I admitted.

Len nodded. "I don't know Satchel as well as you do, but in the little time I spent with her, I grew to care about her. I want you to know that. As a teacher, I've known a lot of kids over the years, but with Satchel—

I don't know, there was just something different about her."

"Something special," I agreed. "She kept saying she was supposed to be with us—with me and the Duttons—but I guess that was wishful thinking."

I started to rise from the table then, but Len stopped me by placing a hand on my arm. "Beth," he said, "I don't want to offer empty words or false hope, but I want you to know that I think, somehow, Satchel is going to be okay. I don't think she's going to go far."

I tried to smile. "I hope you're right, Len."

He gave my arm a gentle, comforting squeeze. And then I rose to go.

CHAPTER 63

Spring flowed into the Delaware Valley with a rush of warm air, bringing with it the newborn colors of the year's early foliage. Seaton's campus became green again, the hills carpeted with grass instead of snow and mud. A myriad of leaves unfurled everywhere, cluttering the treetops and casting shadows on the ground. Soon Chapel Valley would be filled with daisies, a sight that, in my childhood, had never failed to fill me with joy.

I wasn't sure, though, that this present season would hold such promise. My one comforting thought was that with the passing of winter, Satchel would no longer be out in the cold.

Almost every day now, after school, I went to the

bookstore. At first I visited briefly and left, but slowly I fell into a routine of voluntarily helping out, doing some of the odd jobs Satchel had done. Bel needed the help, and I needed to be doing something that made me feel connected to Satchel. Each day when I arrived, Mr. Dutton or Bel or Len would ask, "Has there been any word?" and every day I said no, the police had no leads as yet. We'd let the dread and disappointment pass inevitably through us, some of it settling once again into that empty place in our hearts, and then we'd go to work.

I gained a certain solace from being with the people who loved Satchel as I did, the people who missed her, who feared for her, who prayed for her. We didn't even have to say her name; a certain look might pass between us, and we knew that it was Satchel we were thinking of, her name that we were silently lifting to the One who could see her wherever she was.

The last weekend in April was a long weekend for the students at Seaton, which allowed the boarders time to go home. I should have used that Friday to grade papers and catch up on lesson plans, but I didn't. For the first time in my life, I was very nearly neglecting my job and my students. I was too distracted by thoughts of the one student who was lost.

I spent that Friday at the bookstore, shelving books, working the cash register, helping customers. The Duttons weren't there in the morning because Mr. Dutton had a doctor's appointment, and afterward they stopped to pick up groceries on the way to the store.

At nearly noon the two of them came in the back door carrying paper sacks. I was already in the back room, searching the refrigerator for something cold to drink. When Bel saw me, she said, "The cupboard is bare, I know. Honestly, I think Len's stomach must be a bottomless pit. I can't keep anything on hand anymore, not since he arrived. But, bless him! What would we do without him?"

I laughed and took the sack she handed me. "Good," I said, looking inside. "You got more cranberry juice. Just what I was looking for."

"Help yourself," Bel said. "There should be plenty of ice unless Len's used it all up and didn't make more."

I set the sack on the table and pulled the juice from it. "Are there any more bags in the car?" I asked.

"Just a couple."

"I'll get them." This was from Len, who was suddenly striding into the back room on his long legs. He passed us and disappeared out the door.

Mr. Dutton was busy at the counter, putting food away. I watched as he pulled a glass, bell-shaped cookie jar down from the cupboard. Inside were a few scattered pieces of dried mango. He set the jar on the counter, then untied the twist tie from the neck of a plastic bag.

In spite of the obvious, I asked, "Mr. Dutton, what are you doing?"

He paused and turned to me. "You really should call me Ted, you know, Beth. I'd prefer it."

I frowned and shook my head. "But why are you filling that jar with mango?"

"It's for Satchel when she comes back." He emptied the plastic bag, then put the lid on the jar and lifted it to the cupboard again. "It's just—I don't know—it makes me feel hopeful."

"I see." My response was weighted with uncertainty.

"If you're going to be perfectly honest, dear," Bel chided, her head in the fridge as she rearranged items on the shelves, "you might as well admit that you're the one who's eating it in the meantime."

"Yes, well, I'm afraid I've taken a liking to it."

"As long as you don't eat too much, Ted. Your diet, remember?"

"Speaking of which," Len said, coming inside and dropping the last two grocery sacks on the counter, "how does the doctor say the old man's doing?"

"Amazingly well, for someone in such poor health," Bel quipped.

"He says," Dutton added, "I can expect to live a little while longer. Though I plan to do better than that, of course."

"You will if you watch what you eat," Bel said. "You can't do like Len here—eat everything you want and expect to get away with it."

"Now, Aunt Bel, I'm not such a bad eater."

"Just a big one, which is as it should be."

Len started to say something, shrugged instead, then began pulling groceries from the sacks.

Mr. Dutton pushed a button on the stove to start the

teakettle boiling. By the time the last groceries were put away, he had poured himself a mug of tea and settled into his overstuffed chair. He sank into the cushions with a heavy sigh. "Well, if the rest of you don't mind, I think I'll wait right here for a while."

"That's fine, dear," Bel said absently.

Len gave his uncle a bemused look. "And if you don't mind my asking, Uncle Ted, just what are you waiting for?"

Mr. Dutton looked up and blinked at Len from behind his thick glasses. "Why, I'm waiting for Satchel to come back, of course. Aren't you?"

Len, Bel, and I exchanged glances. Mr. Dutton was right. While on the surface of things we appeared to be going about our lives, our primary activity was waiting. Above all else, we were just waiting for Satchel to come home.

CHAPTER 64

While we waited, something entirely other was happening. In this unexpected and unwelcome place, Len and I were thrown together like two ticket holders watching for an overdue train. We found ourselves, in a sense, sitting side by side on a bench in the station, glancing at our watches, wishing the train would come, tossing comments to each other to commiserate. But eventually we found the comments leading to genuine conversation, until finally our thoughts flowed easily, as though we'd never been strangers at all but had always known each other.

In fact, he did remember us as kids, he said—remembered those nights in his Uncle Ted's cabin when a group of students came around to hang out with Mr. Dutton. "I'd mostly forgotten about those visits," he confessed, "but being here in Delaware again—I don't know—kind of brings it back."

We were taking a break in the back room, drinking raspberry tea from glass bottles and nibbling on mixed nuts Bel had dumped into a candy dish. I leaned forward over the table and looked at Len intently. "What do you remember?" I asked.

"I remember you," he said. His bottle of tea hovered momentarily between the table and his mouth. "And another girl, a blonde—"

"Natalie."

"Yeah, I guess so."

"She was my best friend. Still is."

He nodded. "She was dating Ken, right? The guy that played the guitar."

"Yeah."

"And you were dating the other guy—what's-his-name."

I gave a small laugh. "Ray."

"Uh-huh." The bottle finally reached his lips, and he took a long swallow. After a moment he said, "So what happened to him?"

"Ray? Oh, he became a doctor, got married, had kids."

"Uh-huh." Another swallow, another nod of the head. "But you never did?"

"Get married? No. And you?"

"Came close once. She broke it off."

"I'm sorry."

"Oh, don't be sorry," he lobbed back at me. "I'm not." He laughed and shook his head. "Not at all."

After that, when I was in my classroom in Heath Hall, I realized I was counting down the hours until I could leave Seaton and go to the bookstore. Sometimes when I arrived, Len was at the door watching for me. He'd open the door and welcome me, and we'd go on glancing at our watches and waiting for that train, but at the same time we talked and laughed, and sometimes we got so wrapped up in the moment we very nearly forgot we were waiting for anything at all. It's funny how something bad and something good can be happening at the same time, and even be related, one event springing up out of the other. And I guess that's the funny thing. If the train had not been waylaid, Len and I might never have known each other.

That last Friday in April, the Friday Mr. Dutton replenished the jar with mango, I stayed at the store until about five o'clock. I might have stayed longer, but Natalie had invited me to meet her at a coffee shop for sandwiches and dessert. Since Satchel ran away the second time, Natalie had been taking special care to be in touch with me daily, which I appreciated.

As I was preparing to leave, I carried one last stack of books from the back room to the front counter to tell Len they'd been inventoried and were ready to shelve. Len leaned on the counter, reading the newspaper.

"Any good news?" I asked as I dropped the books beside the cash register.

Len looked up at me and said, "I guess that depends on how you define good." He smiled, and I returned it.

"I suppose you're right," I said.

He tapped an index finger on the open page. "Did you know the U of Delaware is hosting a series of readings by local authors?"

"No. Guess I missed that. I haven't read the paper in a few days."

"The first one's tomorrow night, a guy named Russell Barrett. Ever heard of him?"

I shook my head. "I don't think so. What's he write?"

"Poetry."

"Really? And it got published?"

"Apparently. It says here he'll be reading from his newest release, *Blue Moon Over Autumn*, which is his second volume of poetry. He's a professor at the university."

"I wonder whether anyone will go."

"His students will if they know what's good for them."

"Spoken like a true teacher." I laughed.

"But who knows, maybe the guy's actually good." Len shrugged, then frowned at me. "Hmm . . . you look doubtful. What? You don't like poetry?"

"Me? I love poetry. It just seems like very few people do these days."

"I do," he said.

"Yeah?"

"Yeah, I do." He folded the paper then and put it aside. "Well, would you like to go, then?"

"To the reading?"

"Yes."

"Do you mean . . . with you?"

"Well . . . yes."

I was flustered, and the words felt slippery on my tongue, like a school of minnows that I couldn't wrap my hands around. At the same time I considered responding with that old cliché, *I thought you'd never ask,* because all along I'd been waiting for this too. Satchel, yes, of course, but this too.

"Yes," I said when I finally said something. "Yes, I'd like to go."

Len smiled once more, and I had an odd sensation that Satchel Queen was looking on and laughing.

CHAPTER 65

After the poetry reading we stopped at a restaurant in Newark to grab something to eat. As Len took a bite of his hamburger, he shook his head and laughed silently.

"It wasn't that bad, Len," I said.

"It was awful," he countered. "And the worst part was that everyone in the audience acted like he's some ancient sage spouting off pearls of wisdom."

"Well, he had a few nice images—"

"But did you understand a single one of his poems?"

I sighed in defeat. "No, not really."

"No, and neither did anyone else. But people want to

pretend to understand so they don't look like fools. Classic case of the emperor's new clothes. No one will admit the stuff is drivel."

"The book actually got some good reviews . . ."

"Yeah, which is a sad commentary on those particular literary critics." Len devoured a dill pickle spear in a couple of bites and followed it with a large swallow of iced tea. "Though I have to say—and I hate to admit it—but I kind of envy the guy."

I felt my eyebrows reach for my hairline. "How so?"

"Well, here he was up there reading from his own work, you know? I mean, he's holding in his hands a book he'd written himself."

"You want to write poetry?"

"Great Scot, no," Len exclaimed. "I like poetry, if it really is poetry, but I'm not going to try to write it. No. I want to write history."

"You do?"

"Well, yes. That's why I was in Europe, you know, doing research into the medieval church and the Protestant Reformation. I suppose it sounds like a complete bore—"

"Oh no, not at all."

"But I'd like to write a book about it. Actually, I've been planning to write about it for a long time."

"Really? I think that's wonderful."

He looked at me and smiled. "You do?"

"Yes, I really do."

He nodded as though in satisfaction, then went back to work on his hamburger.

"Well, what's keeping you from doing it?" I asked.

He looked thoughtful a moment. "Nothing, really. Now that I've done the research, I just have to find the time to do it. I've got to somehow carve out time in my teaching schedule, and that isn't going to be easy."

"No, I imagine not. You're going back to Quentin College in the fall, aren't you?"

"Oh yes. I'm afraid so. Don't have much choice about that. Not with a mortgage and a car payment. But like I say, I'm going to get that book written somehow."

Our waitress appeared and poured us both more iced tea. "Can I get you anything else?" she asked.

Len looked at me. "Beth?"

"I'm fine for now, thanks."

The waitress left, and Len poured a couple packets of sugar into his drink. He stirred the grainy cloud of sweetener until it dissolved into the tea. "Guess I should really cut back on the sugar," he said. "I don't want to end up like Uncle Ted."

"I don't think you will."

"No, probably not. He had a huge jump start toward diabetes that I never had."

"What do you mean?"

"Just that he may not have ended up a diabetic if not for all the drinking in his early years. Or at least that didn't help." He looked up at me suddenly and said, "You probably weren't aware of that, were you? I mean, did you know he was an alcoholic when he was teaching at Seaton?"

"Not at the time, no. But Ray recently told me about it."

"Really? You still in touch with Ray?"

"I saw him at homecoming last fall. You know, that's how I got back in touch with your uncle. He ended up in the hospital where Ray works."

"Oh yeah? Small world, isn't it?"

I nodded. "Sometime after that, Ray told me he and Ken used to go over to the cabin once in a while and share a few beers with Mr. Dutton."

"No kidding." Len pushed his empty plate aside and curled both hands around the glass of iced tea. "I'm not surprised, but I hate to hear that."

"Yeah, well, they were young."

"Uncle Ted wasn't. He should have known better. But he was pretty far gone by then."

"You know, Len, what amazes me is that I had no clue."

"A lot of alcoholics are good at hiding it."

"But Mr. Dutton seemed to have it so together."

He shrugged. "Typical."

"Did you know at the time that he was drinking?"

"Sure. I mean, I'd stay right there in the cabin with him whenever I came down to visit. It was kind of hard to miss all the bottles everywhere. I'd get up in the morning and go looking for corn flakes and find Jim Beam in the cabinet instead."

"He didn't try to hide it from you?"

"Not very hard. Listen, tell you the truth, I drank with him sometimes. I thought it was cool. He was so different from my dad—Mr. Shirt-and-tie Conservative. You know how parents look to teens."

"I guess so."

"I just didn't know *how* far gone he was," Len continued. "Talk about not having a clue."

I stopped picking at my grilled chicken salad and looked intently across the table at Len. "What do you mean, you didn't know how far gone he was?"

He glanced sideways. He looked uneasy, but when he turned his gaze back to my face, he tried to smile. "I trust you, Beth," he said. "Listen, Uncle Ted didn't have a heart attack. He tried to kill himself."

The fork I'd been holding landed on the table with a loud clang. "You know that?"

"Of course." He studied me, his eyes narrowing. "You act as if you know it too."

I looked at him hard. "I do know."

Silence. Then, "How? How do you know?"

"I was there."

I told him the whole story then, while he looked incredulous one moment, grieved the next. When I finished, neither of us spoke for what seemed a long time.

Finally he said, "I can't believe you've known what happened all these years."

"Yes. It's never left me. The only thing I don't know is why he did it."

Len shook his head slowly. "I don't know that either, Beth. I've never really understood. But—" He took a deep breath and sat up straighter, as though he'd just snapped out of a trance. "It was a long time ago, and

Uncle Ted has really changed. I mean, he stopped drinking, got his act together, and went on to live a productive life. So, happy ending. What more can you ask for?"

I didn't respond. Suddenly I was thinking of Satchel. I turned to the window and saw my own reflection in the glass. The night outside was dark and overcast, and the clouds had begun to spit rain that looked like scattered gemstones in the lamplight.

"She'll be all right," Len said.

"What?"

"Satchel. You were thinking of Satchel, weren't you?"

I drew in one quivering breath. "Yes, I guess I was. I hope she's . . . inside somewhere, out of the rain."

His hand found mine on the tabletop; his skin felt warm and reassuring. "One thing I can say for sure about Satchel," he said. "She knows enough to come in out of the rain."

He was right, of course. I nodded, squeezed his hand, offered him a smile. "Thanks, Len. I'm glad you happened to be here now while all of this is going on."

"So am I."

We sat quietly then, not needing to talk. We seemed to understand something without saying the words aloud. He'd be going back to New York before too much more time had passed, but that wouldn't be the end of things. His hand in mine was both strange and not strange, unexpected and yet somehow expected. Like a piece of a puzzle finally fitting snuggly into its companion piece. *Of course,* one thinks. *This piece goes with that one. I should have seen it long ago.*

When Len asked me out and the pieces fit, there arose that sense that this was somehow where we'd been headed all along, even when he was a long-haired dreamer and I was an invisible child.

After he drove me home to Pine Glen, he put his arms around me at the door and held me, and he kept on holding me until I felt solid and whole and warm and seen. He didn't let go until I knew that I was there. And then he said goodnight and told me he would call me the next day.

So that when, on Sunday afternoon, the phone rang and the caller ID gave Dutton's home number, I thought surely it was Len. But it wasn't. The voice on the other end of the line belonged to Theodore Dutton. He had never called me before, and I didn't expect him to call me now, so the first words out of my mouth were, "Is everything all right?"

"Oh yes," he assured me. "Everything's fine. It's just that—" he stopped a moment and lowered his voice—"I believe I know where Satchel is. I can't tell you where, Beth, but I want you to know she's safe."

CHAPTER 66

"Why can't you tell me where she is?"

"If I do, you'll go after her, and we can't go after her, Beth. It won't work that way. She'll have to come back to us on her own."

"But—how do you know where she is?"

"I'll explain everything to you later."

"When?"

"After she's back."

"And what if she doesn't want to come back?"

"I think she does. Yes, I think she will."

"But you can't be sure!" The shrillness in my voice was rising along with my anger. Theodore Dutton was a master of frustration, and he had kept me frustrated to varying degrees for a good portion of my life. I took a deep breath to calm myself. "All right, so you think you know where she is."

"Yes. And if she's where I think she is, she's quite safe."

"But you're not sure?"

"As sure as I can be."

"Listen, will you tell me where she is if I promise not to go after her?"

"I think it best not to say right now."

"But Mr. Dutton!"

"You will have to trust me on this, Beth."

"Trust you?" My voice was shrill again. "How can I trust you?"

"It's best that no one knows where she is. I wanted to tell you she's safe just to put your mind at rest, but I can't tell you any more than that. And I'm not saying a word about any of this to Bel or Len."

"But why? I don't understand."

"Like I said, we can't force her to come back. She'll have to want to come back. Otherwise it's no good. We'll just lose her again. All we can do is let her know we love her, and then wait."

"Let her know we love her? But how on earth are we supposed to do that?"

"She'll know, if she listens."

"Listens to what? You're not making any sense."

"Never mind that. Trust me. Everything's going to be all right. Like I said, she's safe at the moment."

"But is she with somebody? Is someone taking care of her?"

"Well, yes and no."

I wondered then whether he had lost his mind. I thought it might be his illness talking, or maybe he had even relapsed and gone back to drinking.

"Just tell me, is she in a shelter, some sort of place for runaways?"

"Well, in a manner of speaking. Though I advise you not to start making the rounds of the local safe houses. That would only be wasting your time."

"Look, Mr. Dutton, Jack Farrell tells me Satchel's parents are beside themselves with worry. If you know something of her whereabouts, I think you owe it to them to speak up."

"No, Beth, no. They're exactly who she's hiding from. You know that as well as I do. They will simply have to be patient along with the rest of us."

"Where's Len?" I demanded.

"Out running errands. He'll be back soon."

"And Bel?"

"Upstairs napping. Which gave me the opportunity to call you."

"Listen, I don't know why you're doing this, and I'm not even sure you really know where Satchel is—"

"Beth!" He sounded genuinely hurt. "I'd never lie to you."

But my experience with him told me otherwise. Why had I tried to forge a friendship with the man after I saw him at the hospital? I should have listened to Natalie. I should have been satisfied to know he was alive while resolving to stay away. And certainly I should never have sent Satchel to work alongside the Duttons in their store.

"So how long do you intend to just wait for her to come back on her own?" I asked.

"As long as it takes."

I wanted to scream. Instead, I said with as much composure as I could muster, "And what if she moves on from wherever she is? What if we lose this opportunity to go after her?"

"I don't think she's going to move on."

My hand was beginning to cramp from my hold on the phone. "If she does, though, and if we lose her, I'm blaming you."

His voice was amazingly calm. "I believe what I'm doing is right, Beth. And I also believe that Satchel is going to come home. Now, Len has just gotten back so I'm going to hang up. But don't worry. Trust me."

CHAPTER 67

But I didn't trust him. And it was a distrust that went back decades. It was a doubtfulness born on an April night when a young girl's heart was broken by her hero. Maybe he had changed. Maybe, as he claimed, he had heard the call of the moments and recognized the voice of God, and it may be that he had paused long enough to listen and respond. Still, something was broken and hadn't been made right.

I stayed away from the bookstore for three days. Because of the depth of my anger, I was afraid of how I would respond to Theodore Dutton if I should see him.

Len called to ask where I was, why I wasn't coming in to the store. I told him I was busy at school and couldn't spare the time. He wondered, I knew, whether it was something between us—between me and him—but I couldn't explain. Not without telling him about the mysterious conversation with his uncle, which I didn't feel free to talk about.

For three days my stomach turned, and I swallowed the anger that burned my throat with bile. Assailed by images of what happens to young girls on the streets, I scarcely ate or slept and thought of little else other than

Satchel and her whereabouts. I wondered whether Dutton really knew where she was, and if he did, I wondered at his insistence on keeping me from her. Once again, he was the man who owed me answers but refused to give them.

On the fourth day I couldn't stand it anymore. I drove to the store at closing time. When I pulled into the lot, Selma Rainbo was getting into her car to go home. She tossed me a pleasant wave, then signaled a right turn and pulled out into a lull in traffic. I was glad she was leaving. One less person to deal with.

I parked my car and went inside. Len stood at the front counter looking over receipts. His face lit up when he saw me. "Beth!"

"I need to talk to Mr. Dutton," I said.

"What? Is something wrong?"

I shook my head, unable to speak.

"He's in the back room with Bel. We're just closing up for the night, you know."

"I know."

"Are you sure you're all right, Beth?"

I didn't answer. I turned away from Len and walked through the musty aisles toward the back of the store. Bel was wiping down the kitchen counter with a dishcloth while Mr. Dutton sat at the table looking over a pile of books.

"Why, Beth!" Bel said cheerfully. "I'm so glad you stopped by."

"I need to speak to Mr. Dutton, Bel."

"Well, all right."

"Alone."

She looked questioningly at her husband. He pushed the books aside and nodded at Bel. "Why don't you and Len go on home. I'll stay and chat with Beth, and then when we're finished I'll call Len to come pick me up."

"No," I said. "I'll take you home, Mr. Dutton. Len doesn't have to come back."

Mr. Dutton looked at me while adjusting his heavy glasses on his nose. "All right."

"Well, then." Bel tried to sound agreeable, but I could hear the hesitancy in her voice. "I'm ready to go home and put my feet up anyway." She looked at the dishcloth in her hand, seemingly not quite sure what to do with it. She settled on rinsing and wringing it out, then hanging it over the faucet. She did this slowly, as though hoping I would change my mind and tell her she could stay.

I didn't. I waited quietly for her to leave. Finally, with a dubious smile for me and a kiss for her husband, she left the room.

As soon as she was gone, I said, "I suppose you know why I'm here."

Mr. Dutton reached over to the chair beside him and pulled it away from the table. "Why don't you sit down, Beth."

I didn't sit. "Where is she, Mr. Dutton?"

The room became quiet, and I heard the tinkle of the bell over the front door, then a key in the lock, signaling Len's and Bel's departure.

Speaking quietly, almost in a whisper, Mr. Dutton said, "I know you're worried."

"I'm way beyond worried at this point. The not knowing is killing me."

Mr. Dutton leaned back in the chair, glanced up at the ceiling, looked back at me. "I can tell you she is safe, and you will only make matters worse if you don't give it some time." He continued to speak in low tones, as though he were afraid Bel and Len were hunched at the back door, listening.

I started to pace then, a few steps back and forth in the small space that was the kitchen. If I didn't move, I thought I might explode. I heard Mr. Dutton say my name, but I didn't respond. I was suspended between that moment and a long-ago night when Ken Cunningham stood under a starry sky running an index finger over his wrist. I heard Natalie scream, saw her fall to the ground, felt again my own grieved astonishment as a distant siren faded into the dark.

I stopped pacing and swung around toward Theodore Dutton. "Why did you do it?" My voice trembled, and my eyes felt like they were on fire, but it was only the tears that had been pressing against them for days, for years.

"Why did I do what?" Mr. Dutton looked up at me dumbfounded, blinking behind his glasses.

"Why did you kill yourself?" I cried. And then I asked it again. "Why did you kill yourself?" It made no sense, asking that question of a living soul, but for me he had been dead for years.

Once the words were out in the open, I found myself gazing upon the face of a man who seemed to be breaking apart into a thousand tiny pieces. I watched as his skin changed hues from red to pink to chalky gray. His eyes widened, his mouth came unhinged, his jaw trembled. He lifted one hand toward me, and it fluttered in the air between us like a wounded bird.

His lips moved. He was trying to say something. I waited and watched as he choked out the words, "What do you know about that?"

Cold tears rolled down my cheeks. "I know everything, Mr. Dutton."

"How?" He shook his head; it seemed a great effort. "How long?"

"I was there that night."

"What do you mean?"

"It was Ray and Ken who found you. They found you on the floor, in the blood . . ."

"Dear God," he breathed, shutting his eyes, and I thought he was indeed addressing God and not me. "They told me it was Fosset. They said Clarence Fosset found me . . ." After a moment he looked up again. "Tell me what you know." He touched the empty seat beside him, and this time I sat.

"Tell me what happened," he repeated.

I told him the story of that April Fool's night, of going to his cabin with Natalie, of the ambulance and the police and the look on the boys' faces as they stood in the chilly air under the midnight sky. I told him the story that Commander Pettingill spun at assembly on

Monday morning, casting it out over the student body like a fraudulent blessing. I told him about the lies and the secrecy and the years I thought he was dead, and how I had grieved for him, and how I had wondered what awful thing would make him want to end his life.

When I finished, he had to moisten his lips before he could speak. He winced as though his tongue were made of sandpaper. "You've lived with this a lifetime, and I never knew."

"I just don't understand what happened, Mr. Dutton, why you'd want to do such a thing."

"I . . . I was a fool, Beth. A drunk and a fool."

"But that doesn't tell me anything. It doesn't tell me *why*."

"How can I explain?" he said, his face wrinkled with pain, his eyes moist. "I really—I had no reason to die. No reason at all. And I think in the end, that's what it came down to. I had nothing to die for. No noble cause, no lofty ideals, nothing like what the poets talk about, like I talked about in class day after day. Not love of God, because"—he waved a hand—"there was no God, you see. Not love of family, because I was alone. Not love of country—certainly not that, not after Vietnam. You're too young to remember, I know. You're too young to understand how we were sent to die in a losing battle, and if we came home we were crucified for going, crucified by the very people we were supposed to be defending. That did something to me, Beth, something irreparable, and though I tried to forget about it all and just go on with my life, something inside of me was lost, or hardened, or changed in some way I couldn't understand. After 'Nam, I had no goals other than getting as drunk as I could as often as I could. And I'll tell you, when you're looking at the bottom of an empty bottle and you start realizing there's nothing worth dying for, you finally decide there's nothing worth living for either."

When he finished, we looked at each other for a long time. He wanted me to understand, but I didn't. I said, "But you were the one who told us life was a gift. You were the one who took us out to the valley and told us to feel what it was like to lie under the sun, to be alive on the earth."

"I wanted you to believe that, even if I couldn't."

"But I trusted you. We all did. We all . . ." I stopped, pressing my mouth into a small tight line.

"What, Beth?"

"We loved you. Didn't you know that?"

He closed his eyes, shook his head. "No." The word was a choked whisper. "No. I couldn't see beyond my own misery. That was all—"

"We loved you, and you betrayed us."

I put my face in my hands and wept. I felt Mr. Dutton gently touch my shoulder. "Beth," he whispered, "my dear Beth. Can you ever forgive me?"

For the first time, I knew that I wanted to. But I couldn't stop crying long enough to find the words. Minutes passed. I took deep shuddering breaths and tried to look at the man sitting beside me at the table. When I finally thought I could speak, I opened my mouth, but before I could begin, I was interrupted by a pounding overhead. I looked at Mr. Dutton, then at the ceiling where the clattering came from. I gasped and started to rise, but Mr. Dutton held me firmly by the shoulder, as though telling me to sit. I watched in surprise as the attic door fell open with a crash. A pair of delicate hands opened the stairs and sent them unfolding toward the floor.

Then a figure emerged from the ceiling, climbing backward down the ladder, stopping at the bottom and staring at Dutton and me with an expression of bewilderment, compassion, and love.

And then Satchel Queen came and put her arms around both of us and, without a word, drew us into a place as tender as mercy and as clean as grace.

EPILOGUE

Satchel stands at the open front door of Pine Glen, looking out. I wonder whether she sees that certain light that settles over Delaware on summer nights, that sigh-of-contentment light that warms you even while it's fading. I think she must. Because it's there for all who look and listen, and Satchel is listening.

She lives here now with me in Pine Glen. She has been here all summer and will remain right here throughout her senior year at Seaton. It is an informal foster parenting situation of sorts. I don't know what happened behind closed doors between Roger and Judy Leeson, but once Satchel came down out of the attic, they agreed to let her stay at Seaton for her remaining year of high school. Their one request was that she live with me rather than in the dorm. Jack Farrell told me later about his phone conversation with Roger Leeson.

"I guess it's an unusual thing to ask," Satchel's stepfather had said, "but that child—she's been through a lot in her life, you know? Now, I just want her to be happy. Yeah, I can speak for her mother too. We want Satchel to be happy. We think the best situation for her would be to live with Miss Gunnar and not in the dorm. It'd be, you know, kind of like having a home. Would you consider allowing her to do that?" Jack Farrell didn't have to consider the request for long. As soon as he hung up with Roger Leeson, he called to let me know I was about to become something of a surrogate mother. I couldn't have been happier.

As for Theodore Dutton discovering Satchel's whereabouts, it was the mango that gave her away. "I kept filling up the jar only to find it empty," Ted said. "Someone was eating the mango, and it wasn't me. I can't stand the stuff myself. And Len can't either."

Satchel had a key to the store, so she simply let herself in and went into hiding. At night she came down from her hiding place and rummaged for food.

"Didn't you think the Duttons would suspect something when there was food missing?" I asked when she told me the story of how she came to live in the attic.

"Naw. Bel kept blaming Len for eating everything. I

figured I could let him take the fall. I didn't know he doesn't like mango."

"So how long did you intend to stay up there?"

She shrugged. "I didn't bother thinking about that. I was just kind of enjoying it while it lasted."

"Enjoying it? What on earth did you do up there all that time?"

"Slept. Read. There were plenty of books, and I found a flashlight down in the store so I could read even when it was dark. And then I spent a lot of time listening to Mr. Ted."

"Listening to Mr. Ted?"

"Yeah, he'd sit down there in the back room reading the Bible out loud. Yeah, at first I couldn't believe he was reading. I mean, that was my job. I was supposed to read to him. But then I saw the Bible where he left it on the kitchen table. It was large print, and he was reading it with a magnifying glass. And then he prayed a lot."

"Did he pray out loud too?"

"Yeah. And he asked God to keep me safe and bring me home. He said, like, 'Please bring her home, because we love her.' "

Her eyes glistened as we exchanged a smile. That very day I started getting rid of the extra books in the guest bedroom to prepare a place for Satchel. This was before I even knew for sure that she'd be living with me. Something just told me things might end up that way. I taped up some boxes and carried the books out to the car and carted them off to Bel's Book Nook. It took three trips. Whether Satchel stayed with me or not, I needed to get rid of the books. And in the end Satchel did stay.

Now she turns away from the screen door, her whole face radiant. "Where's Len taking us to dinner tonight?"

"I don't know. He says it's a surprise." I'm sitting on the couch watching Satchel, content simply to be with her. "All I know is he said to dress in something nice." Which we have done—new clothes for both of us from Lord and Taylor, courtesy of Roger Leeson. He gave Satchel a generous financial gift, telling her to buy what she needed for school. Then he added, "Buy yourself some new clothes, will you? Something that doesn't have holes in it. And Miss Gunnar too—buy her something nice." He's a happy man these days, the father of twin boys. He has given his wife the gift of a fulltime nanny. I've decided he's not such a bad fellow after all.

Satchel moves across the living room and sits down in the wing chair. Wide-eyed, she says, "Maybe Len's going to give you the ring tonight!"

A small thrill of excitement runs through me. "That would be something, wouldn't it?"

"But then . . . maybe I shouldn't be there. If he does, I mean. Maybe you'd rather it just be the two of you."

"Oh no. I want you there. I really do."

Satchel smiles. "It's kind of like we're family, isn't it?"

"Yes," I say, nodding happily, "it's just like that, Satchel."

For a moment she looks dreamy. "You know, it's

going to be really cool to be in your wedding. I've never been a bridesmaid before."

"You'll be beautiful," I say. "And I can't think of anyone I'd rather have with me than you and Natalie."

Dear Natalie. She's beside herself with excitement, insisting that we start planning the wedding right away. I tell her there's plenty of time, as it's at least a year off. Len is going back to Quentin College for another year of teaching. He promises, though, to visit me and Satchel as often as he can. Satchel has already begun working on her application to Quentin. When I move to upstate New York, she plans to be there too.

I will spend this upcoming year teaching at Seaton. Satchel will go on working at Bel's Book Nook. It will be a good year for us both, I think. Pine Glen will be a true home, and we will miss it when we go. But we will leave it in good hands, relinquishing the house to Joel Sexton and his family with the promise that they will never again wake up to find a car in their living room. Joel says he will keep his fingers crossed and hope for the best until then.

Before Satchel and I move to New York, there's another wedding we'll be attending. Ray and Brenda are getting remarried over Thanksgiving weekend. I would tell you that story of love restored, but that is for another book. Suffice it to say that I rejoice for them, knowing that the returning to one's first love doesn't happen very often.

I learned about Ray's impending marriage when he answered Theodore Dutton's request to stop by the store and visit him. Ray did so reluctantly but told me later he was glad. While he was there, a weight he didn't even know about suddenly rolled off his back. It was the rolling off that let him know the burden had been there for years, and he had simply grown used to carrying it. He said the weightlessness was amazing, right up there with being in love again with his wife. He said sometimes restoration comes to us as a gift when we didn't even know it was possible and haven't done a single thing to deserve it.

Ray went on to tell me Ted thanked him for saving his life. "If you boys hadn't come by the cabin," Ted had said, "I most likely wouldn't be here now. I should think I'd have bled to death."

Ray said he deserved no thanks, that he and Ken had gone to the cabin only to pull an April Fool's joke. Ted waved a hand and said no matter the boys' intent, it became an intervention. "A divine appointment," he'd said, "to keep this old fool alive."

Satchel leans her head back against the chair and shuts her eyes. She is smiling pensively, as though at some secret thought. But I can read her mind. It is a sense of satisfaction that leaves her at rest.

I think I hear a car approaching, so I rise and go to the door. A car passes by, but it isn't Len. He'll be here soon, though. Meanwhile, I will take a moment to stand here and drink in the light, for it is full of life.

Which leads me to the final thing I want you to know. It's a small place, this state called Delaware. Small and rather insignificant and often overlooked.

Invisible, even. Kind of like me. Maybe like you. But this is where God met me, raining down goodness on humble ground. So I want you to know that if you stop and listen to the moments, you might realize He is in them, calling your name. And if you're like Nathanael, and if you're like me, you might be surprised and ask, "But Lord, how do you know me?" And He will answer you the way He did Nathanael, and the way He did me, "When you thought you couldn't be seen, I saw you."

Len's car is coming down the lane now toward Pine Glen. I open the screen door and step onto the stoop, waiting for him there with open arms.

Center Point Publishing
600 Brooks Road • PO Box 1
Thorndike ME 04986-0001 USA

(207) 568-3717

US & Canada:
1 800 929-9108
www.centerpointlargeprint.com

Center Point
Large Print

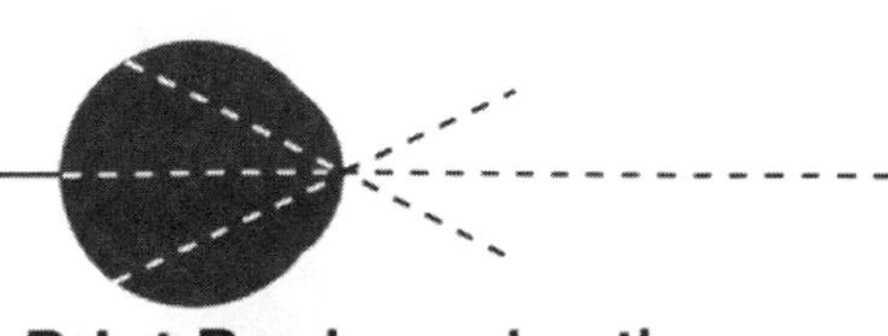

City of Tranquil Light

BO CALDWELL

CENTER POINT PUBLISHING
THORNDIKE, MAINE

This Center Point Large Print edition
is published in the year 2011 by arrangement with
Henry Holt & Company LLC.

The text of this Large Print edition is unabridged.
In other aspects, this book may vary
from the original edition.
Printed in the United States of America
on permanent paper.
Set in 16-point Times New Roman type.

ISBN: 978-1-60285-987-6

Library of Congress Cataloging-in-Publication Data

Caldwell, Bo.
City of tranquil light / Bo Caldwell.
p. cm.
ISBN 978-1-60285-987-6 (library binding : alk. paper)
1. Missionaries—China—Fiction. 2. Americans—China—Fiction.
3. China—Social conditions—20th century—Fiction. 4. China—Fiction.
5. Large type books. I. Title.
PS3603.A43C57 2011
813′.6—dc22

2010042067

For Kate and Scotty and Ron,
real and constant blessings in my life—
with love

CONTENTS

City
of
Tranquil
Light

Shepherd-Teacher

Suppose it is an autumn day, fine and clear and cool. Late afternoon, when the sun nears the horizon and turns the sky into a watercolor of pastels. It is beautiful, as though God is showing off. As you approach the city you first see its wall, an immense gray brick structure that is as solid as it is imposing, nearly as wide as it is high, some thirty feet. If you are coming from the east, it will be in sharp silhouette against the lovely changing sky. Near the city the air begins to smell of smoke, but mostly it has the sweet, clean scent of the ripening winter wheat in the surrounding fields.

From a distance the city may not look like much; only that dark wall is visible, and what can that tell you? Some say the cities in the North China Plain are by and large alike, one indistinguishable from another; to them this one might look like any other. But it is not; I can testify to this, for it is the place on this earth that I love the most, the city in which my wife and I lived for nearly twenty-five years among beggars and bandits and farmers and scholars and peasants, people whom we deeply loved. The name of the city is Kuang P'ing Ch'eng—City of Tranquil Light—and although I now reside in

southern California and have for many years, that faraway place remains my home.

And it is often in my thoughts. Above my bed hang three Chinese scrolls depicting New Testament scenes, painted by our most improbable convert and given to me when we left China. In the first, the prodigal son kneels at his father's feet as the father rests his hands on the young man's head. The son's pigtail is disheveled and his blue peasant's tunic and trousers are dirty and torn, while the father's violet silk robe is immaculate. In the second, an oriental woman lovingly washes our Lord's feet with her tears and dries them with her long black hair, her own bound feet tucked beneath her, and in the third, a slight but sturdy Zacchaeus, wearing a gray scholar's robe and with his long braided queue hanging down his back, climbs a persimmon tree for a glimpse of Yeh-Su, Jesus. A Chinese lantern of bright red silk—red is the color of happiness—hangs over my writing table, and a small carved chest made of camphor wood holds my woolen sweaters. My Chinese New Testament, its spine soft and its pages worn, sits on the table by my reading chair, with a strip of faded red paper, a calling card given to me long ago, marking my place. I still read the Scriptures in Chinese; I find I am more at home in it than I am in English, just as my Chinese name, Kung P'ei Te, given to me at the beginning

of this century, seems more a part of me than my legal name, Will Kiehn.

On my dresser is the photograph taken on our wedding day, November 4, 1908. Katherine and I were married at the American Consulate in Shanghai, and we are wearing Chinese clothes in the picture; our western clothes were too shabby for the occasion, and by then we had dressed in Chinese clothes for two years. Next to the photograph is my wife's diary, a thin volume I never read while she was alive but whose pages I now know by heart. Reading her sporadic entries is bittersweet, for while they bring our years together to life, they also show me my flaws and the ways in which I hurt her, unintentional though they were. But her pages make it seem that she is near, and if the price I pay for that closeness is regret it is a bargain still, albeit a painful one. I was her husband for over thirty-seven years, during which the longest we were apart was thirty-one days. She taught me the self-discipline I lacked, believed I was capable of far more than I did, and loved me as a young man as well as an old one. She was the one and only love of my life.

When I was twenty-one and on my way to China, I tried to envision my life there. I saw myself preaching to huge gatherings of people, baptizing eager new converts, working with my brothers in Christ to improve their lives. I did not

foresee the hardships and dangers that lay ahead: the loss of one so precious, the slow and painful deprivation of drought and famine, the continual peril of violence, the devastation of war, the threat to my own dear wife. Again and again we were saved by the people we had come to help and carried through by the Lord we had come to serve. I am amazed at His faithfulness; even now our lives there fill me with awe.

Last week when I was sitting in the small reading room of the retirement home in which I live, a man selling Fuller brushes visited. It was a hot day, and the man was invited in for a glass of water. He looked to be about fifty years old. There were several of us in the reading room, and as the salesman approached and awkwardly began to show us his great variety of brushes—nailbrushes, hairbrushes, toothbrushes, scrub brushes, whisk brooms—I heard his difficulty with English, and because he was oriental I asked if he spoke the standard language, Mandarin. He nodded and I began to speak in our shared tongue, and when he asked my Chinese name and I gave it, he stared at me in wonder.

"Mu shih," he said urgently, Mandarin for shepherd-teacher—pastor—"you baptized me and took me into church fellowship when I was a young man. I am your son."

I am retired now, and while at the age of eighty-one I know this is as it must be, it is strange not to be involved in active ministry; gone are the responsibilities that filled my life for so many years. I continue my work by praying for those who still serve, which I am able to do as my mind is sound. My physical health is also good; my nephew, John, a medical doctor, keeps careful watch over me, and I am well taken care of in these years, measured and monitored as never before. My niece, Madeleine, and my great-nieces and -nephews and their children also visit, and I am doted on by these younger generations.

I am also in the good company of many who have placed the Great Commission foremost in their lives. I live at Glenwood Manor, a home for retired missionaries in Claremont, California, a small town some thirty miles east of Los Angeles. With its parades on the Fourth of July and Homecoming Weekend, its parks, and its tidy downtown, Claremont is wholesome and wholly American. From my room I look out on a small vegetable garden that thrives despite my come-and-go attention. Beyond the garden are the city's eucalyptus-lined streets, and beyond them citrus groves and the foothills of the San Gabriel Mountains and Mount Baldy. Each morning I walk to Memorial Park and the Public Library, and afterward I answer letters and read a daily

Chinese newspaper and books to which I had no access during my years in China. Once a week I read a newspaper in German, the language of my parents and my childhood. At the start of the day when I read the Scriptures, I see truths I have never seen before, even after several decades of preaching the Gospel. And I dream of Chung-Kuo, the Middle Kingdom: China.

I am an ordinary man and an unlikely missionary. The talents I have been able to offer my Lord are small and few and far outnumbered by my faults. I am often slow in getting things done, and at times I exhibit a marked willingness to avoid work. I have never considered myself an intuitive person, and I am inexperienced in many of the ways of modern life. I have, for example, never learned how to drive—I gave up after twice failing the required test—and I know little about the world of finance. I am absentminded and I often misplace things, and while I struggle with pride, I am rarely angry. Nor am I greedy, for which I have my heritage to thank; I am the son and grandson of Mennonite farmers who came to America for religious freedom, and I was raised to aspire to a simple life of farming the land and following Christ. But despite my ordinariness and the smallness of my talents, I have led an extraordinary life. This is God's grace, His unearned favor.

When I was twelve years old, a missionary spoke at the small schoolhouse in Washita County, Oklahoma, where my three brothers and two sisters and I were taught weekdays for six months of the year. We spoke English at school, but at home and in church we still spoke the mother tongue, low German, though our parents had been in America for more than twenty years. German must be God's language, my uncle told me with great seriousness, because that's what the Bible was written in. He did not see the humor in this.

The missionary was from India and he said he was returning there the following month, which I found startling, for he was old and frail. He told our class that in foreign lands the need for those to share the Good News and to care for people's bodies and souls was great, and that a missionary could be a doctor in the mission field as long as he had a good strong brush and plenty of soap and water. "A missionary brings light to the darkness," he said. "We are called to go where there is little light, and where there are people in need of help."

It seemed he was speaking directly to me; my face grew hot and I felt a pull somewhere inside. At the end of class when the offering was taken, I gave all I had—the quarter I had earned for work on the farm, plus six pennies.

At that time, I had not yet been baptized. As Mennonites we believed that faith comes not as

an inheritance but as a personal decision; it is a gift freely offered and up to each individual to accept. My parents worked hard to help their children be ready to receive that gift; my mother knelt and prayed with us each morning, and in the evening my father read to us from Scripture. I was taught that faith should be apparent in every area of one's life, and I saw evidence of my parents' faith in their actions. They shared what they had with those who had less, they never turned a stranger away, and they showed me that loving our neighbor often meant feeding and clothing him, even if that involved less comfort for us. These things were as much a given in our home as taking your hat off when you were spoken to.

While faith was not my inheritance, it was my heritage. My German ancestors were people who lived apart from the world and much to themselves in Prussia, preferring not to unite with the state and its church. They wanted no part in government affairs and refused to take up firearms, for doing so would violate the commandment *Thou shalt not kill.* Czarina Catherine II of Russia, hearing that the community was skilled in building dikes, offered its members a deal: she would give them large tracts of virgin farmland in Polish Russia and the freedom to practice their beliefs, in return for which the people would improve the land.

Mennonites believe in the dignity of labor, and

they accepted Catherine's offer. Six thousand souls left Prussia for Polish Russia, where they built their own churches and schools and were exempted from military service. They were allowed to substitute an affirmation for an oath—swearing of any kind was forbidden by God—and they were allowed to bury their own dead. They began to work the swampland along the Vistula River, where they built dikes high enough to keep the river's overflow from the lowlands, eventually transforming vast expanses of swampland into thousands of acres of wheat. They continued to speak German and they thrived for many years.

Until 1873, when Alexander II, Catherine's great-grandson, revoked their special privileges, causing the community to look once more for a place where they would be free of the demands of an aristocratic government. The United States seemed to be the answer; its Constitution promised equal rights to all, and Congress had passed a bill that excused conscientious objectors from bearing arms. The community sent a delegation to America to spy out the land, and they returned with good news: fertile farmland could be had for very little, and the state of Kansas exempted Mennonites from military service. The Santa Fe railroad sent an agent to Russia to offer free transportation on a chartered steamer.

Thus in October of 1874, after selling their land for a fraction of its value, it was to America that everyone went. With their families and friends, my parents traveled by rail to Antwerp and from there to New York on the *Netherland*. The group settled in Kansas, but my parents soon found that their one-hundred-and-sixty-acre farm was too small to support a family of six. In 1885, the year I was born, they traveled to the western part of Oklahoma territory and leased a section of land that had never been cultivated.

Again and again, my ancestors said yes to God, and as I grew I saw those around me say yes as well. Over the months then years I watched one person after another in our community walk forward at Sunday services. At times I looked wistfully, even enviously, at the new church members and wished that I, too, could say the words, could produce the faith. But I could not; I was suspicious of God and was afraid that, if I said yes to Him, He would change me in ways I would not like and ask of me things I did not want to do. I thought of the visiting missionary, and of what I had felt as he spoke. What if God should ask me to leave home? That I could never do. So I tolerated the restlessness that dwelt in my heart and decided that faith could wait.

Which it did, for four years, until early one morning in late summer when I was in the fields. I was sixteen years old and farming was what I

loved. I knew how to prepare seedbeds, plow the fields, plant and tend our crops, and harvest wheat and fruit at the optimal time, and I felt a deep satisfaction in watching things grow. Our property was bound by a creek to the north and a line of dogwood trees to the south, with the Washita River running through the center of our land. To the south of the river we grew wheat and to the north was grassland for cattle, with orchards on either side. We harvested more grain and fruit than we could haul to market, and nearly everything on our table came from our farm: cheese and sausage, bread and eggs and jam, apples and peaches and corn.

That morning I fell to my knees behind the plow to pray before I began the day's work, just as I did every morning, for while I was unable to surrender myself to God, I was equally unable to turn my back on Him, and I could not discard my habit of cautious prayer. The day was already hot and the sun warmed my back as I knelt in the cool red dirt and thanked God for my life and asked Him to help me plow a straight line.

I was about to stand when something stopped me. It was the quiet, a deep calm that I did not want to leave or disturb. I stayed very still, and as I gazed out at the wide expanse of rich red earth, my mind and heart grew still as well. I felt a Presence that seemed to surround me and pursue me at the same time, a Presence that I

knew was God, and I had the sense that I was deeply loved and cared for. I had been told of this love since I was small, but on that morning it seemed to move from my head into my heart; knowledge became belief. As I remained kneeling in the red soil, it seemed that the gift of faith was being offered to me. I whispered, "Help me to believe," and a feeling of great relief came over me as I realized how I had been longing for enough faith to give myself over. From somewhere inside I felt a *yes,* and an unfamiliar peace replaced the restlessness in my soul.

Two weeks later, I gave my testimony at our meetinghouse. As I looked out at the congregation, my face grew hot and my voice trembled and I felt myself perspire, but I persevered. Four Sundays later, with our congregation gathered around me, I walked into the clear rushing water of the Washita River. As I knelt, our pastor cupped his hands behind my head and I lay back in the water and felt it rush over me. Then I was up, gasping and wet and cold, and I felt new.

When I finished school three years later, my father sent me to the Gemeinde Schule—community school—a small Bible academy established by the church in nearby Corn, Oklahoma. The younger members of our church community were trained to take on the work of

the older ones; my father hoped that when I finished at the academy I would attend the church's Bible College in Hutchinson, Kansas, then return home to become superintendent of our Sunday school.

But that is not what happened. On a Saturday afternoon in late summer of 1906, a few weeks before I was to leave for Kansas, we had a visitor. His name was Edward Geisler, and he and my father greeted each other with a holy kiss, the custom among members of our faith. He was nearly family, my father said; Edward had left Russia in the same group as our family, and he had given himself to God's service. He had traveled to China in 1901 with five other young volunteers as part of the South Chihli Mission, and a few years later he and his wife and another Mennonite, the first Mennonite missionaries in China, had formed the China Mennonite Missionary Society. Now he had come home from China's interior to seek an increase in support for their work and to take new recruits back with him to China. "Our friend is following the Great Commission," my father said. "'Go out to the whole world; proclaim the Gospel to all creation.'"

The next morning Edward spoke at our church. What God asked of us, he said, was nothing less than absolute surrender. "The Gospel tells us this clearly: 'Whosoever will save his life shall lose

it: and whosoever will lose his life for my sake shall find it.' The question we must ask ourselves is, What are we holding back? What is it that we will not give up?"

I felt found out, as thoroughly convicted as if Edward had addressed me by name. Something tightened in my center, a tense feeling that stayed with me the rest of the day, and at dinner that night I did not speak. My mother asked if I was ill and whether I wanted to leave the table. A part of me did, but I stayed where I was.

I was sitting next to Edward, who seemed to single me out from my siblings. He asked me kindly about school and farming and my baptism, and he said he could see that I loved God and that my faith would bless me all my life. I said no more than what was required, not because I disliked Edward but because I was so drawn to him. He was tall and thin and awkward and not handsome—*unexceptional, like me,* I thought—but when he spoke of China, I could not look away.

He talked of Keng-Tze Nien, the Boxer Year six years earlier when thousands of Chinese Christians and 186 missionaries and their children had been murdered for following Christ by members of the secret Society of Righteous Harmonious Fists. But Christ's message would not be stopped, Edward said; the people's needs were too immense. They suffered from ignorance

about hygiene and lack of medical care. Many infants died at birth, and fewer than half of those who lived survived to their first birthday. Mothers fed their children rat feces to cure them of stomach ailments, men applied the bile from the gallbladders of bears to heal their children's eyes, and opium addicts and beggars slept in the streets.

Yet Edward made no capital of what he had seen. "The suffering is great, as is the need for help, physical and spiritual." He paused, and his expression softened. "But the rewards are also great. The people are the kindest and most generous I have known. They are wise in many ways, and there is much to learn from them and to admire. They have the right to hear the Gospel."

Toward the end of the meal, Edward turned to me. "I return to China in a few weeks. My wife is there, caring for our children and carrying on our work. We need helpers, for the harvest is great, the laborers few. Why don't you come with me, Will? The Chinese language is difficult, but far easier when you are young. Perhaps this is your calling."

I saw my siblings trying to stifle their laughter. Of all our family, I was the least likely to leave. I wasn't good at speaking in front of people; I became nervous and I stammered. I was quiet and shy, I wasn't a good student, and I disliked being away from home.

"I'm needed here," I said, my voice cracking. "I haven't any training or gifts of that kind."

Edward said, "The Giver of those gifts may feel otherwise," and he looked at me, his blue eyes bright. "A torch's one qualification is that it be fitted to the master's hand. God's chosen are often not talented or wise or gifted as the world judges. Our Lord sees what is inside"—Edward touched his chest—"and that is why He calls whom He does." Then he turned to my father and they began to talk about wheat.

In the morning Edward left to visit other churches; he would return in a week. During those days I struggled, for while I felt pulled toward Edward's work, the idea seemed too foolish to even consider. I couldn't imagine leaving home; I suspected I was unfit for anything but farming, and I thought surely God would want me to remain where I had been planted. I decided I was being proud to think I might be remotely capable of meeting the challenges that must face a man like Edward every day, for in the few years that had passed since I joined the church, I did not feel I had made much progress spiritually. I yearned to walk more closely with God, and while I did experience moments of joy, they were often followed by days of despair. I told myself that surely God would not ask me to do work that was

so clearly beyond me, and I fervently prayed that China was not my calling.

The night before Edward was to return, I woke suddenly in the night. When I couldn't fall back to sleep, I crept out of bed and down the ladder that led from the attic bedroom I shared with my brothers. I sat down at the table my father had made from the elm trees that edged our land, and for a while I just listened to the nighttime sounds of our home—the even rhythm of my father's snoring in the next room, the soft rush of the wind outside, the neat ticking of the kitchen clock—sounds as familiar as my own heartbeat.

As I sat there, I suddenly knew I would go to China. The realization was as simple and definite as the *plunk* of a small stone in the deep well of my soul, and despite the fact that it would mean leaving what I loved most in the world, I felt not the sadness and dread I had expected but a sense of freedom and release. The tightness in me loosened like cut cord, and I was joyful.

The next morning I stood nervously in our kitchen, my hands gripping the rough wood that framed the door, as I waited to tell my father of my decision. I was worried about his reaction; I expected disappointment and anger and dreaded them equally. I had not disobeyed my parents since I was a small boy, and the thought that God might ask me to do so now made my heart clench.

I saw my father coming toward me from the chicken house. He had barely entered the yard before I hurried to meet him.

"I have something to tell you," I said. "I feel that God is calling me to serve Him in China. I know it makes no sense; I know I'm unqualified and I'm needed here and my decision must seem all wrong to you. But yes seems the only answer I can give."

I had braced myself for my father's objections, but none came. He stared at me without speaking for a long moment; then he put his arms around me and embraced me tightly. "Will," he said, "you have chosen the better part. How could I refuse you?"

Edward was to leave for Seattle from his family's home in French Creek near Hillsboro, Kansas, in two weeks. My parents went with me to the farewell meeting, which was held at the home of fellow Mennonites, where, with the friends and relatives who were able to join us, Edward, myself, and three other recruits sat outside at rough tables and benches under shade trees while Edward read Scripture and prayed for us and led us in the four-part singing of a few hymns. A few of the group gave their testimonies; then we shared a fellowship meal, and our families and friends wished us well.

At the end of the meeting, my mother took me aside. "Will, do you have money to travel?"

I felt instantly foolish and ashamed, for I hadn't even thought about money; I had somehow thought Edward would take care of it. Out of pride and embarrassment, I said, "I hadn't worked it out. Edward invited me. He'll pay the bills."

My mother shook her head. "Here," she said, and she took my hand and pressed a roll of bills into it, more money than I had ever seen. She smiled at my amazement. "It's my inheritance from my parents, two hundred dollars. Edward says it will cover the train to Seattle and the steamship across the ocean." She held me close for a moment. Then she said, "My sweet boy—I will miss you more than you know."

At the railway station, my parents and I stood together awkwardly. When it was time to board, my heart pounded and I suddenly wanted to change my mind; it seemed that doing something right shouldn't hurt so much. But the conductor called out and waved his small flag, and I knew I had to go.

I embraced my mother and father a last time. None of us could speak. I walked to the train and climbed aboard, then hurried back to the last car and watched my parents until I could no longer make them out in the distance; even my father waving his broad-brimmed felt hat was gone. I worked at committing this last sight of them to memory, so I could call it up at will, and I tried

to console myself with the idea that I would return in five years. But it did not ease the ache in my chest.

My mother had never sent me off anywhere without food, and this departure was no exception. Packed in a small basket were homemade sausage and biscuits, apples from our orchard, spice cake, and tea, all of which I shared with Edward and the three other recruits, whom I found intimidating, for at twenty-one I knew I was the youngest and least experienced. Jacob and Agnes Schmidt were a married couple who had met at the Salvation Army, and Ruth Ehren was a deaconess, which meant, Edward explained, that she had completed a two-year nurse's training program at an orphanage and hospital in Berne, Indiana, so that she could devote herself to the care of the poor and sick. The long black dress and black bonnet she wore signified her training and position. A fourth recruit, another deaconess, would join us in Seattle.

After three days on the train we reached Seattle, where we would spend our last night in America with friends of Edward's. At the railway station Edward asked me to stay with the luggage while he took the others to our hosts' home. While I was sitting on the trunks, a young woman passed by. She wore the same type of

black dress and bonnet that Ruth did, and when Edward returned for me, he brought this young woman with him and introduced her as Katherine Friesen, from the Deaconess Hospital in Cleveland. "She's also my wife's sister," Edward added, and I heard the pride in his voice. She smiled fondly at him but seemed to ignore me, which was fine by me, for I could not speak. Although slight, she was so sure of herself and so imposing in her black dress that I was in awe of her from the start.

October 3, 1906

I am far away from home tonight, the farthest I have ever been, sitting in the comfortable parlor in the home of strangers in a rainy city I do not know on the edge of this continent. Tomorrow at this time I will be even farther away, miles out to sea—I, Katherine Friesen, who have spent my life in the middle of this country with not so much as a glimpse of the ocean, will be in the middle of it! I have surprised myself this evening, for while I thought I would be anxious or afraid, I am neither. Although I love my family and will miss them, and although I have no idea what to expect of the days, weeks, and months ahead, here is my secret: I am happy. My heart beats strangely; I feel more like I am returning home than leaving it.

These giddy feelings seem wrong. Shouldn't a good daughter, a good sister, a good deaconess, be ambivalent about leaving home? But I'm not, which amazes me. I'm amazed that I've made it to Seattle, amazed at my good health, amazed that one obstacle after another concerning money and the details of the journey has been overcome. Here I am, sitting at this cherrywood table by a warm fire, "en route to the Far East," as our hosts put it; how glamorous it sounds!

The other recruits don't seem to share my high spirits; they already look homesick. The married couple appears to be aware only of each other; I haven't seen them more than two feet apart all evening. Young love, I suppose. Ruth Ehren, the other deaconess, is as somber as if our journey were a punishment. She's what people often envision when they hear the word *missionary*—a serious soul who travels to faraway lands to turn heathens into Westerners. I don't understand her; being morose seems like such a loss.

Then there is Will Kiehn, who strikes me as awkward and dreamy, but Edward certainly sees something in him; his strong encouragement is the reason Will is going to China. I can see that Edward loves this clumsy boy, for he already favors him every chance he gets; tonight at dinner he passed Will extra crescent

rolls (the boy seemed ravenous—I kept wanting to ask if anyone had been feeding him) and afterward he made sure Will wrote a letter to his parents. Edward says Will reminds him of his younger self, that when he talked to Will about China, Will's expression of wonder mirrored his own feelings when he was starting out. That's how I felt too when I began to sense the idea of China in my soul, a kind of irrational certainty that I would go, even though it made no sense. Edward says that when Will told him of his decision to go with him to China he felt a bounce of joy inside; he was certain he'd met a like-minded soul. This is high praise, for while my brother-in-law can be impetuous and unorthodox in his ways, he is as wise as he is kind, which makes me believe there must be more to this Will than I see. Perhaps he isn't as bothersome as he seems.

Edward's excitement is a dramatic contrast to the somber mood of the others. His eyes are bright as he talks of leaving in the morning, and I see the energy in his step and his movements, as though this tidy home in which we are guests constrains him. Of course he really is returning home—to Naomi and the boys and the new baby, all of whom I'm eager to see—so there is reason for his joy. But I think it is more than a homecoming. He is excited about the work.

As am I. I have no idea what this life will be like, nor can I guess whether I'll be gone for five years or fifty. I know only that I am happy—in my heart and mind and soul and even my body, which feels strong and sturdy and healthy. I'm weary too, but I don't mind the fatigue; I am on my way to China, and that is enough.

Early the next morning we left for the Seattle docks and for the S.S. *Minnesota*, which was to depart shortly before noon. Edward settled us on board then went to secondhand stores to purchase a few last supplies he knew he couldn't get in China. Noon came and he hadn't returned, a problem because he had the tickets. The whistle blew once, then a second time, and finally Edward came charging up the gangplank, awkwardly carrying a load of folding chairs he'd bought at what he excitedly said was a most reasonable price.

The thick ropes tethering the ship to the dock were untied and we were under way. I stayed on deck, and in my mind I said goodbye to my family once again as I watched Seattle and America recede.

Edward joined me, and for a while we were silent. Then he said, "Perhaps it's time to learn your first Mandarin phrase."

I was immediately anxious; I did not feel at all up to tackling a new language. But when he

spoke again, I was so drawn to the sound of what he said that I couldn't help asking its meaning.

He smiled and repeated it. *"Tsaichien mei-kuo,"* he said. "*Tsaichien* is goodbye, *mei* is beautiful, *kuo* is country. That's the name for America: Beautiful Country."

I tried to repeat it. Then I asked him the word for China.

"Chung-Kuo," he said. "It means Middle Kingdom, because of the people's ancient belief that their country was at the center of a vast square earth, surrounded by the Four Seas, beyond which lay islands inhabited by barbarians. That's us." Edward turned and faced the front of the ship, and the expanse of ocean spread before us, so that America was behind us. "The strange part," he said softly, "is that after you've been there for a while, it truly does feel like the center of the world. It becomes a place you never want to leave."

I nodded, willing to be convinced. For at that moment, despite the homesickness that had accompanied me like a stowaway since I'd left home, I had a dim hope that, given time, I might come to feel the same.

The Journey Inland

1906

We were at sea for thirty-one days, most of which we spent in dank, unfurnished, third-class cabins that had been recently painted with inferior green paint and still smelled strongly of the stuff. As our rooms were in the ship's hold we felt its every move, an experience that took some getting used to for people who had never before been at sea, much less crossed an ocean. Once a day we met to pray and sing a few hymns, but none of us spoke more than necessary. We were always cold, and the sea's roughness sent our belongings sliding back and forth across the floor so much that we gave up putting them back.

We all felt ill, but Katherine seemed to fare the worst. When I mentioned this to Edward, he said she had had health problems from childhood and suffered from headaches the doctors could neither diagnose nor cure. But Katherine's belief that God had called her to serve in China did not waver, even as the intensity of her headaches increased. "She may be weak physically," he said, and I heard the affection in his voice, "but it does not hinder her devotion. She has made it her ambition to please God and believes that, if

she dedicates herself to Him fully, He will take care of her."

During the day I sat in my small airless cabin and worked at learning Chinese. In the written language, each character had as its origin a picture, with simple characters combined to convey more complex meanings. The character for *wife* was a woman with a broom, *good* was a woman and child, *prisoner* was a man in a box, *worship* was a man kneeling. The written language was the same throughout China, but the spoken language varied dramatically by region and was much more difficult. The dialect I was learning was *kuan-hua*, or Mandarin, called the standard language and spoken north of the Yangtze River. It used four tones; some dialects had as many as seven. The first tone was even and flat, the second slightly rising like a question, the third falling and rising, and the fourth falling. A character's tone changed what it meant, so the same word could have four entirely different meanings, depending on its tone. *Ma* could mean *mother, horse, scold,* or *hemp,* each represented by a different character.

Each day I studied three hours in the morning and three hours in the afternoon. I loved the language from the start, and my only complaint was that I could not learn it faster; I wanted to master its strokes and tones and unfamiliar sounds immediately. I had never been much of a

student before, but I became one on that voyage. Immersing myself in this strange new language quickly became my solace.

We reached Shanghai on November third and spent our first two hours on Chinese soil following Edward through the tedious chaos of customs. When we emerged, grimy and fatigued, we found ourselves on a wide boulevard crowded with harried pedestrians and rickshaws. Edward hired rickshaws to take us to Schaftsberry House, an inexpensive boarding house used frequently by missionaries, and when he had settled us there he brought us Chinese clothes to wear. Six years had passed since the Boxer trouble, but there was still hostility toward foreigners; recently in Nanchang a woman medical missionary who had not adopted Chinese dress had been surrounded by a mob and forced to take refuge in a patient's home. The next morning, Katherine, Ruth, and Agnes put on long loose padded cotton jackets over their dresses, and the men dressed like poor schoolteachers: Chinese trousers, long gray padded gowns, and cotton shoes with thick felt soles.

After breakfast we boarded a Chinese junk that would take us fifty miles west on Soochow Creek, and that night we slept crammed together on the center deck of the junk, our luggage

stacked around us and beneath us and a mat of oiled bamboo above us. The next evening we reached Yun Liang Ho, the Grand Canal, which stretched from Tientsin in the north to Hangchow in the south, linking the country's two largest rivers, the Yangtze and the Yellow River, and many smaller canals. There Edward hired a houseboat to carry us one hundred miles north to the city of Yung Nien Ch'eng—City in Pursuit of Happiness—in Shantung province.

The houseboat would be our home for the next few weeks. Sixty feet long and fifteen feet wide, it had a flat bottom and an unpainted hull made of heavy timber finished with tung oil. It sat low in the water, its deck only four feet above the water's surface, with the mast behind the cockpit, where the crew cooked their meals. The six boatmen would eat and sleep on the deck of the wide prow, while the captain, Wen Yeh, and his fifteen-year-old son, Liang, shared the rear of the boat. In the middle were the two small rooms that made up the passenger quarters. Katherine, Agnes, and Ruth shared one room, and Edward, Jacob, and I the other. There was also a small common area with a table and chairs and a makeshift stove made from a square kerosene tin, where Edward would prepare our meals.

Edward supplied blankets and thick cotton quilts for our mattresses, and as we settled into our temporary home I eyed my surroundings

with suspicion, for even with our luggage stowed in the hold beneath the floorboards, the provisions we had brought were everywhere: sacks of potatoes and rice, boxes of wood and charcoal, crates of medical supplies, the chairs Edward had bought in Seattle. I had always been clumsy and was certain I would trip over everything.

We slept on board that night and were awakened early the next morning by a great deal of shouting and running and what sounded like the squawking of a rooster. When we came on deck we found Wen Yeh standing at the front of the boat holding a cock he had just killed, sprinkling its blood on the prow as a way to appease the spirits and ensure a safe voyage. Edward told him that our God was watching over us and that it was unnecessary to appease any spirits, but Wen Yeh was unconvinced. The canal was a dangerous place, he said, plagued by evil spirits and bandits, and threatening for the more immediate reason that none of the boatmen could swim.

The morning was cold and breezy; the crew hoisted the sail and began to row, singing to the wind. Because there was no way to heat the cabins, being inside wasn't much warmer than being outside, so after a breakfast of rice porridge and tea, I sat in the open prow of the boat, studying and looking out at my strange new

surroundings. Most of the other boats on the canal were long narrow sampans, which were made of three planks, and *wupans*, made of five planks, all of them with bamboo roofs over their middle sections. Large eyes were painted on both sides of their bows, for it was believed that, without eyes, boats could not see ahead. Children ran and played on their decks; laundry hung from the awnings. There were also other houseboats, like ours, and junks with square white sails and hulls of red and blue and orange.

On the canal embankment, mules loaded down with large wicker baskets full of vegetables plodded to the nearest market town. Men balanced huge baskets hung from carrying poles stretched across their shoulders, and women walked with swaddled babies strapped on their backs. Beyond the embankment were fields of winter wheat broken up by clusters of earthen houses with black tile roofs.

When his father didn't need him, Liang sat with me and helped me with my vocabulary. I would point to something and ask what it was—*Na shih shen-mo?*—and Liang would give its Chinese name: sky, water, land, foot, hand, head, eye, mouth, rice. At the end of the day, our houseboat and the other boats on the canal anchored for the evening, for no one traveled at night. The boatmen lowered the sail and three of them crossed the wide plank of wood that

stretched to the embankment and pulled the boat toward them with bamboo ropes. In the prow of the boat, Wen Yeh beat a huge brass gong to frighten away evil spirits for the night, for they were said to be afraid of noise.

November 11, 1906

Today is my birthday—I am twenty-two years old—a fact I've kept secret because I don't want a fuss. We are traveling north on the Grand Canal and everything feels wet: my clothes, shoes, bedding, books, hair, skin. I haven't seen the sun since we left Shanghai, and I sleep on a bed of folded mildewed quilts.

None of this bothers me. It's my impatience that nags at me, for I long to be useful. I've been of some assistance to Ruth Ehren, whom I misjudged. She's not morose; she's in pain, suffering from an abscessed tooth, for which I've given her hot compresses. But I can't help the people here until I know at least some of the language, so that is my task for now: learning to unlock this daunting secret code. I spend much of my time bent over C. W. Mateer's *Kuan hua lei pien*—Mandarin lessons—but my advancement is slow. Edward said as much this morning. "Some find the language easier than others," was his comment as he looked over my exercises. True enough: after studying the language for more than a month, I can do

what the others could after only two weeks: write thirty characters, read sixty, and say a few words and sentences and be (mostly) understood. My astigmatism hinders my reading and is partly to blame for my frustration; the characters swim like ink stains and my eyes ache from the unfamiliar strain of reading up and down. To relieve my eyestrain Edward has suggested that for now I concentrate more on the spoken language than on the written. I like this advice—how wise people seem when they give us the counsel we want! I consider it permission to eavesdrop on the boatmen whenever I have the chance, and when I understand even a word or two, I am elated.

When there is a little wind, the boat moves slowly up the canal and our journey is pleasant enough. But when the air is still, the men do the work and pull the boat themselves. All six of them—everyone except Wen Yeh and his son—cross to the embankment and put on harnesses that are attached to the boat with ropes made of hundreds of feet of braided bamboo, bamboo because it's not absorbent and doesn't become heavy when wet. Then, their harnesses in place, the boatmen begin trudging up the embankment, pulling the boat behind them, sometimes so far ahead of us that we lose sight of them, as Wen Yeh steers

and Liang pushes the boat away from the shore with an iron-tipped pole.

The boatmen's labor is excruciating to watch. The burden of pulling the boat makes them stoop over so low that their hands brush the ground as they walk. Their slow chant is a moan, and they work without stopping for rest or food; in the waist of their trousers they keep hunks of dark bread that they chew on throughout the afternoon, not stopping until evening, when they tie up the boat.

Seeing this yesterday was shocking. After breakfast Edward told us to leave the boat and cross to the embankment, why we didn't know—until the boatmen began their exhausting work and we understood that we'd disembarked to lighten their load. I hated the sight of the men so burdened and did not see how we could travel this way in good conscience, but when I caught up with Edward on the towpath and asked if there wasn't a more humane way to travel, he looked at me sharply. "You've been in China for less than a week and you're already overhauling the economy and modes of transportation?" My expression must have registered the sting of his words, for he softened. "Katherine, there are practices in this country that you will dislike, I assure you. But some of these we must accept as they are. We are here to offer

the people the gift of faith, not remake their way of life, even when the change seems necessary and right. It's a question of choosing your battles. Remember that we're guests, and uninvited ones at that." He watched the trackers ahead of us for a moment. "We do what we can. Today that means getting off the boat and walking."

As it turns out, watching the trackers pull the boat is not the worst part of it; that comes at the end of the day when we reboard the boat and I see the toll the work takes on them. Their feet are raw from the rocks on the towpath and their hands are chapped and blistered. If they wash, they do so in the dirty canal water and then dry themselves on their cotton trousers, which are understandably filthy; it's as though their hands and feet become infected right before my eyes. They limp when they walk, their eyes are red and irritated from what I am certain is trachoma, and they have terrible hacking coughs from who knows what.

As the boat's captain does not acknowledge me, I asked Edward to see if I may help his men, but Wen Yeh refuses. I also asked Edward why Wen Yeh did not use younger men for such hard physical labor; I guessed the boatmen to be forty years old or more. Edward laughed grimly. "Subtract twenty," he said. I said, "Excuse me?" and he nodded toward the

boatmen. "The hardness of these people's lives makes them look far older than they are. That's my rule of thumb for guessing someone's age here: subtract twenty years from how old they look."

When we had been traveling for eight days, Wen Yeh told Edward that there were rumors of bandits along the part of the canal we were approaching, and that we needed someone to keep watch at night while the captain and the other boatmen slept. Edward asked me to do this, which I took as a compliment and evidence of the high esteem in which he held me until I overheard him speaking to Jacob. "Will's going to keep watch," he said, and I felt a warm surge of pride. "He's the youngest—he can spare a night's sleep better than we can," he added, and they laughed.

That night after dinner I took my place at the boat's helm, wrapped in my wool blanket and wearing socks as mittens. The water lapped the sides of the boat and I heard the boatmen talking on the prow; later I heard them snoring. The air was wet and heavy and the trees along the embankment were menacing in the darkness. Alone in the night, listening and watching for what or whom I did not know and worrying over what I would do if we came upon them or they upon us, I began to question my call. I felt I had

been foolish and proud to have thought I was meant for the mission field; staying home with my family and working in the church I had grown up in seemed the choice I should have made. My doubts led to regret and worry, and I was soon miserable. The only sort of prayer was one of anger: *I knew I wasn't right for this. Why did You bring me here?*

My complaining eventually led to an uneasy sleep, and I awoke when the night sky had its first wash of gray. I was miserable; my anger was gone, replaced by a sick feeling of shame at my untrustworthiness. I had just enough time to try to look like someone who had been awake all night before the boatmen awoke and got to work.

Later that day Edward asked me to accompany him to the nearest market. He was our cook, preparing simple meals that usually consisted of boiled potatoes with a few vegetables and sometimes a little fried pork or boiled fish. Every few days he disembarked and bought fresh fruits and vegetables, which he then boiled and peeled thoroughly, for the only fertilizer used was night soil—human waste—and parasites and amoebic dysentery were common.

I accepted his invitation eagerly, for I was keen to see as much of this new country as I could. In the area of China we were passing through, the population was so dense that we were never far from a village or town, and therefore a market.

Towns usually held markets every five days, and each town was known by the days of the lunar month on which its markets were held. A town that had its market on the first day would then have it five days later, on the sixth, and again on the eleventh, and so on, and was called a One-Six town. A town with a market on the second day and the seventh was a Two-Seven town, and so on. The people were accustomed to walking long distances to buy their food, so nearly every village had a market within reach every day of the month.

As Edward and I began making our way through the village's crowded streets, I had to work to stay with him, for the sights and sounds were nearly overwhelming. Men loaded down with firewood and huge bamboo baskets of vegetables labored under their heavy burdens while food vendors sold roasted chestnuts and boiled noodles. The stalls were filled with more goods than I'd ever seen in one place before—eggs and fruits and vegetables, steamed bread, chickens and pieces of meat hanging from hooks, black cloth shoes and skullcaps, medicinal roots and iron kettles. Many of the villagers had never seen a foreigner before, and as we passed they stopped and stared and pointed at us, *yang-kuei-tze*, the foreign devils.

Edward bought what we would need for the next few days, and we started back to the

houseboat. A group from the market followed us out of the village and as we made our way through the fields more people joined them, so that by the time we reached the canal several dozen people were following us. I saw from Edward's expression that he was uneasy, and when we reached the boat Wen Yeh was pacing on the deck; the next village on the canal was known to be a bandit stronghold, and he wanted to get a safe distance past it before dark. But when Wen Yeh caught sight of the crowd, his expression changed from impatience to alarm. He motioned for us to hurry across the plank and called to Liang, who was standing on the embankment waiting to untie the boat, to come on board.

A few men started yelling and others joined in. As I was crossing the wooden plank, Edward was in front of me and Liang was behind me. Someone threw a rock, which hit the plank near my feet with a loud thud, startling me and making me jump. I ran the last few feet across the plank, and as I stepped onto the boat I heard Liang stumble behind me, and I realized that my running must have caused him to lose his balance. I heard him cry out, and when I turned I saw he'd fallen into the canal.

Liang couldn't swim; none of the boatmen could. I pulled off my Chinese gown, jumped into the water, and began to move toward him;

though he was only a few yards away, he was sinking. When I reached him I grasped his thick black hair and pulled his head to the surface, then grabbed hold of him with one arm and looked around for help. There were men in small boats nearby, but none moved toward us. Struggling, I pulled Liang back toward the houseboat as he fought against me in his panic. When we reached the plank I felt rocks below my feet, where Liang had landed in the water. Edward leaned down and grabbed my hand, and I pulled Liang closer, and lifted him partly out of the water for Edward to haul him up.

I leaned against the wooden plank, my chest heaving as I tried to catch my breath. I looked to my left and found that the group that had followed us was still there, watching, only now they no longer looked hostile; they were laughing. I had no idea what had amused them; it was as if I were in a play I didn't understand. I hoisted myself out of the water and onto the plank and went aboard the boat. The boatmen quickly pulled up the plank and Wen Yeh poled away from the embankment.

Liang was sitting on the deck of the prow, coughing and trying to catch his breath. Katherine knelt at his feet, and I saw a bright red gash on his ankle. I went below to shed my wet clothes, frantic to get warm. My hands trembled so badly that undressing and dressing seemed to

take hours, and as I worked at peeling my wet clothes off and pulling the dry clothes on, I asked myself angrily what had possessed me to come to this place. *Pride,* I thought ruefully; *you have too high an opinion of yourself.* But there was nothing to be done about that just then, and aside from being plucked from that boat and that continent, I had only one goal: to get warm. I put on nearly every piece of dry clothing I owned, then pulled the rough wool blanket from my cotton mattress and wrapped it tightly around me. Because I thought I was responsible for Liang's fall and I was certain I would be greeted with anger and blame, my second goal was to not have to see anyone for the rest of the night. But I was weak from hunger and desperate for something to eat, so I took a deep breath and went up to the deck, still clutching the blanket.

The sun had set. After making it a little farther up the canal, Wen Yeh had steered the boat to the embankment and the boatmen were tying up for the night. The air was knife-cold; in the darkening sky, handfuls of bright stars seemed to have been flung around a white shaving of moon. When I stepped onto the deck, Wen Yeh approached me and I readied myself for his anger. But instead he stood before me in silence, then knelt and bowed low, resting his head on the deck, and I heard the sound of weeping. I did not move; I had no idea what to do. Finally he began

speaking in hushed Mandarin. When he finished, I looked at Edward, waiting for him to translate.

"He says Liang is yours now," Edward said. "These people believe that if you save someone's life, that person belongs to you, and you must take care of him the rest of his life. That's why no one else tried to help—partly because they couldn't swim but also because no one wanted another mouth to feed. They thought you were foolish to save him."

For a moment, I could only stare at Edward; nothing made sense. "But I didn't do anything."

Edward nodded toward Wen Yeh. "To him you did. He's certain that he's lost his son."

"I would never take his son from him."

Edward nodded at Wen Yeh. "Tell him that."

I took a deep breath. "Wen Yeh," I said, "please get up. You owe me nothing."

Edward translated, and Wen Yeh raised his head and met my eyes. Then he slowly stood, still bowing as he did so, and embraced me.

Liang was sitting on the deck drinking tea, a white bandage on his ankle. He too hugged a blanket tightly around him, and when he saw me he laughed weakly and pointed, first at me, then at himself.

I sat down next to him and touched the white dressing on his leg. *"Na shih shen-mo?"* What is that?

"Peng-tai." Bandage; I repeated it. Then Liang

hesitantly touched my shoulder and said, *"P'eng-yu."* Friend.

I nodded. Then I touched Liang's chest and said, *"Hsiung-ti"*—younger brother—and he beamed.

November 15, 1906

Our ninth day on the canal. A bad day turned good.

This afternoon Liang fell into the canal while following Will across the gangplank. While struggling in the water the boy cut his ankle on the rocks, but good came from it: the gash was painful enough that he allowed me to dress it. Which I did, as gently as possible, talking to him all the while (mostly in English—I didn't want to risk offending him in my piecemeal, unpredictable Mandarin), hoping to keep his mind off what I was doing and allay his fear of me. Almost before he knew it, I had stitched the cut and bandaged his ankle.

The other boatmen watched us suspiciously from a few feet away. A few minutes later when Liang was good as new they were impressed, and finally one of them was brave enough to come forward. He bowed to me, then timidly pointed to his knee, and I saw that he too had a deep cut, dirty and infected.

I told the man to be seated next to me, and I cleaned the cut then stitched and bandaged it

as I had Liang's ankle, once again rattling on in English to distract him from what I was doing. My strategy worked a second time, and when I had finished he turned to his companions and pointed to the wide bandage on his knee. As they marveled at him, he nodded matter-of-factly, pleased with himself, and that did the trick: the men lined up, eager to show me their various injuries and to list their complaints. Despite the fact that I understood little of what they actually said, we were able to communicate enough for me to treat their cuts and boils and blisters and mouth sores and eye infections. As I did, they became less hostile and afraid; they began to laugh as we worked to understand each other, and they thanked me when I had finished. They didn't need to, though, for their gratitude was plain.

I too was grateful—to God for this good turn of events, to the boatmen for their trust, and to Will, who held the lamp above me and did anything else I asked of him. He didn't complain once—not of the cold or the late hour or the dreariness of the night, and his poor arm must have been frozen stiff from holding the lantern for so long. But he said nothing, and in doing so he endeared himself to me, at least a little.

Which is a good thing, for I was angry with

him. Last night I couldn't sleep and I made my way quietly up to the deck, hoping that some fresh air would calm me. The air in our cabin is so thick that it's hard to take a deep breath. Everything was very still, and in the moon's soft light I saw Will sitting alone, keeping watch as Edward had asked him to. But then I heard a sound I know only too well from my cabin mates below, the ruffled sound of snoring, and I saw that Will was fast asleep. I was immediately irate—he was supposed to be watching over us, keeping us safe! I wanted to wake Edward and expose Will's failure. My quick temper surprised me, and I just stood there for a moment, watching him. In that dim light he looked so young that my feelings eased, and the night was so peaceful that I thought perhaps the threat of danger had been exaggerated. I decided there was no reason to cause a fuss then and there—it could wait until morning—so I went back to bed.

This morning Will looked miserable. He kept to himself at breakfast, and when Edward asked him how his night was, he shrugged without looking up. Edward stared at him strangely, and I saw that Will was about to confess. But just then he happened to glance at me, and when I saw the sadness and remorse in his face my desire to accuse him left me.

"His night must have been just fine," I said. "We're here, aren't we?" and somehow the moment passed.

Tonight he proved himself, so I am giving him another chance. I'll at least be kinder to him. I'm feeling kind toward everyone this evening, despite my fatigue and the lack of supplies, light, and warmth. For the first time since leaving home I was useful. And I am content.

The boatmen decided Katherine was a healer, and that night became a routine. Each evening after dinner she sat on a wooden crate near the cockpit, where a few hot coals burned in a brazier, as the boatmen gathered around her, intently watching everything she did and asking questions of one another about their complaints and her cures. Her face looked wan and the circles under her eyes grew darker and her teeth chattered as she spoke, but she never admitted to being tired or cold. Night after night I observed her gentle touch, her kind tone, her careful ministrations. While everything else gave off the pungent, metallic smell of kerosene and canal water, Katherine always smelled like soap. As she worked, I saw the gratitude in the boatmen's expressions, and although their complaints seemed to grow increasingly minor, I could not blame them, for I found myself searching for an ailment of my own.

After three weeks' travel on the canal, we reached Yung Nien Ch'eng in Shantung province. While the boatmen unloaded our goods from the hold, Edward hired two-wheeled carts pulled by mules to carry us and our freight 135 *li*, or 45 miles, to his family's home in Ch'eng An Fu—City of Perfect Peace—on the border of Shantung and Honan provinces, an overland journey that would take two days.

Because the land was flat, I thought traveling by cart would be easy. Not so; the issue wasn't the topography but the roads. While ancient and frequently traveled highways connected major cities, smaller cities and villages were linked only haphazardly. These country roads were nothing more than the legacy of earlier travelers, paths cut randomly through this field and that, rarely in anything resembling a straight line. If the roads weren't muddy, a mule-drawn cart could travel twenty-five miles in a day, but reaching somewhere relatively nearby could take hours or most of a day, simply because the roads wound around so much. In winter and spring they were thick with dust, and during the summer rains they became muddy to the point of being unusable, often becoming rivers, as many of them were lower than the surrounding fields. The springless carts that traveled these roads were flatbeds on two wooden wheels—huge round pieces of wood weighing nearly two

hundred pounds each. The carts screeched horribly as they were pulled; there was no money for axle grease. Padding the floor with bedding made the ride bearable but not comfortable.

On our first day we traveled to Shin Sheng Chou—City of New Future—the home of John and Anna Leicht, fellow Mennonite missionaries. Jacob and Agnes Schmidt and Ruth Ehren were to remain with the Leichts to help them with their work; Edward, Katherine, and I would stay for the night then travel the last twenty miles to Edward's home in Ch'eng An Fu the next day. When we reached the Leichts' home we found a somber household; the couple's only daughter was ill due to an enlarged spleen. After hearing that we would be staying in the home of missionaries I had hoped for a real bed, so when we were shown into a large room with a pile of millet straw I felt a sharp stab of disappointment, followed by shame at my selfish concern.

The next morning we did what we could to help the Leichts. Jacob made the fire and I brought in more firewood than they would need for a week, while Agnes cooked breakfast and Ruth and Katherine examined the sick girl and bathed her. When we said our goodbyes, Edward assured them that he would visit within the month, then he and Katherine and I set off on the last leg of our journey.

As we traveled across the countryside, Edward grew more and more excited. By then he had been away from his wife and two sons for over a year, and there was a new daughter he had never seen. When his home was at last in sight, he jumped down from the cart and ran the rest of the way. Eager for our journey to be over, I got out too and walked next to the cart. When we were still a good distance away from the Geislers' home, Edward's wife, Naomi, ran from the house and to him. When they met, they held each other closely, and as I watched I felt a cloud of envy at what they had.

Dinner that night was a celebration, for tomorrow was Thanksgiving, a fact I'd forgotten until Naomi reminded us. We gathered around the Geislers' kitchen table—Katherine and myself, Edward and his two young sons, Paul and John, and Naomi, holding their one-year-old daughter, Madeleine. Naomi loaded my plate with pork and vegetables and Chinese steamed bread then began cutting my meat, as I looked on awkwardly, unsure about what to do. In a moment, she caught herself. "Oh," she said, and she laughed, "look at me! I am so used to having children on either side. Forgive me, Will."

I nodded. Edward and Katherine laughed, and I felt my face grow hot. But for a moment it felt like home, and Edward, sitting across the table next to Katherine, winked at me. "Consider it a

compliment," he said, and he nodded at his wife. "She sees you as family."

I felt myself grow redder still, and when I looked up, I found Katherine smiling at me. I returned her smile and felt a sudden and unexpected contentment. My homesickness had eased; it seemed I had fallen in with family.

November 27, 1906

We've reached Edward and Naomi's home, and I am elated to meet my handsome young nephews, Paul and John, and my beautiful baby niece, Madeleine. But most of all I'm excited to see my most sisterish sister. I loved sitting across from her at dinner tonight, and afterward when we were alone she made me laugh until I couldn't speak. She has always been the funny one, I the serious one. "Katherine, who's *this?*" she said, and as she walked across the room, I suddenly saw our father trudging to the barn in the morning, pulling his suspenders up as he walked, his short legs bowed outward. "And this?" she asked, and there was Mother, standing at the stove and methodically stirring a pot with her huge wooden spoon, her eyes wide and her lips pursed as she hummed a hymn, her right foot tapping in time. Naomi continued through our family, one sibling after the next, until I was laughing and crying both. Finally she sat

down on the bed next to me and propped her chin on her hand and gazed at me dreamily. “Who’s this?” she asked, barely containing herself. I was stumped, but not for long; she couldn’t hold herself back. “Will Kiehn!” she said jubilantly. “Our smitten new recruit!”

The two of us were in my room during all of this—*my room*. I say it over and over again, for I have never had a room of my own, and it feels like a great luxury. To be able to close a door and be alone! When Naomi and I finally whispered good night—the others were long asleep—I shut the door and knelt.

There is much to thank Him for: a safe voyage across the ocean, a safe journey up the canal, a safe trip inland. A reunion with Naomi, and becoming acquainted with my nephews and niece. I am grateful for these blessings and many others, but I am also troubled, for when I fell to my knees in this small room it was as much from fatigue as from gratitude; I am exhausted. I felt so strong at the start I thought I was finally rid of the weakness I’ve grown up with. But to my disappointment it has accompanied me.

At dinner I saw that I am not alone in feeling tired, for while I can see she is happy, Naomi looks fifteen years my elder instead of five. The sweet softness of her features that made her look like a girl even at twenty is gone; her

face is now thin and angular. I remembered Edward's words about the hardness of people's lives here and thought, *Add ten,* for in the five years since I saw my sister she has aged twice that and now looks ten years older than she is. I can't help but wonder if I am seeing my own future.

But perhaps I'm just chasing my tail; perhaps my being tired is making me worry about being tired. I've been taught since I was small to be grateful in all things and for all things, so despite my feelings I give thanks for this night and this place and for what lies ahead.

Ch'eng An Fu

1907–1908

Both my new home of Ch'eng An Fu and my future home of Kuang P'ing Ch'eng were in the North China Plain, a region that was, strangely enough, geographically similar to Oklahoma: miles of flatness with no mountains to break the horizon, just acres of good farmland well suited to millet and wheat. The plain was bounded to the north by the Great Wall and the hills leading to Mongolia, to the east by the Yellow Sea and the mountains of Shantung, and to the west by the mountains of Shansi. To the southeast there was not such a definite border; it eased gradually into the valley of the Hwang Ho, or Yellow River, and the Yangtze Plain.

The place was also similar to Oklahoma in terms of weather; it too had a climate of extremes. Winter days could be bitterly cold, with the temperature dropping well below zero and the Yellow River frozen for months. In spring the wind covered the plain with sand from the Loess Plateau to the north and the Gobi Desert to the west, sometimes burying whole cities. A sandstorm in Ch'eng An Fu once turned day into night and made everything we touched gritty in the space of an hour, even with the doors

and windows tightly shut. Summers were fiercely hot—110 degrees Fahrenheit is the highest temperature I remember—and late summer brought torrents of heavy rain that made the Yellow River overflow its banks. Autumn was the reward, long and beautiful.

A view of the plain from a small rise was one of green tilled fields punctuated with pagodas and ancestral grave mounds, yellow dried-up riverbeds, and villages of flat gray roofs. Homes faced south because north was believed to be the side of darkness and for protection from the northwest wind. They were built on mounds of earth five to ten feet above the ground because of flooding, a continual threat. A boat sitting on dry ground miles from any river in November might be adrift in a field of water by the following August, as farmers struggled to salvage what they could of their underwater crops.

The plain was ancient; most of the country's oldest capitals had been located there, and it was the birthplace and burial place of Confucius and Mencius. Most of the people were farmers as their ancestors had been, and intensely connected to the earth. Rather than the land belonging to them, they seemed to belong to it, and they tended the fertile brown soil unceasingly, growing winter wheat, millet, cotton, and *kaoliang*—sorghum—working for three harvests in two years. A good harvest meant three meals a

day; anything less meant deprivation. Meals were simple: vegetables with boiled millet, bean curd, steamed bread, or noodles made of wheat. Meat was the exception and rice an extravagance, unlike in the south, where it was a staple.

The region was so densely populated that the next city, village, or town was nearly always in sight. A village could be a dozen homes, a town one or two hundred households and a dozen or more shops. These estimates are my own; the people had no interest in statistics, and, when asked how big a town or city was, the answer was usually along the lines of "not a few." Most cities were surrounded by walls, archaic brick structures with odd curves and angles meant to bring good luck or discourage bad luck, and four arched gates corresponding roughly to the points of the compass.

I came to know the region well during my first few months in Ch'eng An Fu, as Edward asked me to do many errands for him. I went twice to Shanghai to accompany new missionaries back to Ch'eng An Fu, escorted three children to a school for the blind in Peking, delivered a farm wagon that Edward was loaning to a Presbyterian mission in Tsinan, and accompanied him on many of his trips to nearby villages.

When I wasn't traveling, I continued my study of the language with Katherine and our tutor,

which I was eager to do for several reasons, among them the fact that I knew I wasn't of much value until I could speak and understand Mandarin. Our teacher was Li Lao Shih, an elderly gentleman who wore the usual attire of a scholar: a long gray robe slit at the sides, white trousers tight at the ankles, a short black satin jacket, and a black skullcap. The first time we met I greeted him with respect, telling him in Mandarin that I was happy to have come to Ch'eng An Fu and to be able to meet such an honorable teacher, and that I wanted to become a Ch'eng An Fu person. He nodded, unable to hide his amusement at my pronunciation, and replied that he was unworthy of such earnestness in a student.

Li Lao Shih came to the compound each afternoon at one o'clock and worked with us for the next four hours, our primers and dictionaries spread out around us, and when he left I continued studying alone until dinner and afterward. Despite Edward's assurance that I was progressing well, the language seemed to mock me, which was all the more humiliating as Katherine was often witness to my mistakes.

When I voiced my frustration, Li Lao Shih quietly reminded me that the function of study was to build character. At the close of one particularly difficult lesson, he called Naomi. Pulling the long hair on his chin, he spoke to her

softly in Mandarin then asked her to translate, as he spoke little English. Naomi turned to me.

"Your teacher says that the Chinese language has always been this way. It is this way now and it will continue this way. It will be here far longer than you." She added, "I believe he is suggesting that it is for you to adapt yourself to China, not the other way around."

January 26, 1907

I have been in Ch'eng An Fu for two months today and have been treating patients for several weeks. On the opposite side of the kitchen from my room is another smaller room the size of a pantry, and that is my makeshift clinic. Edward put up shelves for medical supplies and brought in a small bench and table. "Pretend you're still on the houseboat taking care of the boatmen," he said cheerfully. He looked around at the cramped space and winked at me. "Only here you can spread out."

This odd little clinic is something he has wanted for some time. Naomi is too occupied with their children and the details of the compound's daily life, so a week after we arrived he smiled at me and said, "Katherine, you're the man for this job," then he posted signs in the city announcing free medical care at the compound. I was apprehensive. I

pointed out several times that I am not a doctor; I've had only two years of nursing training and am very aware of how much I don't know and how limited my experience is. Nor do we have adequate equipment or supplies—or so I thought. Each time I brought up these concerns, Edward listened patiently. Then he said, "You'll see," and moved on to something else.

He's right. The people's needs here are so great that two years of nursing training has indeed given me a good deal of experience, and there is much I can do, even with limited supplies. Each morning I find a few more patients waiting outside the kitchen door in the winter air, their faces drawn, the fear in their eyes showing how desperate they are. I am humbled by their trust; it must take a good deal of courage to accept help from someone considered hostile by so many. But there they stand, each morning a longer line of peasants and farmers and their timid children.

The most common complaints—and all of these seem nearly epidemic—are malaria, jaundice, intestinal parasites, trachoma, and, in infants, lockjaw, but on any given day I see a dozen ailments in addition to these, some of which I can diagnose, some of which I can't, and with these I just do my best. At night I search through the few medical books I have

for diagnoses for what I've seen, neglecting my language study in the process, so that I remind myself of the mediocre student I was when I was younger. I can read medical texts for hours on end, but a page of my primer puts me to sleep.

Which is one reason I'm behind. After two months' study I am expected to be able to converse a fair amount and be understood with gestures, to know the Lord's Prayer, and to have completed two dozen lessons in the primer. I can say the Lord's Prayer start to finish, and because I am talking with patients I am making progress in the spoken language, and my conversation is passable. But it's far from perfect; yesterday at market I thought I had asked for an orange, only to learn I'd asked for a saw. Next I said I wanted to buy a chicken and was told I'd requested a wife.

It's the written language that worries me. We are to take a comprehensive language exam when we have been in the field for six months, and I am significantly behind in my lessons, something I have hidden from Edward, who would not be pleased; he sees one's progress in the language as a gauge of one's seriousness about the work in general. But the people's physical needs are too great, and at the end of the day when I am frantic to get to my medical books to see if the rashes and

coughs and fevers I saw were what I thought they were, I push my homework aside with little trouble.

When I had been in Ch'eng An Fu for three months, Edward asked me to go to Ta Ts'ai Chou, a city to the north. The city's only missionary was an elderly Methodist minister who was going home on furlough and was not expected to return. I would move there with Mu Tseng Lee, an experienced Chinese preacher, and his wife. This was fine with me, and I was packed in less than an hour. I had only just unpacked, and I had few belongings anyway.

In early February we arrived in Ta Ts'ai Chou, a name that meant City of Great Wealth for a place that was far from it. It was a good deal smaller than Ch'eng An Fu, home mostly to poor vendors and farmers. The vacated mission house consisted of a front room large enough for meetings, a bedroom behind the hall for the preacher and his wife, and a small room at the back of the house for me. I had no equipment for cooking, so the pastor and his wife shared their meals with me, usually millet gruel with a few boiled vegetables and steamed bread.

I spent most of my time with Mu Tseng Lee, who was both devout and unorthodox. One afternoon a month after we arrived in Ta Ts'ai Chou, he asked me to accompany him on a visit

to a sick friend. The day was mild for winter, and together we made our way through the midday crowds to the home of the sick man at the opposite end of town, where we found him lying underneath several quilts on the *k'ang*, a low, hollow brick bed connected to the stove so that the heat circulated through the platform. The earthen floor was swept clean, and on a wooden table was a shrine to the family's ancestors. On another table sat a huge teakettle covered with a kind of blue quilted jacket.

Mu Tseng Lee introduced me to the sick man and his family, a wife and two sons and their wives, all of whom watched us warily as they took turns sipping from the teakettle's spout. Mu Tseng Lee sat on a small bench next to his friend, who held the pastor's hand between his own and said something in hushed Mandarin. The pastor turned to me and translated. "He says we are kindness itself, and he prays we do not hurry away."

I nodded at the patient, and he smiled weakly.

Mu Tseng Lee took his soft paper hymnbook from the large sleeve of his gown, turned to "What Can Wash Away My Sins? Nothing But the Blood of Jesus," and began singing a Mandarin version of the hymn to his sick friend, though it was clear he knew the song by heart. Between the lines of the song the pastor also prayed over the sick man, all the while beating

his friend on the head with the rolled-up hymnbook and using it to accentuate lines he particularly liked.

I looked on, shocked but afraid to interrupt; perhaps this was his way of praying, I thought, or yet another Chinese custom I knew nothing about, for one of the few things I did know was how much I didn't know. Mu Tseng Lee had told me that, according to Confucius, this realization was the beginning of wisdom. "'To know what you know and know what you don't know is the characteristic of one who knows.'"

I said nothing, but sat there uncomfortably, as I silently prayed we weren't doing any harm. Finally, after a few verses of the hymn and much enthusiastic and energetic prayer, Mu Tseng Lee stood to leave. His ailing friend took his hand again and spoke, and again the pastor translated. "My friend hopes that favorable winds may accompany us."

Once again I nodded, baffled. The patient did indeed seem somehow more comfortable. Or, I thought, perhaps he was just relieved that our visit was over.

When we left the house, I asked Mu Tseng Lee the reason for his unusual method of prayer. He grunted. "That man, when he is well, turns from the right way. I thought I would beat the devil out of him." I started to laugh, thinking it was a joke, but Mu Tseng Lee stopped walking and faced

me. “You find evil humorous, my young friend?” I could only shake my head.

From there the pastor planned to visit another friend. I felt I had witnessed enough prayer for the day, so after a short distance we parted ways and I continued on alone. A light wind carried the clean scent of wheat from the fields, and I headed toward South Gate so that I could leave the city and walk in the fields, something I enjoyed and did often, as it reminded me of home.

The city was bustling, the streets crammed with people and carts and chickens and pigs. As I made my way toward South Gate, I found myself caught up in a mass of people all headed in that direction. I couldn’t have extracted myself if I’d wanted to; all I could do was keep moving forward, which I did without a fight, thinking I was going that way anyway, and there must be something to see.

There was. Just outside the gate the group stopped and formed a half circle, in the center of which, ten yards in front of me, stood the magistrate and five armed soldiers. Three men knelt in front of the soldiers, their heads bowed with their necks stretched out, their hands tied behind them. They were naked from the waist up, and each of them repeated the same phrase: “Have mercy on me.”

An old man next to me nodded toward the men

and explained that they were begging the executioner not to cut their heads completely from their bodies. If the head remained connected to the body, even if only by a strip of skin, the condemned could be reincarnated. The victims' relatives had spent a great deal of money to persuade the executioner to honor this request. When the old man finished speaking, he waited for me to respond; he seemed to expect me to be impressed. I nodded that I understood, and he returned his attention to the scene in front of us.

I felt a strong sense of dread but there was nowhere to go; people were pressed in tightly on every side of me. Then it was too late: as the executioner stood next to the first man and stretched out his right arm, the onlookers murmured excitedly at the sight of the long knife and its wide blade and in three quick strikes the men's heads were severed from their bodies.

It was horrible. The victims' heads fell to the ground and their bodies went limp. There was the quick red flow of blood, the shocked expressions on the dead men's faces, their black queues lying in the dirt. I wanted to run from the scene like a criminal, for I felt that being an onlooker to the slaughter implicated me. But I saw I was alone in these feelings. The magistrate had departed, the executioner was wiping the blood from his sword on his trousers, and people were chatting casually as they made their way back toward the

city. The mood was as relaxed as if we had just watched a puppet show. A few people glanced at me, and I sensed them gauging my reaction. I saw no choice but to force composure on myself and return home.

I became ill that night, feverish and coughing, gasping for air in my sleep, and in the morning I woke to find Mu Tseng Lee standing over me. I braced myself for his blows, thinking he was going to pray over me, but he only placed his hand gently on my wrist, feeling my pulse, then he asked to see my tongue. He nodded, and he said kindly, "My friend, you are sick from despair. This is how the heart speaks to us, through our illnesses."

I had no argument. My body ached, my chest was tight, my head throbbed. I had never felt so sick.

Over the next few days my strength and appetite diminished, the fever and cough worsened, and the pastor grew worried, for what looked like a simple illness in that time and place could turn serious overnight. A cough could mean the common croup just as easily as a fatal case of diphtheria. I also felt sick in spirit and was home to a deep melancholy. The executions had stayed with me, and I did not see how I would ever feel comfortable in that place. I alternated between blaming my feelings on this backward society and blaming myself for failing

to have the strength to tolerate it. I also missed home—my family, our farm, speaking German, sleeping in a bed, milk, bread, cheese, forks, clocks—and the longer I was gone the more intense my yearnings became. When I looked up at the night sky, it seemed impossible that my parents and siblings saw the same stars I did; I felt too far away to share the same heavens. Each evening when I went to bed I heard music from the flute played by someone in town, mournful, haunting melodies that were punctuated by the sharp clack of the wooden blocks the night watchman struck as he walked around the city wall. In the early dawn, I heard the sounds of animals dying and carcasses being beaten, for we lived near the slaughter man, who killed his pigs just before sunrise. I had hated the slaughter of animals on our farm, and the sounds of these dying animals tormented me.

On the seventh day I was sick, Mu Tseng Lee sent word to Edward, who came to Ta Ts'ai Chou two days later. When he arrived he had only to look at me before murmuring the German word that had been in my mind for many days: *"Heimweh,"* he said. Homesick.

I nodded, embarrassed but also relieved that he knew my secret, and I answered in our mother tongue, my voice hoarse from coughing, *"Garrecht"*—exactly right.

Edward sighed. "It eases with time."

A few days later he took me back to Ch'eng An Fu, and while I felt like a failure, I was too sick to care much. Edward felt I was not well enough to stay in the room I'd occupied before, a small bedroom in the boys' orphanage in the city. Instead I was given a storage room at the rear of the Geislers' home, where under Naomi's care I was able to recuperate from what she diagnosed as a persistent case of croup. I spent ten days wrapped tightly in a wool blanket, hot poultices on my neck and chest, potash tablets in my mouth, praying all the while that I could accept this country and its ways, for I knew I had to if I were to stay.

April 2, 1907

Three weeks ago Will Kiehn returned from Ta Ts'ai Chou. Now that he's well, Edward has decided that he'll remain in Ch'eng An Fu, so Will has moved from his sickroom back to the orphanage, where he is to oversee the thirty boys who live there and help Edward with the work of the mission.

I am sure Will means well, but since his recovery he has been constantly underfoot. I catch him staring at me at odd times during the day and always at dinner, and when our eyes meet, his face reddens instantly. I am uncomfortable being the object of his—what—devotion? I have come to China not to be

gazed at longingly by a farmer's son but to give myself unreservedly to the work at hand. I sense such disquiet in him, and while I know it is not mine to speculate about, I do wonder if China is truly his calling.

But at times I see there is more to him than first meets the eye, for what he may lack in perseverance he makes up for in goodness twofold. He is a sweet boy, kind and gentle. I say "boy" because even though I am only a year older, he seems several years my junior. I see him with the orphan boys, whom he clearly loves and treats not like charges but like younger brothers, jostling them as they walk together, teaching them to throw a baseball, teasing them. Edward is so much older than the boys that this is a new experience for them, and I see them soaking up Will's easy affection like starved pups.

He is also diligent. He has rejoined me in my sessions with Li Lao Shih and he breezes through our weekly language assignments, which are ordeals for me. We are to complete thirty lessons in the phrase book and twenty grammar and idiom lessons in the wretched primer, which asks us to translate odd English sentences into Mandarin and vice versa. ("The thieves made a hole in the wall." "I have guessed his riddle." "They shot him dead with an arrow.") We are also to learn China's

geography and be able to converse with good pronunciation. This we learn through tone drills in which Li Lao Shih shouts a sentence to us and we shout it back to him. The first time we did this I thought our teacher must be somewhat deaf and that I was to shout everything at him. But after the lesson when I yelled, "Li Lao Shih, would you like some tea?" he quietly said that I should not trouble myself about tea, but perhaps I would find it pleasant to lower my voice. It was only then that I realized he's not deaf at all; shouting lessons is just how they do things here. That was my lesson for the day: Don't yell at your teacher except when practicing tones.

Behind the Geislers' home was a large open yard in which Edward planned to build a small school. One evening in April, a month after my return to Ch'eng An Fu, he said the time had come to begin building. I nodded eagerly at this, for I felt here at last was something I knew how to do. I had helped my father then and members of our small church at home raise a simple wooden structure many times, and I hinted to Edward that I was an expert at such endeavors, even implying that he was fortunate to have my help. He smiled wryly and said, "Good. I'll rely on you."

I went to bed that night with the too-sweet feeling of unwarranted pride, and when I awoke

the next morning I was confident and energetic. We would purchase the lumber we needed and get to work, I thought, and be building by noon. But at breakfast when I asked Edward where we would buy the lumber, he laughed.

"We don't buy lumber," he said, "we buy trees."

I nodded; that was reasonable, something I should have thought of. Of course there weren't lumberyards here; we would be cutting the trees down ourselves.

Edward explained that because trees were not plentiful, it was necessary to use a *ching-chi*—an intermediary—to find a landowner amenable to selling the trees growing on his property. A week earlier the *ching-chi* had located a farmer near Kuang P'ing Ch'eng on whose land grew a small grove of elm trees, and after much bargaining, a fair price had been agreed upon.

"So now we dig," Edward said.

"You mean cut."

He shook his head without looking up from his breakfast. "Dig. We don't cut trees down; we dig them up." Then he looked at me evenly for a moment. "You're still thinking as though you were in America, Will, when you're here on the other side of the earth."

I nodded, reminded yet again that I had much to learn.

That morning after breakfast we set out for the

field where the trees grew, carrying as many tools as we could: spades, picks, shovels, saws, and an ax. Because the trees grew at the edge of a family graveyard, men in the city were frightened of disturbing the spirits of the dead and therefore unwilling to uproot the trees. Instead, Edward had asked me to bring along four of the older orphan boys, who, I could see, were clinging tightly to my assurances that there were no evil spirits and that no harm would come to them.

As we walked, people began following us, for our small procession had aroused their curiosity. By then I was used to being watched and followed; it would have been far stranger and even ominous had people ignored us. Someone asked where we were going, and someone else answered, "They are going to dig trees at Lan's farm, near the grave mounds." "How do they dig the trees on a graveyard?" the first man asked. "With them, it is no problem," the second one answered. "When they get to the place, they all kneel and pray. After their prayer, the tree comes out of the ground by itself." Edward laughed grimly and muttered, "Would that it were so."

When we arrived at the appointed spot, we found the trees next to two dozen graves marked by cone-shaped mounds of earth, an eerie sight in the middle of a wheat field. The people believed that the happiness of the dead depended

on a suitable burial, and this site had been deemed an auspicious resting place, despite its being in the middle of a field, forcing the farmer to plow and plant around the graves year after year.

The trees did not come out by the roots as the villager had predicted; rather, we dug them out, as Edward had said we would, hacking through root systems and throwing shovelful after shovelful of dirt to the side. It was grueling, tedious work; I did not think it would end. But eventually Edward told us to put down our tools. He, the boys, and I surrounded the tree, and with all our combined effort and might we pulled and pushed the tree from the earth.

Then we started on the next one, and at the end of the day, when I did not see how we would have the strength to walk home, we gathered everything and took all of it with us—trunks, branches, twigs, sticks, roots, leaves. Everything would be used; what wasn't suitable for building would be used to make farm tools, and what wasn't used for tools would be burned as fuel in the kitchen. Some of it we carried in bundles on our backs, some on carts that Edward had hired.

I went to bed that night bone weary, my back stiff, my arms and shoulders aching, my hands raw with blisters. I knew that much work lay ahead of us; as there was no sawmill, we would saw the trees ourselves, cutting the trunks and

larger branches into boards, some thick for window and door frames, others less so for floor planks. But I was amazed at what we had done: we had dug up five trees, which now lay in the compound yard. The wood was perfect lumber, tough and hard, not prone to splitting, and a nice light brown in color. We could begin building in a few weeks. Despite my aches and pains and exhaustion, I was content; there was now one less thing I didn't know.

In Ch'eng An Fu, I found myself more and more smitten with Katherine. At dinner each night, sitting across the table, I could not keep my gaze from her, and soon I began to think that she was staring at me too, a development for which I was not prepared. When our eyes met, I quickly looked away, then hours later in the boys' orphanage I would lie awake in my small bed, wondering how to approach her, for I had no experience in matters of the heart.

Day after day I tried to muster the courage to arrange a situation whereby we might become better acquainted. Then, one night shortly after the tree digging, I came up with a plan. The next day when Edward said he did not need my help that morning, I casually walked to the front of the compound, where Katherine saw patients when the weather was fair. It was a fine spring day, clear and bright and breezy, and nearing

time for lunch. As I came into the courtyard, her back was to me as she motioned to the next patient. A poor woman brought her daughter forward, a child who looked to be around seven years old. The woman said they had walked two hours to reach the compound, because they had heard there was a healer.

Katherine asked, "What is your complaint?"

The woman said the girl was lazy and would not do as she was asked, and that her laziness had caused a stomachache. Katherine looked at the girl and gently placed her hand on the girl's greatly distended belly while the mother explained that as she had been unable to find any cockroach feces, the usual cure for such ailments, she had fed the girl rat feces, to no avail. Then she had gone to a native practitioner who had slashed the child's wrists, the remedy for intestinal worms, still with no improvement.

Katherine nodded as she listened, her mouth tight, and I saw the concern in her expression. "The child does have worms," she said gently, stroking the girl's hair as she talked. "But slashing her wrists is not the way to rid her of them. There is a medicine we can give that will cure her."

The mother was wary.

Katherine said, "Leave her with us and return for her in three days. Or you can stay with her. You will see a great difference in her."

Seeing the woman was still reluctant, Katherine shrugged. "All right," she said. "You can certainly try your methods again. But they won't help." Then Katherine stepped away from the woman and her daughter and motioned for the next patient.

An elderly man began walking toward Katherine, but the mother blocked his way. "No," she said, "we will try it. Give her your medicine so that she may be well."

I was impressed by Katherine's bluff and at her calm demeanor and confidence. She smiled and called for her assistant, one of the older orphan girls, who would take the girl and her mother to the upstairs of the main house, where there was room for half a dozen patients to stay. As she did so, she caught sight of me watching her. She smiled again, and I saw the color in her cheeks deepen, causing a sudden shakiness inside me.

"Is it lunchtime?" she asked.

"No," I said nervously, "I have a complaint. A medical complaint."

Katherine looked at me with raised eyebrows, and I sensed more amusement than surprise. "Very well," she said. "I'll see this gentleman, then I'll see you," and she turned back to her patient.

I leaned against the wall in agony as Katherine worked, for I suddenly saw the foolishness of my scheme. But there was nothing to do now but go

through with it, and I decided she might as well see me as I was.

Fifteen minutes passed. There were still patients waiting, and Katherine looked at me. "I can wait until you finish," I said, and she nodded and continued working. With each patient, she was gentle and determined. I could see her patients' surprise when they saw her, this healer they had heard of, for she looked far younger than twenty-two. She was small, only five feet tall and perhaps one hundred pounds, with dark hair pulled back in a bun at the nape of her neck and gentle gray eyes. She effortlessly engaged person after person in conversation.

By the time everyone was gone I had been waiting for nearly an hour, feeling more hopeless with every minute. She gathered her instruments and bottles of pills and ointments into a large bamboo basket then turned to me. "We can go to the dispensary," she said, and she walked briskly toward the house. Following her, I felt some slight hope; perhaps I really could be alone with her, even briefly.

What Katherine called her dispensary was a cramped room near the kitchen that held her supplies. She unlocked the door and opened it wide, then turned to me and said, "How may I help you?"

Once again, I was certain I was making a terrible mistake. But it was too late; there was

nothing to do now but forge ahead. "It's my toe," I started. "I have an ingrown toenail. It's hereditary."

Katherine looked at my feet. "Hereditary ingrown toenails? That's quite serious, but you are indeed fortunate. I happen to know how to treat such problems. Let me see the toe."

Speech had left me. I could only nod as I stooped down to take off my shoe and sock, convinced that I had ruined any chance I might have had at romance. My feet! What had I been thinking? I was going to show her my feet, and from that I hoped she would find me interesting and likable?

Katherine tapped a low shelf against the wall and said, "Can you put your foot here?"

My cheeks burning with embarrassment, I did as she asked and rested my bony old foot on the shelf. She leaned down to get a better look, and when I flinched at her careful touch, she laughed softly. "Well," she said, "today is your lucky day. A doctor at the deaconess hospital taught me just how to take care of trouble of this kind." She turned to her shelves of medicines and tonics, tapping the shelf with her fingertips. Her back to me, she said, "It's easy. We just remove the toenail. If that doesn't work, we cut off the toe."

Her tone was so matter-of-fact that for a moment I believed she was serious. Then she turned and smiled at me. She took a small bottle

and held it up to the faint light. "Maybe that's a bit drastic. We could try this. I think there's just enough to do the trick." She leaned close to me and put something on the side of the toenail. The stuff burned and I couldn't help but pull away from her.

"What is it?" I asked, still a little unsettled at the idea of parting with my toenail.

"Iodine," she said. "To clean it so I can trim it back. It will only hurt for a moment. Once I cut away the ingrown part of the nail, the pain will be gone."

I willed myself to relax as Katherine trimmed the nail. As she did, she talked about the patients she had seen that day, and I was so engrossed in listening to her that I was surprised when she said she was finished. She was right: the pain was gone. I awkwardly put on my sock and then my shoe as she watched. Finally I stood and faced her. "Thank you. It was good of you to help me."

She looked at me steadily, her gray eyes kind. "I'm glad to help you anytime I can," she said.

I heard myself blurt out, "In return I could help you with your language studies," for I knew she was struggling, and it was the only way I could think of to have more time with her.

She blushed, and I silently called myself an oaf for embarrassing her. But then she said, "Yes. I could use some help," and because I was happy,

my heart drumming in my chest as though she had declared her love, I grinned at her, despite my bashfulness and embarrassment. She smiled back, and I knew I had found heaven on earth in the North China Plain.

The story of my ingrown toenail proved to be a delight to Edward and Naomi and the three other missionaries in Ch'eng An Fu, and for days afterward my amused coworkers asked about my health.

A week or so later, Naomi took me aside after dinner. "You're recovering well?" she asked.

I smiled. "Very well," I said. "I was in good hands."

She nodded. "You know, Will, if you're truly interested in Katherine, you must make your feelings known. You must also be persistent."

I nodded, bluffing. "Of course."

"I know whereof I speak," she said. "At the start I couldn't stand the sight of Edward. Had he not been determined, I would never have come around."

This surprised me; I had assumed the two of them had been a match from the start.

She shook her head. "I had a great dislike of him. I didn't like his mannerisms or his sense of humor. I thought him clumsy, and his hands and feet too big. But he was persistent. He tried to sit next to me, and if some other girl or boy sat

between us, he just talked over them as if they weren't there." She looked down and wiped her hands on her apron. "Even when he first proposed, I said no. But I desperately wanted to know and follow God's will for my life, so I prayed that if it was His will for us to marry, Edward would propose to me again. A few days later, I found Edward weeping. I asked him what was wrong, and he said, 'You don't love me.' My heart broke to see how I had hurt him. I saw how proud I had been, and I asked his forgiveness, and from that moment I began to see him differently. I saw that although he didn't have a formal education, he was wise in faith; that although he could be impetuous and stubborn, he was far more often considerate and unselfish. I opened myself to him, and soon I began to love him."

She looked at me evenly. "So," she said, "are you concocting other ailments that will allow you to spend time with Katherine, or do you need help?"

I laughed. "I have another plan," I said, and I took Naomi's questioning as a good sign and an indication that she and Edward would not be averse to my attentions to Katherine.

That night I lingered after dinner as Katherine and Naomi cleared the table, waiting for a moment to speak to Katherine in private. Edward was in another room reading, and when Naomi

left the kitchen to put their children to bed, I seized my chance and casually asked, "Would you like help with your studies?"

She looked shocked for a moment, and I realized that while I had been thinking all week about our studying together, she probably hadn't. "In return for your medical services," I said.

She laughed. "Oh, yes. My payment." Amazingly, she motioned to the large dining table and said, "Shall we?"

It was as simple as that. I nodded, not trusting myself to speak, and the two of us sat down at the table.

Thus began the most enjoyable studying I've ever known. Once Edward and Naomi had gone to bed we got to work, sharing a lamp because of the high cost of kerosene, an advantage, I decided, as it forced us to sit close together.

At the start I sat across the table from her, but each night the distance between us diminished and soon we were sitting side by side, talking about our lessons in low voices so as not to disturb anyone. One evening she surprised me by saying she had heard me speaking to the gatekeeper and that I was becoming more natural and comfortable with the language.

"You'll make a good preacher, Will."

I stared at her, unconvinced.

"I think you have a gift."

I was too startled by her confidence to answer.

• • •

May 12, 1907

Today it has been five and a half months since we arrived in Ch'eng An Fu, and what that means nags at me: in two weeks we take the dreaded language exam. I have studied night after night, sitting late into the evening, my lessons spread out in front of me and Will patiently tutoring me. The language comes much more easily to him than it does to me but he is also diligent, and I am the beneficiary of his hard work. He has a gentle spirit that I admire, probably all the more so because of my own impetuousness and impatience. At times I see my opposite in him, and being with him is like taking a cool drink of water. He calms me, and when I am with him I feel hopeful and refreshed.

Late in the evening our conversation meanders away from Mandarin, and we talk about all sorts of things. Last night Will spoke of his time in Ta Ts'ai Chou and of what happened there—of his loneliness and isolation and of the horror of witnessing an execution. As he talked of the condemned men's tortured expressions and their pleas for mercy and of the pain and helplessness he felt as he watched them, I saw his anguish and felt the tenderness of his heart.

I also see his commitment to the work here.

He does everything and anything Edward asks of him—digging up trees, overseeing unruly orphan boys, crossing and recrossing the plain by foot, bicycle, wheelbarrow, and cart to do this errand or that. He never complains or questions Edward, even when Edward sends him right back to a place he just came from. Traveling across this harsh, flat landscape is far from pleasurable, but Will says yes to Edward's requests without question. I see a new humility in him and I realize he's not the person I thought he was. I thought at first I had misjudged him, but it's not that. The qualities I so admire in him now weren't there before; he has changed.

Little by little, I came to know her. Her parents, like mine, had been born and raised in Polish Russia, emigrated to America two years earlier than mine, then settled in South Dakota, where they raised wheat. Katherine was the second girl of twelve children, with her sister Naomi being the eldest; their mother had died while giving birth to the youngest when Katherine was fourteen. Shortly before their mother's death, Naomi had left home to study nursing at a deaconess orphanage and hospital in Cleveland, and soon Katherine began to feel called there as well. But when she told her father of her desire, he said he could not agree to it; he depended on

her to care for her younger siblings. But a few months later he remarried, and because Katherine held a special place in his heart, he said yes to her request and gave her his blessing. She left home a few weeks after she turned sixteen and joined her sister at the orphanage to begin her training.

At the start she worked in the printing press and learned how to set German type; later she became a teacher for the older girls. But her greatest love was nursing; she had known all along that what she most wanted was to care for the sick, and she began her training as soon as the deaconess in charge would allow it. From the time she was seventeen she spent any spare time she had at the hospital, talking with patients, accompanying physicians, observing procedures, assisting the nurses, and learning everything she could about medicine.

When she had been at the hospital for five years, Edward, her brother-in-law by then, visited the hospital and spoke about his work in China. That night Katherine had a dream in which a map was spread out before her. Though she saw no one in the dream, it seemed as though someone was pointing to China, and when she awoke, she felt certain she was being called to join her sister and brother-in-law in their work.

When she found Edward that morning to tell him of her desire, she matter-of-factly listed her

health problems, her inexperience as a missionary, and her lack of funds for travel. Edward did not hesitate; he was returning to China in three months and said she was welcome to join him. Regarding her inexperience, he said she would learn, and that a desire to serve God was the most important qualification. Regarding her health, he said that was between her and God; if she felt this was her calling, he suspected God would take care of her. Regarding money, he was unable to offer her any help, as he had barely enough for his own travel. They would just have to pray about it. Which they did, and within a few weeks a group of Katherine's former patients, hearing of her desire, contributed over thirty dollars toward her transportation, enough for her to travel by train from Cleveland to her family's home in South Dakota.

She arrived home a month later, and there she told her father of her plans. The thought of his daughter going to such an unknown and faraway land without a husband pained him, but she did not back down, and in the end, tears running down his cheeks, he gave her his blessing and said goodbye. From there Katherine traveled to Winnipeg where two of her brothers lived. She gave her testimony at their church, and when a collection was taken, the amount contributed was enough to cover the remainder of her travel expenses.

"The rest you know," she said. "I came to China, and here I am."

May 26, 1907

The exam was difficult; just thinking about it gives me a headache. Edward conducted the written portion, in which we were to translate fifteen sentences from Chinese to English and fifteen sentences from English to Chinese. Next was the geography portion, which asked for the Chinese names of the eighteen provinces, their capitals, the larger rivers, and the treaty ports. There were also comprehension questions on our required reading. The oral exam consisted of conversation with Li Lao Shih, who asked whether my parents enjoy good health, and how long I've been in China, how long it took me to travel here from my home, which countries I have visited, my likes and dislikes. I was then to question him similarly, according to Chinese etiquette, asking him about such matters as his honorable parents, his wife, family, education, and place of birth.

I'm not surprised that I didn't do well on the written portion. I'm disappointed, but it's not a catastrophe. It just means I'll need to keep studying and take the exam again in a few months. At least I passed the conversational part, which I'm certain is due to the patience

of my patients with my well-meaning but flawed Mandarin. Because my pride didn't want Will to know of my failure I avoided him this afternoon, hoping not to tell him, so after dinner tonight when he asked me when I would retake the exam, I assumed Edward had told him. I shrugged and said, "In a month or so, I suppose," hoping to sound as casual as he had and leave it at that. His amused smile told me a moment too late that he hadn't known I'd failed—he'd tricked me into telling him. But before I had time to resent him for it, the affection in his eyes and the warmth in his smile made me forgive him. He said, "You'll be all right. We'll just work a little harder." I saw that my poor performance had brought with it a gift, for I most certainly need to be tutored for another few months by handsome Will Kiehn. And I'm suddenly eager to learn.

On the night before Christmas Eve, Katherine and I stayed up late into the night talking about our hopes for our work in China, of how we had felt called, and of how the work fulfilled us. When there was a pause in our conversation, I said a silent prayer—*Let her say yes if this is Your will*—then I looked at her and what I meant to say was *Will you be my wife?* but I was so overwhelmed by even the possibility of becoming her husband that nervousness got the

better of me and I heard myself say, "Will you be my husband?"

She looked shocked for a moment; then she smiled.

"My wife," I said hurriedly. "Will you be my wife?"

She smiled again. "Yes."

She had answered so easily that I thought she must not have understood, so I took a deep breath and tried again. "Katherine, will you marry me?"

This time she laughed and my heart began to tear. Seeing the look on my face, she gently touched my cheek. "Yes," she said again, and in the late-night quiet of that dimly lit room, we shared our first kiss.

Katherine felt it urgent to tell her sister what she thought was secret, that she was engaged to be married to her brother-in-law's young recruit, but early the next morning when she joined Naomi in the kitchen, Naomi was not surprised. "I knew long ago," she said. "It was obvious from the start."

Katherine smiled. "I certainly found him near me on the houseboat every time I turned around."

As Naomi had told Edward our news before I had a chance to, I was surprised when he came looking for me at the boys' orphanage that

morning. “You know this changes things, don’t you?” he asked soberly.

I stiffened, certain I had overstepped my bounds. “I didn’t mean—” I started, but Edward waved my words away.

“We’ll be brothers,” he said, and he laughed and embraced me warmly.

Katherine and I felt strongly that we should abide by the custom of missionary organizations in China at that time, which dictated that young people who wished to be married not do so until they had spent two years in the field. Custom also dictated that we must not be alone together. As we lived half a mile apart, and our work kept both of us occupied from sunrise to sunset, this was not difficult.

When less than a year remained to the time when we could be married, I suggested that Katherine choose the date. She chose the fourth of November, her mother’s birthday, and I honored her choice. Because we could not be alone together even to plan our wedding and our future, we wrote notes, and in these notes Katherine repeatedly reminded me that it was not too early to plan for how our household would be outfitted. She was right; supplies from the United States had to be ordered well in advance, and she knew that my father had sent us a small monetary gift as an engagement present. But I was often slow in getting to these sorts of practical tasks,

and when I was careless in answering her prompts, Katherine called attention to this in her next note. Still I did nothing. *"Kommt zeit kommt ratt,"* I wrote back, an old German saying meaning when the time comes, there will be a way. Katherine's next note was nothing more than a list of what we could afford to order from Montgomery Ward for our first household, and the assurance of her handwriting told me her tone. I placed the order that day.

As Edward had come to China at such a young age, he had not yet been ordained as a pastor in the Mennonite church, and because there was no American minister anywhere near Ch'eng An Fu, we would need to travel to Shanghai, where we could be married by the American consul. On a beautiful clear day in the second week of October, 1908, we left Ch'eng An Fu accompanied by Ruth Ehren, the other deaconess Edward had recruited when we first came to China. She lived at the mission station in Shin Sheng Chou, a day's journey away, and was willing to accompany us as our chaperone, as was the custom.

I hired a cart to take us overland, and two days after leaving Ch'eng An Fu we reached the Grand Canal then traveled south by houseboat for three weeks. On reaching Shanghai we went to the American Consulate, where we completed the necessary forms and were told by the vice

consul that we would need to secure the services of a qualified minister. When we explained that we knew no one in the city, the consul suggested the Reverend Tennant Wright, who was in charge of the Presbyterian bookstore. He agreed to meet us at the consulate, and the next morning Katherine and I stood side by side in Chinese dress before the minister, witnessed by Ruth and the vice consul's secretary, as we nervously gave our answers when needed. After the ceremony, Ruth treated us to a lunch of fried noodles with shrimp from a street vendor, then tea and dragon beard candy, a sweet made of spun sugar that looked like a white cocoon, and which my new wife enjoyed immensely. It all felt like a celebration feast, and that evening when I held my dear one in my arms in the cramped cabin of our houseboat, I was sure I was the happiest and most fortunate man on earth.

On our journey back to Ch'eng An Fu as husband and wife, we heard historic news: on November 15 the Empress Dowager had died. The Emperor had died the day before, and the heir apparent was an infant, leaving the Ch'ing dynasty in a precarious position. The Middle Kingdom was changing before our eyes.

November 16, 1908

Once again I am on a houseboat traveling north on the Grand Canal. Once again I have

spent the day studying and the evening treating the boatmen's wounds. Once again I often find Will nearby—and I welcome his attention. Twelve days ago we promised each other faithfulness, love, and constancy, and now I am married to a man who is sweet, kind, strong, and most of all good. And he's funny. When during our vows he said, "With all my worldly goods I thee endow," he winked at me. We both knew that in my small purse I had eleven cents while in his pocket he had the grand sum of $2.56. After the ceremony he said he had no doubt whatsoever but that I had married him for his money.

I do feel rich. When I was a child, I never thought I would grow up to be married. I wasn't even certain I would grow up; I knew from overheard conversations between my parents and the doctor that my ill health would most likely prevent me from reaching adulthood; mine would be a brief life. But here I am, twenty-four years old and married to a man I love dearly; perhaps we'll even grow old together.

The vista of my life has changed, and I marvel at what lies ahead.

Kuang P'ing Ch'eng

1909–1911

When Katherine and I returned from Shanghai, I moved from my room in the boys' orphanage into Katherine's small room in Edward and Naomi's home, and on the surface our lives went on as before: she spent most of her time caring for patients while I worked with Edward. But inwardly I felt changed; I was more whole and more myself, because Katherine was my wife.

We had been married for nearly a year when Edward came to us with a question: Did we feel ready for a station of our own? A city three days to the north of Ch'eng An Fu by cart had no mission, and he felt that with increased funding and new recruits the time was right to expand our work. He cautioned us that how we would be received and how the work would proceed were unknown, but Katherine and I nodded without looking at each other. We had been hoping that just such an opportunity would present itself.

Where mission work was concerned, Edward never delayed. Only weeks after that short conversation, Katherine and I packed our belongings, said our goodbyes, and left Ch'eng An Fu. I was twenty-five; Katherine would be twenty-six in a few weeks.

For two days we traveled north by cart, and on the third day, an overcast afternoon in early October of 1909, we reached Kuang P'ing Ch'eng, City of Tranquil Light. When the city's huge gray wall was in sight, we asked people we encountered on the road where the main gate was, as it varied from city to city. We were somewhat guardedly told East Gate, and when we passed through it we found ourselves on one of the city's main thoroughfares, Cheng Chieh, True Street. We found lodging at the Inn of Sweet Water, a damp and dank place whose well gave forth water that was brackish and unpleasant. I later learned that the place had been called Bitter Water Inn, but the people preferred names that were appealing to the ear and that reflected their hopes of good things to come, so the name had been changed. That evening, as Katherine and I sat at a wooden table to eat our dinner of boiled noodles, I thought at first we were alone. Then I saw many pairs of eyes watching us from outside; people were putting their wet fingers to the tinted paper windows so that they could see inside and get a look at the only foreigners for miles.

The next morning we set about finding a place to live. As we walked from the inn toward the center of the city, we saw a storefront on Hsiao Chieh—Filial Loyalty Street—that was available. We were in luck: the owner, a fairly

well-to-do merchant, was willing to rent to us, which was a good sign, as many Chinese were reluctant to do business with foreigners. He was of the Mohammedan faith and reassured us many times that he did not worship idols of wood, iron, gold, or silver but that there was one true God, who was Father to us all. We agreed to his price more quickly than we perhaps should have, but we were eager to get settled, and we signed the lease the next day then began acquainting ourselves with our new home.

The city had two main thoroughfares that were paved with long hand-cut stones worn smooth from centuries of use. Cheng Chieh ran for four miles from east to west while Te Chieh—Virtue Street—ran north to south. Neither these streets nor any others in the city were straight but rather curved unpredictably, for it was thought that evil spirits were unable to make turns. It was also believed that a clear path between two gates let evil spirits pass easily through the city, so East Gate and West Gate were not opposite each other. North Gate and South Gate were, which was acceptable because the well in the center of the city lay between them, creating an obstacle.

Nearly the entire length of Cheng Chieh was lined with eating places, tearooms, and shops. Large wooden boards with bright gold characters on backgrounds of deep scarlet, indigo, or

emerald announced what each shop sold and who sold it. The silk and medicine shops were similar to traditional stores, but most of the others were like fruit and vegetable stands in an American city—stalls that opened onto the street with narrow benches set out in front so that customers could sit down while bargaining. In the tea shops, professional storytellers entertained customers and boosted business in the process; the longer people stayed to listen, the more tea they drank.

Carcasses of whole pigs with blood dripping to the ground hung in the front of the butcher's shop, and at the fishmonger's, live fish circled in large tubs of water. *I-yen t'ang*—"one-word halls"—were like five-and-dime stores, where everything sold for the same price, and the boiling water shop was a small dingy place with half a dozen hot kettles resting on mud stoves. Children carrying teapots hurried in and out, rushing to get home while the water was still hot; the cost of fuel made it cheaper to pay for boiling water than to heat it.

Near the far end of Cheng Chieh, almost to West Gate, was the *tsa-huo-p'u*, the variety store that sold what you couldn't get anywhere else: red paper for invitations, white paper for funeral announcements, paper money for idols, and firecrackers for feast days, weddings, and funerals.

Near the well and close to the center of Cheng Chieh were the city's official buildings, the *yu chen chu*—post office—with a professional letter writer sitting in front, and the *yamen*, a walled collection of spacious courtyards and brick buildings with curved tile roofs that housed the town hall, court house, jail, and official residence of the magistrate, who was in charge of the city's local militia and police and acted as the judge of civil and criminal court. The magistrate's seal was kept at the *yamen*, and the keys to the city gates were brought there after the gates were locked at sundown and kept there until dawn, when the gates were opened. Next to the *yamen* was Cheng-Huang Miao—the City God Temple—the busiest and most important of the city's several temples, dedicated to the city's divine defender, who was believed to protect Kuang P'ing Ch'eng from disasters of every kind.

Roughly parallel to Cheng Chieh was Ma Lu, Horse Road, which was used by wheelbarrows and carts because it was less congested. Behind it was a tangle of lanes named for what the shops on them sold—Shoemaker Street, Lantern Alley, Pawnbroker Lane, Jade Street, Lacquer Street, Chopstick Lane—and behind them was a series of curving and nearly identical alleyways that wound their way to the city's residential areas and eventually out to the city wall.

• • •

November 2, 1909

Six days ago we arrived in Kuang P'ing Ch'eng, where, like Ch'eng An Fu, setting foot inside the city walls is like stepping back into another century. There is no plumbing, running water, or electricity, and the smell in the streets can be so foul that I sometimes hold a small piece of camphor wood to my nose so I can inhale its musky scent. I am ashamed of my reaction; my dislike lessens me, not the city, and I pray that my feelings will change. I desperately want to like it here.

Our new home is a typical Chinese shop, with an earthen floor and close-fitting foot-wide boards that form the front wall. At night we put the boards up to close the storefront tight; during the day we take them down so that the shop opens onto the street and presto! our open-air chapel, where Will can preach and where we can hold services. A door at the back of the storefront opens onto a small brick courtyard, on the other side of which are the three rooms where we live. The owner agreed to sell us the few pieces of furniture that were here for a reasonable price, so we are now the proud owners of six long benches (where our visitors can sit), the woven cane and thin pallet of straw that are our bed, a bedside table, and a wooden shelf.

As the place had been empty for months it was filthy, so we have spent these first few days cleaning and whitewashing. As I walk through the empty rooms and into the courtyard, I tell myself that this is home now, and I pray for the grace to accept the details of my medieval life and do the work I've been called to do.

Eight days after our arrival in Kuang P'ing Ch'eng was a market day, which meant Cheng Chieh would be busy and attracting an audience would be easy. The people loved to be entertained and were extremely curious, and they were interested as soon as a foreigner began to speak. But as I stood in front of our small shop that morning, my heart thudded in my chest and my voice felt tight inside my throat, for I felt completely unequipped for what I was about to do: preach in Mandarin to a group of strangers who would most likely not be welcoming. I didn't see how I could make these people understand why foreigners would leave their own homes thousands of miles away to come to their country, where we knew no one.

I started to turn back inside, thinking I could prepare more, but Katherine, standing behind me, put her hand on my shoulder and looked me in the eye. "Don't worry about saying anything great. Just be a vessel and speak from your

heart." Then she nodded toward the street and I stepped into the autumn sun.

I wore a scholar's gray robe and a black satin jacket and cap but was still so conspicuous that people stopped and stared as soon as they saw me. A small group quickly gathered, mostly farmers in padded jackets and wide trousers of dark blue cotton, along with a few scholars and merchants and business magnates in long robes. I closed my eyes, turned my face heavenward, and began to pray out loud in English. "Father God," I said, "You have brought us here to tell the people of Your love for them. Inspire me and make me wise. Open the hearts of those listening today, that they may know Your Spirit. I ask for this—along with courage, O dear God, please give me courage, and please give it to me now, God—in Your Son's name."

When I finished praying I glanced at Katherine and she nodded encouragement. I could see she was amused at my request for courage; it was not something I had planned to say, but one of those blurted-out prayers that are often most real.

I began speaking in Mandarin. "Good day, my friends," I said loudly, and I heard the trembling in my voice, "I am from Wai-Kuo"—the Outside Kingdom—"a place you call Mei-Kuo. My country is a young country, while yours is many centuries old. Your first emperor, Fu Hsi, lived thousands of years before my country was born."

A few people nodded.

"I have been told that Fu Hsi tamed the animals and taught his people how to live in families; that he showed men how to fish and wrote songs for them to sing while they did. I have been honored to hear these and other stories about your country."

I tried to gauge people's interest and understanding. Perhaps two dozen men sat on the hard benches; another dozen stood at the perimeter, watching cautiously. A few beggars crouched in the corner.

I continued. "I have also been told that many centuries ago there were strict laws for young people who refused to listen to their parents. There is a record of a particular young man who continually refused to obey his parents. This rebellious son was severely punished, but even after everything possible had been done to correct him, he still would not change his wicked ways."

A few of the older men looked pointedly at whatever younger people happened to be nearby.

"The elders of the village were forced to sentence the disobedient son with the ultimate punishment, in the hope that the threat of this punishment would bring about repentance before the sentence was carried out. They decided to dig a hole and prepare to bury the hard-hearted son alive, with the fervent hope that he would at the

last moment plead for forgiveness and promise to change. But when they informed the young man of his sentence, his heart was so hardened that even the threat of being buried alive did not cause him to mend his ways, and he continued to defy his parents and the community. The elders had no choice but to dig the grave and prepare to bury him."

I paused, amazed that my listeners seemed eager for me to continue.

"The elders brought the young man and his parents to the grave. They took hold of him and were ready to throw him into the freshly dug earth, but at the last minute," I said slowly, "at the very last minute, the father leaped to the young man's side and requested that he be buried with his son."

My audience gasped softly.

"It was this act of the father that at last broke the hard heart of the son. He repented, and both father and son came out alive."

The people commented to each other about the rightness of this outcome. I took a breath, and as I looked at the faces of those sitting in front of me, a man sitting on a bench in the second row caught my attention, for he gazed at me with such focus that I found it difficult not to stare back at him just as intently. His appearance was commanding, for even seated, I could see he was tall and very muscular. His face, because it was

pockmarked and in some way fierce, reminded me of a lion's face. I felt hypnotized by him, and he seemed to be drawn to me as well, for he did not take his eyes from me. I had the sense that he was listening with his heart.

I took a deep breath. "I have come here from my country to tell you the Good News: that there is a God who has this kind of deep love for each of us, the love of a father for his son. This God desired to know us and to be known by us, and His desire was so great that He became man so that He could walk and live among us."

A few people nodded, and I was encouraged. I continued, telling of the life of God's Son, the man called Jesus: Yeh-Su. I told of His birth and of His ministry and the miracles He performed. I told of His death and resurrection, and of His promise to never leave us. The people listened intently, and I thought we might have many potential converts.

But when I finished, everyone left without a word or a look back, except for the large man in the second row, who stood and approached me. He was indeed tall, well over six feet, which was common in northern China. I looked up at him, already thanking God for his faith and hoping that his size was an indication of his belief. If only one man was going to accept the Lord that day, I thought, at least he was the size

of two. “Friend,” I said hopefully, “do you want to know more of this man Jesus?”

The man shook his head. “Foreign gentleman,” he said eagerly, “what is the cost of your buttons?”

My spirits fell as I looked down at my chest and understood. Katherine had added leather buttons to my satin jacket, something not seen in China.

“Come back on the next market day and I will have one for you,” I said finally, an attempt to bring him back for buttons, if not for faith. He smiled slightly and went on his way.

I went to bed that night not encouraged by my evangelistic efforts, but my discouragement did not linger. Three days later, on the next market day, a morning so crisp and clear I could only feel hopeful, my button man was back, and once again he stared intently at me as I preached. When I finished he came forward and I asked him to come inside so I could give him his button. He nodded agreeably and told me his name—Chu Chung Hao—then followed me across the courtyard and into our home, where he and I sat down together on a bench near the stove. While Katherine served us tea, I gave him a button and sold him a copy of the Gospel of Mark in Mandarin for one copper coin, less than an American penny. We received these tracts at

no charge from Bible societies, but we had learned that when we gave them away people used them as doorstops or inner soles for their cotton shoes instead of reading them.

My button man seemed pleased with his purchase but even more pleased with his button, and I had no doubt that it was the buttons that brought him back the next day and the day after that and so on. As we made our way through Mark's Gospel, his collection of buttons increased, and at the end of the first week he made an announcement. *"Mu shih,"* he said, "I have read the testimony of Mark, and I accept what he says as true. I believe in this man Jesus; I have opened my heart to him. What must I do next?"

I was wary. In Ch'eng An Fu I had seen new converts who went through the motions of faith to gain the rewards of physical comfort, whether that meant food or shelter or care, adding the Christian faith to the combination of the teachings of Confucius, Buddha, and Lao-tzu that comprised their religion, hoping that belief in Christ might improve the mix. Perhaps this man's question was not a matter of the soul but of buttons.

"Have you given this adequate thought, Chu Chung Hao? Do you understand what your decision means?"

He nodded.

"You do not think it hasty?" I was aware that I was doing exactly the opposite of what I had come to China to do. Here was a man who desired to come to Christ, and I was the barrier, not the entryway. Still I went on. "It has been only a few days since you first heard of Christ."

"Mu shih," he said, and I heard the sadness in his tone. He looked down as he spoke, and he seemed ashamed. "I have been unhappy for many years. My home is full of strife, as is my heart, and my days are difficult and without joy. But since I heard you speak, my soul is host to a strange new peace. I am no scholar, but you say that only this is required: that I believe in this man Jesus, which I do. I have accepted Him in my heart as you suggested, and I am already changed inside."

As I listened to his testimony, I was amazed at his belief. "Chu Chung Hao," I said, "you have been given the gift of faith. You are truly blessed."

December 1, 1909

We have a new member of our household—Will's first convert has come to live with us. Until now he has earned his living by teaching a kind of Oriental self-defense, but two weeks ago he told Will that he has grown tired of fighting and that it saddens his Lord. He said that if he lived with us here he could be of use:

he could get water and coal for us, and buy our food, and cook our meals. Will said yes; he somehow did not think it necessary to discuss the idea with me first. Perhaps he thought it unimportant; I don't know. Marriage is not as easy as it looks.

I understand the logic of this arrangement; I understand what Will means when he says we are fortunate to have Chu Chung Hao with us, that he will be a great help both in understanding the culture and in people's acceptance of us. I also understand that Chu Chung Hao must have experienced a great change of heart to alter his life as he has. And I understand that what's done is done.

But this giant of a man moving in with us came as quite a surprise, and I am struggling to adapt. It is strange enough to be a newlywed; even stranger to be a newlywed in a foreign city in a foreign land where I know almost no one; and stranger still to have someone I do not know living with us. When I greet these two men each morning I sometimes feel that I'm the newcomer who has moved in with *them.* Chu Chung Hao is only two years older than Will, and even though they've known each other for only a few weeks, they seem as comfortable with each as old dogs, so much so that it's a little disconcerting.

I meanwhile am a little afraid of our new housemate. He is an imposing man—tall, lean, powerful-looking, and at first glance frightening in his strength. His name fits him: *Chu* is the last name of an emperor of the Ming dynasty, *Chung* means loyal, and *Hao* means heroic or bold. The combination of the words describes him well: he has a noble bearing, and he seems both loyal and heroic. He is also strangely graceful; he moves so quietly and calmly that it is like living with a leopard. Yesterday when we were in the city square I was listening to the lungs of a stooped old man. When he saw Chu Chung Hao standing beside Will, the old man nodded solemnly toward Chu Chung Hao and said matter-of-factly, "That one can kill a man with his hands as easily as you wipe your brow."

But sitting at our table and sharing our meals with him, I see a kind face and dark eyes that are full of sorrow. I sense a gentle soul and a sweet nature, and I pray that my misgivings will ease.

In return for room and board and modest pay, Chu Chung Hao did much for us. Each morning he did the day's marketing and brought water from the city well for drinking, cooking, bathing, and laundry. He arranged for coal to be delivered and he cleaned and replenished our kerosene

lamps and trimmed their wicks. He prepared meals that were simple but good and he made our donation to the beggar king, a kind of required extortion in the city. Had he not, we would have been harassed by beggars and pickpockets every hour of the day.

Although Chu Chung Hao cautioned us that he was not a scholar and that perhaps someone else would be better suited for the task, he also gave us our Chinese names. The surname was to be a Chinese name that began with the first letter or syllable of our English name, Kiehn. It was also desirable for the name to have a good connotation. For our family name, Chu Chung Hao chose the name Kung, the family name of Confucius and therefore a choice that honored us deeply. Given names consisted of two characters that described some pleasing and admirable quality to be attained, if not already a part of the bearer's character. My given name was P'ei Te; *p'ei* means great, *te* means to attain. Together they mean "he who will attain greatness." Katherine's name was Mei Li, which means "beautiful strength."

Chung Hao had been with us for several weeks when, at dinner one evening, I asked him the question that had been much on my mind. "You have never married, Chung Hao?"

"I am married," he said simply. He did not look up from his bowl.

“Is your wife dead?” I asked, and I was aware of a quick look from Katherine at the bluntness of my phrasing.

He shook his head. “No,” he said, still not meeting my eyes. “She is most certainly alive. She lives in my home with my brothers and their wives.”

This surprised me. “Why have you left her?”

He shook his head again. *“Ta tai ko,”* he said—She is too fierce. “She has a temper that she uses like a weapon. That is why I wanted the buttons—as gifts, to soothe her.” Still he looked down at his bowl. “But her spirit is angry and I am alone. A frozen heart is a great sorrow, *mu shih*.”

“Is there not some path of reconciliation between the two of you? Is she as fierce as that?”

“That cannot be known. She treats me as though she despises me, and she despises herself.”

“What is the source of her anger?”

Chung Hao paused. “We have buried three children,” he said finally. “Two were stillborn; the third died one month after birth. My wife believes she is at fault. After each death she has refused to eat for many days, hoping to join our children in the next world. Time has hardened her sorrow into anger.”

“We will pray for her,” I said, and he nodded halfheartedly. He did not seem convinced it would help.

• • •

Two weeks later on an early morning in late December there was a knock on our bedroom door. When I opened it I found Chung Hao standing in the doorway and I could see he was distraught. *"Mu shih,"* he said quickly, "my wife is ill. She has taken a large dose of opium, with the intention of ending her life."

"When?"

He shook his head. "I do not know the hour. My brother came for me in the night."

"How far is your home?"

Chung Hao pointed to the west. "An hour's walk across the city."

I said, "Take us there."

Chung Hao nodded, his expression pained.

I closed the door and looked at Katherine; she was already dressing. "If she dies while we're there, they'll blame us," I said. "Even if we haven't done anything."

She did not look up. "I know what to do."

Soon the three of us were walking quickly through the city in the soft gray light of early morning, Chung Hao leading us through narrow back lanes to avoid the market-day throng that was already gathering. We did not speak as we walked. The morning was extremely cold, more like the middle of winter than the start of it. To warm her hands Katherine carried a fire basket, a bamboo basket with a saucer of live coals inside.

I had not thought to wear my hat, a lapse I sorely regretted. Chung Hao, walking evenly and easily at my side, seemed unaffected by the cold.

When we had walked for nearly an hour, we reached the western part of the city and turned down a lane that looked like all the others, lined with small windowless mud-brick homes with tile roofs. Chung Hao pointed to the last house. “There,” he said.

Inside it was so dark that I couldn’t see for several moments, and although I was aware that there were other people in the room I couldn’t immediately make them out. As my eyes adjusted, I saw the *k’ang* in the middle of the room. There was a wooden chest at the end of it and a bench against the wall. A large black kettle sat on the stove in the corner, where two men whom I guessed to be Chung Hao’s brothers stood motionless. They looked to be nearly as tall as Chung Hao, but of slighter frames. Their wives were not in sight.

A woman covered with several quilts lay on the *k’ang*. She looked far older than Chung Hao. Her long black hair was loose around her face, which was haggard and pale and covered in perspiration. Her cheekbones protruded sharply, her eyes were sunken. Had I not seen her chest moving with her labored breathing, I would have thought her dead.

Chung Hao motioned to the men in the corner.

"My brothers," he said. "They will bring you whatever you need." The men said nothing, but only nodded uncertainly, their fear of us evident.

"When did she take the opium?" Katherine asked. She was leaning close to the woman, holding her thin wrist and searching for her pulse.

"It has been more than a few hours," one of the brothers said, in the vague way of the people in that place.

Katherine looked at me and said in English, "If she's not in a coma we have a chance. She has to move around."

With Katherine on one side and me on the other, we were able to wake the woman and get her upright. Once she was standing, her padded blue cotton jacket and trousers hung on her as if her body were no more than a few bones strung together, and when I took her hand, it was like cold metal. She looked so frail that I doubted she could support herself, but as she grew alert she began to fight us off, and I saw I had underestimated her and that we were in for a battle.

Katherine nodded as we forced our patient to begin walking. "Answered prayer. Her fighting will save her."

Despite the woman's efforts to resist us, we were able to lead her in circles in the middle of the dark room, holding her between us. After many small laps, the woman cursing us bitterly

and ordering Chung Hao to make these foreign devils leave, Katherine asked for a cup of warm salt water. When one of Chung Hao's brothers brought it, we led the woman to the *k'ang* and seated her on the edge of it. Katherine held the cup to the woman's lips, but the woman pressed her lips together and shook her head. Katherine asked pleasantly, "May we have some chopsticks, please?" and when they were brought, she used them to pry the woman's mouth open. Then, as the woman fought and struggled against us, Katherine poured the salt water down the woman's throat.

It was a success: within minutes the woman's stomach rebelled and the results were abundant, with a great mess to be cleaned up. In the middle of the foulness and the woman's moaning and cursing, Katherine smiled confidently. "More walking," she said brightly. "I believe we are winning her back."

The chill from our walk there was long gone, for this saving work was strenuous, and as we walked the woman around and around the room I was soon as warm as if I had been working outside for hours. Presently she was alert enough to walk unaided, but Katherine was not yet convinced that all was well. Another treatment was needed, she said, and she took a long feather from the bag of supplies she had brought with her, then addressed the woman again.

"Sit down and open your mouth wide," she said, but despite the authority in her tone and manner, the woman refused. So once again, as I held the woman still, Katherine used the chopsticks to pry the woman's mouth open, then poked the feather inside. Again it produced results and was a success; much more had to be cleaned up.

The woman sank to the floor, exhausted. Chung Hao's sisters-in-law had entered the room, and while they got to work cleaning up the mess, Katherine knelt next to the woman and gently wiped her face with a damp towel.

I turned to Chung Hao. He stood back several yards, shaken and afraid, watching his wife. "She will recuperate," I said. "She only needs rest."

He nodded slightly, then walked to his wife, knelt in front of her, and spoke to her in a whisper we could not understand. She gazed up at him for a moment and then began to weep softly.

Wanting the two of them to have some kind of privacy, Katherine and I busied ourselves with cleaning up. Katherine asked for a basin of water, and we washed our hands and dried them with a towel she had brought. I was amazed at all that had happened, but Katherine acted as though this were any other day.

Finally Chung Hao stood. He asked his sisters-

in-law to care for his wife and said he would see us home. I accepted his offer without hesitating; I knew I was not familiar enough with the city to find our way.

The three of us retraced our steps in silence. The days had grown short and the sun was nearly gone, the shops already shuttered tight. I hadn't realized we had been there so long, and while I was tired and suspected that Katherine was far beyond that, I felt deeply content. I thought briefly of my family in Oklahoma: I pictured gifts and a tree decorated with lighted candles and a fire in the hearth, and I felt a quick stab of longing. But it lasted only an instant, for although there were no lights or decorations in our city's dark streets, it was still Christmas Eve, and we were blessed.

February 25, 1910

Now we are four: Chung Hao's wife, Chu Mo Yun, has joined us, the same woman who ingested opium with the hope of ending her life. Early one morning a month after her unsuccessful attempt I found her in our kitchen with Chung Hao, helping him to prepare breakfast, and when they heard me enter, they turned and she bowed to me. In the weeks since I first saw her, she was much changed. Her color was good and her hair was neatly coiled at her neck and held there with a

silver fastener. She wore a clean jacket and trousers and was a little less skeletal. Sewn down the front of her short padded jacket were the black leather buttons that Will had given Chung Hao.

Chung Hao introduced her to me and said she was most grateful for my help. She nodded as he spoke but did not look at me. If I was surprised to see her in our kitchen, I was astonished to hear Chung Hao say that he and his wife had made peace and hoped they could now live as husband and wife—meaning with us. While I was happy to see her in good health and the two of them reconciled, the idea of her moving in did not immediately strike me as a good plan. My hesitancy must have registered in my expression, for Chung Hao quickly continued. "My wife could be of great help to you, Kung Mei Li. She knows much about healing."

Still I hesitated, questioning the wisdom of having someone with such trauma so recently in her past living with us. But then she looked at me, and the earnestness in her expression caught at my heart. "Kung Mei Li," she said softly, "I am greatly in your debt. I owe you my life, and I ask your permission to repay your kindness."

I was uncomfortable agreeing to her request without talking to Will, who had left to preach

at the market early that morning. But even as I was thinking this I heard myself say, "We would be honored to have you." It seemed a decision I did not make.

So now she has joined her husband and moved in with us. She has been here for one month now and she works hard at any task I give her, and does everything quickly and efficiently. Like Chung Hao, Mo Yun's name suits her. *Mo* means lonely, *yun* means cloud, and this sorrowful woman does indeed seem to hover slightly above the earth. My only complaint is that I have no complaints, for she is so quiet that I sometimes don't know what to make of her.

But she is helpful, and help is something I sorely need, for I am now inundated with patients, in large part because of Mo Yun, whose former bad temper had made her infamous in the city. Word of her healing and transformation has spread far and wide, and many people have come to see if the change is real, and to see us, the foreign healers whom they believe are responsible for that change. Many of them have let us help them.

Our clinic is in the courtyard behind our street chapel for the simple reason that we have room for it there, and on days that aren't too cold it's all right. Will was doubtful when I first brought up the idea, especially because

of the lack of privacy. But that is its advantage. With so many myths about foreigners—that we make medicine from babies' eyes is one of the most common—we have a great deal of suspicion to overcome, and doing everything out in the open makes us less mysterious. While I was concerned that those needing care would be uncomfortable with the lack of privacy, it turns out that privacy itself is what would make them uncomfortable, not the lack of it, for it is an unknown concept. As I ask each person about his or her complaints, those waiting their turn press in close to us, wanting to hear our every word. When they can't hear us they call out, "What did he say? What is it that hurts?" and demand that we speak up. They also press in when I pause for a few minutes to eat a hurried meal. As I gulp down noodles and tea (my manners are long gone), I am as closely observed as if I am the patient and they the physicians.

Our courtyard clinic is simple but functional. The examination beds are doors laid across saw horses and covered with pieces of matting. The doors to our home turn on wooden pins, and it's easy for Will and Chung Hao to lift them out and carry them to the courtyard. The dispensary is a few large woven baskets that I carry outside. One holds dressings for wounds—bandages, spools of sewing thread for

sutures, bits and pieces of adhesive tape that's so expensive and hard to come by that I get most of it by peeling it off of packages sent in the mail. In a larger basket are the medications I dispense constantly here: quinine for malaria, santonin for worms, potassium chlorate for mouth sores and ammonium chloride for sore throats, paregoric for intestinal pain, zinc oxide and sulfur ointment for scabies, a tincture of iodine and carbolic acid for minor cuts and bismuth ointment for more serious ones, Dover's powder for opium addicts, ephedrine for asthma and bronchial ailments, and emetine and magnesium sulfate for dysentery.

I cannot help everyone. I can't help those who need surgery—I explain to them that I cannot cure with the knife—and I can't treat those with serious internal ailments. But there are many I can help, even though they have ailments and symptoms I've never heard of or found in American medical texts, but which I am coming to know well. Eye infections are very common, particularly trachoma, which causes such inflammation of the eyelids that they become nearly inverted and the eyelashes rub against the eyeball, causing swelling, blurred vision, and eventually blindness. There is no dentist, so I pull teeth. Last week I delivered my first baby—a girl!

A great number of infants have lockjaw,

which was a mystery to me until I learned that the mothers here don't have diapers for their babies; instead they place the infants feet first in sacks that come over their hips and are tied around their waists. The mothers scoop up dirt from roads so trampled by horses, donkeys, and oxen that it is as fine as talc. They put a little of this at a time into the babies' sacks to absorb any wetness in the sack. When the baby develops sores on its body from rubbing, lockjaw germs from the dirt enter the infant's bloodstream and poison the whole body, usually leading to death. The babies' mouths are shut so tightly that I must use chopsticks to pry them open so I can feed them.

This kind of story is not unusual. Because it's believed that disease is caused by displeased demons, superstition dictates many treatments, and much of the disease here is caused by poverty and ignorance. Nearly everyone is underweight, their eyes dark and sunken, so I work at teaching them about hygiene and nutrition. I explain why we need to keep flies away from food, I show them how to brush their teeth, and I sell soap for one cash, which is a copper coin, per bar. I'd gladly give it away, but then they'd think it had no value.

Each morning when I come into the courtyard I find more people waiting than the day

before. Two weeks ago there were thirty, and now that thirty has become fifty. This is the only place for many miles where people can receive western medical care, and they come from all over. A few are carried from great distances, some as far as six days away. Women with tiny bound feet walk for many *li*, leaning on a walking stick or a family member for help.

When we first came to Kuang P'ing Ch'eng, I prayed for enough patients to keep me occupied for the day. Now I pray for the strength to treat them all.

April 2, 1910

Not everyone who comes to us wants help. Yesterday I had my first social call, a group of perhaps a dozen women, well-dressed and well-kept, who appeared in the courtyard late in the morning. When I asked what I could do for them, a tall graceful woman who seemed to be their representative stepped forward. "I am Feng Chen Mei," she said, and I immediately bowed to her; she is the wife of the magistrate and therefore the most important woman in the city. The meaning of her name describes her well: chaste beauty.

"We have heard much about the foreign healers, and we have come to see for ourselves."

"I am honored," I said. "Are you ill?"

She shook her head but said nothing. She seemed suddenly uncomfortable.

"What is it that I can do for you?"

The women whispered to one another, then Feng Chen Mei looked at me evenly and said, "We would like to see your feet. We have heard that they are large, and that you walk as fast as a man. Can it be true?"

I felt my pride quicken. My feet? I wanted to say. My feet! Do you think I have traveled halfway around the world to show you my feet? But something inside me said, "Show them your feet," and I understood: these women all had bound feet. Seeing a woman with feet as large as mine was an event.

Somehow I held my tongue (I am given many opportunities to do so) and I said, "It's true. My feet are quite large." I looked down and raised my skirt high enough to display my ankles, exposing my heavy old size-five walking boots, which were two or three times bigger than the tiny embroidered shoes worn by my guests.

The women gasped and began talking all at once, marveling and commenting freely on the size and ungainliness of my feet. Then I said, "Would you like to examine them more closely?"

The women glanced at each other excitedly, as if this was too good to be true. Feng Chen

Mei nodded. Then, as if mindful of propriety, she added, “We are unworthy of such generosity.”

“It is I who am unworthy of your visit,” I said, which seemed to seal our deal. I welcomed them into the courtyard and invited them to sit on the benches that surrounded the examining tables. When they were settled, I hoisted myself up onto the examining table and took off my boots and my long stockings, and there were my bare feet for all to see in the warm spring air.

The women were fascinated. I stretched out my legs, I flexed my feet, I wiggled my toes, and my audience giggled with delight. I handed my shoes to Feng Chen Mei, who took them as gingerly as if they might dissolve in her hands, and the women giggled and talked to each other about how large they were and how awkward and how high the heels were, though they were no more than an inch. When Feng Chen Mei handed the shoes to the woman next to her, I asked, “Would you like to examine my feet more closely?”

Again the enthusiastic nods. I motioned for them to come forward, which they did hesitantly, then one at a time they touched my feet. They were most fascinated by my toes and wide arches, for that is what they don’t have, what foot binding steals when the feet of

three-or four-year-old girls are broken, forced backward, and tightly wrapped in the name of beauty.

As my guests ran their fingers over the soles of my feet I struggled to keep a straight face, for everything they did tickled horribly. Finally I could contain myself no longer, and I started laughing as I hadn't in months, a big belly laugh. This startled them, and they froze for a moment and looked at each other in alarm. They must have thought I was unbalanced. As I had no idea what the Mandarin word for "ticklish" is, I ran my fingers lightly over my forearm to try to show them. They looked at each other then repeated my gesture on themselves, which of course doesn't tickle when you do it to yourself. They looked at me blankly. I gently took Feng Chen Mei's hand and ran my fingers across the underside of her wrist, and she laughed and pulled her arm away and I pointed to my feet and nodded. She laughed; she understood! I was elated.

It was a good day.

May 1, 1910

My visitors have returned so often that I finally asked them to come at an appointed time so that I don't neglect those in need of my help. We have agreed on a schedule: they come on Monday afternoons. They gather in

the courtyard or in our home and it seems there is no end to their fascination with me. In addition to my feet, my skin, and my hair, they want to examine my shoes and stockings, my dress, my wedding ring, and much in our home—and they want to know the cost of all of it. They are especially enamored of the sewing machine, which they call the iron tailor. I had a yard or so of yellow gingham left over from a tablecloth, and I cut some squares of it and sewed them together so that my guests could see the machine's even, straight stitches. The women were delighted; they asked me to do it again and again, and in the end I gave each of them a square of yellow gingham to keep. They thanked me profusely and ran their fingers over the stitching in wonder.

Yesterday when they came I was anxious; they had visited enough that I felt I had run out of novelties to share with them. I showed them in and asked them to be seated, praying that something would come to me. When everyone had a cup of tea and we were all settled comfortably, I took a breath and said, "Well. What would you like to see today?" thinking that perhaps they had suggestions of their own.

They exchanged looks and I could see they were amused. Then Feng Chen Mei smiled at me. "Kung Mei Li," she said gently, "we have

not come to see your possessions. We have come to see you."

"Me?" I asked.

The women nodded and she continued. "We have many questions. Why is it that you would leave your home, where you surely must have everything you desired, to come here? Did you leave your family? What was your life like before you came here? Tell us, please."

I stared at all of them for a moment, trying to think what to tell them. Help me, I thought. Then I said, "I first thought of coming here after my mother died." The women looked interested, and I went on. "I loved my mother deeply, and I felt lost after her death. I felt as though I had wandered far from home and did not know how to return."

Feng Chen Mei seemed pleased. "Continue, Kung Mei Li."

"With my mother gone, it was my responsibility to start the kitchen fire early in the morning. I sat near the stove so that I could add fresh wood when it was needed, and as I kept watch I read my mother's Bible." I picked up Will's Bible, which was lying on the table near me, and held it up for the women to see. "It's a book of stories about God. I usually read what we call the Psalms, which are poems about God. The poet speaks often of his pain, and this comforted me. But he also

speaks of love for his God, and this gave me heart." I opened Will's Bible and translated part of the ninth Psalm: " 'I will praise thee, O *LORD*, with my whole heart; I will shew forth all thy marvelous works. I will be glad and rejoice in thee; I will sing praise to thy name, O thou most High.'

"One morning almost a year after my mother's death, I turned to a different part of our book." I opened Will's Bible to Luke and found the place I wanted. "My eyes fell upon a story I knew well, in which this man Jesus, whom we believe to be God's Son, showed His followers that He loved them in a surprising way: He washed their feet." The women glanced at each other and I could see they thought they had misunderstood me. "Yes," I said. "He washed their feet. He did this because He loved them and because He wanted to show them that serving others is honorable, and what God wants us to do—what we are created to do."

I looked down at the pages open before me. "I had read this story many times, but that morning was different; the story seemed written especially for me. Jesus was suddenly very real, as if He were in the room with me, washing my feet as I watched. I was so overcome that I fell to my knees. I was certain that God was asking me to serve Him, and I

wanted to do that more than anything in the world. I said yes."

I stopped. I was surprised I had said so much and was embarrassed. I looked at Feng Chen Mei, waiting for her to respond.

"Kung Mei Li," she said finally, "we are most grateful that your Jesus God has washed your feet and brought you to us."

I started to correct her, thinking I had misspoken. "Oh, no, He didn't really—" but I stopped. Truth seemed to trump fact; perhaps He was speaking through me in spite of me. "Thank you," I said. "As am I."

We talked for a while longer, and when it was time for my guests to leave I walked with them out to the street then stood there for a while, watching them make their way slowly toward their homes on their bound feet. The daylight was fading; a storm was moving in and huge rain clouds darkened the afternoon sky. The gray light softened the city's dinginess and turned the grimy old city beautiful. As I looked down the street—our street—I felt a wave of affection pass through me and I thought, I love it here. The realization brought me up short; I found myself in awe of the sudden loveliness of the very city I so disliked only a few months ago.

That was yesterday. This morning when Chung Hao came back from market, his basket

was full. I was alarmed when I saw this; we have been short of funds for a month and I have asked him to buy only what we truly need each day, a little flour and a few vegetables. He set the full basket on the table and I looked inside and found potatoes and apricots and eggs and millet and pork, more food than we've had in weeks.

"Chung Hao," I asked, "how did you pay for this?"

He said only, "Do not be concerned."

Then something in the basket caught my eye. I reached inside, and underneath a bag of millet I found a small square of my yellow gingham with rows of stitches crisscrossing it, and I knew we had been taken care of. We, who came to help the people here, are the beneficiaries of their kindness.

On a cold day in late January of 1911, a messenger from the post office came to our home, saying that a large crate had arrived for us and that I needed to arrange for it to be delivered. I knew what it was; my mother had written that my family had sent us supplies. But I wanted it to be a surprise for Katherine, so I tried to be casual as I set out with the messenger.

As the crate was three feet long, two feet wide, and nearly two feet high, I had to hire a cart to transport it to our home so there was no hiding

the surprise, but it didn't matter. Katherine beamed as soon as she saw it, eager and impatient as a child, her eyes bright. Packages were always an event, and we had looked forward to this one even more than most; we were in short supply of just about everything and had been tightening our belts for several months.

Once the crate was inside, Katherine handed me the claw hammer to pry open the lid. We were alone; the next day was the first day of the new lunar year—New Year's Day for the Chinese, the most important day of the year for a Chinese family—and Chung Hao and Mo Yun had gone to his brothers' home for the traditional family New Year's Eve meal of fried fish and dumplings. Chung Hao had invited us to accompany them, but I had declined. I had seen the hurt on his face when I did, but I had told him we did not wish to intrude.

When I pried the lid off the crate, we found a treasure chest, with every gift evoking home. There were cans of apricots and peaches and pears, German sausages, and a tin of churned butter, a welcome change from the stuff we made from scalded goat's milk, which tasted odd and looked like cottage cheese. I knew my mother would have made all of these. There were new shoes and a patchwork quilt, a clock, a bolt of good wool and a box of paper, toothbrushes, twine, bread tins for baking, needles and thread,

a tin of coffee, woolen gloves for Katherine. Tucked underneath everything was a thick knitted cap that had been my father's and was now mine.

We were ravenous, and Katherine immediately began slicing into one of the sausages, which we ate sitting on the floor, our loot spread out around us. I put on my father's cap and knew I should feel satisfied and content, but in the quiet amid the packaging mess, I couldn't ignore my conscience. I knew it had been an honor for Chung Hao to invite us to his home on this of all days, and therefore an affront to be refused.

I stopped ogling everything and eating, and I looked at Katherine. "I think I've offended Chung Hao."

Katherine's face was flushed and her hair mussed. The quilt was spread across her lap and she was happily pulling on her new gloves. She looked at me quizzically, her mouth full of sausage. "What?"

I took off the cap and looked at her uneasily. "Chung Hao invited us to go with them to his brothers' for the New Year's Eve feast. But I said no, and I believe he was hurt."

Katherine froze. "Oh, Will." She shook her head. "Of course he was hurt. Why did you refuse?"

"My pride. We had nothing to bring, and I didn't want to go empty-handed."

Katherine looked around at our gifts, then took

off her new gloves and began gathering a few sausages and cans of fruit. "Well, we do now. Perhaps we can make things right."

I watched, chagrined. "It's your fault, you know."

She stared at me with a Where-do-I-start? look on her face.

"For marrying such an oaf."

She laughed. "At least he's a repentant oaf," she said. "There's something to be said for that."

We packed some of the fruit and sausage into a large basket and set off quickly through the darkening streets, where people were making their way to their family homes for the celebration. We reached Chung Hao's home nearly an hour later. As we stood at the gate I smelled garlic and meat cooking in oil and heard laughing and talking from inside and I faltered, questioning the wisdom of our plan. But Katherine looked at me so sternly that I felt like a scolded child, and I decided the punishment fit the crime; I had acted childishly indeed. I knocked and called Chung Hao's name.

When he opened the gate, I said, "My friend, I trust you will pardon us for interrupting your celebration. But I see I was most ungracious in declining your invitation. I have been told that the New Year is a time to right wrongs and forget grudges, and it is my hope that you will forgive my rudeness."

Chung Hao hesitated. "I feared I had insulted

you. That perhaps it was not fitting to ask you to come here as guests."

I shook my head. "I was foolish and ungrateful. Please forgive me." Then I held out my father's cap, which I had brought with me on impulse. "I believe this would suit you well."

Chung Hao carefully took the cap from me and looked at it in wonder. Then he laughed, a deep joyful sound, and put the cap on. I felt a pang of regret; I loved that cap. But he smiled broadly and the sting eased. "I would welcome a man with a gift like this any day of the year, no matter how foolish." He laughed again and held open the gate and escorted us inside.

Several months later we had a celebration of a different sort: on a windy afternoon in May we held our first baptism service and welcomed five new members into our church—Chung Hao, Mo Yun, and three of Katherine's first patients. The fact that our converts were so few did not discourage us, at least not for long. As the wind blew dust circles around our feet, we led these new believers to our courtyard for what they called the "ordinance of washing." Chung Hao had helped me haul the large tub we used for bathing into the courtyard and fill it with fresh water, for the practice of the Mennonite church was baptism by full immersion. One by one our new believers came forward. I helped them into

the tub one at a time and held their hands as they knelt and ducked their heads underwater. When they stood from the immersion and opened their eyes and professed their faith in Christ as their Lord, they looked at me with an earnestness and joy that filled my heart.

The last to be baptized was an elderly woman whom Katherine had cured of lameness. I led her to the tub and began to sprinkle her head with water, rather than helping her into the tub, for she was well past sixty and very frail, and I worried about the consequences of immersing her.

But she stopped me and pointed at the others, who were soaked and happy. "Why am I not like them?" she asked.

I explained that because of her age, she might not stand the shock and that instead I would pour a small amount of water on her head.

She smiled and shook her head. "*Mu shih*, if I should die during the act of receiving baptism, would I not be most blessed of all?"

That fall was the start of a time of great change for China. On October 10, troops in Wuchang in the south forced their commander to rebel against the Manchu regime, which had ruled over China since 1644. Soon afterward the rebels declared a new republic, with the southern cities of Wuchang, Hanyang, and Hankow under their control. The government regained control of

Hankow by the end of October, but those few weeks were enough for the rebellion to gain strength. By the end of the year, China's southern and central provinces had declared themselves free of Manchu rule and the leaders of the movement established the Republic of China in Nanking, naming as its temporary president Sun Yat-sen, a western-educated doctor and the leader of the revolution.

On a cool day in late November of 1911, as Katherine and I were walking home through the city, we saw a group of people gathered at the *yamen* on Cheng Chieh, and as we made our way closer we found ourselves gazing at something we could never have imagined. In the center was a large dark heap of something, and when we drew closer we saw that it was a pile of queues, the long braids worn by Chinese males. Men all over the city were cutting them off, an act that had been forbidden by the Manchu empire since the seventeenth century, when the queue became a symbol of Manchu domination of the Chinese and required by law. The new republic had abolished the law. Two months later, in February of 1912, the last Manchu emperor, a six-year-old boy named Pu Yi, would give up the throne of China and a more-than-two-thousand-year-old dynasty would come to an end.

My own life changed as well. In December I received a letter from my mother, and as I had

not heard from her since we had received the crate of gifts, I opened the letter quickly, eager for news from home. Because the postal service in China was so unpredictable and usually so slow—a letter could take as little as three months to reach us or as long as two years—I looked first at the date, which was six months earlier. Then I slipped the letter into my pocket to save it for later.

After dinner, while Katherine was talking with Chung Hao and Mo Yun, I went into our bedroom and lit the lamp. I sat down on our bed and carefully unfolded the letter.

June 7, 1911

My dear son,

It has been some months since we sent the crate of supplies to you, and I hope it arrived safely. You have made many sacrifices for your work, and we hope that our gifts have brought you and Katherine much joy.

I write to you now with great sadness, and the fact that you must hear this news so far away from all of us compounds my grief. Last evening, shortly after dinner, your father passed on. It was his heart, and we had no warning. He came inside from checking the animals and stood at the kitchen window,

looking out at the fields. Because he seemed winded I asked if he was all right. He smiled at me and he looked very peaceful, and he said he could not be better. I left the kitchen for a moment, and when I returned he was on the floor, as sudden as lightning. I knew he was gone.

I have taught you since you were a small boy to trust God in everything, and I am praying that you will trust Him now, with your father's death. It is a difficult request, I know, for I am struggling to do the same. I cannot conceive of our lives without him. I do not always feel God's Presence, but I know He is with us, and I cling to that fact. It will have to suffice for now.

The letter continued, but I read no further. I sat for a while in silence, picturing my father the last time I had seen him, five years earlier as the train pulled out of the station when I was leaving for China. I could see him waving to me, his arm around my mother, and I could hear him calling goodbye to me, his voice growing hoarse until it was lost in the distance and the sound of the train.

I heard laughter from the next room. I read the letter again, and again after that. I do not know how much time passed before Katherine came into the room to see what was keeping me. She

had only to look at my face to know that bad news had arrived. I handed the letter to her, and when Chung Hao appeared in the doorway and Katherine told him my news, he wept for my loss.

For several months my father's death felt like a blow that might level me. But one night when I went outside after dinner and stood looking up at the stars, something changed. I was breathing in the scent of wheat from the fields beyond the city wall, a smell that usually made me miss home and long for the time when Katherine and I would return to Oklahoma after our time in China to help run my family's farm, a future I'd always seen as a given.

Until that night. Despite my grief I found a gift in my father's passing: it severed my ties to my old life and freed me for my new one. From that time on I ceased thinking of my time in China as an interlude, and I no longer dreamed of returning home.

Firstborn

1915–1917

October 9, 1915

Six years ago today we arrived in Kuang P'ing Ch'eng. Some days it seems I've lived here for decades, while on others it's as if we've just arrived. It's the same with the work: one day I'm amazed at all that has been accomplished through us, and the next day all I can see is what hasn't.

Our church has fifty-six members now, and we meet three times a week—for worship on Sunday mornings, and for Bible study and prayer during the week. We ask our women members to take a vow that they will not bind their daughters' feet. In nearby villages are a dozen outstations that Will has established with Chung Hao's help; I visit them once a month as well, as sort of a traveling clinic. Will estimates that Mo Yun and I have treated thousands of people for one ailment or another, including thirteen attempted opium suicides. All but one of these survived, and while I know the one who died was too far gone when I was called, she haunts me still.

Last month we received an unexpected donation from a couple in Kansas who had

read of our work in the quarterly newsletter sent to Mennonite churches in the United States. It seemed like a small fortune, and in the letter that accompanied the check our new benefactors promised to send another gift before year's end. As the tile roof of our storefront on Hsiao Chieh leaked so badly that rainy days were as miserable inside as out, we used the money to rent a Chinese ancestral home just inside East Gate on Ch'ien Chia Chieh, Thousand House Street, an odd name as ours is the only house here, but the people see the name as a good omen. The house is unusual for a Chinese home: the design of most Chinese buildings emphasizes breadth rather than height, and many of the homes are wide U-shaped structures that are really a series of rooms. But our new home has two stories and is therefore a real find. Downstairs there is a large room suitable for a meeting hall, and upstairs are bedrooms for us and Chung Hao and Mo Yun. But best of all (to me, anyway) is the medium-sized room downstairs behind the hall, which is now our clinic. No more courtyard!

The night after we moved into our new home was Chung Chiu Chieh, the Moon Festival, which is a celebration of the autumn harvest and the end of summer, something I'm all for because of the relentless heat. (We are among

the few foreigners who tolerate the high temperatures instead of migrating to the coast, partly because of finances but also because neither of us wants to be away from Kuang P'ing Ch'eng for so long.) The Moon Festival falls on the fifteenth day of the eighth month of the lunar calendar, September 23rd this year. It's believed that the moon is brightest and fullest on this night. The people see the moon's round shape as representing the family circle, and they gather with their relations to stare up at the full moon together. This perhaps sounds silly, but it isn't; it's beautiful, and it is my favorite night of the year.

The night was quiet and clear and the moonlight so bright that the evening was like an enchanted version of day. Red paper lanterns hung from the towers of the city wall and from houses and shops on every street, as if the city were dressed up for the celebration. Chung Hao and Mo Yun and Will and I hung our own red lanterns in our courtyard then sat together outside and admired the moon, which truly was a marvel: white and perfectly round, and so big it seemed to be right above us and shining only for Kuang P'ing Ch'eng, as if our city was the moon's favorite place on earth. Chung Hao and Mo Yun recited poems about the moon and we shared moon cakes, sweet rich pastries filled with ground lotus seeds and

the yolk from a salted duck egg in the middle. The cakes are beautiful; they have a thin crust and a shiny glaze, and the top of them is imprinted with the Chinese character for harmony. They are all the more special because we have them only on this one night of the year. It was a magical night, and the fact that Chung Hao and Mo Yun celebrated with us instead of with Chung Hao's brothers touched us both deeply; we truly are a family.

Those are the rewards; there are also disappointments. Although Will is known and greeted in many parts of the city, there are days when people stop only to curse or spit at him as he preaches, and his discouragement tears at my heart. We have had converts who are faithful and enthusiastic for a few weeks then drift back to their old lives when their curiosity has been satisfied and the novelty worn off. I have patients whose ailments are too serious for me to treat, and of the ones I can, there are often too few hours in the day for fearsome diseases I've never heard of, rashes I can't diagnose, strains of malaria unmentioned in my textbooks. All we can do at these times is keep moving forward.

And dream. Although he has no idea where we will find the funding, Will dreams of building; he envisions a whole building for a clinic, instead of a room, and a school for girls

as well as boys. I too dream, but not of building. My dreams concern something else entirely—or rather someone else. I know that our lives are about to change.

Our daughter was born on an unusually warm day in May of 1916. Katherine felt unwell when she awoke that morning, but because this had happened several times in recent weeks I was not alarmed; she usually improved after a period of bed rest. By mid-morning she said the pain was gone and I went to work in the garden, partly because the work needed to be done, but more because I wanted to be nearby but not underfoot.

A few hours later I was seeding cabbage when I looked up to see Chung Hao walking toward me. There was an urgency in his gait that caught my attention instantly, and I stood motionless for a moment, just watching him. Each stride covered nearly three feet. When our eyes met, I knew he had news.

"It is time, *mu shih*," he said. "Kung Mei Li is calling for you."

For a moment I was at a loss; the day had come a week sooner than we had expected. We had made plans for Katherine's sister, Naomi, to be with us when Katherine's time came, but that useless concern fell immediately away. I dropped the hoe and ran to the house.

Mo Yun could be of some help, but she had

assisted Katherine in only two childbirths. Chung Hao said his brother's wife gave much of her time to midwifery and he would bring her to us at once, if we so desired. "Yes," I said. "Quickly."

When I went into the bedroom to wait with Katherine I was suddenly struck by the sparseness of our home and the lack of medical care available to us. But there was no time to worry; there was only time for Katherine. She smiled weakly and said, "There's a package on the floor of the dispensary. Everything is sterilized. Get it, but don't open it yet."

The calm in her voice calmed the nervousness in my heart. I went to look for the package, found it where she had said it would be, and took it to the bedroom. Then I sat down on the bed next to her and held her hand.

Nearly two hours later Chung Hao arrived with his sister-in-law, and Katherine instructed her to wash thoroughly with very hot water. Not long after, Katherine suddenly cried out in pain. Mo Yun led me from the room and told me that all was well and there was no need to worry. After this I felt certain that everyone would be better off if I stayed out of the way, so I went back outside to pace and to suggest to God that He stay very near just then.

I cannot say how much time passed before I was called inside. Though it seemed like at least

a day, it could not have been more than a few hours before Mo Yun appeared at the back door of our home. *"Mu shih,"* she called, "your firstborn is a daughter!" I hurried inside, wishing I had roses or a gift for my dear Katherine, but when I entered our bedroom and saw her holding our child, my worries left me. I knelt at the bed, weak with gratitude and relief.

July 1, 1916

We have struck gold, we have found treasure, we are rich beyond anything I have ever imagined. Her name is Lily, and she is six weeks old.

I cannot stay away from her. When she falls asleep and I place her carefully in the basket she sleeps in (the beautiful crib Will made seems far too vast for one so small), I have every intention of leaving the room to read or sew or be productive in some other way while she is asleep, but I rarely do. I don't like being away from her, and I love to watch her sleep.

She is quite a celebrity. Word of her traveled far and wide almost as soon as she entered this world, and the next day neighbors brought us noodles wrapped in red paper, a sign of prosperity, despite the fact that our firstborn was a girl, far inferior to a boy in their eyes. Now she's the one people come to see; Will and I are yesterday's news. When Lily was two

weeks old, Feng Chen Mei and her entourage returned, asking to see "the silver baby" as they call her, because of her pale skin. The women have never before seen a foreign infant, and everything about her amazes them: her blond hair and wide blue eyes, the white gown and booties I sewed for her, her crib. Even diapers! They say she is pretty and well fed, and when I enter the room holding her wrapped in a clean white coverlet, they gasp and are speechless for a moment. Then their questions begin. What does she eat to grow so big and strong so quickly? What is her sweet scent? How does she stay so clean? Why is her skin so pale, like the moon?

The women are fascinated by her, but no more so than I. No one told me that having a child is like falling in love. I feel giddy and light, and I never tire of gazing at her. She is a marvel or, as Mo Yun says, she is our Pao Pei—our Little Precious. The world seems blessed and beautiful and charmed, and I cannot remember my dull old life before our Lily. How did we live without her?

As December approached, Katherine longed to spend Christmas in Ch'eng An Fu with Edward and Naomi and their children. She was fatigued and I worried about her getting sick, but I could not refuse her. We set off two days before

Christmas, with Katherine sitting on the bench of the wagon holding our seven-month-old daughter wrapped tightly in woolen blankets. To lighten the load for the donkey, and to keep warm, I walked.

Late on the first afternoon we reached a village in the low hills of Shantung province where, because of the cold, we stopped at the first inn we came to, the Inn of Great Bliss, a dismal place that I suspected was no worse than any others. After a dinner of noodles with vinegar, we purchased millet straw from the inn's owner, a small stout woman whose manner let us know that having us as guests did not please her. In our room we spread a thick layer of straw on the earthen floor and covered it with the bedding we had brought with us, then Katherine and I lay close together on our makeshift bed with Lily nestled between us. Katherine was exhausted from sitting in the springless cart all day, and she and the baby quickly fell asleep.

I was in that vague state of half-sleep, half-wakefulness when something woke me. I looked at Katherine and saw she was asleep, which did not surprise me; she was slightly hard of hearing due to ear infections she had suffered as a child. I lay very still, listening, and heard men talking loudly in the inn's main room. I knew what kind of place we were in—rough, unfriendly to foreigners, far from the larger roads—and I knew

the group had been drinking rice wine all night. The voices grew louder and someone called out, *"Shah, shah!"*—Kill, kill!—followed by raucous laughter. My heart began to race; I was afraid not for myself but for Katherine and Lily next to me. If the situation worsened, I did not know how I would protect them.

The shouting and coarse conversation went on for a while, then suddenly there was a moment of quiet followed by a heavy thud, as though something or someone had been knocked to the floor. The voices stopped except for one man, speaking in low, even tones. Then I heard the sounds of men leaving the place, and everything became still. More time passed, and I heard only a dog barking in the distance.

I finally fell into an uneasy sleep, and when I awoke the winter sunrise had lightened the room's darkness to sepia. Outside it had begun to snow, and snowflakes had drifted in through the tile roof, leaving a thin layer of white that covered Katherine and Lily and me like a blessing. I knew we had been saved.

An hour later when I asked the proprietor for tea and noodles, she treated me very differently than she had the night before. She seemed frightened; she would not meet my eyes, and when I tried to pay for our breakfast, she shook her head vehemently. In answer to my confusion, she held out a long strip of red paper, eight

inches long and four inches wide. It was a calling card, and its size indicated that it was from a person of some notoriety; the larger the card, the more important its bearer. Two black characters were printed vertically on it, and when I read them I felt a wave of apprehension. I had heard of this person—Hsiao Lao, or Laughing Tiger—a well-known bandit chief. On the back of the card was a Chinese proverb printed in neat black characters: a *good neighbor is a found treasure.*

I had no idea what to make of the message or the card, and while I hoped not to cross paths with the bandit chief again, I decided that if I did I would be better off if he considered me a friend. I carefully folded the calling card and hid it in the lining of my woolen hat. I said nothing to Katherine.

At that time bandits were a constant and very real threat. The young republic was in turmoil; the new government established in 1911 had been unable to unite the country, leading to a period of violence and unrest that would last for decades. Without a strong central government or military presence, banditry became widespread, and men like Hsiao Lao did as they pleased. They held up travelers, taxed everything and everyone, and raided villages, towns, and cities at will, injuring or killing those who resisted and burning villages and crops to the ground.

Kidnapping was a means of increasing their income, and they targeted anyone they thought might bring a good ransom, particularly foreigners, all of whom were believed to be wealthy.

For these reasons, I worried for several months after our stay at the Inn of Great Bliss that Hsiao Lao could appear at our home at any moment, demanding what I couldn't imagine. Then our lives changed so profoundly that I didn't think of bandits or anything else in the world; I thought only of our child.

In early April of 1917, when Lily was eleven months old, she woke crying and feverish in the night. She would take neither water nor the canned milk we ordered from the United States, and the way her abdomen tensed and contracted made it clear that she was in pain. Katherine bathed her in cool water and held her, and Lily grew calmer and fell asleep.

But by next morning the fever had returned, and it remained throughout that day and evening, despite everything we did to relieve it. The next two days continued like that, Lily frighteningly hot, we trying hard to cool her.

On the third day Katherine came to me, still holding Lily in her arms. I had hardly seen her not holding Lily for those three days. Katherine's face was pale and drawn, her dark gray eyes anxious. "I know what's wrong," she said.

"There's mucus and blood in her stool. She has dysentery."

I sat down as heavily as if I had been struck. At that time and place, dysentery was nearly always fatal in an infant.

That night began our vigil. We placed wet towels on Lily's feverish body, trying to keep the fever down, and we held her close when she seemed to be in pain. She was becoming dehydrated and losing vital body salts, but there was no doctor to call and no hospital to take her to within hundreds of miles; we were everything. No matter what we did, she grew weaker by the day, sometimes experiencing bowel movements every hour. We did not have the only medications that might have helped, emetine and magnesium sulfate. Katherine had ordered both of them from Parke-Davis a year earlier, just as she always did, but we had missed several shipments of supplies, presumably intercepted by bandits. We sent a messenger to Edward in Ch'eng An Fu, but they too had missed shipments and had nothing to offer.

I had never felt such helplessness or despair. On the sixth night, unable to sleep, I went outside. In my exhaustion, I had not noticed that Katherine was not in the bed next to me, so I was surprised to find her next to me in the darkness. As I stood there, I began to question everything I had done since coming to China. Every decision

I had made—save asking Katherine to be my wife—seemed foolish and ill-conceived, and I saw that we should have gone home when we had a child. Surely we had done enough in China by then.

Finally Katherine spoke. "I have been pleading with Him," she said. "All my life, I have tried to be obedient, to say, 'Thy will, not mine.' But I can't say it tonight. For the first time since I was a child, the words won't come." She paused for a few moments. "It's my fault that we don't have any emetine or magnesium sulfate. I should have ordered them earlier. I should have ordered more." She shook her head and began to weep.

I held her close to me. "You did nothing wrong," I said, and I thought, *It's Your fault, not hers*.

Katherine was trembling in my arms, and I wished for something more to tell her. But I had no answers; all I could tell her was what I felt. "I don't understand either," I whispered, and she nodded.

Three more days passed. We held Lily constantly, for if we laid her in her crib, she cried out in pain. Mo Yun asked if she could give Lily an herbal remedy made from shepherd's purse, a weed that grew in the west of China. We said yes without having to discuss it; we had seen much evidence of Mo Yun's abilities as a healer. She charred the surface of the herb's leaves, mixed

them with honey and water, and fed them to Lily. Katherine and I were hopeful, and we watched for the slightest sign of improvement. Lily did seem better; she had a more restful night and was more peaceful in the morning. But by the next evening she was worse again.

Word of her illness spread quickly, and people brought us food we had not asked for and for which we had no appetite. On the tenth night Lily grew less fretful, which I thought to be a good sign. Then Katherine said, “Look at her eyes.” They were half open and glassy; she did not seem fully conscious. Her breathing had grown irregular and her pulse weak, and I understood that our child was dying.

At sunset Katherine asked me to hold her, a first; I usually had to convince her to rest. I took our infant in my arms then watched in disbelief as Katherine devoured a bowl of noodles, more food than she had eaten in a week, then washed it down with a cup of tea so hot it must have scalded her mouth and throat. Minutes later, when she had finished, she held her arms out, ready to take the baby back. Seeing my confusion, she said, “I need my strength.” I understood: she was eating to gain strength for Lily’s death.

Our firstborn died the evening of April 11; I cannot say the hour. I know only that it had been dark out for some time. We were in our bedroom.

A small piece of camphor wood burning in a saucer gave a soft light and a musky scent. Katherine sat in the rocking chair I had made, holding Lily in her arms; I was kneeling on the floor next to her, praying, my hand on Lily's head. Lily's breathing had become increasingly shallow and more labored.

I do not know how long we sat like that. At some point Katherine said, "She's gone," and I nodded. But we still stayed like that for some time, the only sounds in the room that of Katherine weeping and the creak of the chair as she continued to rock.

When Katherine finally laid our child's body on our bed, I could see that it was painful for her to do so. It was very late at night, but Chung Hao went for the carpenter who had helped to make our new home habitable, and as I watched, he worked in our courtyard, making a small coffin of hard Chinese elm, the same wood I had used for our furniture. Katherine and Mo Yun bathed the body and dressed our daughter in a gown of white silk that Mo Yun had made. When the carpenter had finished, he sealed the bottom of the casket, rough and unvarnished, in quicklime; then we took it to Katherine in the bedroom, where she lined it with a white coverlet. When there was no longer any excuse to wait, I carefully laid our child's body inside the coffin, the most difficult thing I had ever done.

When the workman had sealed the lid with quicklime, Katherine covered the coffin with a white coverlet my mother had sent us and with chrysanthemums brought by Mo Yun, who said they were a symbol of longevity, and that because of Christ she knew Lily's soul would have eternal life. We held a small service in our bedroom with Mo Yun and Chung Hao and a few other church members. The whole room had the clean scent of freshly cut wood, a scent that would from that time on awaken in me a sense of great loss and great love.

In the morning I visited the magistrate for permission to bury a foreigner in a Chinese cemetery. Because the magistrate's wife was Katherine's friend, she pled our case and convinced her husband that we should be allowed to bury our daughter in the family graveyard of Chung Hao, who said that it should be so because he and I were brothers.

That afternoon, Chung Hao and I visited the cemetery, a small plot of land surrounded by pine trees an hour's walk outside of the city. Katherine did not accompany us; she said it was a decision she could not make. Chung Hao and I decided on a space near his mother—so that, he said, she could watch over Lily—and Chung Hao hired workers to prepare the grave.

Early the next morning, we prepared to take the

coffin to the cemetery. When we opened the door of our home and stepped outside, we faced a large crowd, some sixty people standing closely together in the chill morning air. Word of our loss had traveled in the night, and our church family had come to accompany us. Katherine and I were stunned by the gathering, most of whom were peasants and farmers. For a few moments I could only look at them, unable to take in the fact of their presence. "Thank you," I murmured at last, and they nodded silently.

We began making our way through the city. People walked next to us and behind us and in front of us, and at the cemetery they surrounded us as I prayed aloud and read Psalm 121. Then, as Katherine and I watched, Chung Hao and two other church members lowered the coffin into the freshly dug grave, and we said goodbye to our firstborn.

April 14, 1917

We buried our daughter yesterday, and I am brought up short by the harshness of Your ways. I have given my all for You and in return You have taken the gift I love most—my sweet child. But perhaps I am mistaken; perhaps I haven't given my all but have held something back. Did I love her more than You? I know You are a jealous God, but are You that jealous, that You would take the other object of my

devotion? I feel broken, as though there is a great gash inside of me, and my only prayer is a question: "What have You done?" I ask not from anger but from confusion, for I truly do not understand.

Perhaps You are a flawed God, imperfect as we are. We are, after all, made in Your image. Perhaps it was not Your intention to take Lily, but Your inattention. Did You look away for a moment? Was Your mind elsewhere? Many times a day I ask myself what else I could have done and search for some mistake I made. But perhaps You are at fault, not I. It seems there is so much You could have done.

When I have railed against You and worn myself out, I ask You to receive me again, for I have nowhere else to go. You are my God, my only God, and for now that must be enough. I don't understand You, but I am here, as are You. That is my prayer for now.

May 20, 1917

Grief has made me a recluse. I don't like to leave our home, and while I force myself to visit those who are too sick to come to me, were I to have my way I wouldn't leave for many days. I know Will bears the same sorrow I do; I see the deep sadness in his eyes and how distracted he is when speaking to people and the way his shoulders stoop when he

doesn't know I'm watching. But what has hollowed me out seems to have given him wings. He travels now, walking miles and miles from one farming village to another. In the past either Chung Hao or I accompanied him on these treks, but he goes alone now, by choice. At first his ardor and faithfulness for our mysterious Lord made me wistful, even envious. But now I wonder, for while he says he makes these trips because there is much to do and time is short, I have begun to believe that he leaves because being here is too painful.

In a way his absences are a respite, for I keep my grief to myself when he is home. Will has a tender heart that is tenderest of all toward me, and I don't think he could bear to see the depth of my sorrow. I suspect he feels the same, which is probably for the best. I think the sharp edges of our loss and our gutted spirits make us unable to comfort each other. We are just surviving, each of us too wounded to ease the other's pain. And so I let Will see only the quiet tears—my courteous, moderated, composed grief. The rest I save for when he is away, and once he is gone I give in to my sadness and am able to do little else.

Nine days ago I was sitting at the window, trying to darn a sock. Simple tasks like these take me a long time now; I cannot keep my mind focused on what's in front of me. That

afternoon I alternated between staring down at the sock and looking out the window. I wasn't looking for anyone; Will would not be back for several days. But I kept watching anyway.

It was sometime after lunch when I saw Chung Hao go to the front gate that opens to the street and admit someone into our courtyard. I felt a wave of dread for a moment, fearing the magistrate's wife and her entourage were paying a visit. They have been extraordinarily kind to me since Lily's death, bringing all kinds of gifts: pickled eggs, apricots, candied lotus seeds, ivory chopsticks, embroidery. I am touched by their kindness, but my conversational and social skills are greatly diminished, and I did not see how I would greet them cordially. Then I saw that it wasn't the magistrate's wife or any of her companions; it was my own sister walking across our courtyard.

I am usually careful about appearances here in Kuang P'ing Ch'eng, even in our home, but I ran to Naomi like a child and fell into her arms. She held me close and whispered, *"Ach, meine Beistand"*—standby, her name for me from childhood—and I whispered the question that torments me: "Why?"

Naomi led me inside, then faced me and looked me over, taking stock. The moment was

familiar—she used to do the same thing each day when I was little, before I set out for school or church. But the sadness and worry in her expression were new, and her appraisal made me appraise myself. I saw my soiled skirt with its creases and stains and my dirty nails, and I touched my hair and could not remember when I had last brushed it thoroughly, let alone washed it.

Naomi kissed my cheek and smoothed my hair. "Come," she said, and she guided me toward the stairs. "It is as when you were little. First we wash you. Then we feed you. Then you rest." I nodded, completely willing to be taken care of. All I wanted was for her to talk more; the sound of her voice and of her faint German accent, somehow still present all these years and miles away from home, were a salve I had craved without even knowing it.

Beistand. When I was a child, I was Naomi's constant helper and assistant, ready to do whatever she asked. She was my confidante; nothing felt real until I had told her about it. I adored her, and after she told me the meaning of her name—my sweetness—I decided she was my sweetness, God's gift especially for me. When she left our home to begin her training at the orphanage, I was bereft. Her departure seemed to herald bad news; six months later our mother died, a loss I could

not take in. It wasn't until Naomi came home several months later that our mother's death became real to me.

So it was again, but with a mother's grief instead of a mother's death. Naomi called for Chung Hao and asked for hot water to be brought, and when the tub upstairs was full, she helped me undress and step into the bath. The water and Naomi's careful ministrations seemed to unloosen something in me, and as she bathed my back and unpinned my tangled hair and washed it, I wept and finally gave in to what I had refused to accept: that our child was gone.

Once I was clean and dry, Naomi helped me into fresh clothes and brushed my hair and coiled it at my neck. "Now for some food, yes?" and she led me downstairs. As I followed her, I caught sight of myself in the mirror. I never have spent much time looking at my reflection, but I've purposefully avoided it since Lily's death; I could not look at myself. So what I saw in the mirror shocked me: the dark circles under my eyes, the sharp cheekbones, my sallow complexion. But most of all, the eyes—the sorrowful eyes. I had the look of a refugee, someone far from comfort and home and unable to return.

Naomi is gone now; she left this morning. Paul and John were ill when Lily died, which

was why she was unable to come any sooner, and although they are now recovered, she is needed at Ch'eng An Fu. It was difficult to see her leave, but I am much the better for her visit. I was taught that we are Christ's hands and feet on this earth, and Naomi certainly was for me, for while my heart still aches, I feel deeply loved and cared for. If I don't feel like myself, that's all right. I have hope that someday I will, and that is enough for now.

On a hot and humid day in July I found myself in a town that looked familiar, though I could not at first recall why. It was a particularly out-of-the-way place, and as I stood in the one main street and gazed at the dingy inn in front of me, I was even surprised to find myself in a town; I couldn't remember exactly how I had gotten there. This was my state of mind at that time, always somewhat lost. In most villages and towns, people gathered around me as soon as they saw me, wanting to get a good look at the foreigner, and I would immediately begin speaking to them. But in this place the people glared at me.

When I saw the sign on the inn across from me—Inn of Great Bliss—I remembered the night at Christmas with Katherine and Lily on the way to Ch'eng An Fu: the threatening voices during the night, the delicate blanket of snow covering

us the next morning, the bandit chief's red calling card. I felt a wave of apprehension pass through me, and a voice inside told me I should continue on my way. But I chose to ignore it; I told myself that I knew best, and that I was so desperately tired and hungry that I should go inside and rest.

I stepped inside the inn as a paying customer, eager for shelter from the relentless heat and thinking I would eat a bowl of noodles before I slept. But when I entered the room, my apprehension returned, for I sensed such darkness in the place that I immediately changed my plans. I breathed in the odor of stale men and spilled wine, and the odor had the effect of smelling salts: I woke up. I found myself facing a dozen or so men seated on the benches that lined the walls, men who stared at me with hate in their eyes. The one closest to me spit noisily at the floor just in front of where I stood.

I did not hesitate; I turned and left. Outside I stood for a moment trying to decide on the best course to take. To my right I could see a sign for another inn, but I was not hopeful that I would fare any better there. My only choice seemed to be to retrace my steps and try to find another village before dark. Fatigue was no longer a problem; the feeling of threat had awoken me and I felt uncomfortably alert, almost ready to run.

As I stood there, the men from the inn came outside and gathered around me. "He thinks he is a healer," said one, and the others laughed harshly. "These foreign devils," the man went on, "you know them by their light eyes, their big noses. They are clever; do not be tricked by them. They can look at the ground and know where you have buried your silver. They make their medicines from our bones."

The man's companions murmured in agreement. A few others joined the group, and as they closed in on me, I felt their hate. A rock landed on the ground a foot away from me, and it was like a signal, for immediately rocks and hard clods of dirt began to hit me from every side.

I was strangely calm inside; my main thought was how thankful I was for the old pith helmet I was wearing, which I was never without in the summer heat. Suddenly I knew what to do: I took off the helmet and swung it in circles around my head and began to sing at the top of my lungs in the less-than-tuneful voice that God gave me the German song "O Christmas Tree." *"O Tannenbaum, O Tannenbaum, Wie treu sind deine Blätter."*

"O Christmas Tree, O Christmas Tree, Your branches green delight us."

The leader looked furious, and others watched me without speaking. For a moment I thought

they would rush me and kill me on the spot. Someone threw another rock, which hit my shoe, and another, which hit my chest. I took a deep breath and started the second verse even more off-key and with even more gusto: *"O Tannenbaum, O Tannenbaum, du kannst mir sehr gefallen":* "You give us so much pleasure."

I would not be guilty of holding back.

Then someone in the back began to laugh, and a moment later all of them joined in. "His mind has left him," the leader said with scorn. "He's a harmless fool! A barking dog seldom bites." With that my audience began to disperse, and as I finished the third verse, amazed that I remembered it, I found myself alone. I turned toward the main road and left the place, pleased with the way I had handled a difficult situation.

But my good mood did not last. It was very hot, and the dusty road was unpleasant. It was now late in the afternoon, and the road would be more dangerous at dark. In a field of tall grass on my left I saw that what I had at first thought was a dog watching me was a wolf. I knew I had to find the nearest village, but I had no idea where it was; I was lost. I had not eaten at the inn as I had planned, and the burst of energy I'd felt earlier had left me. I was hot and my head ached and my heart was beating fast, and I desperately needed to rest. I could not remember how long I had been away from home this time—six days or

seven, I thought—and I knew I should return. I tried to keep control of my thoughts by holding tightly to the words Katherine said to me each time I left home: *He knows the way that you take, Will.* But I found myself answering her in my mind: *Does He? Then where is He? Why does He let me wander like this?*

As I asked these questions and let myself dwell on them, I became angry. At first it was the heat that angered me. Then it was the dust, and the fact that I was lost. Then I was angry that I was hungry, and that I was tired, and that I was alone. I was angry that I had not started for home that morning instead of pushing on, and I was angry at Katherine for not talking me out of this trip in the first place, and I was angry that I had not turned back. I was angry at our constant struggles with money, and at our struggles with our work and our daily lives, and I was angry about our great loss, our daughter. I realized I was angry at God for all of it; I decided He had neglected us, and I felt betrayed.

My anger propelled me, and I listed my complaints and elaborated on them as I walked. I became so engrossed in my grievances that I paid no attention to where I was going, and when I finally emerged from my anger, nothing was familiar—not the road ahead or behind, the fields on either side of me, the horizon. I looked at the sun and my compass, and I realized I had

been heading west instead of south. Seeing my error encouraged me; I decided to retrace my steps until I reached another road or someone to ask.

When I turned to walk back in the direction I'd come, I saw a pool of water some distance from the road. An elm tree grew next to it, and as trees were rare, I decided to go and sit in the shade for a few minutes so that I could think more clearly about what to do next. As I neared the pool, I saw something at the edge of it, a dark gray bundle of clothing, I thought. But I knew it wasn't clothing, the way you know things without knowing them, and I could not take my eyes from it but went closer. When I stood over it I was unable to look away; it was an infant.

I knew she was not alive; I say *she* not because I knew it was a girl; I just thought *she* when I saw the child. The skin on her face was gray and slack, and I knew she had drowned. When I looked across the pool, I saw another dark bundle, which I knew was another infant, and that she, too, had drowned, and I realized it was a drowning pool, where people disposed of unwanted infants, usually girls. I had heard of such places—some towns had a tower from which parents threw their infants to dispose of them, others had pools like this. But I had never seen one, and the sight of it made me double

over. I could not get my breath; I was suddenly too weak to stand and I fell to the ground, sick in body and mind and soul.

I woke in a place I did not know, a room so dark I couldn't tell if it was day or night. The air was cool and smelled of earth, and I was lying on a low pallet with a dirty gray quilt covering me. A chipped cup was on the floor and I reached for it and drank lukewarm tea that I hoped wouldn't make me sicker, but I was too thirsty to care. My clothes were torn and filthy, and I was barefoot, my sandals gone.

I was weak and sore, but I sat up and tried to recall what had happened. I remembered being lost and thought I must have had a fever because I recalled being very hot, not only outside from the sun's heat but inside as well. I no longer felt feverish, but my body ached. Breathing deeply was painful, and as I touched my arms and legs and shoulders and chest, testing, I found I was tender and sore in many places. I had been dreaming that I was being beaten, but as I took stock of my physical condition I understood that it was not a dream. Then I remembered the drowning pool, but I recalled nothing after it.

I stood and tried the door and found it bolted from the outside. There were no windows in the room; the walls seemed to be made of packed earth, like a cave. A few lines of gauzy light

came in through the cracks in the door. Since I saw no way of escape, I decided that all I could do was wait, and I sat down again, and as I sat there I remembered the anger and resentment I had felt while walking. I saw that my anger had come from self-pity and a lack of faith, and my failings grieved me. I asked God for His forgiveness, and for His strength for whatever were the consequences of my actions. My father had told me when I was young that courage was not strength in the absence of fear but strength in the presence of fear, and I asked God for the courage to withstand whatever lay ahead. I felt His forgiveness wash over me, lessening my remorse.

Perhaps an hour later I heard the door being unlocked and an old man entered the room. His garments were rags, and he was lame and stooped over with arthritis. He said nothing, only held out a cup to me, and I took it and thirstily drank more lukewarm weak tea. The old man left but returned shortly with a wooden bowl of boiled sweet corn, which I ate like a dog, as I had no chopsticks. It wouldn't have mattered; I was starved.

My jailer watched me eat, and when I had finished, he motioned that I should come with him. With a shaky courage and trembling legs, I followed him through what I supposed was a large ancestral home, albeit in ruins and not a

typical residence, but a maze of rooms that seemed to have been added on over time. At least some of the structure seemed to be built into the earth. I had for a moment entertained thoughts of escape, but when I saw my complicated surroundings, I gave up those ideas, not only because of the crazy structure of the place but also because there were men everywhere I looked, too many to count, lounging like large rats in room after room.

I was led outside and across a large courtyard where the air smelled cleanly of the mountains, a fact that added to my apprehension, for it meant I was far away from the plain, and therefore from home and familiar territory. My guide and I entered a large room with a few rough tables and chairs and with several mattresses on the floor along the wall. The mattresses surprised me; real mattresses were unusual in that part of China, especially outside of large cities, and as I looked at them I realized they were the narrow types used in train berths, and I knew they'd been stolen. A dozen or so men sat at the tables, talking and drinking and cleaning their rifles. They looked at me with a mix of mild curiosity and scorn.

Next we came to a larger room, where my ancient escort motioned to a wooden bench by the door and told me to wait, then left me there. The room smelled of opium, a thick, cloying

odor like burnt chestnuts. Low wooden platforms lined the walls, and men lay on them in twos, facing each other with an oil lamp between them. Each man held a long narrow wooden pipe with its bowl over the lamp's flame. In the bowl of each pipe was a dark ball of opium paste that sputtered as the men sucked in the fumes, lost in their smoky dreams.

My jailer returned and again motioned for me to follow him. We passed through a smaller courtyard, then through a short hallway and into a room that seemed to be at the back of the residence. The air grew cooler with each room, which confirmed my suspicions about the house being built into the side of a mountain.

When I entered this inner room, I faced two men sitting across from each other on low wooden chairs with a battered table of Chinese blackwood between them. The man on the left was large and imposing, with thick black hair and high cheekbones. The first thing I noticed about the man on the right was that he was wearing my pith helmet; the second was the rifle that lay across his lap. He and the larger man were quietly playing fan-tan, a simple betting game in which players place a pile of coins under a bowl, then bet on what the remainder will be after the coins have been counted off in fours.

The smaller man seemed to be in charge. As I stood there he looked me over coolly and seemed

unimpressed with what he saw. A boy of perhaps ten sat on the floor at his feet. He turned to the young man and asked pleasantly, “Shall I kill him for you?”

I looked quickly at the leader to gauge the seriousness of the boy’s offer, but he shook his head, laughing. “A good neighbor is a found treasure,” he said, and he watched for my reaction.

I knew the phrase immediately; it was the proverb from the back of the calling card that had been given to me at the inn at Christmas. I also knew that this was the bandit chief Hsiao Lao—Laughing Tiger—my benefactor that night, and the realization brought a rush of fear.

The bandit chief smiled broadly and took from his sleeve the same calling card, now battered and worn. He held it out to me, and when I did not reach for it, his expression turned serious. “I left this for you at the inn so that you would know your benefactor, *mu shih*. I suggest you take it. Who knows when you will need it again?”

I nodded. My hand shook as I took the card.

The bandit chief turned back to his game, and he and his companion continued to play as I looked on. I was hesitant to stare openly at him but unable to do otherwise. Chung Hao had once seen a bandit chief who lived in the northwest, toward Mongolia, a man who was feared by all

who knew of him. His hideout was in the ruins of an abandoned temple, where he and his men lived on boiled mutton and wine from leather flasks. He wore padded sheepskin trousers, a peaked wool hat, and a bandolier across his chest, and he led his gang as they attacked caravans at dawn.

My bandit chief was nothing like this. He was younger and smaller than his companion, slender and small-boned, with pale skin and delicate features. His eyes were alert and intelligent, his face round, his lips thick and wide, his expression jovial and relaxed. He seemed incapable of frowning. His attire was bizarre: a dirty white dress shirt and green brocade vest, gray pinstripe trousers, and black rain boots that looked English. A long string of pearls hung around his neck, and diagonally across his chest he wore what I first thought was some sort of black satin sash but which I realized was the cummerbund for a tuxedo. The white garment fastened around his waist was a woman's brassiere, which he was using as a sort of two-compartment coin purse.

Finally Hsiao Lao looked at me and gestured to the coins in front of him. "Come," he said. "Play awhile." He blushed as he spoke, and for a moment he looked too boyish to be a threat to anyone. Then he growled a command at the man sitting across from him. The man jumped up and

hurried out of the way, and I saw fear in his movements and menace in my bandit chief's eyes.

"I do not gamble," I said cautiously. "It is against my teaching."

Hsiao Lao regarded me evenly and rested a hand on the rifle in his lap. "You may play without gambling. If you are using my money and not your own, it is not gambling, *mu shih*. It seems you owe me this courtesy, does it not?"

I sat down. The bandit chief counted out a dozen coins from the brassiere fastened around his waist, and the two of us began to play in silence. His hands were graceful, with ornate rings on each long slender finger, and he gave off the scent of cologne. Except for the sounds of men laughing and shouting from other parts of the house, the room was silent.

Fan-tan is a game of pure luck; even so, I tried to lose and succeeded many times by betting on the number three over and over again. The bandit chief did not speak while we played, but stared intently at the coins and the bowl, deliberating over which number to choose and smoking a long-stemmed pipe with a bone mouthpiece.

While we played, I assessed my future. I assumed I was being held for ransom, a chief means of support for bandits. Katherine and I had very little cash, every dollar of which was desperately needed for our work, but even if we

had had a larger sum, I would not have wanted it spent on my safety. My one hope was that I was more valuable to my captor alive than dead.

When perhaps half an hour had passed, Hsiao Lao nodded to his large companion, who took the bowl and coins from the bench. The bandit chief looked at me and, blushing again, he said, "I am honored you have visited me."

I did not hesitate. I knew how conversation worked in that time and place: one compliment was answered with a greater one. "It is I who am honored to be received," I said, as if visiting royalty.

"Your stay here was not planned," the bandit said.

"I do not remember how I came to be here," I said, trying to make my lapse sound casual.

Hsiao Lao smiled wryly. "Perhaps your God was watching over you. I have heard stories of this God you believe in: that you speak to Him as if He lives with you here"—he touched his chest—"and that you believe He cares for you as a father cares for a son."

"Yes."

"Then perhaps you are right, for you have been most fortunate. You were very ill when my men brought you here two days ago. The heat had overpowered you, as often happens with those who do not know the strength of our sun. But you were not only ill; you had been beaten, and you

lay near a road that is heavily traveled. You had no shoes, but you are fortunate: you still had your clothes. You also had these, which I assumed you wanted me, your benefactor, to have." He held out his wrist, on which he wore the watch my father had given me, and from the brassiere around his waist, he took my compass. "And you had your excellent hat." He grinned and tapped my pith helmet on his head. "When my men examined your hat, they found my name, so they brought you to me"—he laughed gently—"as though you were a belonging I had misplaced. You were not in possession of your senses. You were at a drowning pool, and I believe you would have died had you been left there."

"I am grateful to you."

He went on. "There was also the inn some months ago. Foreign-born, do you know what would have happened to you and your wife and child at the inn that night had I not intervened?"

"I suspect we would have been killed."

The bandit chief smiled; he seemed pleased. "Correct. So it seems I have saved your life twice now, *mu shih*, first in the dark of night, and now in the heat of day."

I winced at the thought of being indebted to this man, but I knew my life was in his hands just then. "It was most honorable of you," I said.

He laughed. "Lest you be misled, be assured

that my reasons for helping you were not mora but practical; I view you as an investment tha could prove useful. Life is unpredictable; w never know what we will need." He regarded m carefully for a moment. "You have a child. Were you blessed with a son?"

"A daughter," I said. "She passed on."

He shook his head, and for a moment his expression seemed truly pained. "It is unfortunate to lose your firstborn, even a girl."

I said nothing.

The bandit continued. "So you know how it is for a father to see his child ill. I suspect fate has brought us together again, for I have heard of your healing and my eldest son—my firstborn—is in need of your attention."

I shrugged, hoping to make myself appear useless. "I have only the clothes on my back. Nor am I trained for that kind of work. I am only a teacher, not a healer."

Hsiao Lao shook his head. "I think not. There are many stories about the foreign-born's healings."

I suspected he had heard stories of Katherine, not me, but I did not correct him. "I have no supplies," I said.

Hsiao Lao stood and picked up a kerosene lamp. "That we can remedy," he said. "Come."

I followed him out of that room and into another next to it, inside of which were two

immense wooden cabinets side by side, the largest pieces of furniture I'd ever seen. Chinese homes had cabinets such as these instead of closets, but I had never seen any so big. Each one was perhaps twelve feet high, four feet wide, and very deep, with a heavy brass lock on its doors.

Hsiao Lao unlocked the first cabinet then opened its doors and stood aside. "Are we not well stocked?" he asked.

I looked inside and saw that the cabinet was crammed with stolen foreign goods: a rolled-up rug, leather suitcases, a mantel clock, a camera, a silver tea service, several quilts, and shoes and stacks of clothing piled high. There were also opened Red Cross relief boxes that held provisions I had not seen in years—cans of bully beef and ham, boxes of raisins, canned fruit. It was the sort of bandit's loot I had expected. I said, "There's nothing here I can use for your son."

Hsiao Lao smiled slyly. "Perhaps here," he said, and he unlocked the second cabinet and opened its doors wide. I found myself staring at boxes that said CHINA MENNONITE MISSIONARY SOCIETY, MONTGOMERY WARD, and SEARS, ROEBUCK AND CO., all of which I knew were ours, supplies sent by our mission board twice a year and that Katherine had ordered: household goods such as sandpaper and twine, needles and

thread; personal items such as toothbrushes and toothpaste, safety razors and shaving cream, fountain pens and pocketknives, all things that were ordinary at home and precious here and that we had waited for and missed month after month.

Then, high on the cabinet's top shelf, I saw boxes from Parke-Davis and Burroughs-Welcome, the companies from which Katherine ordered medical supplies. My heart beat faster as I reached up and took one down. Inside I found gauze bandages and plaster of Paris and adhesive tape, tubes of ointment and bottles of powders and pills that Katherine used every day, among them emetine and magnesium sulfate—the medicines we had needed for our daughter.

I said nothing but stood there in silence, demanding of God an answer to the question in my heart: *Why is this man's child alive and mine dead?*

"Are you not impressed, *mu shih*?" Hsiao Lao asked.

"Yes," I said softly. "I am most impressed." It felt like an admission of defeat.

"Now you have the honor of helping my son," Hsiao Lao announced grandly. "His cheek has been badly cut. Take what you need and we will go to him."

I saw no choice but to do what he said. I took a box that held gauze bandages, tape, and plaster

of Paris, and I followed Hsiao Lao out of that room and through the maze of his home.

When we reached what seemed to be the opposite side of the dwelling from where we had started, we entered a small room where a boy of perhaps twelve sat playing cards with a young woman. When we entered, the woman quickly rose and stood with her back to the wall, her head bowed. Hsiao Lao growled something I did not understand, his tone harsh, and she hurried from the room as if she'd been struck.

The boy looked up at us solemnly. He had his father's wide lips, but where they made the father seem jovial, they made the son seem arrogant and scornful. The boy regarded me coolly, with an expression that told me he considered himself my superior. I did not have time to dwell on this, for a dirty rag was tied around his head covering the left side of his face, and I was dreading what the crude bandage concealed.

Hsiao Lao stood behind the boy, his pride evident. "My first-born, Pao Hsing," he said—Precious Star—and he rested his hand on the boy's head and gazed down at him with great tenderness, as any father would. Then he knelt and began to gently remove the cloth from the boy's head as the boy sat there, unmoved. "He and another boy were out in the fields yesterday," Hsiao Lao said, "and they had their

knives. While they were playing, the other boy cut my son's cheek. The culprit has since been punished for his carelessness." The bandit lifted the rag from the boy's face, and I saw that he had indeed been badly cut. A long deep gash ran from his cheekbone to the corner of his mouth.

Hsiao Lao looked at me expectantly. "Well, healer? What can you do? This is perhaps your most important patient."

I nodded, fully understanding him, for I had no doubt that I would be killed if I failed to help the boy. As I knelt next to him, he looked at me with wide dark eyes that were at once imploring and demanding and defiant; he knew well who he was. I asked God for guidance and tried to think of any of Katherine's patients who had had similar wounds. "The wound can heal," I began, "but the upper and lower parts of the corner of the mouth will not grow together if the boy is constantly opening his mouth to eat and speak."

Hsiao Lao's tone was impatient. *"Wai-kuo jen"*—outside countryman—"your words do nothing. Can you help him?"

I gave the only answer I could: "Yes."

Hsiao Lao nodded, and I got to work. I took the package of plaster of Paris from the box I had brought with me from the cabinet and asked for a pot of boiled water. He called out and the young woman he had sent from the room opened

the door, nodded at his command, and ran off.

While we waited for her to return, Hsiao Lao played cards with his son as I looked on. When the water was delivered, I carefully cleaned the wound, then mixed a generous amount of plaster with the water. I brought together the edges of the wound and, as Hsiao Lao held them in place, I covered the length of the wound with a thick piece of gauze followed by first one and then another layer of plaster. The boy was patient during all of this, staying very still and watching my face.

When I had finished, I stood up and looked nervously at Hsiao Lao. Probably less than an hour had passed, but I felt as though I had been working all afternoon. I gave whatever instructions I could think of, dictated by common sense. "He cannot have solid food, only liquids. If he must open his lips, he must hold the corners of his mouth together with his fingers."

The bandit nodded knowingly, as if these were his thoughts exactly. "In how many days will he be healed?"

I had no idea. "Three weeks," I said, because it sounded reasonable. "Twenty-one days."

Hsiao Lao shook his head. "Twenty-one is an unfavorable number. Twenty-four is more fortuitous."

I was feeling flexible. "Very well," I said. "In twenty-four days his wound will be healed."

The bandit chief looked satisfied. “If you are correct, you may then return to your home. If not, you will stay until the boy has healed.”

I stared at him in disbelief. “I cannot possibly remain here.”

The bandit waved my words away. “Oh, but you can, *mu shih*,” he said, and he paused. “If I wish it.”

I shook my head. “My wife is in Kuang P’ing Ch’eng. She is still recovering from the loss of our child. She will worry; she will be tormented.”

He said nothing.

“Hsiao Lao, I beg you to allow me to go home, and I will return when it is time to remove the plaster. I am a man of honor and of God.”

Still he said nothing for perhaps a minute. Then he said, “You will send word saying that you are safe. I do not wish to worry Kung Mei Li.”

He watched me closely as he said my wife’s name, and I understood the unspoken threat. It had the desired effect; I was afraid for her, and I nodded obediently.

“You will not say where you are, only that you will be here helping others, which I believe is the reason you came to our country.”

I nodded again.

“There is much for you to do here. My men are plagued by all manner of maladies, which I am

certain you can cure. After twenty-four days, if my son has healed and my men are in good health, you may go."

My spirits sank at the uncertainty of remaining in that place, but I understood there was nothing I could do. The bandit chief called again to the woman outside, and she brought paper and pen and ink to me. Hsiao Lao looked on as I wrote to Katherine. I started in English, but he snatched the paper away from me and told me to write in his language. I started again, this time writing Chinese characters, and when I was finished, I handed my work to my taskmaster, who read it with disdain. I said that I had been sick, and that strangers had taken me in and would care for me until I was well enough to return home. I said I was safe, that I would be home in four weeks, and that I prayed for her peace of mind.

I was taken back to my room and left alone. I had no idea what time it was; it felt very late. I heard shouting and loud carrying on in other parts of the house. For the most part I could not understand what they were saying, but a few times I heard the bandits playing a game in which one man quoted a line of poetry, then someone else supplied the next line. This went on for what seemed like hours. Finally the noise died down, presumably because they had had enough opium to make them doze, and I too fell into an uneasy sleep.

• • •

I was awakened by my jailer. I guessed it was still night; the room was very dark. The old man motioned for me to go with him, and once again I followed him through the maze of the bandits' home. At one point I thought how foolish it was to be up so late; how was I going to get up in the morning to do all that needed to be done? Then I remembered where I was, and I realized that for perhaps the first time in my life it did not matter what time I got up in the morning.

I could not imagine that being summoned by a ruthless bandit in the middle of the night was good, and I tried to brace myself for whatever was next. But when we entered Hsiao Lao's room I found him sitting alone, quietly cleaning his rifle, and he seemed genuinely glad to see me. He greeted me like an old friend. *"Mu shih,"* he said graciously, "how good of you to visit me again."

I nodded cautiously. "It is good of you to receive me."

"What kind of health does your honorable grandfather enjoy?" he asked.

It was custom to inquire after a guest's ancestors. "My grandfather left this world many years ago."

Hsiao Lao nodded and then seemed to register my confusion at the late hour. "Ah," he said, nodding, "I am often unable to sleep." His tone

was gentle, as though explaining something difficult to a child. "My great intelligence keeps me awake. So you and I will talk and pass the night until I can rest. We have much to discuss." He eagerly motioned for me to sit across from him, and when I had seated myself, he looked at me for a long moment and I met his gaze.

"You are looking at my eyes," he said. "The color surprises you."

"It does. I have not met anyone in China with eyes like yours."

"What color would you say they are?"

"Golden brown," I said. "Like amber."

He nodded, pleased. "Just *so, mu shih*. My ancestors believed that amber contains the soul of the tiger, and that it gives strength and courage to anyone who wears it. The color of my eyes is a sign that I have the tiger's soul, and with it his courage and strength. I am named for him."

I was somewhat taken aback at the bandit chief's high opinion of himself, but I answered politely, *"Ni t'sa ch'ien'la"*—You are too modest. Then I added, "Perhaps over time you will gain his confidence as well."

He missed my tone. "That I have as well," he said matter-of-factly. Then he regarded me for a moment and said, "I believe you are a man of education, *mu shih*. Where did you receive this gift?"

The night seemed more and more dreamlike,

but the rifle at the bandit chief's side and the intensity of his gaze were both very real, so I answered his question. "The Mennonite Bible Academy in Corn, Oklahoma."

Hsiao Lao nodded as though he knew the place well and said, "As I suspected, an excellent institution." He was quiet then, and I knew he wanted me to ask him the same question; it was characteristic of Chinese conversation to ask a question that you wanted to be asked.

"And you, Hsiao Lao?"

"I studied at the university of the green forest," he said, and when I did not respond, he smiled broadly. "Bandits have been my teachers."

He went on to tell me about his life. He was born into a peasant family, and in an attempt to provide for his children, his father joined the imperial army. A harsh and cruel man, his father enlisted Hsiao Lao in the military when he was just ten. In an effort to better himself, Hsiao Lao vowed not to drink alcohol or use opium, as both would dull his senses and his talents, a vow he had continued to keep, though he did not require it of his men. He learned to read because as a boy he had heard stories about the region's bandits and warlords, men who were wild and fierce and noble, and he had wanted to read those stories for himself. Those led him to the tales of famous warriors in the Chinese classics, which awoke in Hsiao Lao a strong feeling of love for China in

general and for the northeast in particular, the region that was home for him and for many of the great warriors. He had gone on to read and memorize many of the classics, and he encouraged his men to do the same.

In comparison to the warlords of the past, he considered the military leaders of his time to be inept and corrupt, seduced by the lure of power and wealth. He came to revile them and, because he would not compromise, he left the military and joined a bandit gang whose leader possessed passion and courage. Because the military had paid him almost nothing and because he had grown up poor, he was determined not to grow old that way.

Hsiao Lao was then not yet twenty, but White Wolf, the leader of the bandit gang, recognized his intelligence and made Hsiao Lao his confidant and advisor. White Wolf soon consulted Hsiao Lao on every decision: when to attack, where to attack, how to treat his men, how much opium to buy, how to punish disobedience. Hsiao Lao found he had the gift of foresight: he could examine a situation and see in his mind exactly what to do at that moment. White Wolf was superstitious; his previous advisor had been a Taoist soothsayer in whom Hsiao Lao placed no trust. Hsiao Lao explained that he made his recommendations not by looking at the stars but by looking in his heart

and mind, and the soothsayer was dismissed.

When the bandit gang was attacked without warning by a small band of imperial soldiers, White Wolf's trust in Hsiao Lao wavered, and he secretly met with his former soothsayer. After that night, the soothsayer was not seen alive again; his headless body was found outside the next morning. With the soothsayer's murder, White Wolf grew more nervous and became fearful of everything and everyone. Hsiao Lao quietly pointed out the chief's weaknesses to his men and said that their leader's caution was cowardice, that his plans were doomed. When White Wolf mysteriously died after eating dinner with only Hsiao Lao, the men were not surprised. Killing one's enemy during a feast was a well-honored tradition of war.

"Since that time I have been the guardian of Feng Hsiang Chou, the town in which you and your wife and daughter stayed, and where you became ill." Feng Hsiang Chou—City of Felicitous Winds—was a place Hsiao Lao said he owned, which was very nearly the truth, as he demanded large payments from its residents, payments he called taxes but which were really simple extortion. He taxed weddings and funerals, wealth and profits, livestock and land. There were taxes on everyday items such as grain and salt and firewood, and on luxuries such as tobacco and opium. If he needed additional

funds or if he sensed disloyalty in his citizens, he created new taxes, or he required his citizens to pay their existing taxes years in advance. Just then he was considering a tax that would pay for a shrine to the benefactor of Feng Hsiang Chou—himself. In return for these payments, he offered the village protection from other bandit gangs, mostly through his reputation for swift and brutal retaliation.

I listened without speaking, and when he paused, I knew I was expected to respond. "You are indeed a benefactor," I said carefully. I did not want to praise him for his robbery; I also did not want to anger him.

"Continue, *mu shih*."

"You are a forward-thinking man in many respects, but there is a practice here that is very backward and that therefore puzzles me. In my country it would be most shameful."

Hsiao Lao narrowed his eyes.

"It is the drowning pool. The killing of infants is barbaric, and it is most surprising that someone as enlightened as yourself would permit it. No doubt it is an outdated practice that has been overlooked."

Hsiao Lao still did not speak; he continued to stare at me for perhaps half a minute. Then he started to laugh. "I will close the drowning pool, *mu shih*. It is a simple enough matter. I have many more important matters to think of." He

yawncd and looked around as if getting his bearings. "Tomorrow you will begin treating my men, who are in great need of your care." Then, whether from fatigue or irritation I did not know, he waved me away, and my first night with the bandits finally came to an end.

The next day I was taken to a large room toward the front of the residence, where I began my brief career as bandit physician. The rolled-up rug I had seen in Hsiao Lao's cabinet had been spread out on the floor of the room, a rich oriental tapestry of crimson and deep blue, far more beautiful than anything in our home in Kuang P'ing Ch'eng. A large old wooden table had been set on the rug, and boxes of Hsiao Lao's confiscated medical supplies had been arranged around the table. A pair of worn Chinese cloth shoes lay on the floor and I put them on eagerly, as my bare feet felt raw.

Along the walls were benches and crude chairs, where a few dozen bandits sat glowering at me. As they watched I began to take stock of my supplies, trying to look competent. My unfortunate patients passed the time by showing off their stolen possessions to one another, playing poker and fan-tan, cleaning their guns, and drinking hot rice wine from leather flasks.

Their laughter and talking suddenly stopped, and when I turned from my boxes I found that

Hsiao Lao had joined us. As he looked around him, he seemed very proud of the setup, and I could see he expected me to express my amazement, which I did. Then he stood before me, inhaled and exhaled deeply a few times, and said, "I would like an examination."

"Very well," I said. "What is your complaint?"

He stared at me blankly.

"Your ailment?"

"I have none," he answered.

"Then what is it I can do for you?"

"Examine me," he said impatiently, "so that my men will see what it is to be in perfect health and therefore be given proof of how rightly I live my life."

The bandits nodded as if they thought this wise. As there seemed to be only one way forward, I said I would be honored to give the bandit chief a thorough and modern western-style physical examination. I did not say that it was also the first I had ever performed.

I started by gathering my tools: a stethoscope, thermometer, and package of tongue depressors. I set these things out carefully on a wooden crate and asked the bandit chief to lie down on the table, which he did with much show. I glanced at my audience and saw they were transfixed, and I thought how elated I would be with such rapt attention when I preached.

I then began to do whatever I could think of to

the bandit chief, not knowing exactly what I was doing, but not worrying about it much since he didn't either. I started by pressing the stethoscope to his chest and listening to his heart. I nodded. "Very strong," I said. "Like a tiger."

Hsiao Lao smiled proudly at his men, and once again they nodded.

I pressed the stethoscope to his back and told him to breathe deeply as I listened to his lungs. "Excellent," I said. "The lungs of a stallion."

Next I took the thermometer and explained to Hsiao Lao how to hold it under his tongue. I read his temperature and pronounced it perfect as well, then used the tongue depressor to look into his mouth. I did this quickly, as many of his teeth were black and his breath foul. Once again, I said all was well.

During each of these tasks, Hsiao Lao regarded me as seriously as if he were gravely ill, then seemed elated and relieved by each assurance of good health. His men watched with equal parts apprehension and fascination, and cheered at my pronouncements.

Lastly I placed my hands gently around the bandit chief's neck. I saw a flash of suspicion in his eyes, but as I began to check the glands under his jaw and in his neck, he relaxed. "Once again, perfect," I said finally, and I turned to the men. "Your leader is indeed in excellent health." At this the men began to cheer as loudly as if a great

victory had been won, and the bandit chief stood and smiled broadly at them, relishing their praise. What was odd was that I was telling the truth, for while I was no doctor, I knew enough to know that despite the foul breath and awful teeth, the bandit chief truly was in good health, all the more remarkable because of the life he lived.

When the men were quiet, Hsiao Lao looked at them somberly. "A man's good health is his gift to himself," he said. "A leader's good health is his gift to his men." He announced that I was a wise healer, then he glared at his men and told them to obey my instructions, and finally he left.

Then his men and I were left alone, and my real work began, for unlike their leader they had complaints that were all too real, and I spent that day treating one man after another. I lanced their boils and cleaned their cuts and sores, swabbed their throats, and applied hot compresses and ointment to their bloodshot eyes. I treated mouth sores, scabies, ringworm, and intestinal parasites. Many of them had bullet wounds, some minor, others that should have been fatal, and I addressed the gastric complaints caused by the constant use of opium, for the majority of the men were addicts. But unlike most opium addicts, who were emaciated and skeletal, these men were strong and hardy, which was even more remarkable given their hard lives.

As I treated each man, all the while praying I wasn't killing any of them, those waiting their turn watched warily. I desperately tried to recall the hours I had spent assisting Katherine, and sometimes I imagined her watching me. The alarm I knew she would feel at the idea of me acting as physician was the only thought that made me smile.

July 21, 1917

Will has been gone for nine days, the longest he has ever been away. I expected him home three days ago, but a letter was left at the gate during the night—by whom we don't know—in which he says he is safe but that he has been ill and will be home in four weeks. This has never happened before, and while Chung Hao tells me that all is well and that *mu shih* is most certainly needed somewhere for legitimate reasons, I am not convinced.

This morning as I sat with Mo Yun at breakfast, I stared out at the courtyard, waiting to see Chung Hao come toward the house with news of Will. I had no interest in my meal. Without looking at me, Mo Yun pushed my bowl an inch closer to me, then continued eating in silence. I pushed the bowl away. She pushed it toward me again. Once more I pushed it away.

Again she pushed it toward me. Then she

said, "Worrying this way does you no good, Mei Li. It is drinking poison to quench your thirst. I know that I am young in my faith and there is much I do not know, but of this I am certain: if your fears rob you of your strength and conquer your heart, it is the people of Kuang P'ing Ch'eng who will pay the price. Surely you do not wish to punish them." She nudged the bowl a little closer to me. "You must eat. If not for yourself, then for them."

I started to reply, to ask her crossly when had she lost a child and possibly a husband, but before the words left my mouth I tasted their self-pity and recalled that the woman speaking to me has buried not one but three children and has felt such pain that she wanted to end her life. In fact, nearly everyone I know in Kuang P'ing Ch'eng has known more loss than I, and I saw that even now my life is blessed.

So I ate, and today I gave myself to my work with a concentration I have not felt since before Lily's death, and therein found some relief for my anguish.

For many days after that I treated one man after another. I prayed each morning to do God's will, then treated men who had burned whole villages, stolen from us, and demanded extortion money from peasants who had never in their lives had enough to eat. My ministrations were often given

through clenched teeth and with an angry and bitter heart. But each morning when I asked God for the grace to obey Him, I remembered a story from my childhood. A man sees a blacksmith hammering a sheet of metal. The bystander, after watching the blacksmith's efforts for some time, says, *"Schlag nur zu. Es gibt eine Schaufel"*—"Keep knocking away, a shovel is taking shape."

I estimated that somewhere around eighty men lived in that strange house, and as I saw at least a dozen men a day, I thought my work would soon be done, and I hoped I might then be able to persuade the bandit chief to release me. But I was mistaken, for the bandits surprised me: they liked being treated. Day after day I found them waiting for me, sometimes with new complaints, sometimes just wanting me to repeat whatever I'd done before, seemingly on the theory that if a little was good, more was better. I also began to suspect they were becoming hypochondriacs, for some of them invented new and vague illnesses that tended to disappear the moment I applied ointment to whatever part of their body they claimed was hurting.

As I spent time with them, I began to know them. Some were just local hoodlums; some were farmers who saw stealing and kidnapping as quick ways to make money. Others had had no other way to make a living and found themselves forced into banditry by necessity, or they were

ex-soldiers who, after going for months without pay, left their units and joined whatever bandit gang was strongest. Their main topic of conversation was opium: how much they had and when they might get more. On the days when their supplier brought his usual amount—two hundred egg-sized lumps wrapped in oiled paper—the bandits were cheerful and content. But there was no guarantee as to the quantity: soldiers sometimes confiscated much of the region's available opium, in which case the supplier might bring half or less of the normal quantity. At such times, the bandits were like men possessed, wailing and shouting and abusing one another until dawn.

Each evening after delivering my ministrations, I was returned to my small room until Hsiao Lao demanded my company. In my cell, I was given a bowl of moldy-tasting boiled corn and water from an earthenware jug that looked ancient. Most of the time Hsiao Lao ate what his men ate, but there were exceptions. One day he grandly offered to share with me some half-cooked pig tripe, which I could not stomach. Another time he gave me soup with pieces of tough meat that he said was "young cow" but which I learned from my jailer was Shantung dog, and still another time he offered me a thin flat *kaoliang* cake stuffed with boiled scorpions minus their stingers and shells. I refused these

and ate only what the men ate, partly because I couldn't tolerate Hsiao Lao's offerings, but also because I knew they were stolen. When I mentioned this to him he only shrugged, but the next night when he sent for me, he smiled. "I have solved your problem. You may eat our eggs. Those we do not steal. We raise the chickens ourselves." Then he handed me an egg, took one himself, poked small holes in both ends of the shell, and sucked out its contents. He motioned for me to do the same, saying, "Eggs bring longevity." I refused at first, but Hsiao Lao regarded me sternly and said, "Surely you are not so foolish, *mu shih*. Is a long life not something you hope for? If not, I can arrange otherwise."

His bluntness surprised me. I took the egg from him, not for longevity but for protein. "If you kill an American, Hsiao Lao, will your life not be short as well?"

For a tense moment he glared at me. Then he began to laugh as if both of our lives were a wonderful joke. From that night on, he gave me an egg each night.

His attire each evening was a puzzle I had to stare at for some moments to decipher, with each ensemble stranger than the last and accessorized with jewelry, belts, scarves, and sashes worn in all kinds of strange ways. One night he wore a bowler hat, a silk kimono, and a mohair scarf tied around his waist; the next night he appeared

in a cardigan sweater, pajamas, and a straw hat. Along with the rifle across his lap, the only certainty was that he would be wearing some kind of hat. Had I seen a photograph of him, I would have thought him comical, but the rifle and his unpredictable moods made me take him quite seriously. I had the feeling he put a great deal of thought into his ensembles and that he hoped to impress me, and I complimented him on his choices. I admired his foreign shoes, his wristwatch (which was mine and which I showed him how to wind), his necktie, and whatever else he wore. He was the only one who dressed in this fashion; his men might wear a trinket or two, some new possession of which they were particularly proud, but their clothes were limited to layers of loose brownish-gray rags whose original shapes and colors I could no longer discern.

August 4, 1917

Twenty-three days and no word. I read and reread Will's brief letter, looking for some clue I didn't see before, but I find none. I try to think of good reasons for his being away but can't, and I become convinced that he is in danger and that I am going to lose both of them, first her and now him, which terrifies me. I was raised to believe that a loving God directs my steps and that, for those who love God, all

things work together for their good. But each morning when I wake and remember my circumstances, I question Him: This is Your design for my life, this agonizing subtraction?

I want help. I want someone to go looking for my husband, I want to send out the cavalry, I want good news, I want him home. But there is nothing; no action to take, no one to send, no news—no Will. All I can do is wait and pray, and when I have ranted and raved in my mind and worn myself out, I ask God to receive me again.

My faith feels tattered and threadbare and I am ashamed. What good is it if it does not see me through pain? But a scrap of faith is better than nothing, so I cling to it tightly. With as much trust as I can muster, I ask Him for the thousandth time to keep my dear one safe. Somehow the day passes and I am able to be useful, and at night He lets me sleep. In the morning we begin again.

During the hours I spent with my host (mostly in the middle of the night, owing to his insomnia), we discussed a wide range of subjects. There was much he wanted to know about America—the distance from my country to the moon, what we ate, how we lived, what kinds of guns we used, how we protected ourselves from foreigners, what our city walls were made of. He wanted to

know what my life had been like when I was young, and whether I was wealthy. When I told him I wasn't and that I would not bring any ransom at all since our mission, like many, refused to pay ransoms, the bandit chief became indignant. This was most offensive, he said; how could I not be wealthy, given my extensive knowledge of western medicine? He said he was most ashamed for me; it was a great affront that I was not worth a large sum of money.

He also wanted to know about this God I believed in. When I learned that the bandit chief could read, I gave him copies of the Psalms and New Testament in Mandarin. Hsiao Lao seemed to understand the Psalms, which, I told him, were written by a great warrior. I also told him stories of Christ's life. These stories amused and fascinated him, and at times he seemed even wistful as he listened. "You are fortunate indeed," he said once, "to have someone such as this as your God, *mu shih*." But when I explained that this same God was his Father as well as mine, the bandit chief only shook his head.

On the nights he didn't ask questions, Hsiao Lao held forth about his own life and philosophy. He was articulate and intelligent, and he could be charming when he wished. He was a skilled storyteller, very theatrical and a good mimic of the people he described. He had a gentle side that I did not see often, but which was genuine; when he

looked at his son, I saw the same love in his expression that I had felt for my daughter. He was also cruel, impetuous, moody, and selfish, but he did not see these qualities in himself; he considered himself a man of reason, passion, and action, and what I considered superstition he believed was innate wisdom given him by the gods. He demanded complete and uncompromising loyalty from his men, and he severely punished the slightest aberration. A bandit who, when I had successfully treated his trachoma, came to me after nightfall to tell me I was the wisest man he had ever met was found dead the next morning. Another came to me with a large package of opium that he wanted me to sell in Peking for him so he could go to America. When I said I could not do this, he looked completely without hope, and he too was found dead the next day. If I mentioned these deaths to Hsiao Lao, he became angry and would not discuss them.

While it is true that he terrified me, he also fascinated me, and late in the day when I had seen to my unfortunate patients as best I could, I found I looked forward to his summons.

August 8, 1917

Since Lily's passing, I have many moments when I think she is here. It can be anything—a bundle of clean laundry on the bed whose curved shape is so like that of her body when

she was wrapped in a blanket; the sight of a mother carrying her own baby, though the child looks nothing like mine; the sound of mourning doves cooing on the tile roof, so like the sounds she made. For a moment I am elated; I think there has been an awful mistake and that she is here. Then I see the laundry or the other child or the doves, and I remember that she is no longer on this earth, and my heart contracts.

This happens with Will now. He has been gone for twenty-seven days, and frequently I think I see him striding across the courtyard or coming into the house or sitting at his desk, only to realize that I'm seeing a shadow or a tree or a man who actually looks nothing like Will. Then the torment begins. What if he has not returned by next week? By next month? What if he never returns?

At times my fear overwhelms me. Last night I woke in the dark and the panic seemed unbearable. All sorts of horrible possibilities presented themselves in my mind, fantasies that I would not entertain in the daytime but that took hold of me in the dark of our bedroom and seemed completely real. As I lay there alone, I became convinced that Will had been killed, and my breathing quickened and my heart began to beat so hard that it was all I could do not to cry out.

I heard the door open. Then I heard soft footsteps and knew it was Mo Yun; I smelled the ocher-colored sesame oil that she massages into her long braid each night. I heard her move toward the bed and I felt her leaning over me. I was ashamed of my lack of faith, but I whispered, "I am so afraid."

Mo Yun didn't speak; she just rested her hand on my back then began to trace circles with her fingers—across my shoulders and down my spine, back and forth, up and down, again and again. As she did, my heartbeat slowed and my chest relaxed, and I began to feel calmer. When my breathing was normal, Mo Yun lay down next to me on our bed and I heard her inhale deeply, then exhale. She did it again, and her breathing was like an instruction: Do this, she seemed to be saying, breathe. So I did, and as I matched my breathing to hers, my fears subsided and I fell asleep.

When twenty-four days had passed and I felt I'd examined every bandit several times, the bandit chief himself came to my small cell, a first, and escorted me to his son. I had checked the boy each day, and each day there had been indications that he was healing, or at least that there was no infection: his color was good, his eyes were alert, and he had no fever, each a small

miracle. Another miracle: the plaster remained just as I had applied it.

I congratulated the boy. "You have taken good care of yourself," I said. "It has greatly helped your healing."

He glared at me.

I asked for boiled water, and when it was delivered I began to wet the adhesive, my fingers shaking under Hsiao Lao's scrutiny. Finally I removed the plaster and saw yet another miracle: the cut had healed, not perfectly but adequately, leaving a bumpy and fairly prominent pink scar.

Hsiao Lao was pleased. He let out his breath and examined his son closely, then looked at me. "*Mu shih*, you are indeed a healer. From this time forward you are also my friend, and I am releasing you. In the future, you need not fear any harm; you have my protection. I have saved your life twice; you have saved the life of my son. These things are equal, and our fates are now linked." He looked at me intently for a moment then, as if seeing the future. "It is said that in times of peace one should not forget danger. I am certain that one day you will value my help. We will meet again."

I bowed slightly, from sarcasm more than respect, for I was tired of him and worn down inside. "Something to look forward to," I said.

My bandit gazed at me for another moment. Then he turned his back to me, and I was free to go.

• • •

I was made to walk blindfolded for several hours with two bandits, the three of us walking single file, so that I was continually tripping on the heels of one and being shoved by the other. There were so many turns in the road that I wondered if we were going in circles; perhaps it was a trick and I was to be killed after all. But finally we passed through what felt like a narrow gorge; I felt walls of rock on either side of me and the air became cool. Not long after that, one of the men removed my blindfold. I shielded my eyes with my hand, waiting for them to adjust to the daylight, and when they had, I looked out on a long narrow valley I had never seen before. Hsiao Lao had made a great show of returning my compass as a parting gift, and I took it from my pocket and saw that I was facing slightly southeast. One of the bandits pointed due south, then the two of them turned and left me standing alone on the narrow path. For a moment I didn't move; I couldn't believe I was truly free. Then I started for home.

As the bandit chief had kept my watch, I had no idea what time it was when I was released; I guessed it was mid-morning. I walked until late in the day, when the sun had dissolved and the sky was drained of its color. On another day, I would have stopped for the night then, but I kept walking, certain that I was close enough to make

it safely to Kuang P'ing Ch'eng and unwilling to rest until I was home. I walked longer and farther than I ever had in one day, stopping only at village inns along the way for a drink of weak tea.

I estimated I had been walking for twelve hours by the time I saw the outline of Kuang P'ing Ch'eng's wall against the horizon, and out of joy I ran until my strength failed me. When I couldn't run anymore I walked, more and more slowly, but I made progress and at last I reached the wall and made my way to East Gate.

The city's four gates were locked at sundown, after which there was no way in or out of the city except by permit or special favor from the magistrate. But East Gate had a smaller gate within it that had a peephole and was guarded all night by armed soldiers. It could be opened after the large main gate had been closed, and when I finally reached it, I leaned heavily against it, the wood rough against my face. "I am Kung P'ei Te," I called weakly. "My home is on Ch'ien Chia Chieh, just inside East Gate." Nothing. "I am Kung P'ei Te," I said again. "This is my home."

I heard hurried conversation, and I was asked if I was alone. I answered yes and said the magistrate was my friend and that he would give them permission to open the gate.

I was amazed then to hear Chung Hao's voice,

telling the guards to let me in. More conversation followed, words I couldn't make out, and finally the smaller gate was opened, and I was allowed to enter the city.

Chung Hao was waiting for me. "Each night I have been keeping watch," he said quietly. "My heart has been gray, *mu shih*."

I could only nod. With Chung Hao supporting me, we walked the short distance from East Gate to our street, and soon our home was in view.

It was by then very late at night, and when we reached the house I was surprised to find Katherine in the kitchen, her back to me. I was extremely weak, but the sight of her gave me strength and I remained standing instead of collapsing on a chair, which was what I had looked forward to doing for several hours.

Katherine turned when she heard my steps and dropped the wooden spoon she was holding when she saw me. Her face was thin and drawn, her eyes wide and anxious, and she looked very thin. For a moment we stared at each other without speaking, and I saw in her expression the same fear that had lived in my heart: that we would never see each other again. Then she ran to me and nearly knocked me over, and I held her close and breathed in the scent of soap and something else that was only her, and I felt her tremble in my arms. She whispered, *"Chu liao fan mu yu?"*—Have you eaten?—and I laughed

and felt delight and relief, for it is the first thing the Chinese ask, a sign of hospitality, and it meant that I was home.

Late that night, after my first bath and real meal in thirty-one days, I lay in bed next to Katherine, grateful for her embrace and the welcome of her body. I was exhausted in every way and was sure sleep would quickly overtake me.

But it didn't; something kept me awake, and I realized it was the stillness. The quality of the silence in our home was different; there was a feeling of absence in it that until then I had not allowed myself to register. As I lay there in the dark, I began to fathom the permanence of our daughter's death, and I felt as though I had been struck. I said something or moaned, I don't know which, and I was afraid I had disturbed Katherine. But she was awake, and I felt her turn toward me. She put her arms around me, and for a moment all I heard was the sound of her breathing. Then she said, "I know."

Something inside me gave way and I could no longer ignore the sadness I had been carrying with me like a stone every day since April 11. Katherine held me to her, and for the first time since burying our child I surrendered to my grief, and to my wife's consolation.

Famine

1918–1922

My wife was the kindest and most generous person I have ever known, devoted to helping the people around her. She worked long hours during the day, and at night she read medical texts and pored over pharmaceutical catalogs, carefully choosing which supplies we could afford, knowing that some or all of what she ordered would never reach us due to banditry. She was also one of the most stubborn people I've ever met, often determined to do things her own way, regardless of the toll it took on her health.

Once at the end of a long day of seeing patients, when I could see she was exhausted, I suggested that perhaps those remaining could wait until the next day for her help. She regarded me sternly.

"Which of these would you send home?" she asked, and she motioned to three men sitting in front of us. "Him?" She pointed to a man whose eyes were so inflamed they were nearly swollen shut. "Or perhaps him?" The next man was coughing hoarsely. "Or him?" The third man was bent over in pain, holding his stomach. She faced me again. "Will, would you have us care for their souls and ignore their bodies?"

I had no reply, for she was right; we communicated our faith less by preaching than by acting, less through our words than through the work of our hands. I abandoned my argument and made myself useful.

But as Katherine worried over her patients, I worried over her, for I had begun to understand that, if we were to stay in Kuang P'ing Ch'eng as long as I hoped, she would have to learn to spend her energy more carefully. The threat of overwork was a concern for anyone in the mission field in China, for the simple reason that there was always so much need. But the life was particularly hard on women, and especially on those with Katherine's temperament, for while others rested when the work began to take its physical toll, she did not. She pushed herself until she finally collapsed from sickness or fatigue.

January of 1918 was one of those times. Her illness started with her old headache accompanied by abdominal pain and a high fever, with chills so severe her teeth chattered. Her symptoms led her to believe that she was experiencing a worse-than-usual episode of malaria, which she had contracted during her first year in China and of which she was never completely cured; she suffered repeated attacks over the years. This time, despite treating herself with quinine, she continued to run a fever and

became weaker by the day. One morning she said she felt a bit faint and a moment later her legs gave out underneath her, leaving her unable to walk. Still, she wouldn't stay in bed; she wanted to lie on the couch in the sitting room so that she could see through the large window that looked out on the courtyard. There she would stay until I carried her back to bed later in the day. She had always been small, but with the illness she lost weight, so that picking her up was like lifting a child.

She tried to diagnose herself and wondered aloud in a matter-of-fact way about typhoid or some type of bacterial infection. She prescribed for herself various pills and tonics, which concerned me a great deal as I was not convinced that her mind was clear. But I also knew there was no point in arguing with her; doing so when her mind was set only made us both unhappy.

It seemed that to fully recuperate and regain her strength she would need an extended period of rest. Because I could not imagine this happening in China, I suggested to her that when she was well enough to travel, we return to the United States for a furlough. By then we had been in China for nearly twelve years, twice the time missionaries typically spent in the field without furlough. We had not planned it this way; we had simply never wanted to leave, even briefly. But a furlough was now a good idea for

several reasons, I told her: we could see our families, and we could visit American Mennonite churches and tell them of our work and perhaps increase our financial support. While we were gone, we could leave our work and our home in the care of Chung Hao and Mo Yun. The only argument I didn't make was the real one, the one that kept me awake at night: my fears about her health.

Katherine didn't like this plan when I brought it up, but I was persistent and eventually she agreed. The next problem was money: we couldn't afford the tickets to the United States. Over the next month she began to regain her strength, and around that time a businessman from Tsinan heard from mutual friends of our plans. This man offered to advance us the money for the journey, saying that his wife was in the United States and that we could repay her there. With his loan we had enough for overland travel to the coast, steerage passage across the Pacific, and train fare from Seattle to Oklahoma.

We left Kuang P'ing Ch'eng in March of 1918, and arrived two months later in Clinton, nine miles from my family's farm on the Washita River in Bessie. I had written to my family that we were coming, but my letter had not arrived, so that when I telephoned home from the station, they were shocked to hear from me. My mother said my brother Henry was in the fields but was

expected home with the wagon soon and would come for us then. When he finally did, he drove the same spring wagon my father had used to plow the fields for many years. He looked distressed when he saw us, and I apologized for the lack of warning. Henry forgave me but I felt him thinking *You are still the same slow negligent old Will that you always were,* which was exactly how I felt. In Kuang P'ing Ch'eng, I shouldered responsibilities I had never imagined I could, but the moment I returned home, I felt like my old self, doubtful and insecure.

When I stepped through the door of my family's house, the fact that I was home hit me as abruptly as if I had been awakened from a dream. I smelled coffee and freshly baked bread and my mother's lavender talc, and the spring afternoon light fell in through the windows and made the inside of the house glow. From the kitchen I heard my older sisters laughing and talking together as they prepared a dinner I'd grown up on and that now seemed an extravagance—baked ham and green beans, candied sweet potatoes, cucumbers with vinegar and sour cream. My sisters, slender girls when I left home, were now stout wives and mothers.

My mother was in the living room, sitting in the bentwood rocker my father had made when they were first married. The room had not changed: the sewing machine and a basket of

mending were by the window where the light was good, the rocker was near the fireplace for warmth, and the curtains were as crisp and white as if they had been washed and ironed that morning. When my mother heard me enter, she stood with difficulty and I saw how frail she had become. I had tried to warn myself that she would have aged while I had been gone, but I was still shocked by her appearance. She was a widow and an old woman; her hair was white and her eyes were cloudy, and her hands shook as she reached out to me. When we embraced she whispered, *"Mein lieber Junge"*—my dear boy—and I was overcome with missing home and being there at the same time, and the fact of my father's passing years earlier was suddenly painful and new again.

We had arrived at the start of the winter wheat harvest, and because there was a shortage of labor I took a job working in the field. When the harvesting was complete, there was more work to be done; some of the large fields in the area had never been cleared of their shrubs and small trees, and I worked at cutting down blackjack oaks, using our wagon and horses to haul the wood home, which made me feel I was earning our keep.

In late August, after spending three months with my family, we left to travel to Katherine's family farm in South Dakota. As my eldest

brother drove us to the train station, Katherine asked him to stop in the apple orchard. The trees had been almost completely stripped of fruit; all that remained were the apples in the highest branches, out of reach. "The best ones are the hardest to get," Katherine said. She got out of the wagon and, with her long skirt hiked up, climbed tree after tree as easily as a boy, adding a dozen ripe apples to our stash. The sight of her high in the branches warmed my heart; I had not seen her so healthy since our first years in China. In South Dakota, Katherine's family welcomed us and we stayed with them for another few months, and with familiar food and more rest than she'd had in years, my wife's health continued to improve.

When we left Katherine's family, we traveled across the central United States, visiting the Mennonite churches and communities who supported us, as well as others we hoped might become interested. Our mission organization, the China Mennonite Missionary Society, drew its recruits and supporters from three of the Mennonite church's many branches: the Krimmer Mennonite Brethren (Edward's church), the Mennonite Brethren (my family's church), and the Evangelical Mennonite Brethren (Naomi and Katherine's family's church). We spoke to one community after another about our work and the needs of the

people of China, just as Edward Geisler had done years before, and we had moderate success: some churches pledged ongoing support, others took offerings for us, and a few individuals promised us aid in the future.

Our furlough had a bittersweetness I had not anticipated. I had expected to feel at home the second we stepped onto American soil, but instead I felt out of place. The farm I had grown up on felt familiar but also foreign, the abundance of food and goods uncomfortable. Every meal was a feast—pot roast and new potatoes, spareribs and sauerkraut, fried chicken and dressing, spice cake, rhubarb pie, cherry cobbler—and while I had never thought of my family as wealthy, we certainly were compared to the way Katherine and I lived in China. But the longer we stayed in our old home, the more I longed for our new one.

April 30, 1919

We left Seattle nearly six weeks ago and arrived in Kuang P'ing Ch'eng late last night. As we neared the city, people we met along the way greeted us and accompanied us on our way, and by the time we reached East Gate word of our return had outdistanced our cart and we found a hundred people waiting for us. When we could finally see the city wall it was nearly dark, and I worried the guards wouldn't

open the gate for us. But when we reached it we found it open, with Chung Hao and Mo Yun and so many friends waiting for us that it took nearly an hour to reach our home.

I never expected such a welcome. We had returned to China on the *Tenyomaru*, the same ship that carried us to America last year, and as I went to bed late last night I thought of one of our fellow travelers. A large group from the Mennonite church in Seattle had escorted us to the dock, and as the ship made ready to leave, Will and I stood on the deck, waving to our friends below, who were singing loudly. A portly woman standing next to us eagerly searched the passengers on deck, then turned to me and asked, "Who are they singing for? Is there a famous evangelist on board?"

I didn't want to draw attention to us, so I answered hesitantly. "We're missionaries returning to China."

I needn't have worried; I might as well have said we were hoboes. The woman's face fell, and without a word she turned her back to me and waved to her friends across the deck. "They're just missionaries!" she shouted, and left us, for another part of the ship and, I presume, more interesting shipmates.

Just missionaries. The prideful part of me wishes she'd seen our welcome last night. I don't think I have ever been so happy to reach

a place. It's more than happy; I'm relieved to be here, for I feel like a dog retreating to lick its wounds. While Will worked on his family's farm, I underwent treatments for malaria in Moundridge, Kansas. The doctor there gave me betony root, and I feel (and hope) that I am finally rid of this tenacious illness. But with that hope came sorrow, for I learned that malaria has made me unable to conceive again. I can't have children, simple as that.

My faith tells me that God is in all things and that good can come even from this, but I still feel that I've failed at something. I feel that I've failed Will, though I know he doesn't see it this way. I find myself questioning my Lord's ways; I do not understand why He would place a longing in my heart that He doesn't plan to fulfill. But whys don't get me anywhere; they just lead me around in circles. So I pray I can accept this painful lack, and if my prayers are halfhearted, I know they are still heard.

In May of 1919, a month after our return from furlough, we heard of a small compound that was for sale. The compound had been the site of a pottery business that had gone bankrupt, and now the owners, who were originally from another province, had decided to leave Kuang P'ing Ch'eng for good and were eager to sell the property as soon as possible, and at a very

reasonable sum. Though they did not say this, there was a reason for their low price: a man who had worked at the kiln had been murdered there and his skeleton still lay where he had died. The whole place was now considered haunted, and no Chinese would think of buying it as they were deeply afraid of evil spirits, whom they believed to wander unhappily through this world, pestering the living.

With the contributions and promised support we had received on furlough, we were able to buy the compound, which was a great find. Just outside the city's East Gate, it occupied some four acres surrounded by a fifteen-foot wall. As Katherine and I walked around the property and its two buildings, we talked excitedly about what we could do with so much space. We envisioned clean, well-stocked examining rooms, a large worship hall filled with believers, and a vegetable garden in the space behind the house where the soil was good and the plot slightly raised so it would not flood during the summer rainy season.

The main building was a sturdy two-story ancestral home with a curved roof, made of wood rather than mud bricks, which was an advantage because of Kuang P'ing Ch'eng's harsh weather and frequent flooding. On the lower floor, which was surrounded by a wide veranda, were the kitchen and a large open room that could

function as a worship hall. Upstairs were three smaller rooms with low slanted ceilings—enough living space for us and for Chung Hao and Mo Yun, and even for a small study. The other building on the property, an old one-story wooden storehouse with an earthen floor, could be made into a suitable clinic and dispensary. Behind these two buildings was a large open lot with a deep well and space for another structure, if and when we had the funds.

Because of the belief that the gate to a home or business indicated the value of what it protected, the compound's imposing gate was also an advantage. A compound such as this always had a gatekeeper, who lived in a small house adjacent to the gate, and Lao Chang, the gatekeeper for the previous owners, asked to stay on with us. I was skeptical; he looked to me to be an old man, and I doubted he would be able to work for much longer. But when I asked his age, he smiled broadly. "We are the same, *mu shih*. My thirty-fifth year will soon begin." He was right—he only looked many years my senior—and I agreed to his request.

Once the deal was made, Katherine and I and Chung Hao and Mo Yun celebrated our good fortune with a dinner of tangerines, dumplings, and fish, a combination that sounds odd, but one that Mo Yun chose with care. Tangerines symbolized wealth and peace, dumplings good

fortune, and fish abundance, with the skeleton signifying a surplus, and the head and tail a good beginning and a good end.

The buildings on our new property needed a great deal of work, and we spent the rest of that spring and early summer repairing them. I replaced the windows and loose tiles on the roof of our home, we whitewashed the interior walls, and we had screens made for the windows, something that was viewed with great suspicion but which we knew would be a hygienic necessity in the summer heat. As the roof of the building we would use as a clinic was beyond repair, I spent much of that summer going up and down a ladder laying a new tile roof, and each evening Katherine cleaned and bandaged my tough old hands, cut raw from the rough edges of the tiles. We put in a wooden floor and new doors, we placed benches along the walls for patients, we lined the small room that would be the storeroom with shelves, and we set up two examining rooms, each with a large wooden table.

By the end of June we were able to hold Sunday services in the large downstairs hall of our home, and a week later Katherine posted a sign at the compound gate announcing that the clinic was open every day except Sunday at no charge. She was soon seeing sixty patients a day,

many of whom came a great distance. With the facilities of the new clinic and the help of Mo Yun and four of the older orphan girls she was training, she was able to treat far more patients than she had in the past. We were the happiest we had been since Lily's death, and I began to believe we had survived the worst; surely the years ahead would be easier.

I could not have been more wrong.

In the North China Plain, summer was the rainy season, with a great deal riding on how much rain fell in those months. Too little rain caused long, painful droughts, while too much rain caused the Hwang Ho—the Yellow River, also called "China's Sorrow"—to flood. These extremes of drought and flood often followed one after the other, and either could lead to famine. It had been that way for two thousand years, with famine in one area or another nearly every year.

The Yellow River runs for twenty-four hundred miles east then northeast from the interior of China toward the Yellow Sea. The river's name comes from its color, the result of the large amount of silt it carries, making it the muddiest river on earth. The silt accumulated at the river's embankments, and despite constant efforts to build up the embankments to contain the river, the land was so flat and the drainage so slow that

heavy rainfall made flooding inevitable. Time and again, cities, towns, and villages were destroyed, crops flooded, and millions of people left homeless and starving.

On a hot and humid day in July of 1919 we had cloudbursts late in the morning. By noon those showers had become a downpour, and by afternoon there was word that the Yellow River was already rising. Although our compound was a good twenty feet above normal flood level and many miles from the river, we moved everything from the dispensary to the highest point in the compound—the top shelves of a large locked cupboard on the second floor of our home. I thought we were being overly cautious, but by evening there were reports that the river was overflowing its banks and people living near it were leaving their homes, carrying as many of their possessions as possible on their backs.

Over the next weeks, the Yellow River flooded extensively, entirely covering the lower-lying areas of the plain. Hundreds of villages and towns disappeared, thousands of people died, much of the region's livestock drowned, and crops were lost overnight as fields of corn, millet, and summer wheat became acres of watery mud. The earthen walls of many of Kuang P'ing Ch'eng's homes crumbled, and several inches of mud covered the floors of most houses, including ours. It seemed there was

water everywhere I looked; everything felt wet.

While it was quickly clear that the flood had destroyed the summer crops, it was thought that the harvests of the coming spring would be enough for the coming year. But the flood was followed by a devastating drought in Shantung and Hopei provinces. By the following spring the ground was too hard and parched to be plowed, and by the end of that rainless summer, our region was experiencing a severe famine.

September 17, 1920

We are living in the land of naught: no rain, no crops, no food. Month after month has been dry. The cleared fields are only stubble, picked clean months ago of even the scraps of last year's crops, but emaciated mothers and their children still scour the ground for anything other than dirt. They make thin porridge from roots and weeds, and they mix chaff and dried leaves into a cake that looks like baked mud. Farmers can't feed their livestock, so they slaughter their cattle and sell their horses and mules. Families sell everything they own, and once that money is gone they beg and steal and live on whatever they can find—dog meat, a small bowl of parched barley flour. There are rumors of cannibalism.

Until I experienced a famine I thought

starving to death was a slow process, which by itself it is. But a weakened body welcomes all kinds of quickly fatal diseases, and a person deprived of nourishment can die in only a few days. The dead lie in the streets and are carried out of the city at night, and some days when I am in the city they seem to outnumber the living. Babies whose parents are unable to feed them are discarded, usually in a ditch outside of North Gate, where wild dogs fight over their corpses.

Many people have left the city, walking three hundred miles or more to relatives in other parts of the country, taking only their clothes and sleeping in abandoned temples along the way. Many others have come to us; each day at our gate we find a dozen or more refugees from the city as well as from places farther away, and we have taken in nearly two hundred people. We are somehow able to feed them all, though I'm not sure how; every meal seems like the loaves and fishes. Each morning we cook five large kettles of a porridge made of millet and beans and do all we can to make the food go further. We buy the coarsest grain so that we can buy more and have more to share, and as we've run out of cooking fuel we've begun to burn whatever we deem least necessary—old furniture, doorframes, wooden crates.

Perhaps half of our refugees are infants and children, their ribs showing through their ragged tunics, their eyes sunken and hollow. Some are orphans whose parents have starved to death; others have been abandoned by parents who can't feed them and decide it's better to leave them here than take them along, only to bury them down the road. The parents bring their children to the compound gates then just disappear, or they plead with us first then tell their children goodbye and turn and walk away as the children cry and try to run after them while we hold them back. It is horrible, and I wake each morning with dread.

Not all of these desperate parents bring their daughters and sons to us; some send them to live with relatives, others tie them to trees and leave them there. Still others sell their offspring, either because they want the money or as a way to keep the children alive. At first this was a clandestine affair, but now the selling of children, especially young girls, is a brisk business with its own stand at the market, where anyone can buy a girl for three dollars. Buyers say they'll keep their charges, but they rarely do; most return to the coast cities they've come from to resell their purchases for a profit. Will and I visit the stand each day and buy every child offered for sale.

I cannot stand to see them shipped off to the grim future of prostitution and slavery that I know awaits them.

Our guests have transformed the compound into a city of its own. The grounds are covered with temporary shelters for the adults; at first we set up cots in the worship hall for the abandoned or orphaned infants and children, but those were all occupied in a few days. So now the clinic is our orphanage and the meeting hall the clinic; it's musical chairs on a larger scale. Will and Chung Hao moved everything out of the clinic and into the large downstairs room of our home, and we filled the clinic with as many cots and bamboo baskets set on rockers as would fit. Our worship services are now outdoors. As we had only just put the finishing touches on the clinic, dismantling it seemed like going backward and I admit that it pained me. But with more than one hundred children in our care, it was the only choice.

Tonight before I came upstairs I stood in the doorway, looking at the dozens of cots and baskets and the sleeping children and babies that they held. The room smelled of them, a dusky, heavy scent, and the sound of their breathing was like a distant ocean. After seeing so much hardship and death in the last six months, I have found the nearness of the

children to be a salve. When I had soaked up as much of it as I could, I went upstairs to bed, unexpectedly calmed and consoled by our charges.

Since returning from furlough, the word "childless" has taken up residence in my mind. It sits in the room of my thoughts like an unwelcome guest. But tonight I found a different word lingering my mind: "childfull." I'm no longer childless; I'm childfull, for although I have not one child of my own, I have the unexpected gift of a hundred who are like my own, a fact that fills my cracked heart with purpose.

While we believed that some of the children in our care would be reclaimed by their parents, we doubted that most would, and we needed a permanent place for them to live; they could not sleep in the clinic indefinitely. As building an orphanage would provide work as well as housing, I began drawing rough plans for one, and soon Chung Hao and I were marking out the foundation. We bought building materials and organized men into companies of twenty, with one man serving as leader of each company. In this way, we were able to employ several hundred men.

Each day I went out to oversee tasks about which I knew little and for which I had no

training. When I woke in the morning and thought of what faced me in the coming day, it seemed impossible. There were no sawmills; everything was done by the men in our compound. We hired local men to make adobe bricks; I ordered doorknobs, hinges, and screws from the United States and glass, nails, putty, and lime from Shanghai. We would use calcimine as paint to cover the plaster on the building's interior.

On the first Sunday that followed the start of this building project, we invited all whom we employed to attend our outdoor service. The day was clear and cool and I hoped that a few dozen souls would attend, which was why I was amazed when nearly one hundred men sat on the benches in front of me. Ten minutes later every seat was taken, and by the time I began to preach, several hundred men faced me.

At the end of the service, I followed my usual custom of inviting those who desired to receive Christ in their hearts to come forward so that Chung Hao and I and five other leaders of the church could pray with them. I was floored when every man present in that throng of several hundred stood and began to move forward, and I restated my invitation, thinking they had not understood. "If you desire to have Christ reside with you," I said loudly, but the men were already on their feet and pressing forward as

though they were in line for something valuable in short supply. They called out loudly, "I want Christ! I want Christ!" and as many of them as could fit climbed up on the platform and joined us there, so that we were quickly surrounded. While I knew that many of them did not fully understand all that was involved in accepting Christ, I felt unable to turn anyone away. I decided that if their motives were suspect, the matter was between them and God, and I left it to Him as we prayed with one man after another.

Two hours later I stood ladling out millet gruel to a line of people that seemed endless. Finally our gateman, Lao Chang, stood before me. Katherine had cured his nearly blind son of trachoma and restored the boy's sight, and Lao Chang had come to know the God we preached. He was devoted to us and to the mission, and he insisted on eating last while his son stood guard at the gate.

Lao Chang watched in silence as I ladled porridge into his bowl. When I inquired after his health, he said, "I am most fortunate, *mu shih.*"

His answer surprised me. "How so?"

He smiled, showing his few remaining teeth. "Because I am alive and I am well. My God is good to me." He paused for a moment then said, "But you, *mu shih.* Why do you stay with us here when you could so easily go to your home and eat your fill?"

"My home is here. And if my belly were full but my heart empty, what would I gain?"

"Ah," he said. "It is a marvel nonetheless for a foreign-born to endure our pain."

By the fall of 1921 we had had no rain for more than a year. No crops had been sown that spring, the yield of the previous year's crops had been severely diminished, and millions of people across northern China had died from starvation. The new orphanage, which we had thought would be so spacious, was already cramped. We had envisioned it as a home for fifty children and soon had one hundred and fifty living there.

As the famine wore on, our spirits wore down. Widows whom we had clothed and fed cursed us to our face, claiming we had killed their husbands then eaten them. Some of the boys in the orphanage complained that we weren't feeding them enough, but they were certainly in better shape than they had been when they came to us; the mere fact that they were alive when so many were dying was a miracle in itself. Other boys began to lie and steal, taking food, plates, cooking utensils, tools, pens, anything small that could be sneaked out and sold. When I confronted them they claimed they'd done nothing wrong, which was just about true in their eyes. Many of them were the sons and grandsons of bandits, where stealing was considered a

perfectly legitimate way to earn a living. Others said that because I had saved their lives I was their father, and everyone knew that taking something from your father wasn't stealing.

The starving continued to come to us for help, and by autumn we were feeding more than four hundred people each day. We also traveled to outlying towns and villages to provide medical care and to distribute grain sent by the American Red Cross Relief Fund. These travels became more and more painful; the devastation seemed endless.

On an early morning in December of that year, Chung Hao and I planned to travel to distribute grain to a few villages a day's journey away. I did not want to go. The thermometer in our kitchen read 38 degrees, and the day was what Chung Hao called "five coats cold." Underneath my padded Chinese jacket, I wore as many layers as I could manage, and I knew that even so the day would be miserable.

After breakfast Chung Hao and I loaded the cart we had hired with bags of grain and set out. The earth was cracked and dry and the fields were bare save the few that had wells for irrigation; even those thin plants of winter wheat would give a meager harvest at best. Where the road ran near the railway lines, I saw flatcars carrying refugees headed in both directions; anywhere was better than where they were. We passed men and

women pushing wheelbarrows that held their household goods and their children, leaving behind abandoned villages and empty homes.

We traveled until late in the day and stayed at an inn that night, then spent the next morning distributing grain. As was the custom, the village elder took us to those in the greatest need, and we gave them rations of grain. This imperfect system of giving food to those who most needed it left a few people with a little something to eat and a great many other people angry. That afternoon as we were leaving the village, several women came running after our cart. Shouting and crying, they climbed up onto it, pushing against us and demanding grain. We had no more and I begged them to get off, but they refused. It was getting late and we needed to start home; we had many miles to travel. I said we would return as soon as we could, but still they would not get off the cart. The carter, anxious to be finished with his long day's work, began to drive out of the village, and the women standing on the side of the road who had not managed to get on the cart began to curse us, something to which I was growing accustomed, for never in my life had so many people cursed me as during the famine. In desperation I offered to pay a Chinese silver dollar to each of the women on the cart if they would get off. They agreed, and we were able to continue on our way.

• • •

December 20, 1921

I am waiting for Will and Chung Hao to return, and they cannot arrive soon enough. It has been a harrowing two days.

Yesterday morning, Yang, a peasant farmer who is known to be a good man, was walking with his two young sons from the city to our compound. Since his wife died at the start of the famine, Yang has done everything possible to feed his boys. First he sold his mule, then his tools—his plow, harness, sickle, and flail. Then he began dismantling his house; he sold the adobe bricks, roof tiles, doorframes, hinges, anything he could carry. Next he sold his small plot of land, and last week he sold all his clothes except those he wore, which gave him enough to feed his sons for another few days. When that ran out, he decided to bring his sons to us until he could support them again.

Which is what he was doing when he met Pao Hsing on the road. Pao Hsing is the son of Hsiao Lao, the bandit who held Will captive. Hsiao Lao has become extremely powerful: he controls a large area in the southern part of the province, including Kuang P'ing Ch'eng, and he is said to be a man of great wealth, more of a bandit king than a bandit chief. It is also said that because he was born in

Shantung he feels a strong loyalty to it, and he seems particularly protective of Kuang P'ing Ch'eng. While it's true that shipments of supplies to our area still disappear and his men take what they want whenever they please, they rarely harm anyone. A bandit raid is more like locusts coming through than an attack. Thus we are considered fortunate.

Pao Hsing, Hsiao Lao's son, is a different man altogether. Though not eighteen he is arrogant, violent, and cruel. Whole villages have been destroyed at his order, usually because someone has not shown him the respect he expects. He is vain and prideful and he makes certain people know he is responsible for his acts of violence. Sometimes he leaves his calling card; other times he makes sure that those who survive see him clearly. He is easy to recognize and difficult to forget; there is a pronounced scar across his left cheek that is curved like a scythe, from a wound that my own husband bandaged for him four years ago. Because of the scar, Pao Hsing is also known as Kou Shan—Contemptible Scythe—a fitting name, since he cuts down whatever blocks the path of his desires.

When Pao Hsing met Yang and his sons, he demanded that Yang pay for the use of the road. When Yang explained that he had neither

money nor food nor goods, the bandit accused him of lying and threatened him. When Yang still said he had nothing, the bandit slashed the faces of Yang's sons, just as his own cheek had been cut when he was a boy, and left the three of them in the road.

Yang somehow managed to bring his sons to us, and I fear I was unable to hide my reaction to what had been done to them. The boys are five and seven and their cheeks were almost slashed through; the cruelty of the act left me first shaken then furious. They were both in shock, trembling and bleeding so profusely that I was amazed they were still conscious. Yang was weeping and extremely distraught, and in the hope of calming him I forced myself to act as though these were minor, even common injuries that would most certainly heal. While Chung Hao took Yang to another part of the house to give him food and drink—he did not remember when he had last eaten—Mo Yun and I got to work. We gave the boys saffron tea, the same tea Mo Yun has given me many times to calm my distress, and we were able to suture and bandage the boys' wounds.

Two hours later I went into the city for saffron and *cong*—green onion, whose value Mo Yun has taught me. The leaves help to heal traumatic injuries and *cong* bai, the bulb,

helps restore vital body functions following trauma. I had nearly reached the apothecary when I stopped at a teahouse on Cheng Chieh, for the conversation that spilled into the street immediately caught my attention. The men sitting inside—only a few of whom were actual patrons, as no one has money to buy tea anymore—were arguing loudly about a suitable punishment for Pao Hsing, for word had spread about his brutality to Yang's sons. Those in the teahouse were outraged; it has been assumed that in return for the constant taxes Hsiao Lao demands of the people here, they are safe from harm.

I stood at the doorway, listening. The more the men talked, the angrier they became. All of them, I noticed, except one. Sitting alone in the corner was a beggar, and his shoes caught my eye. It is unusual for a beggar to have shoes at all, much less the sort of shoes this man wore, a soldier's worn but sturdy boots. I looked at the beggar's face and saw his eager, fascinated expression, and then I saw the scar across his cheek, and I froze. It was Pao Hsing himself, enthralled and delighted by the telling of his offense.

For a moment I was too surprised to speak, but I didn't need to. One of the men in the place noticed my expression and followed my gaze, and he recognized the bandit instantly.

He jumped up and shouted the bandit's name and pointed to him, and he and the other men in the place moved toward the bandit as one.

There was no escape; Pao Hsing was trapped, and the men caught him easily and began to beat him. I have never before seen a man beaten, and I watched in horror, unable to look away. First they hit him with their fists; then, as he slumped to the floor, they kicked every part of his body, the sound of their blows making a terrible dull thud. The proprietor of the teahouse saved him; a man dying in his establishment would bring disgrace and bad luck for many years, so he demanded that the bandit be taken to the magistrate.

The blows stopped. Pao Hsing looked barely conscious and the two men closest to him bent down to lift him. As they did, the bandit turned toward me and I caught my breath. His face was bloody and raw, his body limp, and as the men stood him up between them, I cringed at my role in the beating; even the worst criminal deserves a trial. But then he glared at me hatefully and a chill ran through me. I have never seen such evil in a man's face.

Forced out of the teashop by the proprietor, the mob followed the bandit and his assailants through the city. People along the way joined in, so that by the time the procession reached the *yamen*, there were perhaps one hundred

people, many of them yelling and shouting, cursing the bandit and demanding justice. I followed; I cannot say why.

When we reached the gate to the *yamen* and the hall of justice, the guards sent word to the magistrate. The group was allowed into the *yamen*'s principal courtyard and when the magistrate appeared, he listened intently to the story, all the while staring evenly at Pao Hsing. The magistrate then faced a difficult decision: if he ruled with the people and had the bandit beheaded, he would undoubtedly incur the wrath of Hsiao Lao. But releasing the bandit or doing anything less than killing him would probably incite a riot.

The magistrate is a wise man; he did neither. He said Pao Hsing was guilty of worse crimes than those he had committed in Kuang P'ing Ch'eng; in a village only a few *li* to the northeast he had burned parents alive in front of their children and set houses on fire with families locked inside. Accordingly, the magistrate said, the decision about the bandit's fate belonged not to him but to the *ti-pao*, the principal elder of that village. The magistrate would send a messenger there to explain what had transpired and ask what should be done.

As the magistrate spoke, people grumbled and shifted impatiently while Pao Hsing lay motionless on the ground. At a signal from the

magistrate, two guards lifted him onto a chair in the middle of the courtyard and tied him to it. Men immediately began cursing him and spitting at him, and as I watched, it was as if I awoke from a trance. I turned and hurriedly made my way out of the *yamen*, then somehow remembered to go to the apothecary for the saffron and green onion before returning to the compound. I was ill for much of the night and slept little.

Today Lao Chang brought news from the city. Eight emissaries from the wronged village came to Kuang P'ing Ch'eng with their elder's reply: because Pao Hsing had burned people alive, he should suffer the same fate. The magistrate acquiesced, and as the bandit remained tied to the chair, slits were cut into his body and lighted candles were inserted into his skin. After enduring great pain for several hours he lost consciousness and was beheaded. His head was placed on a spike on the city wall, a common custom for criminals.

These events torment me—the violence of the man, the violence of the crowd, the horrendous cruelty of the punishment. Nor is it over; now we await a father's revenge, which terrifies me. Had someone been at fault for our daughter's death, the rage I would have felt stops me short and makes me pray for Hsiao Lao as well as for us.

• • •

At dawn six days later black smoke rose in the northeast, and we learned that the village raided by Pao Hsing was under attack. More than one hundred bandits had burned every house and shot or stabbed anyone who tried to escape. As the news spread through Kuang P'ing Ch'eng, people began leaving at once; the city's only protection, the magistrate's guards and the militia made up of local men, would be no match for the bandits. When Chung Hao and I went into the city, we found an exodus in progress. People were slamming storefronts closed and running toward West Gate, infants and young children in their arms and possessions strapped to their backs, taking with them whatever they could carry. Those who remained were frantically hiding whatever treasures they possessed—silver dollars, gold, pieces of jade—then locking their doors and piling whatever they could against them from the inside.

By noon the streets were barricaded with furniture and carts and the city seemed deserted. Dozens of people had fled to the compound, seeking protection within our already crowded walls, and when Chung Hao and I returned we locked the gate and gathered everyone in the downstairs rooms of our home. We pushed tables and chests against the front and back doors, and everyone sat close together on the floor and

passed an uneasy and uncomfortable night that way. Waiting seemed our only choice, for while there were some two hundred men in the compound, I had no doubt that we would all have been killed had we tried to fight.

They came at dawn. We first heard distant gunfire and muffled shouts, then the sound of men running, a terrible sound like a fierce wind coming upon us. I went upstairs and from our bedroom window I saw the bandits charging toward us and the city, a dark mass of bodies moving steadily closer. I looked out at more than one hundred men, all running in a way that seemed both orderly and chaotic, like some great being barely contained. The sound of rifle fire drew nearer, and as the bandits approached our compound they seemed to slow, or perhaps I imagined it. For a moment I expected to see them crash through our gate, but they passed us by and moved wildly toward the city, and a few minutes later I saw them scaling the city wall near East Gate.

For the rest of that day and throughout the night we heard them taking our city, and the sounds of destruction and people crying and screaming tore at my soul. The women's voices haunted me; I could not get them out of my mind. We passed another night crammed together, and at dawn when I went again to the upstairs window, I looked out at black smoke rising from

within the city wall. There was no more screaming, only some subdued shouts. I saw the bandits leaving through East Gate and heading northeast. They took with them a long line of prisoners, some carrying the bandits' plunder. It seemed our compound had been spared, and when I went to unlock the compound gate, I learned the reason: Hsiao Lao's red calling card was nailed to our gate.

Chung Hao and I loaded food and medicine onto a cart and set off with Katherine and Mo Yun for the city. When we reached the gate we began making our way through the ransacked city to the well, where people gathered on market days. Doors were smashed in, homes looted and burned, and the air was thick with ash. A few parents and their children dug through the debris and still-warm cinders of their homes, searching for whatever could be salvaged—bricks, mud stoves, pieces of tile, tools. When we reached the city well, I was amazed to see a small table in the midst of the destruction, where a teahouse proprietor sold tea, though his home and shop had been destroyed. Next to him a vendor set up a table and mud stove and was soon selling hot noodles to standing customers, and nearby a woman fried cakes in a small cauldron over a charcoal fire.

We set up a makeshift clinic with a few charred boards spread over rickety sawhorses for

examining tables. Soon several dozen people were waiting to be seen. Most had burns; many had been shot or stabbed. I glanced at Katherine's face as she looked at the growing number of people needing her help. She was rarely daunted, and she showed it even more rarely, but on that day, her pain and discouragement were evident. Still, she did not hesitate but began speaking to her first patient, an elderly woman whose left arm and leg were badly burned. As Katherine began cleaning the burns and treating them with tannic acid and silver nitrate, I heard her reassuring the woman, telling her she was safe now and that she would soon heal.

By noon there were clusters of businesses throughout the city where people sold what they had: oranges, vegetables, steamed bread, baskets, brooms. Those who had lost their homes were building huts of old boards and straw matting to sleep in, and the city grew busy as those who had fled the city before the raid returned.

Katherine and I continued to treat the injured throughout the afternoon. I had just bandaged a gash on a boy's arm when I turned and found myself facing a man wearing the ordinary gray gown that shopkeepers wore. I was puzzled; he did not seem hurt. But when I looked at his face I could not speak, for it was Hsiao Lao himself.

He was much changed. He seemed to have

aged many years since I had last seen him, and when our eyes met, I saw his anguish and pain.

"Mu shih," he said quietly, "I have suffered a great loss."

I nodded, intensely aware of the dangerous position in which he had placed himself. But no one recognized him; few people had ever seen him. I said, "I understand your loss."

He said, "I have such rage," and although he whispered the words, his voice was fierce. "The madness in my heart demanded *po sau*. Do you know this feeling, *mu shih*?"

"Yes." *Po* was return, *sau* was hatred; together they meant revenge. In my mind I saw the medicine for our child in Hsiao Lao's cabinet and I felt an old anger stirring in my heart.

Those around us grew quiet, and I sensed their curiosity about this stranger; our conversation was gaining interest. I took Hsiao Lao's hand in mine, pretending to examine a wound. He let me take his hand, then made a tight fist. "I had no choice but to avenge my son, dishonorable though he was. This I have done. Now I must receive the punishment for the disgrace he has brought me."

"Your son was a hard and cruel man. His character was not your doing."

Hsiao Lao shook his head. "'The superior man blames himself; the inferior man blames others.'"

I nodded; it was Confucius.

He continued. "And a father is reflected in his son the way the sky above is reflected in the water below. My son's failings are my failing, and for this I must pay."

I was about to disagree with him, but he did not give me the chance. Without warning he turned and faced those around him, and his life changed. "I am Hsiao Lao," he said loudly, "the father of Pao Hsing."

A raw energy ran through the gathering, and what had been a quiet scene became instantly chaotic. Three men threw themselves on the bandit chief and began to beat him wildly. Those around them shouted and cried out, and it seemed that everyone there wanted to beat the bandit chief himself or at least get a good look at others doing so. With great effort, Chung Hao and I were able to pull the attackers from their victim, but not before his head was bloody, his body limp.

We stood holding Hsiao Lao between us, facing a crowd that teemed with rage. "My friends," I said, and a few men jeered in response, "this man deserves justice, whatever his crime. Let Hsiao Lao be taken to the magistrate to learn his punishment and his fate."

Someone called out that he should be killed, and I stood my ground. "Do you want his blood on your hands?" Silence. "Do you?" More silence. "Chung Hao and I will escort Hsiao Lao

to the *yamen*. Accompany us if you must. This is the magistrate's decision."

The group was suspicious; I had suddenly become a not-to-be-trusted foreigner again, and not the man they had treated as a friend for many years. But after some discussion they agreed. Two of the angriest men demanded that they accompany Chung Hao and me, and the four of us set out for the *yamen*, the crowd following us.

Beaten and barely conscious, Hsiao Lao, like his son, was carried through the streets to the *yamen*. Once again the magistrate refused to make an immediate decision; he had Hsiao Lao sent to the jail, then ordered everyone to leave until he had settled on the bandit's fate.

Despite Hsiao Lao's guilt, the cruel death that awaited him sickened me. When the magistrate had sent everyone away, I sent word to him that I urgently needed to speak with him, hoping that the fact that Katherine's friendship with his wife and the fact that she had attended to his family many times over the years would cause him to honor my request.

I waited for an hour then returned home, but the next afternoon a messenger from the *yamen* came to the compound, saying that the magistrate would see me. At the *yamen*, the guard escorted me across the main courtyard and into the magistrate's residence, then through a maze of hallways to a rear chamber.

The magistrate was seated at a low table, drinking tea, and he nodded to me when I entered. He seemed to be in a better humor than he had been the day before. I bowed and stated my business. “Magistrate, my heart is heavy. Hsiao Lao is guilty of great wrongs, but he does not deserve the torture that awaits him. No man does.”

The magistrate said nothing.

“You are an enlightened man, Magistrate. You rule the city of Kuang P’ing Ch’eng with justice and wisdom, and I know you must see that torture is most backward.”

The magistrate remained silent. He appeared bored and I thought he was about to send me away.

When a minute had passed and he still had not spoken, I said, “I suspect Hsiao Lao will die from his beating. If you do nothing, he will pass to the next life in a very short time, and his death will not be the result of your actions. It is wrong to cause any man, even a man like him, to endure great and unnecessary pain. Surely you see this.”

When the magistrate still said nothing, I relinquished my ideas of what should happen to the bandit and the idea that I had any control over his fate. I surrendered him to God, and I whispered in English, “Your will be done.”

The magistrate leaned forward, suddenly interested. “What did you say, *mu shih*?”

I was drained and answered with the Mandarin translation of my prayer.

I saw approval come over his face. "You are wise, *mu shih*," he said, and I saw that he had misinterpreted my prayer; he thought I had been speaking to him. He nodded appreciatively at what he took to be my submissiveness and he began to laugh. "I know of your love of humanity. Unlike you, I believe Hsiao Lao deserves to endure great pain. But because of the respect you have shown me, I will honor your request. The people of this city have suffered a great deal at his hands, but we will delay his punishment one day. If he does not die by morning, he will endure the fate he has earned." He looked at me. "You would like to see him?"

I nodded.

"You may go to him." He motioned for his aide and whispered to him. "He will give you my seal and pass."

I left the magistrate and went quickly to the nearest eating house, where I purchased as much cooked food as I could pay for—noodles and vegetables in soup—then had the proprietor pack the steaming food in wooden buckets padded with a rough towel. At the jail, which was within the *yamen* walls, a guard led me into a dark and cramped wooden enclosure where perhaps thirty men crouched together on a brick floor behind wooden bars. The place was dank and horrible,

the air foul, a home to nothing but misery and despair. I felt its hopelessness as soon as I entered.

At first the men would not let themselves be seen, but after some minutes, a few of them began to move toward me from the darkness. I told them I had brought food and I asked them to hold their bowls out to me, and when they did I began to fill bowl after bowl. They were ravenous, and as I passed the bowls back into the darkness, the room grew quiet except for the noisy sounds of them eating, which was like the sound of mongrel dogs being fed. Some of the men were there for crimes they had committed, but many others had been imprisoned for far lesser reasons, such as being unable to pay their debts. One man, old and infirm, was an honest shopkeeper, now disgraced; he had been jailed because his son was a bandit. Another was jailed because his neighbor claimed he had talked of joining a bandit gang, while others were imprisoned for their opium use.

As one man after another handed his bowl forward, I looked in vain for Hsiao Lao. When I did not find him, I asked the jailer, who laughed and said the famous bandit had warranted special treatment. The guard would take me to him when I was ready.

When I had served all of the food except for the portion I saved for Hsiao Lao, I motioned to the

guard, who led me farther back into the jail, down a crude hallway with almost no light at all. At the end of the passage was a wooden gate, which the guard unlocked with a huge iron key. He opened the gate then stood aside and said, "Here is your great bandit chief."

Behind the gate was a small enclosure that was like a wooden cage. I saw nothing there at first, but as my eyes adjusted to the dark, I saw a bent-over form in the corner. As I moved forward, I saw it was indeed Hsiao Lao, though so changed I am not sure how I recognized him. He cowered as I came near, and I said, "Hsiao Lao, it is *mu shih*."

He did not move. I knelt next to him and he turned toward me, and as my eyes adjusted and I was able to look at him, I was shocked by what I saw. Without meaning to I asked, "What have they done?"

He looked far worse than he had when the magistrate's guards had taken charge of him the day before; his face was bruised and bloody and raw, his eyes nearly swollen shut. He had been stripped of his gray scholar's gown and the shoes he had worn and was now clothed only in a pair of ragged trousers. He shivered from the cold and shock and pain. He was filthy, his hair matted and caked with blood, and when I reached out to touch him, he shook violently and recoiled from me.

"Hsiao Lao," I said. "Do not be afraid. I will not hurt you."

He turned and squinted at me, and I saw recognition come into his face. I asked the guard for water, then asked again when he did not bring it, and when he finally did appear with a wooden bowl, I took the towel that had padded the bucket of food, wetted it, and began to wash Hsiao Lao. He pulled away from me at first, but I spoke to him softly and continued, cleaning some of the caked dirt from his face and head and his arms and legs as gently as I could. By the time I began to bathe his feet, the towel was as filthy as the bandit chief's trousers, but I continued. I had brought ointment and bandages with me, and when I had washed him as best as I could, I began dressing his wounds, all the while trying to ignore the anger I felt at what he had endured.

Hsiao Lao said nothing all this time, but he gradually stopped trembling. Finally he spoke, his voice hoarse. "You are my physician once again, *mu shih*. Only this time I am the captive."

"It would seem so," I said.

The bandit smiled slightly as he watched me pour vegetables and noodles into a bowl. I fed it to him in small bites, and when he had finished it, he lay back and seemed to be in less pain.

I said, "I have asked that there be no torture."

He shook his head. "The magistrate will not

agree to this," he said matter-of-factly. "He will want my punishment to exceed my crimes. As do I—for the crime of raising a shameful son."

"The magistrate has agreed to wait one day," I said. I paused, trying to think how to phrase the rest of it, but Hsiao Lao did it for me.

"I suspect my spirit will leave for the other side during the night."

"If God wills it."

"And perhaps I will meet your God." He swallowed with difficulty and closed his eyes. "I believe He will judge me harshly, *mu shih*. But I am not afraid."

"You are His beloved son," I answered, "and He is a Great Mystery, far beyond my knowing. He does not abandon what He has lovingly created, and what happens next is up to Him. I will pray for you."

Hsiao Lao looked at me. "Why would you pray for me, *mu shih*? I have read of your God in what you gave me and I have learned a good deal about Him. I have come to know that I am a sinful man, whereas you are a man of great faith. You have honored me by being my friend, and this mystifies me."

"Why is that?"

"I think it likely that I had medicine that would have saved your firstborn so long ago. How is it that you do not think me your enemy? How can you wish me well?"

In my mind, I saw the bandit chief's boxes of loot so many years earlier, and the box from Parke-Davis. I remembered the pain in my heart when I saw it, and I felt it all again, fresh and hot. "Yes," I said. "You did have the medicine. Had we had it, my daughter might have lived."

"Yet you do not despise me."

"No. I forgave you long ago. My God forgives me and asks that I forgive others in turn."

Hsiao Lao smiled weakly. "He is a foolish God, *mu shih*, to ask you to treat your enemies in this way. Your God does not behave in the way I would expect."

I laughed suddenly, for I had thought the same many times—how foolish God is with me, my sweet, spendthrift, profligate Lord, bestowing on me more gifts than I can number and certainly more than I deserve, believing in me more than makes sense, asking of me things I would not have thought myself capable of. "It may seem that way, Hsiao Lao. He is foolish in His giving and in His care for us. He has spoiled me throughout my life."

"I saw this same foolishness in you when I forced you to treat my men. I did not expect you to help them. I thought at first you might try to kill them, then I saw you were not devious enough. But as I watched I saw your kindness to them. I do not understand this."

"They were hurt and in pain. I have learned to

do what God places in front of me, whatever that is."

"Were you not angry? They had stolen from you."

"As had you," I said. "But I asked Him to help me not act on my anger, and to concentrate on the work at hand instead."

Hsiao Lao nodded. "This is an enlightened view, *mu shih*. Foolish but enlightened."

"My friend, do you not find that the foolish and the enlightened are often one and the same?"

The bandit chief smiled slightly, then became so still that I thought he had lost consciousness from his beatings. Finally he opened his eyes. "*Mu shih*, since I met you, I have had moments when this God of yours has seemed very real to me, times when I have felt that Someone I cannot see is very near. He seems so now; I sense Him in this place with us, and while I should be consumed by fear, I am not. I cannot explain this."

I was caught by surprise both at Hsiao Lao's admission and at the truth of it, for God did seem very present in that wretched cell. "He does not ask us to understand Him, only to trust Him."

"I find myself in a place I do not know. Certainty has always been my companion. But now I cannot say that I truly believe, nor can I say that what you teach is false."

"Faith is a gift," I said. "All we can do is be

open to it. The rest is up to the Giver of that gift. And it is never too late to receive it."

The bandit regarded me evenly and put his hand on my arm. "Goodbye, *mu shih*. You will not see me again."

I placed my hands on his head and blessed him. "You are God's son," I said, "His beloved son, and you are in His hands. I release you into His care."

Our compound was perhaps an hour's walk from the city jail, but it seemed far longer that night. While I knew that Hsiao Lao was responsible for the deaths of hundreds of people and for much suffering, I grieved for him, for I had come to love him.

When I reached home, Katherine was waiting for me, and when she looked at me, she nodded as if she knew everything that had transpired. She embraced me and then motioned for me to sit down at the table, and she placed a bowl of steaming noodles in front of me. When I started to say I had no appetite, she picked up the chopsticks she had set out and handed them to me. "You won't do others any good if you have no strength of your own," she said. And so I ate.

That night I dreamed I was riding in a cart on a freshly plowed field, crossing the furrows at right angles in a manner so violent I was nearly thrown from the bench of the cart. I knew that

going across the furrows rather than through them made no sense and I didn't know why the cart was going in this direction, but I could not turn it around. Then I realized that Katherine was trying to wake me and that it was our house that was shaking violently. We were in the midst of an earthquake. As I got out of bed, the room rocked and the tiles on the roof knocked loudly against each other and the window glass rattled, and for a moment I was irritated at how difficult it was going to be to replace it if it broke, not comprehending that we might have far more serious worries. One of the walls of our bedroom seemed to be at an odd angle and the floor shifted under my bare feet, but by the time Katherine and I had hurried downstairs and outside into the courtyard, the world was somehow still again, and everyone in our compound safe.

In the early morning light when we were able to survey the damage, we found it was comparatively small. The compound's buildings had been well built, and they were for the most part unharmed. A few dozen roof tiles were scattered around on the ground, and there were new cracks in many of the walls. Broken plates lay on the kitchen floor and broken bottles on the dispensary floor, but the buildings themselves were intact.

When I went into the city later that morning the damage was more substantial: many of the mud

walls that comprised the city's houses had caved in, and dozens of homes had collapsed, so that it was even more a city of ruins than it had been the day before. The morning was beautiful and clear and eerily peaceful until tremors shook the earth and made roof tiles drop crazily to the ground. The streets were busy with people cleaning up and talking about how their fate compared to their neighbors' and wanting to put forth their ideas on which gods had been angered and were therefore to blame for the wreckage.

I had not planned on going to the jail and found myself walking in the direction of the *yamen* almost against my will and with a sense of dread. I was thinking I could ask to see the magistrate again and plead with him once more to let Hsiao Lao die in peace, and I was anxious about how I would do this.

But when I turned toward the *yamen*'s entrance, my dread and anxiety turned to wonder, for where I had expected to see the imposing west wall of the jail, I saw nothing but rubble. The outer walls had come down, and with it the interior walls and supports, and although most of the *yamen*'s other buildings remained, the entire jail had collapsed. Men were using poles to push in what remained so that those nearby would not be injured, and in front of me were the jail's ruins, a heap of broken stones and mud bricks and debris surrounding nothing but

hazy dust in the bright afternoon sun. But no wall was needed, for the chaos of the trembling night had set the captives free.

We felt tremors from the earthquake for three days afterward. Eventually we learned that the earthquake's center had been far to the west, nearly to the Tibetan border, with catastrophic effects. Villages were destroyed, the topography permanently altered. Streams became lakes, mountains grew from plains, and the event came to be known as "the time when the mountains walked."

In Kuang P'ing Ch'eng the debris was cleared, and over time the houses and jail were rebuilt. Only two bodies were found in the wreckage, neither of them Hsiao Lao's; no one knew what had happened to him or to the other prisoners. They simply disappeared.

But the earthquake and the prisoners were both soon forgotten, for on a cool morning in March of 1922, three months to the day after the earthquake, it started to rain, the first precipitation in nearly two years. People stood outside with their hands outstretched, their faces turned upward to the slate gray sky. Men hurried to put out every vessel they had to catch the rainwater while children played in the mud and mothers laughed. A week later it rained again, and ten days after that a third time, softening the earth enough to plant spring wheat, and the

Psalmist's words took root in my heart: *He shall come down like rain upon the mown grass; as showers that water the earth.*

In that short time, life began to change. Men once again got to work selling whatever they could, from the clothes off their backs to bricks from the walls of their homes, but now it was with a purpose and a plan, for they used whatever cash they could come up with to buy what had become precious overnight: seeds. We began distributing seed grain sent by the Red Cross to increase the likelihood of an extensive sowing of spring wheat, and by May the landscape was transformed. We no longer lived in a desert; the fields were lined with long even rows of what looked at first like grass. A few weeks later we were surrounded by verdant fields graced with healthy young plants, glorious in the morning sun.

Civil War

1925–1928

By 1925 the lawlessness and turmoil of the previous decade had grown into widespread civil war between south and north. The south was largely controlled by the Kuomintang party in Canton, which hoped to establish the new republic and unify the country under one central government. The north was in the hands of warlords, renegade military leaders who ruled the regions they controlled like small kingdoms. They punished trespassers, executed traitors, and grew rich by taxing their subjects and raiding their villages and towns.

In July of 1926, Chiang Kai-shek, the leader of the Kuomintang, launched the Northern Expedition, a military campaign whose goal was to unify China. Southern troops were sent north to Peking to conquer the northern warlords and establish the Kuomintang as the country's central government. Laborers were promised that the new government would mean higher wages and better living conditions, and as nationalistic feelings spread, so did hostility toward foreigners, who were viewed as opportunists who threatened China's culture and way of life and profited at the people's expense.

While this characterization was certainly true of many foreigners, it wasn't true of all of us, but we nevertheless became the enemy, and there were soon reports of violence against foreigners and their property. American and British missionaries were particularly denounced as agents of capitalistic countries, and as hostility toward them—us—grew, mission boards began to advise their workers to leave the interior for the port cities. The American Consulate followed with its own warnings. In Kuang P'ing Ch'eng, we soon began receiving telegrams that became increasingly ominous in tone, stating that those who remained in China did so out of personal choice and at great risk.

And so the exodus began, with each week bringing news of more foreigners leaving the interior. The first to go were the elderly and those in poor health, then those whose furloughs were due soon, or who had young families, or who simply did not find it in their hearts to stay. Some went to the coast and hoped to wait things out there; others returned to their home countries for good. I did not blame those who left; I understood their desire for safety and for relief from the physical and emotional hardship of our lives. We were all worn down.

By the summer of 1927 the majority of the American and British missionaries were gone. I could not have said exactly how many had left

because keeping track so disheartened me that I stopped doing it. Of the fifteen Mennonite missionaries who had been in China at the start of the decade, six of us remained: Katherine and myself, Edward and Naomi Geisler, and Jacob and Agnes Schmidt, the young married couple Edward had recruited and brought to China when we came. For Katherine and myself, the decision to stay wasn't difficult. It wasn't even a decision, really; we never talked about leaving. I suspect Katherine felt as I did, that even if we had been tempted to leave for our own safety, we could not have deserted those who looked to us for protection. Our Chinese community saw our decision as evidence of our faith.

With the southern army's move north during the spring and summer of 1927, the provinces of Hunan and Shantung became a battleground. The army controlling a particular area changed so frequently that during the next four years of civil war some cities would change hands ten times. Travel became even more difficult than usual, as the trenches the soldiers dug cut deep into the roads, causing them to flood during heavy rains. Prices rose almost daily; the cost of a week's supply of wood, charcoal, vegetables, and wheat was soon what a peasant earned in a month. Communication with the rest of the country was severely disrupted by the fighting. We saw no mail trucks for months at a time, and a wire to a

city sixty miles away took five days to get there, a wire to the coast twenty days or more. A rare message from Edward Geisler in Ch'eng An Fu said only, TROUBLE THERE? TROUBLE HERE.

As anti-foreign sentiment spread, people in Kuang P'ing Ch'eng changed toward us. We had by then lived there for nearly twenty years, but we were suddenly suspect, and I felt a new hostility when I made my way through the city. Women clutched their children close to them as I approached, and men scowled at me then turned their backs.

The war grew nearer to Kuang P'ing Ch'eng, and we grew accustomed to the sight of long lines of exhausted northern soldiers, wounded and bandaged. The officers were followed by single lines of burden bearers, civilians forced to carry supplies, struggling under the weight of their loads and tied together with a rope around their necks or waists. Northern troops began to camp out in our compound, coming and going as the battle lines changed, causing the compound to resemble a barracks more than a mission station. Soldiers slept in our clinic, the orphanage, and the first floor of our home, wandered in and out of worship services, and pocketed whatever caught their eye—canned fruit, tools, blankets, hairbrushes, toothbrushes, cooking utensils—seemingly unaware that they were taking what wasn't theirs. Many of them

were boys, really, no more than seventeen, and the burden bearers were as young as ten. But given the fact that they did us no harm, we considered ourselves fortunate. As Edward said, we bought it cheap.

In November the southern army took Ch'eng An Fu and Shin Sheng Chou to the south and began moving toward Kuang P'ing Ch'eng. When the fighting reached the city's outer suburbs in early December, the northern soldiers in our compound were ordered to battle, and many people in the city and the surrounding area began to flee the southern army, which was greatly feared; while the northern troops were far from loved, they were the enemy we knew. People who chose not to leave the area sought safety at our compound, and the soldiers had no sooner left than we were inundated with refugees: men, women, children, and infants, along with chickens, dogs, furniture, boxes, and baskets stuffed with personal belongings. Once again we had more than two hundred people staying on our grounds, along with thirty-seven patients in the clinic, forty-one children in the orphanage, and our ragged staff of seven.

That winter was the coldest in memory. We slept in our clothes, bundled up in coats and anything else we could find. Food was scarce, and with the freezing weather and the threat of war the city's poverty became more desperate.

Soldiers took whatever scraps of food people had; peasants scrounged in the barren fields for anything possibly edible, while beggars froze in the snow.

January 2, 1928

We are at war; we hear gunfire and cannon, we taste gunpowder, and Kuang P'ing Ch'eng has become a city of the wounded. Teams of men bring the fallen from the battlefields on wagons and carts to the city square, where we attempt to care for them. There is so much suffering I cannot take it in; many of the men have lain on the battlefield for several days after being shot, stabbed, or mutilated and are barely alive by the time they are brought to us. Those with a chance of recovering are taken to the *yamen*, where the magistrate has given over one of the large halls as a clinic, while those whom we know will not live—and these are many—remain in the square, where at least they are not alone as they die. Will arranges for the bodies to be carried out of the city in the middle of the night and buried in the darkness. Some days it seems we save almost no one.

While there is an abundance of suffering, we are short of everything else: help, funds, food, supplies, hope. We've hired women in the city to scrub the dead or wounded soldiers' worn

uniforms until they nearly fall apart, then iron them to kill the vermin that survive the laundering's strong soap and heavy rubbing. We are short of medical supplies—bandages, dressings, sutures, medications—partly because of the great need but also because the war has so disrupted transportation that we receive only a few of our orders. When we began caring for the wounded, I tore strips of white cloth into bandages, but we used those up in two days. I have found horrifying ways to economize; we salvage the used bandages from the living and the dead, wash them in great tubs of water that becomes instantly red, then use the bandages again. We are short of anesthetics, and I must reserve our limited supply for those who will live, no matter how intense the pain of the dying. It is as simple and harsh an equation as that, and although it nearly makes me ill, there is nothing to be done.

Almost nothing. In times such as these one must be flexible, and for those who are too injured or ill to recover I have looked no further than our own backyard for something to relieve the pain of passing from this life to the next. I give them opium. Mo Yun arranges its procurement from a man whose name I do not know and whom I have seen only from afar. He looks like an ordinary beggar, except that

around his neck he wears, of all things, a long string of pearls. Every ten days or so he delivers to Mo Yun a small package containing several dozen opium pills. These I dole out carefully to our dying, not to hasten death but to lessen the pain that accompanies it. I have read of the liberal use of opium pills as an anesthetic for pain during the American Civil War, and I see no reason why the soldiers in China's Civil War should not be afforded the same relief sixty years later. If I had syringes of morphine or unlimited chloroform or ether, I would gladly use any or all of them, but whatever I have must go to those who might live. What I have for our dying is small black opium pills, and giving them to these brutalized men so their deaths become less agonizing is the kindest and holiest act I can perform, and one that I cannot imagine God disapproving of.

I'm less sure of what Will would think, so he is unaware of this practice and I have no intention of telling him. I don't think he could stomach it or, if he did, it would take too great a toll on him. He is a principled man who finds compromise painful, and it's better that he doesn't know, for if it got out that Westerners, not to mention missionaries, were purchasing opium even for use as an anesthetic, we would most certainly lose the trust we have so carefully cultivated for nearly twenty years and

be sent packing by both the Mission Board and the magistrate. This thought terrifies me, but when I begin to question my decision I have only to look at these men dying their awful slow deaths to be sure of the rightness of my course. Many are missing arms and legs; most have been gruesomely stabbed or shot and have lost too much blood to survive. And so I move quietly from one man to the next, offering the blessings of opium and faith and thanking God for both.

Early each morning before going to the city square I went first to a large locked elmwood cabinet in the upstairs of our home to load wicker baskets with medicines, antiseptic, bandages, and other medical supplies. With so many people in the compound we felt it necessary to secure what was most valuable—our medical supplies and our cash—so the cabinet in our bedroom had become our dispensary and our safe. One morning, chilled through and slow with fatigue, I stopped short when I reached the cabinet and could only stare stupidly ahead, trying to make sense of what I saw. The two halves of the round brass medallion that had held the lock to the cabinet doors had been neatly removed and now lay on the floor in front of me, the lock still in place. Next to them were the small brass pins that had fixed the

medallion to the doors. Rather than breaking the lock, someone had simply removed it.

I was furious at what I could only guess was a cruel joke. With more maimed soldiers being brought to us each day, we couldn't afford to lose any of the meager supplies we had, and the thought that we had been robbed made my fists clench. But when I opened the cabinet doors to survey the damage, I received my second surprise of the morning. Instead of the ransacked mess I expected, I found everything intact; nothing had been taken. Rather, the cabinet was more crammed than it had been the day before. Boxes filled its shelves, and the printed names made my heart beat faster: Montgomery Ward; Sears, Roebuck and Co.; Parke-Davis; Burroughs-Welcome; Red Cross; China Mennonite Missionary Society. I began to open them and found dozens of rolls of gauze bandages and adhesive tape, tubes of ointment and bottles of powders and pills—more supplies than we had ever received at once. I felt richer than I would have if the cabinet had been stuffed with cash and I laughed out loud. On top of it all was my battered old pith helmet, which I had not seen since my stay with my bandit chief.

It was freezing outside but I put my pith helmet on anyway, hoping our anonymous benefactor was Hsiao Lao himself and that he would understand my thanks. I had heard many rumors

about him over the years. Some said his men had disbanded after the death of his son, some said he had lost his mind, others said he had moved to the remote west of China and lived there in seclusion. I had come to accept that his fate was a mystery I was not to know, but as I went about my duties that day, I watched eagerly for a glimpse of him.

Six days later we received bad news we had expected. On a late afternoon in the second week of January, Lao Chang, our gatekeeper, came running from the compound gate to the house to repeat what he had just been told by those fleeing the city: except for a garrison of one hundred soldiers within the city, the northern army had fled to the northeast and scattered into the countryside, leaving Kuang P'ing Ch'eng and its suburbs unprotected. The southern army had surrounded the city and the commander had offered the northern soldiers full amnesty if they surrendered immediately. His offer was rejected, and the southern army was now attacking the city with all its force. The city itself was in chaos; during the night scores of residents had fled through North Gate, and now all four gates were locked. The magistrate had stayed in the city out of loyalty, and residents had volunteered to fight alongside the northern troops, arming themselves with whatever they had—ancient guns, homemade swords, large rocks.

Despite being greatly outnumbered and lacking in weapons and experience, the northern army dug in for the siege and the battle was fierce. Southern soldiers who tried to scale the walls were beaten back and slaughtered; those who tried to dig under the city wall were buried alive when their tunnels caved in. The sounds of gunfire and cannon continued through that night, so loud that at times it seemed the fighting was on the other side of our compound wall. An hour before dawn, Lao Chang came running to the house again. Katherine and I were upstairs, unable to sleep and settling for rest. We hurried downstairs when we heard Lao Chang's steps, not needing to dress as we were still in our clothes, and found him with Chung Hao in the kitchen. Lao Chang turned to us as soon as we came into the room and told us what he knew: during the night the southern army had breached the city wall and taken control of the city. Their desire for vengeance was great: captured northern soldiers were tied to trees and burned alive or tortured until they revealed the whereabouts of their commander, who had managed to throw himself from the city wall before the southern troops arrived at his hiding place. The southern officer still sent soldiers to retrieve the body so that it could be shot and hung from the east tower, a cigarette stuck in his mouth. Many of the southern officers were new

and inexperienced, and the soldiers under their command, trigger-happy and drunk with victory, were now hunting down any remaining northern soldiers hiding in the city and shooting them on the spot. It was rumored that once the southern army had killed every remaining northern soldier in the city they intended to come to the compound to kill every foreigner they found.

Lao Chang paused and looked at Chung Hao as if prompting him. Chung Hao stared at me evenly and said, "*Mu shih*, you and Kung Mei Li—"

I did not let him finish. "No," I said, for I knew he was going to urge us to leave the area for safety elsewhere, and this we would not consider. "We will not leave."

It was just getting light out, and we knew the army would soon be at our gates. Lao Chang set off immediately to wake everyone on our grounds and direct them to the large meeting room downstairs, just as we had during the bandit attacks. A few days earlier we had boarded up the windows and moved the benches against the walls to afford us as much space as possible. I had woken in the night in panic several times that week, thinking that gathering those in our care in one room with boarded-up windows would do little to slow an army. But it was the only plan I had.

Lao Chang and his son ran from building to building in the freezing air and hurried everyone

into the worship hall: half-asleep children who were shivering and confused, exhausted refugees, the patients who were able to walk. Then the two of them returned to the clinic with a few of the older orphan boys and carried those who were unable to walk. The hall was soon filled with people. Mo Yun attended to the sick, making them as comfortable as she could and talking softly with them while Katherine gathered the children in the far corner of the room, where she settled them on straw mats on the floor. She gave them blankets to share and began handing out small pieces of the luxury she had saved for this day: one dozen Hershey bars sent to us by a Sunday school class in Oklahoma City whose members had read of our work. The chocolate had the effect she had hoped for: as the children tasted it they grew silent, mesmerized by the cool dark squares.

Chung Hao and I brought in the provisions we had set aside in the cellar—jars of water, canned fruit and cheese, dried beef, and a dozen large tins of crackers. When we had carried everything in and stacked it along the long north wall, I stood in the doorway for a moment to take stock of our progress. I had expected to be surrounded by confusion and fear and noise, but as I stood there the room grew silent and my heart ached, for I looked at a roomful of people who stared at me with utter trust.

"We'll be all right," I said, as much to myself as to them. "Everything will be all right."

Chung Hao and I ran to the other buildings to be sure that everyone had come to the hall, and when we were certain of this, we made ready to close the hall's double doors. We were about to do this when Chung Hao said, "We must speak to you," and he motioned for me to follow him to the kitchen, where I found the leaders of our church: Mo Yun and our four evangelists and three Bible women, their expressions somber but calm. They all looked at Chung Hao, who began to speak.

"Mu shih," he said, "we have given our situation much thought and prayer, and we have decided that when the southern army comes we, the leaders of our church, should be the first to die."

I was overcome by what he said as well as what he left unsaid; they were proposing that they die with Katherine and me.

Chung Hao continued. "It will make it easier for the others," he said gently.

As the others nodded in agreement, I found myself unable to speak for a moment. Finally I said, "My brothers and sisters, we would be honored to die with you." With those words, I felt an unexpected peace come over me; it seemed to enter the kitchen like an unseen guest, and the others' expressions told me that they felt it as well.

Together we returned to the large hall and closed the doors behind us, then stacked benches nearly six feet high against the doors. The room became dark; it was by then light outside, but only a few thin lines of gray light from cracks in the boarded-up windows found their way into the room. The darkness seemed to deepen the room's quiet, and the only sound I heard was that of a roomful of people breathing.

An hour passed. Everything was eerily quiet, the sounds of battle muffled and distant. The darkness slowly lightened as the winter sun rose outside, bringing everyone into focus. In the far corner, Katherine and two of the older girls quietly played guessing games with the younger children, trying to keep them occupied. In the corner diagonally across from the children, Mo Yun wiped the brows of two men who had the fevers of malaria. Katherine had worried about the healthy being in such close proximity to the sick but saw nothing we could do about it, and she had finally shrugged and said, "If God's going to protect us from soldiers, He's going to have to protect us from our own sick as well. We'll do what we can." In the center of the room, filling every space between the corners, were old people and young, parents holding their children, older siblings holding younger ones, all of them waiting for what we didn't know.

Shortly before noon we heard shots being fired.

We had not heard gunfire for several hours, and the whole room tensed as fear spread through it. I asked God to give us the strength to endure whatever He allowed to happen next. Two of the older boys who were acting as lookouts upstairs called down that no soldiers were in sight; the shooting was still coming from within the city walls. We learned later that the southern army was finishing off a dozen northern soldiers they had shot earlier and left for dead but who had somehow survived.

Another hour passed. We took turns standing to stretch and walk around the room, a few people at a time. The youngest children had fallen asleep; the older ones warily watched the adults. A baby cried softly and a few people whispered to each other. A woman near me held her sleeping child in her arms. When the mother looked at me, I saw fear and pain in her face, which caused me to speak.

"Christ is with us," I said quietly. "He is with us now and He will see us through this crisis. When our Lord was in the boat with His disciples and the storm came up, He said, 'Let us go over to the other side.' He did not say, 'Let us go to the middle and be drowned.' He will see us safely to the other side. Whatever happens, whether we live or die, we are victorious."

As if on cue, we heard the faint even tread of marching feet, still at some distance. The sound

of gunfire grew louder and we heard wood being hacked by swords, and I knew the southern army was destroying the compound gate. We heard shouting and the heavy sound of men running hard. The sound of gunfire became unbroken, and I could only think that for reasons I could not understand the battle was now being fought in our compound yard. The firing grew louder still. I saw Chung Hao's lips moving and knew he was speaking to me, but his words were lost in the noise.

"Lie flat," I said loudly. "Everyone lie flat on the floor and do not get up." Almost immediately every space on the floor was covered with bodies. I made my way across them, carefully stepping to a small side window toward the front of the room that looked out on the entrance to the compound. When we had boarded up the hall's windows I had left a crude peephole, and I looked through it and saw several northern soldiers lying on the ground. Another six stood between the house and the compound wall, where a mass of southern soldiers charged into the compound. A dozen more were closer, advancing on those few northerners standing, firing heavily as they moved forward so that as I watched, one after the other of the northerners fell to the ground. Within a minute only one was left—Chang Li, one of the boy soldiers who had made himself at home in our compound six

months earlier. I heard him shout, “You must not harm this place or these people. This is the Jesus church!”

The shooting stopped for the briefest moment. In the sudden stillness the boy looked wildly around him and saw that he was alone, and I saw courage in his expression. Then he fell to the ground, the last to be shot down.

I stood frozen at the window, staring out at the bodies of fourteen northern soldiers. A wave of raw anger ran through me, a rage unlike anything I had ever felt. I had been taught since I was a small boy to abhor violence, and that the use of force against anyone, whatever the reason, violated God’s word. As an adult I had honored that belief and made certain that our compound stocked no ordnance whatsoever. But at that moment my convictions fell away. Nearly everyone I loved on this earth was in that room and I knew that had I had access to a weapon of any sort, at that moment I would have used it without hesitation.

I breathed; I forced my attention to God and asked Him to direct my thinking, and my emotions quieted enough to think more rationally. If we did nothing, I was certain we would be killed; some action was required. I walked to the double doors and motioned to Chung Hao, and the two of us shoved aside the pews blocking the doors. I looked at the roomful

of people again and in my mind I saw them running into the courtyard and being shot down like the soldiers in a matter of seconds. "Do not move," I said. My eyes met Katherine's and I stared at her hard and in English I said to her, "I beg of you, stay where you are," and she nodded. Then I opened the door and closed it behind me and hurried through the house to the front door and the compound yard. I had no plan; I knew only that my choice was to wait for the conquering army or go out and meet them myself. As sitting in a closed room while victory-crazed soldiers hacked down our door did not seem like much of a strategy, I chose the latter.

When I stepped out of the house and into the courtyard I found myself facing a line of southern soldiers advancing toward me, bayoneted rifles and swords drawn. I raised my hands above my head and called out, "I am unarmed. This is my home."

The soldiers paused, their guns still raised, and for a moment they stood motionless. I raised my hands higher above my head. "If I am to die," I said loudly, "allow your officer to kill me."

I saw movement among the soldiers as they made way for their commander, who came forward and stopped a few yards in front of his troops as his soldiers kept their guns trained on me. The commander stared at me for a long moment, sizing me up, and I feared he was about

to grant me my request and kill me then and there.

"Kuan-chang," I said—officer—"I am Kung P'ei Te. I have lived in this city for eighteen years."

He said nothing at first; I was aware of gunfire some distance away, but mostly what I heard was the sound of my own hard breathing. A hundred rifles were pointed at me, and I realized they were not pointed only at me; I felt the presence of others around me and found Chung Hao on my left and Katherine on my right. In my fear, I had not felt them joining me.

Katherine glanced at me. "I will not sit by in a boarded-up room while you die," she said quietly. "If this is your time, it can be my time as well." She looked behind her. "Perhaps there is strength in numbers."

I glanced behind us and saw the leaders of our church, those who told me in the kitchen they were ready to be the first to die if it came to that. Behind them others were joining us from the safety of the hall, so that within moments the whole assembly from inside stood behind us—old people and young, mothers holding infants, fathers holding their children. My breathing became shallow for I thought surely we had arranged ourselves perfectly for an efficient and wholesale massacre, and I was deeply afraid.

All this time the commander continued to stare

at us without expression as his men remained at the ready, their rifles trained on us, their swords at their sides. Finally he said, *"Nu-shih"*—miss—"step forward."

It seemed as if someone had grasped my heart tightly within my chest, but if Katherine felt anything like the fear I did, she did not show it. She walked forward a few paces without hesitating, her back straight, her gaze forward. I started to go with her, but Chung Hao grabbed my arm and whispered, "Wait."

The commander said, "What is your name?"

Katherine said loudly, "My name is Kung Mei Li."

"You are a foreigner."

"Yes, by birth. But this city has been my home for eighteen years."

"Not such a long time in this country. Why have you made this your home? Were you invited?"

Panicked, I began to step forward again; I knew she could be taken from me in an instant. But Chung Hao tightened his grasp on my arm and I stayed where I was.

"We came to be of service," she said.

The commander laughed. "I suspect that is not all you came to do, Kung Mei Li. You preach the man Jesus, do you not?"

"I do," she said.

"Are you not aware that what is well suited to you may be ill adapted to others?"

"I am," she said again. "But it is not a question of what is suited to me. It is a question of obeying my God and passing on what has been given to me. I would be remiss if I kept it to myself."

"You believe it is your duty to impose that truth on other nations?"

"Not to impose it, sir, like a law. To share it like a gift, freely given."

"Your feet are set on the wrong path, Kung Mei Li. Foreigners have shown themselves to be pirates and thieves who pose as civilized peoples dealing with barbarians."

"Yes. Some have. But a man's face does not always tell you what is in his heart. All foreigners are not alike."

The commander took several steps toward my wife. "You are different, Kung Mei Li?"

I was staring intently at Katherine's back. Her voice was strong and sure but I could see she was trembling. I had rarely seen her frightened, and I was about to shake free of Chung Hao's grasp when someone pushed past me and stepped forward.

It was Lao Chang. He stood a few feet away from Katherine, facing the southern troops. "Sir," he said. "I have lived in this city all of my life. Kung Mei Li and Kung P'ei Te have done good things for us. They are *chuan shan ti*"—teachers of virtue—"and they teach us how to be good. They have brought us great good news,

and for this we are in their debt." He paused and looked at Katherine. "Kung Mei Li healed my son and caused his sight to return."

"Then you will not mind repaying that debt by giving your life for hers," the commander said easily.

Everything seemed to stop; Lao Chang looked back at me and I was struck by the peace in his expression. "*Mu shih*, all is well," he said softly. He faced the southern commander and said, "If that is what is required, no, I will not mind," his voice calm. Then, before anyone could move, the commander gave a curt command and the soldier next to him raised his rifle, aimed, and shot.

Lao Chang dropped to the ground, and the sound of the shot echoed in the compound yard. I looked from Katherine to Lao Chang's body and was frantically trying to think of what to do next when someone else stepped forward. The soldiers immediately trained their rifles on this new target, but the officer motioned for them to hold their fire.

I saw only this man's back and I did not recognize him. He wore an old gray woolen cap pulled down low over his forehead and his clothes were layers of dark gray rags. He was slight of stature and greatly stooped over; he used a cane as he walked forward. I assumed he was one of the dozens of refugees who had come to the compound over the last week.

When he had walked a few yards forward, he stopped, facing the commander. He sniffled loudly and with the nasal whine of a professional beggar he said, *"Ke-hsia"*—you, sir—"pity me, pity me." He bowed to the commander, then made a great show of standing upright again, groaning and leaning on his cane, and when he began to speak, he kept his eyes on the ground. "The pastor is honored to have you and your men as guests, and he welcomes you to the city of Kuang P'ing Ch'eng. He has prepared a gift for you and he says you would greatly honor him by accepting it. Would you indulge this servant by allowing me to bring it to you?"

The commander appeared interested. He looked at me and gestured toward the beggar. *"Wai-kuo-jen"*—foreigner—"does this man tell the truth?"

Katherine turned toward me, and when I looked at her she nodded slightly; I had no idea why. Nor did I understand why, with complete certainty, I heard myself say, "Yes, he speaks the truth."

The commander looked back at the beggar, whose gaze was still downward. "You may bring these gifts. My men will accompany you." He said something to the two soldiers next to him, and they walked toward the beggar, their bayonets pointed at him.

The beggar sniffled loudly and shuffled

backward a few steps, bowing repeatedly to the commander. As the southern army and all of us from the compound watched in tense silence, the beggar walked to the side of the house, where there was a run-down old shed in which I kept my gardening tools. During the winter, when I could not garden and had no need for the tools, I boarded the shed up. But to my surprise, the beggar opened the door without any trouble; the boards I had nailed up had been removed. As the soldiers looked on from a few steps behind him, the beggar went inside and came out pushing my wheelbarrow, which was full of something and covered with an old quilt that was neatly tied down.

With effort, the beggar pushed the wheelbarrow across the compound yard to the commander then stood before him, a soldier on either side.

The commander seemed wary. *"Mu shih,"* he called to me, "come. Let us examine your gift together." I walked forward, and when I stood next to the soldiers and the beggar, the commander motioned for one of the soldiers to cut the rope and pull back the quilt. The soldier did so, and as the quilt fell to the ground the beggar met my eyes and something jumped inside me. It was Hsiao Lao.

The commander did not notice my surprise, as he was transfixed by what he saw, and when I

looked down I too was amazed, for the wheelbarrow held luxuries I had not seen in years: a large bag of coffee, a tin of tea, four jars of jam, half a dozen cans of milk, a box of chocolates. I saw thick white towels, a pair of men's shoes, a silver picture frame, and beneath them more items I couldn't make out.

The commander was clearly pleased. He rummaged eagerly through his new possessions, marveling at them, and held up a tube of Pepsodent toothpaste as if it were the greatest treasure of all. "*Mu shih*, you are perhaps a wise man after all. You have as your helper a beggar who gives instead of takes. You are also a fortunate man, for the gifts he brings are worthy offerings, which I will accept. For my men."

"Certainly," I said, knowing full well that this was as close as any of his men would get to anything in the wheelbarrow.

"You have won my favor, though we still have business to discuss. Come, let us reason together. Your charges will wait inside while we agree on what is next." He was about to say something to his troops and I spoke up quickly.

"Kuan-chang," I said, "may we have the honor of burying our dead while there is still light?"

The commander glanced casually around him at the bodies in our yard; he seemed not to have noticed them until then. "You inspired great loyalty in these soldiers, *mu shih*. They had made

it safely out of the city gates and could have escaped. But they chose instead to come here to protect you, for which they were killed."

I repeated my request. "May we bury them?"

"You may. But do not linger." He shouted commands in a southern dialect I did not understand and a soldier approached us and chose eight men from behind me whom he led to the side of the yard. The commander shouted something else and two soldiers gave Hsiao Lao a rough push then led me away to the edge of the yard with the other men. When I looked back, the soldiers were herding Hsiao Lao, Katherine, Chung Hao, and the rest of our group into the house.

The eight men and I were made to wait in the yard until everyone else was inside. By then it was afternoon and the air was a cold, gray mist that hurt my lungs when I breathed it in. The day's pale light was fading; soon it would be gone and the fields outside of the compound would be nothing more than flat black earth. I guessed we had less than two hours of daylight to bury fifteen bodies. With the soldiers' permission I went to the toolshed and took the battered gardening tools I kept there: two spades, a shovel, a pickax, a hoe, and two trowels. We had two carts at the compound, and together the men and I laid the bodies of the northern soldiers carefully on the carts. I picked up Lao Chang's

body and held him for a brief moment before I laid him gently on the cart also. I could not remember ever being in the compound without him.

The soldiers walked us out of the compound and into the nearest field. They gave no thought to an auspicious burial place and I did not ask them to; we were fortunate to be allowed to bury our dead at all. While the men with me began to dig a large grave for the soldiers, I worked at digging a resting place for Lao Chang a few yards away. We worked for nearly three hours, at the end of which I could see only directly in front of me. I heard the other men digging but could not make them out in the darkness. I finally laid Lao Chang in the earth, praying for him and the northern soldiers.

It was dark when we returned to the compound, where we were marched through the gate and across the yard like criminals. In our absence the compound had been transformed. Soldiers were everywhere, taking what they wanted and wreaking havoc. When we reached the house, the men with me were taken toward the large hall, where the door was opened quickly and the men shoved inside. Then the door was slammed shut again and a soldier moved a bench across the doors and sat down heavily and began eating canned peaches from our cellar.

My escorts pushed me roughly toward the

stairs and fear washed over me for the hundredth time that day, for I could think of no good reason to be forced upstairs. When I reached the top step I found the floor of the upstairs hallway carpeted in feathers and saw our limp bed pillows at my feet.

I was led to the small room I used as a study, which had been appropriated by the commander, whose name, I had learned from my escorts, was Colonel Wang. When I entered the room I found him leaning back in the rocking chair I had made when Lily was born, his legs stretched out in front of him, his feet propped up on a cardboard box that contained Mandarin New Testaments. He wore the shoes from the wheelbarrow, brown leather wingtips that had probably cost what our mission spent on food in a year. A few feet away from him, next to his muddy boots on the floor, was a small galvanized aluminum stove that we valued because it was so efficient at heating small spaces; I could get a fire going in it with only a few scraps of paper and a handful of twigs, and in those freezing winters, I treasured it more than I like to admit. The colonel had it burning nicely; the room was warmer than I had ever felt it in the winter. I saw ripped-up New Testaments on the floor and understood the reason for the warmth.

The colonel stared coolly at me for a long moment. Then he said, "*Mu shih*, I am well

aware of who you are. You and those in the room below will all benefit if you are forthcoming about what you know."

For a moment I stood there mute. I understood the words he had used, but not what he was saying until I realized he was accusing me of being a spy. I was exhausted and my judgment lacking, and my first thought was my family's reaction at home. *Will? Our clumsy Will a spy?* My response surprised me as much as it surprised the colonel: I laughed.

The colonel's expression did not change. "This amuses you," he said flatly.

I shook my head and forced myself to focus on where I was. "Forgive my lapse, Colonel. I am fatigued and not myself." I took a deep breath. "I have lived in Kuang P'ing Ch'eng for eighteen years. I am not here for politics or war. My wife and I came here to serve the people and to tell them of a God who loves them. We knew no one when we came; we now know many of the city's residents. We have provided them with medical care; we have taken in many children, especially during the famine. We have taught the people about hygiene and the prevention of disease. We have committed no crimes."

Colonel Wang nodded and I thought for a moment that our conversation was over. Then he asked, "Is this not exactly the claim a northern spy would make?"

When I started to answer he stopped me. "We know you are a spy for the northern army. You and those in the room below will benefit if you are forthcoming about what you know."

I was stumped; it was almost exactly what he had said the first time. As nearly as I could remember it, I repeated my response.

We went on that way for some time, back and forth, the colonel repeating his accusation while I repeated my defense. He sometimes added specific questions about the northern army's supply of ammunition, their casualty rate, and approximately how many troops had been in the area before their retreat, questions for which I had only the vaguest of answers, all of them more guesswork than fact. But he didn't seem to pay much attention to my responses; he simply kept repeating his accusation and his questions, and I repeated my defense and my guesses.

By then it seemed the day would never end, but finally, after perhaps an hour, the colonel leaned back in my chair and answered all of his own questions in great detail. He knew his enemy well. When he had finished, he looked at me for a long moment. Whether he was deciding my fate or the fate of our city or thinking about what he would like for dinner I could not tell. He said, "I do not believe you are a northern spy; you do not appear to have the mind for such things, nor do you have the cleverness to tailor the truth. As you

yourself have said that you are here to serve the people and that you have not taken sides in my country's conflict, I am certain you will not mind giving over your compound to my soldiers."

Seeing no choice, I nodded grimly.

He smiled. "Good. This compound is now the property of the Kuomintang. You and your"—he paused for a moment, searching for a word—"what is it they call you, goatherd?"

"Shepherd."

"Ah, yes. A shepherd has a flock. So you and your flock will leave the compound immediately. You may take what you can carry. Nothing more. My soldiers will escort you to the gate."

"Colonel Wang, an intelligent man such as yourself must see—" I started, but he waved me away.

"You are a fortunate man, Kung P'ei Te. You and yours have been spared." He smiled then. "You may go now and tell them this good news, since you claim that that is what you are here to do."

I left the room, but when I was in the hallway, he called me back. "*Mu shih*, take the potatoes. My men are tired of them, and your provisions will be a welcome change. Consider them a gift from the Kuomintang."

I was led back downstairs and into the large hall, where everyone waited. A few kerosene lamps burned, and in the dim light I found

Katherine and Chung Hao and Mo Yun and the other leaders of our church and I felt a tightness inside of me loosen a bit at the sight of them. "We may go," I said tentatively. People looked relieved and began to stand and I corrected myself. "We must go. The southern army has claimed the compound and we have been ordered to leave as quickly as possible. We may take only what we can carry."

I instructed the older boys to help the sick to the compound gate, some of them on the straw mats we used as stretchers. Katherine made her way to me and said, "The upstairs cabinet," and I nodded. Food and clothes we could replace in the city; medical supplies we could not. We hurried upstairs to our cabinet dispensary where we frantically crammed two small suitcases and two large baskets with as much as we could while a soldier stood in the doorway, haranguing us to be done with it and leave.

Fifteen minutes later, three hundred of us were escorted across the compound yard to the gate. Just before we reached it, I looked back at our home and saw Colonel Wang standing at our bedroom window, watching us as though we were squatters he was glad to be rid of.

Our compound was a short distance from East Gate, an easy walk on any other day but a difficult journey on that long night. Many of those with us needed help: the children, the

elderly, the sick, those who were simply worn down. As we neared the city, the bodies of southern soldiers lay in the fields that surrounded us and the air became thick with ash. The bodies of four northern soldiers hung from the tower at East Gate and there was almost no sound from within the city walls, making me wonder if anyone had survived. The gate was unlocked, an eerie first for night. In the city, dead soldiers lay everywhere, and for several blocks we saw no one. The streets felt so strange that those walking with us who had houses in the city continued on with us, reluctant to go home alone.

We made our way cautiously toward the *yamen*. I was hoping many of us could stay in the large hall that the magistrate had allowed us to use for the wounded only a week earlier. As we neared the center of the city, I began to sense movement behind the walls that enclosed people's homes, but we still saw no one for some distance. At last a gate opened and someone peered cautiously out. I called out, "I am Kung P'ei Te. The battle is over. The army has taken our compound and we are seeking shelter in the city." As an afterthought I added, "We are unarmed," and I saw Katherine's grim but amused look. We were hardly a threat.

The gate did not move, but I began to see others open ahead of us, and soon people began emerging from their homes, greeting us and

telling us of what they had witnessed: the fear and destruction, the torture and death. By the time we reached the *yamen*, word of our coming had preceded us and the magistrate awaited us. The place was wretched; it had become a morgue, with the slaughtered—the soldiers we had nursed and cared for—lying everywhere, killed in their makeshift beds.

Two of the large halls in the *yamen* were empty, and with the magistrate's permission, we directed the women and children to the hall on the left of the courtyard and the men to the hall near the magistrate's living quarters. Those who had survived the attack in the city brought food and bedding and clothing, and those who were returning to their homes also brought what they could.

When I finally lay down late that night on the floor of the *yamen*, I was grateful to be alive. As I fell asleep a question lingered in my mind: in the compound yard, Katherine had seemed to know the beggar, Hsiao Lao, and I could not understand how this could be. I told myself I would ask her later, but I never did; the tasks at hand overshadowed such a trivial-seeming question, and I soon forgot it.

February 15, 1928

We, too, are refugees now, staying at the home of Chung Hao and his brothers and their

wives, the same house where we first met Mo Yun. After being booted out of our compound by the victors, Will and I camped out at the *yamen* for four days then came here. As the southern army has claimed the compound as its own, there is no way of knowing when we will be able to return there. In the meantime we have at least the start of some order to our lives. We have established a schedule of care at the temporary clinic and orphanage at the *yamen*, and the magistrate has granted us permission to hold worship services there for our ragged church. I am astonished at how quickly this battered city has come back to life. Even with the ground still stained with blood, the market is busier each day, and while the people may comment on their fates, they do not complain. Their lack of self-pity inspires and humbles me, and I admire them.

We have been with Chung Hao and his family for a month now, eleven of us in four rooms. I am grateful to be here, and grateful to have Will beside me. Thirty-four days ago when the southern army reached our compound and Will went out to meet them, I did not think I would see him alive again. As he left the hall and closed the door behind him, I glimpsed my life without him—I glimpsed *myself* without him—and I did not see how I would bear it, or how I would sit there without speaking as I

waited for the sound of shots fired at my husband. I could not breathe, and I felt waves of panic and fear go through me. But because I knew there was far more at stake than Will's life, I forced myself to stay still.

Chung Hao stood up then. He walked calmly to the door then turned and faced us, and there was a fierceness about him I had never seen; he looked like a warrior. "If my friend dies today," he said, his voice strong, "I will die with him. Those who wish to stay here, do so. Those who wish to stand at *mu* shih's side, whatever the cost, come."

He looked directly at me then, and I have never been so grateful to anyone; his words gave me strength and permission, and I got to my feet. As I did I saw Mo Yun and Lao Chang and the leaders of the church stand, then one after another of our friends. Within moments everyone in the room was standing, and a current of energy ran through us.

Chung Hao said, "Let us pray," and the adults dropped to their knees, closed their eyes, and began speaking all at once, as is the custom for prayer here. Their murmuring filled the room. I heard *"mu shih"* again and again, and as I looked around—I could not help myself—I saw not the fear of only a few minutes before but faith. Then, in the compound yard when the southern

commander ordered me to come forward, I knew we were safe, for the beggar who stepped forward was my beggar, the same man who brought us opium for our dying wounded. I didn't know his name, but I knew he was from God.

On our second morning here with Chung Hao's family I rose early to go outside to pray before the day began. It's so cold that I can't bear it for long, but even a few minutes of solitude strengthens me. That morning, when I stepped from the house into the courtyard, I thought I sensed someone nearby, and I heard footsteps on the other side of the wall. Fear washed over me and I told myself I was being foolish, but as I started to walk toward the bench against the wall, I tripped on something. My first thought was that it was a body, and I looked down with dread. But when I knelt I found a small basket of eggs, which I had somehow not broken. When I took them inside, our morning became a feast; none of us had felt full for months, but that morning's breakfast left all of us sated.

Three days later when I went outside I found a large sack of flour at that same early hour and in that same place, and four days after that a basket of vegetables. There have been more gifts since—pears, noodles, persimmons, steamed buns—and once, the greatest luxury,

a tin of English shortbread. After the first deliveries I began to check the doorstep before I retired at night, hoping for a glimpse of the giver. But there is only silence and the empty doorstep in the still night; my benefactor is adept at coming and going undetected, and he seems to know my habits. I have come to understand that I am being watched or, rather, that I am being watched over. I have no idea why, but I do not dwell on it. I accept his gifts gratefully and I pray for him in return.

In March of 1928, three months after the battle, the southern army vacated our compound. As long lines of exhausted soldiers headed north, I felt I had seen a million men pass by. In the months that followed, the Kuomintang army took Tsinan, the capital of Shantung province, and Peking, the country's ancient capital. The new government named Nanking as the new capital, and the warlord era seemed to come to an end.

With the soldiers gone, we reclaimed what was ours and got to work. There was much to be done; our guests had thoroughly ransacked each of the buildings: our home, the clinic, and the orphanage. They broke our windows, hacked down our doors, ripped out the wooden door and window frames, and destroyed our furniture. The

few items not deemed worth taking had been thrown on the floor and trampled on, and our carefully stocked pantry had been completely emptied of the onions, squash, carrots, apples, and canned goods that were supposed to sustain us for a year. I was enraged about all of this until I noticed dozens of holes burned into the floors from the charcoal heaters the soldiers used, and I realized that we were fortunate that the whole place hadn't burned to the ground, with or without intent.

Appraising the damage was painful, not only because of the hard work it would require but because the time and money required to fix everything meant time and money not spent on our real work. But we got busy. We swept out the dirt and scrubbed the walls and floors with pailfuls of hot soapy water and stiff scrub brushes. We whitewashed every wall, and our home and the other buildings slowly began to look as they had before the war.

On a cool, breezy afternoon in late April, Katherine and I were whitewashing the last room of the orphanage when Chung Hao appeared and said we had been summoned to the *yamen*. He did not know why we were needed; he said only that the magistrate desired to see us. This was not unusual, and as there was nothing to do but comply, Katherine and I cleaned ourselves up and walked to the city with Chung

Hao and Mo Yun, our hands still ghostly from whitewash.

It was a beautiful day, the kind of spring afternoon on which the world feels new, and once we were walking on that rutted dirt road I had come to love, I was glad to be in the open air. The winter wheat was nearly ready for harvesting and we were surrounded by fields of deep golden stalks that were almost as tall as Katherine. The breeze blew the plants back and forth in even waves, and I breathed in the scent of ripe wheat. I had no idea why the magistrate would summon us, but I chose not to dwell on it and concentrated instead on the feel of the sun on my back and the unexpected pleasure of taking a walk with my wife and friends.

When we entered the city through East Gate and turned toward the *yamen*, the city seemed strangely quiet for late afternoon. We walked by shops whose owners we knew and whom we would usually greet as we passed, but even though it was still afternoon, the shops had been boarded up and no one was in sight. The city's unusual stillness made me uneasy.

We turned onto Hsiao Chieh, which ran straight into the *yamen*, and I heard people talking and laughing, though I still saw no one. The *yamen* itself was on Te Chieh, and when we reached the entrance I was about to knock at the huge doors but stopped, for as I looked to my right I did not

understand what I saw: more people than I could count were sitting at long tables that stretched far down the middle of the narrow street, nearly as far as I could see. Everyone was laughing and talking, and I saw that they were our friends and acquaintances and members of our church, and that the tables were laden with more food than I had seen at one time in many years.

Suddenly everyone grew silent and I was afraid we had intruded on a private celebration. But then the magistrate came forward and smiled at us, and when he had greeted us, he began speaking loudly.

"*Mu shih* and Kung Mei Li," he said. "I am pleased you have answered my request for your presence." He paused, waiting for me to answer.

"We are honored to do so," I said.

He then did something he had never done before: he bowed to us. Then he said, "My friends, you have brought western medicine to us, fed our hungry, healed our sick, eased our pain. You have buried our dead, as well as your own. Our debt to you is great, too large for us to repay." He paused. "But we ask one thing more. Will you do us the honor of being our guests?"

"Magistrate," I said, "doing so would give us great joy, as would anything else you asked of us."

The magistrate smiled broadly and once again faced the citizens of his city. "Let us welcome

our friends," he said, at which people began to cheer and to come forward to greet us.

We sat down to a feast that was like a grand family dinner. There were platters of whole fish fried in batter, baskets of persimmons and apricots and pears, trays of roast goose, hard-boiled eggs preserved in salt and vinegar. When evening came, lanterns were hung along the storefronts, casting the street in a lovely golden light, and I saw the magistrate signal to one of his servants, who left the celebration. He returned sometime later followed by two men carrying a large object covered with a red cloth. They set it down behind our table.

The magistrate stood, and when the crowd had quieted, he addressed Katherine and me once again. "Most foreigners left our country for safety before the war; we know that you could have left as well. That you chose to stay honors us deeply, and I present you with this gift, in gratitude for the safekeeping of Kuang P'ing Ch'eng." He nodded to his servant then, who lifted the red coverlet from the mysterious object, and I was astounded at what I saw. It was a carved chest of *chang mu*, camphor wood, and although of a common size—approximately two feet high, three feet wide, and two feet deep—I had never seen another like it. I knew it well, for it had been made for the magistrate when he arrived in Kuang P'ing Ch'eng thirty years

earlier, and I had often admired it in the *yamen*. Its top was carved with hydrangeas, a symbol of abundance because of the abundance of the flower's petals, while the chest's front, sides, and back depicted Kuang P'ing Ch'eng's city wall with its uneven turrets and odd curves and corners. Each side of the chest showed one of the wall's gates, with South Gate on the front, West Gate on the left side, North Gate on the back, and East Gate on the right side.

The chest's brass fittings and polished wood gleamed in the lanterns' soft light. Katherine knelt next on the ground and ran her hands over the intricate carving, transfixed by it. When she looked up at me, I saw that she was as overcome as I was. "Thank him," she said in English. "Tell them how generous this is, how kind he is."

I nodded; I wanted to do just that, but had no idea how. "Magistrate," I said to him, "the city owes us nothing, and we are humbled by your exquisite gift." Then I turned to the crowd and looked out at scores of people I'd known for decades. I had seen their children grow up, and I knew their joys and their sorrows. I said to them, "Since coming to Kuang P'ing Ch'eng we have received far more than we have given. We came to serve you and to teach you of our faith, but it is we who have been cared for and taught. We came to devote our lives to the work here, and you have given us lives we never imagined. We

know of no place on earth more blessed than this city. And we are blessed that it is our home."

We stayed at the celebration until late in the evening. Again and again I found myself looking up and down the long line of tables at the faces of people I loved. *Remember this well,* I thought; *this night is the gift.*

When I was a child in Oklahoma, neighbors brought food with death and flowers with sickness and other things in between. In China we received noodles on the occasion of our daughter's birth and chrysanthemums at her death; lotus seeds for health and ginseng for longevity; and, at the New Year, tangerines for good fortune, fish for abundance, dumplings for wealth. The siege and occupation of Kuang P'ing Ch'eng and the year following it brought gifts as well. Neighbors gave us chickens and eggs, noodles and cakes, winter wheat and fruit and half a butchered hog, and at the feast we were given, in addition to the magistrate's chest, four hundred dollars from the city's merchants to refurbish and expand the clinic and dispensary.

There was another gift, less tangible but just as real—the gift of trust. Feelings of apprehension that we had never truly overcome in nineteen years seemed to give way after the war. Attendance at services grew to twice or even three times what it had been, and the number of

believers increased by the month. It was as though a wall came down; sometimes during a worship service I felt we had a bond we had not shared before, like people who had been rescued from a sinking vessel and were now grateful for the simple blessing of standing on solid ground.

But those gifts came at a price, and although I was a grateful man after the siege of Kuang P'ing Ch'eng, I was also a haunted one. The image of Katherine, standing alone in the compound yard with thirty rifles trained on her stayed with me for many months, and each time I recalled how close I had come to losing her, a rush of fear and panic nearly brought me to my knees.

Beautiful Country

1932–1946

In the spring of 1932, I began experiencing a strange kind of unrest inside. At first I thought it came from neglecting some responsibility, and I looked for a task I was avoiding or a leading of the Spirit I had ignored. When I couldn't find anything that I had or hadn't done that would cause this disquiet, I worked harder at what was in front of me. I preached in the marketplace from morning till evening, I traveled to the outlying villages with a zealot's fervor, I wrote letters to churches all over the United States telling of our work, I attended to every maintenance chore I could think of at our compound. But nothing helped.

Then one night I woke suddenly with the strange sense that Katherine and I would soon leave China. The thought sparked instant dread in me; I had come to imagine us growing old in Kuang P'ing Ch'eng and living out our days there. These hopes seemed reasonable; missionaries who returned to the United States usually did so to be near their families, but Katherine and I had neither children nor grandchildren, our parents had long since passed on, and our years in China had made only distant

relationships possible with our siblings, except for Naomi. Who was there to welcome us in America? What was there to return to? My middle-of-the-night thoughts of leaving seemed foolish and wrong, and I dismissed them.

But as time went on, my unrest continued and I began to feel a distance from God. I told myself this was natural, a phase of my spiritual life that would pass. I did not spend more time in prayer; I considered my spiritual distress an embarrassing weakness I should be well past or at least able to fix on my own, an attitude similar to a sick man thinking he should heal himself.

When these thin rationalizations gave way, I attributed my anxiety to the general precariousness of our lives and the country's political situation, which was, once again, unstable. The reunification of 1928 had been short-lived; the country was soon in turmoil again as the new government, headquartered in the south, tried unsuccessfully to control the northern provinces. The Communists, once supporters of the Kuomintang but now its enemies, regained strength and essentially established their own government and military in Kiangsi province in the south. In September of 1931 the new government faced a new and even greater threat: Japan took Manchuria and began to move south in an attempt to occupy China.

The Kuomintang already rejected all things

foreign, and Japan's invasion increased feelings of nationalism and anti-foreign sentiments. Attacks against foreigners became more frequent, and in early 1932 we received news that shattered us: Ruth Ehren, the deaconess who had come over to China with us in 1906 and had accompanied us to Shanghai when we were married, was kidnapped and held for ransom by a band of soldiers said to be Communists. The mission in Shin Sheng Chou received a ransom note from the kidnappers along with a bloody finger wrapped in a dirty scrap of blue cotton. The mission staff tried frantically to negotiate with the kidnappers, but two weeks later word came that Ruth had been killed. She had been tortured each day and was said to have lost her mind.

A few months later a messenger from the *yamen* came to the compound with word that the magistrate desired my presence. I was replacing the last loose tiles on the roof of the clinic, an annual chore, and when I finished the task I walked into the city alone. When I reached the *yamen*, I was escorted through the first, second, and third courtyards to the magistrate's living quarters, where I found him in an agitated state. He motioned for me to be seated and asked his servant to leave us, and once we were alone he paced the length of the room for a few minutes, not speaking, his tall form bent over as if beneath

a burden. Finally he sat down across from me, and I saw how much he had aged since the war.

"Mu shih," he said, "my country is changing."

I almost laughed; he seemed to be stating the obvious. "It has been so for many years, Magistrate. Certainly, since I have been here, change has been the one constant."

He shook his head. "That has been change on the surface. The change I sense is far deeper, a transformation of our most basic beliefs. China will be a different place before long; our very core is being altered."

"Surely, Magistrate—" I started, but he shook his head, and when he continued, it was as if he were speaking to someone sitting next to me, for he did not meet my gaze.

"In the past, you have been a refuge for those who came to your compound in times of danger or want. We have been grateful for your protection, but that, too, is changing. I fear that in the future the reverse will be true: your presence will put those near you in peril." He paused for a moment; then, his voice low, he said, "My friend, if the Communists gain power, they will try to kill every missionary in the country; they have said as much. Mission stations will become the most dangerous places to be, rather than the safest." Finally he met my eyes. "I believe the time is coming when you will need to leave us to protect us."

His words stunned me. But I knew what he said was true, and at that moment I saw that the feeling I had had in the middle of the night a few months earlier had been correct. The magistrate was voicing what I had known but had not wanted to acknowledge: Katherine and I would soon leave China. "Do you believe that time has come?"

He shook his head. "Not yet. But I sense it on the horizon and it saddens me, which is why I felt the need to speak with you." He paused and seemed to weigh his words. "When the time comes for you to leave—and it will come, of this I am certain—you must know that your leaving will bring our city great sadness, and that it is not our wish."

I nodded; the truth of what he said sank in me like a stone. My throat tight, I said, "I understand."

The magistrate gestured to a servant standing at the door. The servant left and returned with tea, which he served to us. The magistrate motioned for me to drink and seemed relieved to have the conversation over with. He changed the subject, and we spoke for a while about his youth in the country to the northeast. But our exchange was strained—I could see he felt grieved—and I soon left him.

I told no one about our conversation, not even Katherine. Broaching the subject of leaving

seemed premature, so I waited and watched for a sign. I thought the decision might be made for us, and I half expected to hear that the Consulate or the Mission Board was once again urging evacuation and that Katherine and I would be forced to leave. At night as I lay in bed staring at the worn beams of our ceiling, I tried to envision our departure, and I prayed that when the time came I would be able to freely let go of this great gift from my Lord—this place that had become my home, and the people who were my family.

Six months later, on a fall day in 1932, the magistrate's servant once again came to our compound. When he found me, he was frantic: the magistrate was in grave trouble, he said; I must come at once. I did not hesitate, and together we hurried to the city, where I followed him through streets that, as we neared the *yamen*, became strangely empty. It was mid-morning, a time when the city was usually busy.

When we entered the *yamen* gates the servant ran through the courtyards as I followed. Normally the *yamen* was busy with the city's merchants conducting their business, but that day it was eerily still. We were about to enter the fourth courtyard when two strangers came out of the magistrate's living quarters. The servant and I stopped. Each of the men carried a large sword,

and as the servant and I watched, they casually wiped blood from their swords on their trousers. They seemed very much at home; they were relaxed and calm, even jovial. When they saw me, they seemed surprised to see me. I could not recall ever meeting them, but they smiled and greeted me by name.

"Mu shih," said the taller of the two, "how do you come to be here at such an early hour? Is there not enough to occupy you with your church?" He glanced at his companion and the two of them laughed easily.

"The magistrate requested my presence," I said.

The shorter man smiled. "Kung P'ei Te, you are mistaken. The magistrate is well, but he is unable to welcome you. Let your heart down and come away from this place. My friend and I were here to speak with some spies we found hidden in the *yamen*. Return to your compound in peace." Then the two men took hold of the magistrate's servant and me and began to lead us roughly out of the courtyard. At the *yamen*'s huge outermost gate, they nearly threw us into the street before closing the gate and locking it.

I saw no choice but to return to the compound. I urged the servant to come with me, but he wanted only to be away from the *yamen*—and perhaps me—and he ran off through the city, his footsteps echoing behind him.

• • •

October 23, 1932

Yesterday when Will came from the *yamen* he looked drained and nearly sick. He said he was just tired and went upstairs, and it was Chung Hao who told me what had happened—that the magistrate and his wife had been murdered in their rooms. Who killed them and why is not known; the murderers could be bandits or "the others"—a name for Communists—or warlord soldiers or even Kuomintang. They could be anyone, really.

When I learned the news I went upstairs and found Will in our bedroom. I thought he hadn't told me because he didn't want to upset me, and I was cross; I don't like it when he tries to carry too much by himself. But when I entered the room, my anger left me. Will was sitting motionless on the edge of the bed, staring out the window, his expression anguished. I sat down next to him and he looked at me but did not seem to see me. I took his hand and said, "This was not your fault," for I know how my husband thinks. "They were not killed because they knew us," I said, not at all sure it was true. Will said nothing; he just continued to look at me. Then he began to weep, and as I held him in my arms, I too gave in to my tears. The magistrate and his wife had been our friends and advocates for many years, and

their deaths were a loss I could not take in. Nor could I dwell on the horrible deaths they had faced.

But my tears came from fear as well as grief, for I knew the murderers could have just as easily killed my husband too before going on their way. I have lost count of the number of times I have nearly lost him. When we were younger, the dangers of our lives here were a given: bandits and disease, warlords and violence were realities I didn't question. I rarely let myself think about the risks, and when I did I assumed we were invincible. When Lily died I saw it as a fluke—our one misfortune. But each year I have understood more clearly how vulnerable we are, and I find myself longing for something I've never cared about before: I want us to be safe.

I think of my father when I told him I wanted to come to China. I was twenty-one years old, and he said he feared it was not safe for a woman alone. I think I laughed when he said this, for the thought had never occurred to me; safety seems irrelevant when one is young. But now it's what I want; I want to grow old with my husband, who becomes more precious to me each year. I would have thought younger love was the stronger force, but my feelings for Will have put down roots whose depth I'm only beginning to sense, and while I think of our

marriage as still young—nearly twenty-four years does not seem possible—I see it's not a sapling but a sturdy old oak.

When I catch sight of him striding across the compound yard, I stop what I'm doing to watch him. I see his familiar walk: the efficient steps, his long legs, the way one shoulder is a little lower than the other, the way he taps his fingers against his thighs as he walks when he is puzzling over something. At breakfast when I look across the table at him I see the great kindness in his expression as he listens to Chung Hao's concerns about this young church, and I see his wisdom, which is well beyond his years. I see compassion in his blue eyes, and I see the fatigue from too many years of too little sleep and too much work in the way he stands, resting, when he thinks no one sees him. When he is asleep, I see the growing gray in his blond hair and the furrows in his brow as he worries in his dreams. The term "middle age" fits where we are, for I see in him both the young man I fell in love with and the old one he will be. I see my own dear husband and I am struck by how deeply I love him, by how many times I have nearly lost him—and by how lost I would be without him.

Then I ask where my faith is. I decide I'm being selfish and that fear rather than faith is

leading me, and I scold myself for my lapse; I buck up and work harder and turn my back on this yearning for calm. But it will not be silenced, and once again I am asking God: Would You give me a desire You do not plan to fulfill? I don't receive an answer, but the Silence that greets me is somehow gentle, and I stop battering myself for my lack of faith and accept my desires as a mystery, to be felt rather than solved.

A month after the deaths of the magistrate and his wife, I was upstairs in the study writing to American churches when I suddenly wanted some air. The room seemed to be closing in on me, so much so that I almost felt panicked. I stood and went out into the hallway, not understanding the feeling that had come over me, knowing only that I needed to get out of that room.

I went downstairs to the back door of our home. I was about to step outside onto the porch that wrapped around the first floor when I stopped. Katherine was in the enclosed yard behind the house, hanging clean wet laundry on the lines that stretched between the two elm trees we had planted for just that purpose. She could have had help with this, which, knowing how fatigued she became, I had often suggested. But she always refused, saying that the task reminded

her of growing up, and that she loved the smell of the clean wet clothes.

I was about to go help her when something stopped me and kept me frozen at the door, watching my wife, staring at a scene I had witnessed hundreds of times. But it was different that day; Katherine was different. She looked so exhausted that I almost didn't recognize her. I had never seen despair in her, but that was what I saw that afternoon, that and brokenness. The sight of her made me ache inside, and I wanted to go and comfort her, to repair whatever was wrong and dispel the sadness and exhaustion I saw. But something prevented me from opening the door; I had the feeling that I was supposed to see Katherine like this, and I watched intently as she picked up sheets and skirts and trousers and shirts from the wicker basket at her feet, shook them out, and pinned them to the clothesline.

Several minutes had passed when I realized that Mo Yun was standing next to me. She said, "Are you seeing her, *mu shih*?"

"Yes."

"Do you see the fatigue?"

I nodded.

"Kung Mei Li's life here is very hard on her," she said gently. "She cannot do all that she could even a few years ago. She tires easily and experiences a great deal of fatigue." Mo Yun

paused for a moment. Then she said, "I do not believe she can recuperate here; she will not rest. She must return to America, where she can live a quieter life." Mo Yun took a deep breath and let it out slowly. "I believe that by staying here, you cut short her life."

I nodded, trying to take in Mo Yun's words. I felt a deep sadness, both at what she was saying and at what I was seeing, and I was baffled as to why this exhaustion had appeared so suddenly, as if overnight. "Has her life been more difficult recently? Does she need more help?"

Mo Yun shook her head. "It is not only the physical difficulties that take their toll; her life here is hard on her spirit as well. Kung Mei Li's faith is strong, but it does not always protect her from worrying about those she loves."

As I continued to watch Katherine, I understood that this was the sign I had been waiting for. It was time for us to leave China, and the reason had been right in front of me: my dear wife's slow deterioration, the gradual wearing down of her body and soul.

Mo Yun rested her hand gently on my arm. "Perhaps God is asking you to give up what you love most for whom you love most."

Katherine hung up the last sheet then picked up the basket and began to walk toward the house, and Mo Yun and I retreated inside before she saw us.

I went back upstairs to my study. Only fifteen minutes had passed, but everything felt changed. I sat down heavily and held my head in my hands. I was ashamed of myself, of my callousness and my neglectfulness, and I scolded myself for not having been more attentive; I should have seen her anxiety and fatigue long ago. As I let myself dwell on my shame, I decided that I was responsible for Katherine's health and that we should leave China as soon as possible. My thinking was desperate and frenzied enough that had it been possible for us to go that afternoon I would have tried.

Finally I prayed the only thing I could: *I don't know what to do. Please help me,* and at that moment I gave up. I gave up my plans for the rest of our lives and my hopes to die in China and my desire to direct it all, and I gave up my feelings of shame and responsibility for Katherine's health. I asked God's forgiveness for my willfulness; I asked that He show me what He wanted for our lives, and that He help me to carry out those wishes. As I sat in that still room, I felt the peace that had eluded me for many months. I knew that not only was it time for us to leave; it was right.

The next evening I asked Katherine to come and sit outside with me, something we did often. Our days were so busy that by evening I often felt I

had barely spoken with her that day, even if we had been working side by side, and I enjoyed sitting with her in the after-supper quiet.

The two of us sat side by side on a bench in the garden. A breeze stirred the leaves of the poplar tree above us, and when I inhaled I could smell the familiar smoky odor of the city.

"Do you remember how strange everything was when we first arrived here?" I said. "At night I used to lie awake in the dark trying to decide how soon I could go home without looking like I'd given up. I decided six months was the minimum, and I didn't think I'd last that long, but I also couldn't imagine going home any sooner and facing everyone."

Katherine laughed. "I could see that in you then. See that you were struggling, trying to force yourself to like it here."

I turned to look at her in the darkness. She was staring straight ahead at the gate to our compound, and in the light that spilled out from the windows of our home I saw her profile, delicate and fine. "Didn't you feel the same?"

She shook her head. "Not so much. I was determined to stay and decided that homesickness was a temporary inconvenience that wouldn't last if I ignored it."

I laughed at her down-to-earth practicality, a constant with her. "But did you like it here at the beginning? Didn't everything seem strange?"

She shrugged. "It was China," she said. "I didn't think about it more than that."

We were quiet for a while. Finally I took a deep breath and said, "Katherine, I think it's time to go."

She nodded and started to stand, thinking I wanted to go inside. "If you want."

I took her arm. "No. Not inside."

She looked at me, puzzled. "Where is it that you want to go?"

I looked at her and was surprised at the sense of peace I felt as I said words I had never thought I would. "I think it's time to leave Kuang P'ing Ch'eng and go back to the United States."

She started to speak but I shook my head.

"Wait. I believe the time has come for the mission to make the transition into a native church. I've been feeling this for some time, and I believe it would be in the church's best interest for us to leave. With politics as they are, in the future our presence here may become more of a liability than a help." I paused. "There are other reasons. But no matter what they are, I'm afraid that what I'm asking will break your heart."

She looked at me with such seriousness that I could not tell what she was thinking. Then she said, "I don't want to leave but I'm afraid to stay."

I thought she was referring to the political

danger. "I don't think the situation is dangerous yet."

She shook her head. "It's not that." She gazed straight ahead and seemed to see something far away, then she took my hand and squeezed it, and when she looked at me, there were tears in her eyes. "I find my strength isn't what it used to be," she said, "and I'm afraid I'll become a burden here instead of a help. I don't think I could bear that." She wiped her eyes and would not look at me for a moment; then she smiled weakly. "I didn't think I'd feel old so soon."

Her words caught at me, and I could only nod. Then I said, "Our life here hasn't been easy. Wonderful, but not easy."

She looked around us at the garden, the house, the compound. "Can you imagine leaving? What will we do?"

I shrugged. "I haven't gotten that far."

"When I picture going back, I'm worried I'll be sitting in a rocking chair on a front porch for the next twenty years. Then sometimes I think that's all I'll be able to do."

I shook my head. "Doesn't sound so good. I'm counting on history: each time God has led me away from one thing, He's led me toward something else. Away from home and toward China. Away from the familiar and toward you."

"We'll be leaving home, you know. America's going to be the strange new place this time."

I looked at her and held her hand to my lips and kissed it. "My home is with you, *Meine liebe Herz*. What more do I need?"

Katherine laughed. "You're very good at that, Will Kiehn."

"What?"

"Saying just the right thing. To me, anyway."

We stayed outside much longer than usual that evening, listening to the sounds of the night and chatting quietly about this and that, none of it to do with leaving our lovely City of Tranquil Light. I knew we were comforting each other as the idea sank in, and helping each other to make peace with it. When we went inside, I felt different, as if something inside me had shifted slightly, as though I'd already taken a few steps away from my beloved home.

The next morning I wrote to the Mission Board in the United States, notifying them of our feelings and asking that we be allowed to return to America, and that evening we gathered the leaders of the church together and told them of our decision. While they were saddened, they understood and supported us, and they agreed it was in the church's best interest. As the magistrate had said, not only was the country becoming more unsafe for foreigners; our presence could endanger those around us as well. In serious trouble, it would be impossible for

them to hide us without jeopardizing the safety of their own families.

There was one aspect of our leaving that encouraged me: the end of our work in Kuang P'ing Ch'eng would mean the transformation of the mission station into a native church, a transition I had dreamed of for many years and that was essential to the church's survival and growth. Without native support, mission stations closed or disappeared once the missionaries left, and at a time in which all foreigners and even those associated with them were suspect, the transformation of the mission station into a native church was even more important. I began reading reports from other mission stations that had made this transition successfully and envisioning how it could occur in Kuang P'ing Ch'eng. A native church would need to assume responsibility for all church matters and govern and support itself. We would sign over the deeds to the mission property to the national church, which could then decide whether to continue employing the mission's national workers, who numbered around twenty. Those the church decided not to retain would be given severance pay by the mission, and the church would be free to choose its own leaders and other workers.

At that time, our baptized believers numbered somewhere around nine hundred people, spread out around the church in Kuang P'ing Ch'eng

and seven outstations in surrounding towns and villages. The elders of the church discussed a name for the new church and decided on The Church of His Beautiful Strength. We were also leaving a modern clinic with running water, thanks to an electric pump donated by a church in Kansas City; electric lights, thanks to a Delco generator donated by a Sunday school in Cleveland; and indoor plumbing, thanks to the city's wealthier merchants. The clinic had four well-equipped examination rooms, a full dispensary, beds for sixty patients, and a staff of eight nurses and nurses-in-training, and it would continue to be managed by the church for the time being, with two Chinese doctors, trained at Peking Union Medical College, to work with Mo Yun. Most exciting was the orphanage, which was nearly empty by then, as the dozens of children who had come to us during the famine and civil war had either returned to their parents or grown up. Many of the girls had married, and the older boys had been apprenticed to tradesmen and businesses in the city. Now it would be a school.

As I lay in bed each night thinking of leaving Kuang P'ing Ch'eng, I also found myself remembering our arrival there—the day we came to the city, our small storefront on Hsiao Chieh, our tentative beginnings—and as I did, I was amazed at what God had done, sometimes

through me, sometimes with me, frequently in spite of me. I could not exactly reconstruct how it had all come to pass—where we had found the money and the knowledge and the perseverance to do what we'd done. It didn't add up; it made no more sense than it did to have leftovers after feeding five thousand with a few loaves and fishes. But I had stopped trying to explain it. Mysterious abundance was not the exception to the rule. It was who God was, when we gave Him half a chance.

Two months later we received word from the Mission Board in the United States that we should return when we were able to. We would be supplied with temporary housing in Glendale, California, a suburb of Los Angeles, while we rested and awaited our next assignment. I made arrangements for our travel to the coast, and we continued with our normal lives for as long as we could.

Then suddenly it was the week of our leaving, and I woke each morning with a feeling of dread. Word of our departure had spread far and wide, and people we had known for more than twenty years traveled from country villages and towns all over the region to say goodbye. Our compound was busy from morning until night, and there were many farewells: feasts, eloquent speeches, gifts of candies and cakes, seaweed

delicacies from the coast, and a huge ginseng root, considered very precious. From Chung Hao and Mo Yun we received a red silk lantern so that, they said, our new life would have happiness and much light. There were also contributions made to the mission-turned-church in our honor: eggs, pork, chickens, cash. On our last Sunday our worship hall overflowed with well-wishers. The people of Kuang P'ing Ch'eng valued long friendships, and that morning I looked out at scores of old friends.

There was one goodbye we did not say: we were not able to see Edward and Naomi Geisler, who were in the midst of moving to the far northwest of China when Katherine and I made our decision to leave Kuang P'ing Ch'eng. Edward and Naomi's three children were by then adults; Paul, the oldest, was serving as a missionary in the south of China, while John and Madeleine had settled in the United States after completing their educations there. Edward had written that it was his desire to preach the Gospel to those who had never heard it, a desire Naomi shared, and with their children grown and independent, the time seemed right to leave the church at Ch'eng An Fu in the hands of native workers and move west. I had thought that leaving China without seeing her sister would greatly trouble Katherine, and I had begun devising a plan for seeing the Geislers, even if it

meant traveling four days each way to be with them for an afternoon. But when I proposed it to Katherine, she said no. "We'll see each other sometime, either here or there," she said. I did not understand her meaning, but when I pressed her, she shook her head. "I've said goodbye to Naomi twice: once when she left home and again when she left for China. I don't think I can do it again."

We did not spend a great deal of time packing during those last days; we left our Chinese clothes and our housewares and linens and filled only two large suitcases and the chest that had been given to us at the feast several years earlier. This seemed right, as we were leaving much of ourselves. In the midst of packing I noticed Katherine holding her medical bag, a black leather satchel I had ordered from a catalog in the United States and given to her as a wedding present twenty-seven years earlier. I remembered her opening it when I gave it to her, and I saw it in my mind as it was then, the stiff leather smooth and shiny and ink-black. Now the case was battered and worn, its leather soft and dull and scratched.

She held it for a long moment, just staring at it.

"You don't have to keep that if you don't want to," I said.

"I think it belongs here." She looked at me to see if I agreed, and when I nodded, she began to

clean the bag inside and out then pack it with supplies.

That evening Katherine gave the bag to Mo Yun. In return, Mo Yun took from her hair the silver clasp she had worn every day for as long as we had known her. The clasp had been given to her by her mother, who had received it from her mother, and so on for many generations. In China at that time, a woman who married gave up her own family and, to a large extent, her identity, so the gift was one of sacrifice and self.

Mo Yun held the clasp out to Katherine. "When you leave a place you love, you leave a piece of your heart." She closed Katherine's fingers over her gift. "But you take with you the hearts of your beloved."

On the morning of our last full day in Kuang P'ing Ch'eng, I left the compound early and set out for the cemetery where our daughter was buried, something I did several times a year, always alone. It was Katherine's choice not to accompany me; where I found solace, she found sorrow, and she had not been to the cemetery since Lily's death.

The fields were pale and still in that first light, the air cool and wet. I walked northwest on a rutted hard-packed dirt road that was mostly a rough path cut through fields or around them. It was a road I had come to love; it followed the

curve of the city's wall, then branched off to the northwest and toward the hills far in the distance, barely visible. The occasional elms and poplars were my signposts, the crows my companions, and God seemed very present.

I walked for nearly an hour, and it was still early morning when I reached the cemetery, which consisted of some twenty-five grave mounds in the middle of a field of wheat and surrounded by a grove of pine trees. Lily's grave was in the southwest corner of the cemetery, a location chosen by Chung Hao. He had said she would be near his mother, whom he had loved and who would now watch over my child, and while in my heart I did not believe in that view of the afterlife, the idea still gave me comfort.

At the grave I found what had surprised me a few years earlier but what I had now come to expect: fresh pine branches placed carefully on my daughter's grave, covering it. When this had first happened several years earlier it had troubled me, but I found the branches again the next time I visited and every time thereafter, and I came to understood that someone who cared for us was caring for her. Pine trees were believed to keep evil spirits away and to bring protection and peace to the dead; I could only guess that the branches were left by a patient of Katherine's or someone else we had helped in some way.

That day once again the branches covered the small grave. I knelt in the dirt and told my daughter a final goodbye.

The next morning after breakfast Katherine and I walked together through the house for the last time. We did not speak as we walked from one room to another, touching the walls and furniture. Despite the furniture and books and rugs we were leaving, the house no longer looked or felt like our home; it was already changed into something else, except when we looked outside. In each room, we gazed out at ordinary views we loved. From the kitchen we saw the compound yard, from the meeting room we saw the garden that had sustained us, from our bedroom we saw the city wall, and from the small study where we had prayed together most mornings we saw the compound gate and, beyond it, the plain to the south. Katherine wept softly, and when we left the house and pulled the door shut behind us for the last time, she kissed it. We were leaving holy ground.

A few dozen people were waiting for us in the compound yard, and when we reached the front gate we found many more waiting for us there. Together we walked through East Gate to the *yu chen chu*, the post office, which was next to the *yamen* in the center of the city. We would ride in a postal truck to Handan, and from there we

would travel by train to Tientsin on the coast.

When we entered the city, we were met by an even larger gathering, so that by the time we reached the post office we were surrounded by several hundred people, many of whom had come to us as patients years earlier and were now friends. There were members of our church, and men and women whom we had treated and cared for when they were children and who now held their own children in their arms. There were people we did not know by name, only by face, but whom we still loved.

We embraced people and cried with them and told them we would pray for them. A woman holding an infant in her arms hesitantly approached Katherine, but when she said Katherine's name, Katherine did not seem to recognize her. The woman began to explain that Katherine had delivered her when we had first arrived, and as the woman named her parents and the place she had lived, Katherine smiled and embraced her. Katherine looked at me and said, "She was the first baby I delivered." The woman held her infant daughter out to Katherine and said shyly, "Her name is Mei Li. For you." Then the woman held out a Chinese silver dollar. "For you, Kung P'ei Te. Perhaps you may buy a cup of tea on your journey. "

Someone took my arm then and said, "*Mu shih*, a word with you." I turned and followed a man in

a peasant's blue cotton tunic and trousers. I had not seen his face, so when we were twenty feet away from our friends and he turned toward me, I was astonished to see my bandit chief.

"Hsiao Lao," I said, and I glanced around me, suddenly afraid for him again. "How have you come to be here?"

He looked pleased. "You are surprised to see me?"

I laughed. "Yes. And delighted."

In the day's dim light I looked at him curiously. His clothes were worn but clean, his hair still thick and black, his high forehead smooth and unwrinkled. Although his face bore the scars of his beating that day in jail, his expression was alert and thoughtful, as it had been when I first knew him. But there was something different about him.

He said, "I am greatly in your debt, *mu shih*. I am a changed man."

"It is I who owe you. You protected my wife when I could not." Speaking was suddenly difficult. "You saved her life."

He shook his head. "I am greatly in her debt. And you have given me more than you realize, *mu shih*. You have given me new life."

"I don't know how," I said, for I had often regretted not speaking to him more ardently about my Lord when I had been his captive so long ago. Whether I had been afraid of doing so

or just young I didn't know, but something had made me reticent. "I have thought often of the days I spent with you. I had many opportunities to speak to you about my God, and yet I did not. I have regretted my silence."

He shook his head. "I learned from what you did, not what you said. You healed my son; you cared for my men; you talked with me when I could not sleep."

I thought, *I had no choice,* and I laughed to myself, knowing my behavior had been motivated far more by fear than faith.

"*Mu shih*, I saw your face when you fed me and bathed me and dressed my injuries in the jail. You had every reason to despise me and no reason to care about me, yet I saw not hate but love in your face that day. I saw that this God of yours was real to you. I decided that if He was real to you, perhaps He could be real to me as well. So I asked Him that: I asked Him to be real to me, and He answered my request. My life changed because of the life I saw in you."

He took something from his large sleeve and held out three rolled scrolls to me. "I have studied the art of portrait painting and now earn my living this way. These are a small return for the gift you have given me. Take them with you to your new home." Then he took my other hand and put something in it and I saw that I held a great deal of cash. "For your journey," he said,

and I must have looked alarmed, for he laughed. "Do not fear, *mu shih*; this is not stolen fruit. I earn my wages now." He paused for a moment. "I have also come to say goodbye, for I too am leaving."

"Where will you go?"

He smiled broadly, and his expression was as alert and animated as when I first knew him. "I am going to the north. The people there have the right to hear what I have heard, and I have a great desire to tell what has happened to me. I want to speak of this God I now know and of the new life He has given me."

I was amazed at my sweet Lord's ways. "Hsiao Lao, you have been called."

He nodded. "I have felt an invitation," he said, "and I have said yes. I have believed since I was young that every life has a purpose. Now I have found mine."

He seemed suddenly restless and he glanced around him nervously. Then he said, "You must know that I will always visit her when I am near. And that I will make a point of doing so." I did not understand his meaning at first. Seeing my confusion, he said, "You need not worry about your firstborn's grave."

Firstborn; even then, the word stung. Only-born. "You have been tending her grave?"

He nodded. "I know you do not believe in the needs and desires of the deceased as we do.

Perhaps you are right; my beliefs are changing. But perhaps there is truth in the old as well as in the new. So I will keep watch over her, in case God is busy one day or in case she is lonely. You have my word that I will not leave her alone for long, *mu shih*. From this time forward she is my own, and I will care for her."

I was deeply moved. "You are most kind, Hsiao Lao."

He shook his head. "I am no longer Hsiao Lao. I am Hsieh Kuang Sheng."

I nodded. It was common to rename oneself at turning points in one's life, such as when leaving home or starting a new business, and I was moved by the bandit's choice for his new name. *Hsieh* was to thank, *kuang* was wide or vast, *sheng* was life; his name meant he was thankful for his vast—everlasting—life. "A good fit," I said, "and one that I am certain pleases our Lord."

He smiled broadly. "When you return to your Beautiful Country, *mu shih*, take with you my gratitude to its people for sending you to us." He bowed then, and I did likewise, and as I straightened the battered old postal truck pulled up and I turned toward it for a moment. When I turned back to Hsiao Lao to thank him, he was gone, and before I could call out to him—*Thank you; goodbye; God bless you, my friend,* or any of the other things I wanted to say—I saw him

striding easily toward the city's North Gate. He did not look back.

I returned to the crowd and found Chung Hao, and when he met my eyes I felt how deeply I loved him, and I felt the great hole inside me that his absence would leave. He was wearing my father's cap, the one I had given him on New Year's so long ago, now worn thin. He took a deep breath and, in careful English that I knew he had worked hard at, he said, "You have brought us great blessedness, *mu shih*. It is a difficulty to speak my goodbye."

I couldn't answer at first. When I found my voice, I said in Chinese, "It is I who have been blessed by you." We were silent for a moment, and several times Chung Hao seemed about to speak, but stopped. I asked, "What is it?"

He put his large hand on his chest and spoke again in English. "My heart is a wound," he said softly.

"As is mine," I answered.

He said, "But you are right to go," and he looked toward Katherine.

I nodded. She was a few yards away, saying goodbye to a group of children. We had not even begun our journey, but she looked exhausted; her eyes were sunken and dark, her skin pale, and her coat hung on her thin frame. In the midst of my sorrow, I felt a wave of relief and hope for her recuperation.

Chung Hao looked back at me and said what no one else had. "I do not believe you will return to us, *mu shih*. Be happy in your new home with your wife." Then, with tears in his eyes, he patted my chest and said, *"Chih chi."*

I nodded. *"Chih chi."* It is a Chinese term not easily translated into English, meaning something like intimate friend, confidant, soulmate. But those words do not express the essence of the Chinese. *Chih* means to know, *chi* means self; together they mean to know self—a friend who knows your self—which was exactly the description for Chung Hao.

He smiled broadly, clasped my hand tightly, and said, "We will meet again on the other side."

I could only nod, then embrace my companion and my helper, my brother and my friend.

I helped Katherine into the back of the postal truck and climbed in after her, and we sat with the other passengers and their belongings on hard wooden board benches along each side. The truck's back doors were closed, the truck's motor started, and we began to move. I felt panic run through me, and I took Katherine's hand and we stood at the doors, holding on to them and to each other to keep our balance. The doors didn't quite meet, giving us a narrow view of people in the square waving, with some even following the truck through the city. The truck reached and passed through East Gate's huge arch then

followed a road that used to be a footpath and which we had traveled for more than twenty years, in heat and dust, in rain and mud and sleet. I knew the landmarks along our way by heart: the way the road curved to the right just outside the city, the large stone that marked the end of one man's land and the beginning of another's, the poplar tree that had offered me shade on countless afternoons, the deep ruts where the road dipped a little and became six inches of mud in heavy rain, the grave mounds that dotted the fields.

We passed our compound on the right, and the farther away we got, the more my heart seemed to tear. The road turned sharply south and I strained to see our home one last time. Then I saw the city wall, just as I had seen it hundreds of times when I returned from every possible direction, at every odd hour of the day and night. I remembered the first day we had come to Kuang P'ing Ch'eng, and how its name had led me to expect a graceful city bathed in a gentle glow. It had not appeared like that at first sight so long ago, but as I looked back for the last time, that was exactly how it looked: beautiful, and filled with grace.

Four days after leaving Kuang P'ing Ch'eng, we stood at the dock in Tientsin. As we waited to board the ship and leave Chinese soil, I looked at

a city that should have been familiar but wasn't; in the past I'd always been too preoccupied to notice my surroundings. I felt Katherine's gaze resting on me and our eyes met, and I read in her expression the feelings in my heart: grief, sadness, exhaustion, and comfort at the sight of her.

She started to laugh then. I thought she was crying, which would have been unlike her in such a public place. But she was laughing, and she kept laughing harder still, until she couldn't speak. I was at first irritated, then worried that her mind had been touched.

"What is it?" I asked.

She laughed harder.

"Katherine, are you all right?"

She nodded and when she had almost stopped laughing, she said, "Look at us! In Kuang P'ing Ch'eng, we were sent off like royalty. Look at this king and queen!" And she started laughing again.

Still perplexed, I looked at her. She was my own sweet wife, whom I had looked at dozens of times a day for many years. Her hair was in a bun at her neck, with Mo Yun's silver clasp holding it in place. Her cheeks were flushed, her eyes bright despite fatigue, and her smile was cheerful and familiar and strong. In her hand she held our extravagant purchase for the journey: a Sunkist navel orange from California, which we planned to share when we boarded the ship.

Then I took in the rest of her: the shapeless gray hat I did not recognize, the nondescript tweed coat I remembered buying on furlough twenty years ago, the flat black hand-me-down shoes I knew were too big. I looked down at myself: brown shoes with holes in the soles, patched woolen trousers sent from home a dozen years ago, a worn gray overcoat that had been given to me by an American doctor who had been passing through years earlier. We had tried to dress up for our journey, but I saw how shabby we looked, and how bereft, and what a contrast our appearances were to the rich lives we had led in Kuang P'ing Ch'eng. I too began to laugh, so that the two of us must have appeared greatly disturbed to those about us. But we did not care.

When we boarded the ship a short while later I recalled speaking at Mennonite churches in the United States the year we had been on furlough. People often spoke of the sacrifice Katherine and I had made in going to China. This had always sounded odd to me, for I had never thought of it as sacrifice; I had only been following the desire of my heart. But on that cool November afternoon I understood that there had been a sacrifice nonetheless, a surrendering of one thing of value for the sake of something more valuable. The sacrifice wasn't in going to China; the sacrifice was in leaving.

• • •

In December 1933, twenty-seven years after leaving for China, Katherine and I returned to Seattle, which seemed right, as it was the place from which we had embarked. We booked passage on a train to Los Angeles, and five days later we arrived at Union Station. From there we took a bus to Mission Road in Glendale and the Suppes Missionary Colony, a nondenominational community of thirty furnished bungalows available to retired missionaries, those home on furlough, and those like us—betwixt and between and in need of temporary housing.

I was gloomy during our first few weeks in Glendale; it seemed the best part of our lives was behind us. I was also disoriented, for we had returned to a country we did not know. Perhaps time affected my perceptions, but adapting to life in the United States upon our return seemed far more difficult than adapting to life in China had been when we were young. Everything was new and strange and modern and expensive, and there was much we did not know. Neither of us had ever voted in an election, used a washing machine, seen a motion picture, or learned to drive. We felt we'd come not only from another continent but from another time. When we had first arrived in China, we had learned to go backward; now we struggled to jump ahead.

What we would do next we did not know, a fact

I worried over more than I cared to admit; I could not imagine anything that would fit us or fulfill us as much as mission work. I also knew I would not be easy to place; I was too young to retire and had never pastored an American church. But then a Mennonite church in Los Angeles surprised me by inviting me to meet the congregation of a small nondenominational church that was looking for a pastor. The Mennonite church was assisting them in their search, and the pastor would not say why he thought I might be suited for this particular congregation; he said only that it was an unusual church, young but growing rapidly, and one I might find interesting. Its congregation had recently split off from the Mennonite Church to form their own community, moving to a large room on the second floor of a wholesale market.

Despite not knowing what had prompted the group to separate from the Mennonite Church, the idea appealed to me. I was finding that as I grew older I saw less need for denominations, which I viewed as human institutions, each with its good and bad. Nor did I see the need for expensive sanctuaries or complicated services or boards and committees. I had come to believe that a church was not a building or an organization but a gathering of believers, and less time spent on the extraneous meant more time to give to service. Simpler meant better.

When I expressed my interest, the pastor who telephoned arranged for two of the members of this young church to come for Katherine and me the following Sunday, so that we could attend their service, meet some of their members, and see everything for ourselves. We both woke early that day, wondering if this would be the right place for us. We were excited but also anxious; this was the closest thing either of us had ever had to a job interview and we felt suddenly young and inexperienced, though we were in our early fifties.

At nine o'clock a car pulled up in front of our bungalow and we looked nervously at each other. As we watched the driver and passenger get out of the car, we looked at each other again and began to laugh, for the man and woman walking toward our front door were Chinese. We said hello in English; then the gentleman asked if we spoke Mandarin, and when we said we did, the English portion of our morning ended.

In the car, the gentleman told us about his congregation. It was a young Chinese church that had been started by a small group of recent Chinese immigrants who, unable to find a Mandarin-speaking group, had decided to start one of their own. They had at first met at the Mennonite church; when the group became too large for that space, they moved to the wholesale market, which could seat one hundred people.

The Mennonite church had been supportive and welcoming of the new group, but the group's members felt that being independent of an established church would allow them to grow as they saw fit. They were now a non-denominational Chinese Christian church with Mandarin as their common language.

A sign in front of the warehouse read CHINESE COMMUNITY CHURCH—SUNDAY SERVICE AT 9:30 A.M. with the same information in Chinese characters underneath the English. The service was upstairs, and when Katherine and I were introduced to the congregation, we looked out at more than fifty Chinese worshippers. I bowed to the group and said, *"Ni hao."* How do you do?

A few people in the congregation nodded, but most stared at me solemnly, some suspiciously.

"Ch'eng chieh-chien," I said—I appreciate your receiving me—and saying even that short Mandarin phrase gave me joy. A few more people nodded tentatively. The kindness in their expressions brought Mo Yun to mind, and I repeated her words to us shortly before we left Kuang P'ing Ch'eng. "When you leave a place you love," I said in Mandarin, "you leave a piece of your heart."

It was as though a barrier came down; people nodded at me and smiled, and I continued. "My wife and I have left much of ourselves in China, in a city called Kuang P'ing Ch'eng in the North

China Plain. I suspect many of you have done likewise; a piece of your heart remains far away, in your home in the East. We lived in China for twenty-seven years, more than half of our lives, but God has brought us here now, to this new home. We do not know why; our future is unknown. But we have learned that He knows better than we, and that He is always worthy of our trust."

After the service we were surrounded by people, all speaking Chinese, and the sadness that I had carried with me since leaving Kuang P'ing Ch'eng eased. A few weeks later I was asked to preach at the morning service, and when I again gazed out at that Chinese congregation, I felt as nervous and unsure of myself as I had when I was a young man in China. I asked God to make me a vessel and to give me the right words, and as soon as I began speaking I felt peace and joy settle inside me. A week later I was asked to be the pastor of the church, a position I gladly accepted, and Katherine was asked to work with the women and children.

The church was growing quickly, and as the wholesale market was available to us only on Sundays, the church rented two houses nearby, the larger one to serve as the church's office and meeting rooms and the smaller one as a residence for Katherine and me. When we had been with the church for a year, a second minister joined

us, a Chinese-American preacher who spoke Cantonese, which allowed us to reach a much larger portion of the city's Chinese community. As the church continued to grow and the 9:30 service became better attended, we added additional ones and learned to make use of every bit of space. Sunday school classes met in the rental house, on the stairs or in the kitchen when necessary, and, on one rainy day, inside of a school bus. The church took a new name—First Chinese Church of Los Angeles—and a few years later, when we needed still larger quarters, we were able to purchase an old warehouse nearby and convert it into a meeting hall that could hold three hundred worshippers.

The people at First Chinese Church captured my heart from the morning we met. Because we knew where they were from, we knew them; we knew what they had left and what their customs were and what made them laugh, and to an extent we knew their pasts. I began to see that if we could not grow old in China, perhaps we could grow old with Chinese friends. And with family: for the first time in our adult lives, we had relatives nearby. Although Edward and Naomi Geisler and their older son, Paul, were still in China, the Geislers' second son, John, and their daughter, Madeleine, had settled in Southern California. John practiced medicine in Ventura, and Madeleine and her husband and children

lived in Sierra Madre, a small town east of Pasadena in the San Gabriel foothills. Our nephew and niece were kind to us to a fault; they visited often and included us in their family celebrations, and we shared any news we had from their parents and brother. To be able to know as adults the children we'd known in China was a gift I had not foreseen. It seemed a gift for them as well; we were stand-in parents and grandparents, and we knew firsthand what others never could: their lives in China.

The joy I derived from our work in Los Angeles surprised me, as did the ease of our lives, and I felt a tightness within me unravel for the first time in decades. It had to do with Katherine; I had not realized until I stopped worrying about her how concerned I had been in China. Her improved physical health in Los Angeles led me to believe that she felt the same about me. She gained weight and for the first time in her life the angles of her face softened and her body grew round and even a little plump. She slept soundly through the night, sometimes not waking until nine in the morning, formerly unheard of in our married life.

June 23, 1939

Late last night a woman from our church appeared on our doorstep. She was very distraught, and when Will brought her inside

and she had calmed down a bit, she confessed that she had stolen a pair of shoes from Woolworth's. The shoes were for her daughter, who wants to be, as she said, an up-to-date American-not-Chinese girl. The daughter had seen the shoes at Woolworth's a few days earlier and wanted them desperately, and when the woman had seen them again that day she had thought of her daughter, a good and dutiful girl. The woman didn't have enough money for them, and in that reckless moment she took them. She regretted it as soon as she was outside of the store, but was too afraid to go inside and right her wrong. Instead she hurried home and told her daughter she was ill, then hid the shoes in her closet and locked herself in her bedroom for the afternoon, crying, certain that the police were going to appear on her doorstep any moment. Only after several hours had passed and it was dark did she risk venturing outside and coming to us.

Will and I listened to her story, and I saw the kindness in Will's expression. When she finished, he spoke to her in simple English—as she is from the south of China, we don't understand her Cantonese nor she our Mandarin. "What you did was wrong," he said gently, "but your reason was your love of your daughter." He began to speak to her of faith

and of asking for God's help, instead of relying on our own flawed solutions when faced with need. He said he could see that she felt truly remorseful, and as he was concerned that if she confessed to the store she might be prosecuted, he worked out a plan with her so that she could keep the shoes and pay for them anonymously. An imperfect solution, he said, but perhaps the right one. She listened to him gratefully and agreed to his plan.

As Will spoke, I sat next to the woman on our sofa. I had made tea, and I stroked her back as she spoke, trying to calm her, for I felt her turmoil and wanted to ease her pain. In China, I helped to alleviate physical suffering; here the people suffer not so much from those ailments (though some do, and I have found myself acting as unofficial nurse) as from those of the heart. They are homesick and displaced; with their minds and hearts still in China or Hong Kong or Formosa, they work at adapting to their new lives and American ways with a determination that awes and moves me.

They have a great friend in Will, for I know he feels the same at times. I see a sadness and a sense of loss in him, despite his efforts to hide them. I know if it were not for me he would return to China, and I ache for him. He borrows the same book from the library over and over again and pores over it, rereading the author's

descriptions of life in China at the beginning of this century. I see the wistfulness and longing on his face as he reads then pauses to gaze out the window at our tidy American garden. Sometimes at the church when he is speaking in Mandarin he becomes more youthful before my eyes.

I see as never before that he would do anything for me. He already has; he's left China.

In June of 1941, our telephone rang late in the night. This was not unusual; our congregation felt the liberty to call when they needed help, whatever the hour. The caller that night was not a member of our church but our niece, Madeleine, who had herself just received the sad news she was relaying to us: her mother had passed away three days earlier. It had taken that long for Edward to send word halfway around the world from their home in the far northwest of China to southern California. Madeleine knew little of the circumstances of Naomi's death beyond the fact that she had died in her sleep.

For the next few days Katherine waited anxiously for more information about her sister's passing, from Madeleine or even from Edward himself. What she received instead was completely unexpected and unlikely: a letter from Naomi, written four months before her death.

February 12, 1941

Meine liebe Katherine,

You must be wondering whether your older sister has forgotten how to write a letter or whether she is just plain negligent. The truth is that I have sat down to write to you many times, but with the postal service as disrupted as it is due to the war, the likelihood of a letter making its way to you in faraway California has seemed so slight that I have given up before I started. So yesterday when a doctor passing through our town said he was traveling to Shanghai and would be willing to deliver my letter to someone leaving for the U.S., my heart leapt. I will send this off with many prayers and hope it finds its way into your hands.

We have moved farther west to escape the Japanese occupation and are now in the mountains of the southern part of Kansu province. Our surroundings are remote, to say the least. I see a wolf lurking about now and then, and our home is primitive—two rooms with an earthen floor, straw on wooden boards for a bed, oiled paper for windowpanes—with an assembly hall elsewhere. Edward says the house is so small that he must step outside to change his mind,

and that is just about right. Some would say we are moving backward: our lives are becoming less comfortable rather than more so, and I will admit to you that this undertaking has been more difficult than we expected. I feel older than my sixty-two years; breathing is often difficult and I am nearly always cold and uncomfortable in one way or another, all of which have caused this visiting doctor to believe I have a weak heart that is strained by the higher altitude here. Perhaps he is right, or perhaps I am simply fatigued. Whatever the case, I am at peace. My life has been fuller than I ever could have dreamed: to serve in China for forty years! I know our children are well and grounded in the faith, and I love Edward even more as we get older. His zeal increases with his age, and we are keeping on keeping on. Please pray for him, Katherine. He is not so young either.

There is but one thorn in my side: that you are not here. When you and Will came to China I imagined the two of us growing into stout old ladies together. That is not to be, but I thank God for the years we shared this continent. It is a great blessing to have a sister, and a greater blessing still when she is a sister in Christ.

Last week we had a feast, and I thought of you so. Some departing soldiers of one army

or another—bless them, whoever they are—had hidden then forgotten a stash of delicacies in the assembly hall, which they used as a barracks. Time passed and along came Edward, taking the last few pieces of wood the soldiers had stored in the cellar and finding underneath them treasures we've not seen in decades: coffee, sugar, condensed milk, and chocolate. Chocolate, Katherine! When Edward burst in on me with it all, we laughed like children, and I wished you were here so that I could share it with you. As a youngster you took such pleasure in even the smallest of treats I would bring you—a flower, a scrap of cloth, a fresh pencil, a sweet. You would hold your treasure so carefully and stare at it with such awe that I wished I could bring you something every day of the year. I would have if I could.

The doctor is waiting for my letter, and as patience does not seem to be one of his gifts, I must close. Embrace my sweet Madeleine and John for me when you see them, and forgive my brevity, little sister. But you have always known what is in my heart without my having to speak it. You are with me always, dear Katherine, as I am with you.

In Christ Jesus, our dear Lord,
Your Naomi

• • •

July 30, 1941

When I learned of Naomi's passing, I was tormented by questions I could not answer. I wanted desperately to know her state of mind, and whether she had been in pain, and if she had been unwell. Then her letter arrived, and in her peace I found my own. While her absence leaves a great chasm in my life, there is also a strange kind of relief; when I wake in the night and think of her, I am no longer afraid of the illnesses and accidents that might befall her. I know she is safe and at peace, and that I will see her again, in Paradise.

But there is sadness nonetheless. Each new loss makes the pain of earlier losses fresh again, and I have thought often of Lily's death. I've also recalled how Naomi comforted me, and I have tried to do the same for Madeleine, who is bereft without her mother on this earth. I sit with her and stroke her hair while she cries, I listen to her, and I tell her what I have learned, which is that we grieve deeply because we have loved deeply, and that we do heal. As she dries her tears, Madeleine thanks me, but when I leave her, I know it is I who should be thanking her. In consoling her I am consoled, and my sister feels as close as my breath.

Pastor Yee, the Cantonese-speaking pastor who joined our church six years after we did, was a

truly wise man, a strong Christian with a Buddhist's calm acceptance of both the world as it is and God's will. I learned a great deal from him. At one of our first meetings together, as I explained my ideas about how the church might continue to grow and thrive, Pastor Yee listened patiently without saying a word. When I finished, he still did not speak. Somewhat annoyed, I asked for his thoughts on my exciting and (to my mind) forward-thinking plans. He smiled kindly and held his hand out to me, palm up, fingers open and relaxed. "Pastor Kiehn," he said, "I have learned to hold my plans like so, with an open palm. This reminds me that they are my ideas, not God's. For when I begin to think that my thoughts and God's are one and the same, I sense amusement from my Lord."

I smiled too, for I suspected God had smiled over many of my plans. My plans for old age, for example, and for the quiet decades Katherine and I would spend together as we aged gracefully side by side. These were my plans, not His, as I was to learn.

When we had been at First Chinese Church for ten years, Pastor Yee's wife took me aside one Sunday after church and carefully asked if Mrs. Kiehn was feeling all right. Had she been ill lately? I said no, but that she was perhaps tired, and I cut the conversation short, for it was one I did not want to have.

That Katherine was failing no one knew better than I. The changes had begun so slowly that they were at first easy to ignore. At times she seemed disoriented and she struggled over small decisions such as what to wear or what to eat. She had begun to repeat things to me, sometimes in the space of several minutes, and she was becoming quieter and more withdrawn around others, whether because she couldn't hear them or because she couldn't follow the conversation I didn't know. She tired more easily, but when I encouraged her to get more rest, she bristled at my concern.

For some months I didn't worry about any of this; or, more accurately, I didn't let myself dwell on it. Because I did not want to know what I knew, I told myself that age and fatigue accounted for the changes I was seeing. I could certainly feel myself getting older, and I decided Katherine was probably seeing the same sorts of odd behaviors in me. But as time passed, I had more trouble believing my watered-down reasoning. Then Katherine's sixtieth birthday came and, with it, the end of my denial.

To supplement our income, I worked as a gardener on the days I was not needed by the church. I enjoyed this work a great deal and found it strengthened me physically and encouraged me spiritually. I had worked outside all my life, first on the farm and later in China,

and continuing to do so gave my life continuity. I pruned trees, shaped hedges, picked oranges, and weeded and mowed lawns, on Mondays at the Presbyterian Church down the street from us and on Saturdays for an elderly woman who lived in a large home surrounded by beautiful grounds, a bus ride from our home in Altadena.

Mrs. Henley was a lifelong Episcopalian and the well-to-do widow of an insurance executive, and she let me know when she hired me that she considered gardening to be beneath the pastor of a church. She said surely there was more fitting work for a man with my experience, and she often asked how much longer I would need to continue with it and seemed embarrassed when she paid me on the last Saturday of each month. I ignored her concerns; Katherine and I needed the extra income and I was grateful for the work, particularly during war time. Because of my fluency in Mandarin, I had been asked by the government to assist in translation relating to the war effort, but my Mennonite background had made me a pacifist and I declined. I had never so much as carried a firearm, and assisting the military in any way did not seem that far removed.

The second Saturday of November of 1944 was Katherine's sixtieth birthday. As I gardened that day I was glum; I had no gift for her and no money to buy one. In China we had lived from

hand to mouth because we wanted as much money as possible to go into our work; the less we spent on ourselves, the more we were able to spend on those around us. In the United States we found ourselves still living hand to mouth, for although our salary was adequate there was still much need around us and our day-to-day living was more expensive than we had ever known. We accepted these things and for the most part weren't bothered by them.

Because we had paid our rent and utilities the day before, I had no money on that Saturday, and I would not have any for another week. This wasn't the first time in our marriage I had been unable to buy Katherine a present; in thirty-six years of marriage she had received precious few gifts at all and even fewer of any value. She had always made it clear that she didn't care about possessions, but the thought of going home empty-handed that day grieved me nevertheless.

I was so downcast as I pruned the roses and trimmed the bottlebrush and bougainvillea that I didn't notice Mrs. Henley standing in the driveway until she spoke.

"Pastor Kiehn," she said solemnly.

I turned away from the bougainvillea. "Mrs. Henley?"

She seemed to evaluate me and said, "You are not yourself today."

Her comment startled me, though it shouldn't

have. She was very observant, and I was often aware of her watching me work from the bay windows on the south side of the house. "I suppose I'm not," I said.

"Is there a reason?" she asked.

I hesitated. Mrs. Henley had the ability to see through half-truths, and in the past when I had not been completely forthcoming with her, she had found me out immediately. I did not repeat my mistake. "Today is Mrs. Kiehn's birthday and I am short on funds," I said.

Mrs. Henley looked pained, and for a moment I was afraid she was going to offer to pay me early, which I didn't want, though it wouldn't have mattered anyway; it was late Saturday afternoon, and the stores had all closed. She smoothed her hands over her skirt, a habit she had when giving instructions, and said, "Then you must make do with what you have." She gestured to the garden behind me. "Take what you like, Pastor. Cut every flower, if you want. All women love flowers; surely Mrs. Kiehn is no exception."

Mrs. Henley stared out at the garden. I followed her gaze and saw blue and green hydrangeas, orange birds of paradise, red bottlebrush, and pink camellias. Along the lawn were coral roses, white hibiscus, fuchsia gerbera daisies, and yellow chrysanthemums. For a moment I felt my pride take an interest in the

proceedings, wanting to turn down Mrs. Henley's offer, but I ignored it. "That would be wonderful," I said. "Thank you."

She waved my words away and went inside.

I turned back to my work, and when it was done I took the pruning shears and several sheets of newspaper from the gardening shed and began to gather flowers in Mrs. Henley's beautiful garden for my beautiful wife. When I had wrapped it all in the newspaper, the enormous bouquet looked like a small shrub and was so large I had to hold it in both arms. As I was leaving the yard, I glanced up at the bay window and saw Mrs. Henley at her post, watching me. I held the bouquet out toward her, and she smiled and nodded her approval.

I hugged the flowers awkwardly to me as I rode the bus home, and when I got off at my stop and started toward our house, I saw Katherine waiting for me in our front yard half a block away, something that didn't surprise me, for while she didn't care about expensive gifts, she had always loved any kind of party or celebration. As I walked toward her, my heart beat like that of a young man newly in love, and when she began to walk toward me and to see what I held, she smiled as if she felt the same.

When I reached our front gate, I held out my huge bouquet and said, "Happy birthday!" I would have liked to have been holding more than

flowers, but the bouquet was truly beautiful and I expected her to be surprised.

She was, but for the wrong reason. She looked at me quizzically and said, "My birthday is in November."

Now I was confused. "I know," I said. "It's today."

"What month is it?" she said softly, her expression pained.

I felt a rush of fear at her question. Not what day is it, which I could have explained away, but what month is it. "It's November," I said, as matter-of-factly as I could. "The eleventh." And as I looked at her, I thought, *Please remember; please don't be like this.*

She nodded, but I could see she was struggling. "Of course it is," she said, and she laughed weakly. Only she didn't meet my eyes, and I was afraid to meet hers. I wanted to say, *What's wrong, Katherine? How can you not know what month it is?* But I couldn't, whether because it would be too painful for me or for her, I can't say. I know only that it was the first moment in our married life that I felt something dishonest pass between us: her not admitting her eerie confusion, and me not admitting I saw it.

But the moment passed, and we celebrated her birthday that evening with Chinese dinner and angel food cake brought by our closest friends at church, Thomas and Rebecca Kung, the couple

who had taken us there that first morning. It was a good night; Katherine's eyes were bright and she laughed and seemed very much herself, and I pushed my concerns to the back of my mind.

I awoke that night to find our bedroom lights on; Katherine was getting dressed, humming as she did. It was sometime after three o'clock in the morning.

"Are you ill?" I asked.

She seemed content, as if nothing were out of the ordinary. She did not stop humming, only shook her head. She was putting on a dress she did not much care for because she said its light-brown color looked dusty.

I was feeling irritated. "Katherine, why are you up?" I asked.

"I'm going to the grocery store," she said matter-of-factly. "We're out of milk. I'm going to call a taxi."

"But it's the middle of the night. The market won't be open for hours."

She nodded. "That's what I can't figure out. Why is it so dark?"

I was tired and cross, and beneath the crossness I was afraid. But because she seemed genuinely perplexed, I wanted to comfort her. "It's a little early," I said. "The market isn't open yet."

She was not convinced. She dressed and brushed her hair and put her shoes on and said she was going outside to wait for it to get light.

For a few minutes I stayed in bed, admitting to myself for the first time that something was truly wrong and wondering what it could be.

But I had no answer. I put on my robe and slippers and went outside and sat down next to her on the top step of the porch. I commented on how dark it was, and she agreed that this did not make sense; she couldn't understand why the sun wasn't up yet. I tried other observations, hoping she would see she was mistaken.

When my reasoning had no effect, I just held her hand as we waited together in the darkness, listening together to the sounds in the night. I don't know what Katherine was thinking. Her left hand rested on her purse, and she tapped her fingers to the hymn she was humming. As I held her other hand in mine, I thought of many other times when I had held her hand, and how familiar it was, and how, when our fingers were interlocked, I could not completely tell the difference between my fingers and hers.

After some time, she leaned her head on my shoulder, something she did in China only involuntarily, such as when she fell asleep next to me on a long train ride, but which had become habit here. I heard the familiar sound of her breathing as she relaxed.

"I had the strangest dream," she said softly. "We were in China and I was baking bread for you. Do you remember that, when I made bread

for your birthday when we were first married?"

I nodded, surprised at the sudden vividness of a memory I had not come upon for many years. She was right; we were newlyweds. I had come home late in the day after being gone for nearly a week. As I approached our home, I had thought I was crazy because I smelled bread baking. The Chinese didn't bake bread as we knew it—only steamed wheat buns called *mantou*—and in China I had longed for real bread more than just about any other food. "It was perfect. I never knew how you did it."

"It took some doing, and that's what the dream was. I had bought the wheat and was taking out the sticks and stones and clods of dirt. Then I washed the grain, dried it, and milled it by hand. I sifted the flour and mixed the dough, then kneaded it and baked it in an oven Chung Hao helped me make from a five-gallon kerosene can. It was very real."

"You did all that in your dream, or you did all that to make the bread for me?"

"Both," she said, and I felt a wave of remorse as I recalled eating nearly the whole loaf at one sitting, completely unaware of the time and effort it had required.

"In the dream I put the bread on a table for you, and after I did, I realized it was time to leave the house I was in. It wasn't really our house, just a house. But the owner had said he would not keep

repairing it, and that I should get ready to move. I didn't like this news at first, but then I saw that the owner was right; the house was wearing down. So I was getting ready to leave. When I woke up, I was just beginning to be excited about where I was going." She held my hand tightly and was quiet for a moment. Then she said softly, "I'm afraid of what is happening to me."

Because my heart ached and I had no answer for her, I said only, "I know. But we'll be all right."

A short while later we stood and went inside. Katherine put her nightgown on again and we got into bed and she fell asleep as quickly as a tired child. I did not; I lay in bed and watched the window lighten, sensing the possibility of a loss I could not fathom.

That night was a turning point, the beginning of my wife's slow leave-taking of this earth. The following week she had another episode. We were taking a walk, and with no warning whatsoever her right leg gave out from under her. She would have fallen had I not caught her; we were near a bus stop, and I helped her to the bench, where we sat down. She was very pale, and I could see she was shaken. But after a few minutes she insisted that the problem was her knee and that she felt well enough to walk home.

The next morning she gave in to my request to

see the doctor, who, after questioning her and ruling out other possible causes of decreased mental function such as thyroid disease and infections, concluded that she had experienced a series of small strokes, occurrences that seemed harmless—there was no paralysis or permanent weakness—but were nevertheless taking their toll and would in all likelihood increase in frequency and effect. Their cause, he said, was essential hypertension—high blood pressure with no known cause or cure—which was also responsible for many of the ailments that had plagued Katherine throughout her life: the headaches and fatigue and shortness of breath. When he listened to her heart, he heard an abnormality in the rhythm of its beating, and an X-ray confirmed his suspicion that the work of pumping blood at that elevated pressure had resulted in the enlargement of her heart, another possible cause of her dizziness and shortness of breath. His chief suggestions were to slow down and avoid stairs.

Before we left his office, he also spoke to me privately. My wife's symptoms, he said, would most probably worsen as the strokes intensified or became more frequent. There were, however, things I could do to help. A consistent schedule and environment helped; there should be no changes at home or in her daily routine. She might need help with familiar tasks, which could

become difficult for her; she might completely forget to do everyday things or do them incorrectly.

And so we adjusted. In an attempt to protect her from failing at things she'd done for years but might not be able to do now, I found reasons for her not to do them. I balanced our checkbook, I made out the grocery list and went with her to do the shopping, I kept our calendar. I watched her carefully and was even more careful that she not notice my observation. But try as I would, I could not stop her decline. Each month she seemed a little older and more frail, more forgetful and less herself. Her handwriting lost its sharp precision; her step faltered; her mind slowed. She was at times childlike; the woman who had stood bravely in our compound yard with the southern army's rifles trained on her became anxious when she was alone. When I left the room she watched me uncertainly, and when I left the house—which I did for shorter and shorter periods—she asked nervously when I would be home. I understood that I was losing her not all at once but a little at a time.

There were also times of clarity, moments when she was suddenly her old self. One evening a year after our visit with the doctor, she was sitting at the kitchen table slicing apples for an apple pie. She had nearly finished when I came in for a glass of water. When she saw me, she put

her knife down and smiled. "I have been having the most wonderful time," she said. "I've been in China, seeing many of our old friends."

I must have looked alarmed, because she tapped her head. "In my mind," she said, and as I sat down at the table she asked, "What do you remember the most?"

I nodded; this was the kind of question she asked often, I suspected as a way to gain information without directly asking for it. I said, "I think of the evenings. Of walking through the city at the end of the day, when the shops were closing and it was beginning to get dark. Or of nearing the compound when I was returning home from far away. I would be so tired; I would have spent all day in the city, preaching and talking to people, or I would have walked twenty miles from some little village. Maybe the day had been good, and people had seemed glad to hear something about God; maybe the day had been bad, and I had been cursed and spat on."

Katherine laughed softly. "We never could tell which it would be, could we?"

I nodded. "But either way, whatever kind of day it had been, I always felt peaceful when evening came. I liked the sounds of people talking and calling to each other in the streets as they went home. I loved evening and all those things because they meant I was coming home and that I would soon be with you."

She smiled. "You were smitten with me from the start, Will Kiehn."

"No question."

She was quiet for a time. Then she looked at me anxiously and whispered, "What if none of it was true?"

I started to laugh but her expression stopped me, and when I realized her question was serious I was shocked for a moment. But I took her hand and looked into her eyes. "I would do it all again," I said. "It was worth it, every moment."

"Yes," she said, and I could see she was relieved. "I think that's right." She was quiet for a moment, and when she spoke again her eyes were clear, her expression calm. She said, "You'll be all right without me, you know."

I could only nod, for my throat was suddenly tight, and I felt the nearness of a great fear. But I saw such compassion in her that I also felt hope, though I wasn't sure for what.

"If I'd had my choice, you would have gone first. I know how you'll be. You'll lose things and forget to eat, like you did in China when I was sick."

I nodded again.

"But He'll see you through." She squeezed my hand, a gesture as familiar as breathing, and said, "Do you remember in Kuang P'ing Ch'eng when the southern army was nearing the city and we had everyone in the worship hall?"

"Yes." It suddenly seemed more real than our kitchen.

"As we all sat there, you began to speak. Do you remember what you said?"

"Vaguely."

She nodded. "I suspect you've forgotten a lot of your best moments. That was one of them. Your faith had firm hold of you that day, *mu shih*. Without making a fuss, without standing up or really doing anything at all, you calmed everyone and gave us courage. You said, 'Whatever happens, we are victorious. Whether we live or die, we are His. We have nothing to fear.' " She squeezed my hand. "That's how I feel—that there's nothing to be afraid of. For either of us." She gazed out the window for a moment. "This growing old is the great test, you know—the challenge we've been preparing for all along."

"Yes," I said, but what I was thinking was how foolish I had been. When we left China, I had believed our trials were over. I understood at that moment that my greatest challenge lay ahead: life without my dear one.

"But God will see us through. He has never failed me—especially when he gave me you."

December 3, 1945

Last night I could not fall asleep. The world seemed dangerous and our room did not feel safe. You and I lay in bed together and you

were very still, your breathing even and deep. I thought you were asleep, and I lay next to you, praying. I could not remember how to fall asleep; there seemed to be some trick I'd forgotten. So I decided I would just stay awake all night.

After a few minutes, you said, "Katherine, is something troubling you?" I said no because I was embarrassed; I couldn't explain why I was afraid. You said, "Are you sure?" and I told you my secret. I said, "I'm afraid."

You sat up and switched on the light and turned toward me and took my hand. I thought you would tell me there was nothing to be afraid of, but instead you said, "We never know what we'll be afraid of, do we?" and you kissed the back of my hand. You said we could rest in the other room, and you took the extra quilt from the closet and we went into the living room and you let me curl up next to you on our sofa, and I fell asleep and slept through the night. I dreamed of a river, with beautiful, clear running water and big shade trees on both sides and air that smelled of narcissus.

My sweet Will, my sweet, sweet Will. A few minutes ago you brought me roses from the garden. You are so kind to me, so good. How will I ever thank you? How can I ever repay you?

I believe I could write a book about the goodness of God.

• • •

A month later, she awoke one morning with a headache. After breakfast she did the nearly unheard-of and went back to bed, and as I sat with her in the darkened room I knew that something was very wrong. She lay still when awake, but when she dozed she pulled at the sheets and seemed to be wrestling with something I could not see. My sense of foreboding was strong enough to cause me to phone for a taxicab, and Katherine did not argue. As we rode in the backseat she seemed confused about where she was, but when I reassured her that she was safe she nodded and seemed satisfied.

At the hospital I helped her to a seat in the emergency room then went to the triage nurse to try to explain what was wrong. I did not know what to say, other than that Katherine was acting strangely and that she had a headache, but when I started to speak to the nurse and motioned to Katherine, the nurse immediately called out for help and fear shot through me, for my wife was slumped in the chair, unconscious.

Almost immediately, Katherine was surrounded by nurses and a doctor who lifted her onto a gurney and wheeled her away. Their voices were urgent and hurried; I was not permitted to follow them but told to stay where I was and wait, which I did, sitting in the chair that was still warm from Katherine's body.

I do not know how much time passed before a doctor I did not know called my name. He explained that my wife had had a cerebral hemorrhage and that her condition was serious. He then led me through double doors to a room at the end of a hallway, where I found my wife, silent and unresponsive. An hour had passed since we had left home.

I sat with her throughout that day, holding her hand, speaking to her, praying as much for myself as I did for her, for I was terrified of losing her. In my heart I clung tightly to her and knew I was not leaving her in God's care, but I was afraid to do so. I had telephoned John and Madeleine, and Thomas Kung from our church, and many members of our congregation came and went during that day, praying for Katherine. I could not name any of them. I was aware only of my wife.

Her skin became cool to my touch, her breathing irregular. At eight o'clock in the evening visiting hours ended and hospital rules dictated that I leave. In the several hours since she had lost consciousness her expression had become relaxed and peaceful, the lines of worry and fatigue fading from her countenance. Before I left for the night I kissed her and gave thanks for her for the hundredth time that day. Then I went home alone.

A few hours later the telephone's loud ring

broke the stillness of our home. I was awake and knew before I answered it what the call was: my dear wife had passed away. She had not suffered; she had not regained consciousness. She had simply not awoken and was now no longer on this earth.

For many years I had had the sense that Katherine's time would come before mine. I had in a way accepted this, and I had asked to be strong when that time came, for I was certain I would be with her when she died. That I wasn't grieved me deeply.

The days immediately following her death are unclear in my memory. I know that Madeleine and Pastor Yee's wife dressed her body for burial in Chinese clothes and black felt shoes that had been purchased for that purpose. I know I also wanted her to have Mo Yun's silver clasp in her hair, and I nearly drove myself mad trying to find it, berating myself severely when I could not. I know I was surrounded by people and food; more than three hundred members of our congregation attended her funeral at our church and filed in and out of our home for several days. I know I slept very little and wept a great deal; I was bereft, home to a sorrow more painful and profound than anything I had ever imagined.

For a while her passing felt like a temporary absence, as though she had simply gone away for

a few days. She had been my sounding board and confidante for so many years that I thought constantly of things I wanted to talk to her about—a news item or something that was bothering me—and again and again I thought, *I must tell Katherine*. Then I would remember she was gone, the realization new and painful each time.

The absence deepened, and for the first time in my life, I felt old. I had trouble paying attention to people, but being alone was no better, and I came to dread the emptiness and the quiet of our house. In the past there had never been enough time for all I wanted to do, but with Katherine gone I had no idea how to pass the hours in each day. I saw how much she had encouraged me and pushed me, how she had kept me on track. Now I wanted only one thing: for her to return. I wanted her to sit next to me and ask about my day, to walk with me after dinner, to be asleep next to me in our bed. But the more I longed for her, the more my ability to vividly recall her faded. I could picture her, but I could not recall her voice, and it tormented me.

As those first months passed, I began to question many of the decisions I had made in my life, and my prayer became a petulant litany of complaint; I spoke to God as though He were an incompetent employer, pointing out how things could have been better if Lily had lived, if

Katherine and I had had more years together, if we had been able to grow old in China. I had read that many of the churches built by missionaries were being destroyed by the Communists or used for other purposes, and I began to feel we had labored in vain. None of our work seemed to count from so far away. With so little to show for it, what had it all been for? I had no answer, nor, it seemed, did He. My doubts shamed me and I chastised myself for what I saw as my lack of faith. What had been the point of all my years of believing if my trust faltered when I needed it most?

On an autumn morning nine months after Katherine's death I received a call from Madeleine with news of her father. I knew Edward had suffered a fall several months earlier, and that his health had become such that he felt it necessary to return to the United States. Madeleine was calling to say that he would arrive on the *President Madison* at San Pedro Harbor the following Saturday; the family would meet the ship then welcome him at a party at her home in Sierra Madre, and she was hoping I would join them.

I had not seen Edward since before Katherine and I left China thirteen years earlier, and that Saturday I awoke early, filled with anticipation about the prospect of our reunion. As I sat at the

window watching for my niece's blue Packard, I became so immersed in thoughts of the past that when she greeted me I had to stare at her for a moment to reorient myself. Seeing my strange look, she asked, "Uncle Will, are you all right?"

"How old are you, Madeleine?"

She laughed, and in that moment she looked so much like her mother that I was stunned. She said, "Just between you and me, I'm forty-one."

I shook my head, trying to put things together. It did not seem possible that the middle-aged woman standing in front of me was the baby Naomi had held on our first night in Ch'eng An Fu. "Don't ever get old," I said. "It can be most disconcerting."

Madeleine's husband and two children were in the car. We drove to the harbor and waited with her brother John and his family and dozens of other onlookers for the ship to appear on the horizon. When it came into sight and then docked, I felt a burst of hope. Passengers began to disembark, and although I knew it was irrational, I watched eagerly for the man I had known in China: the tall frame and long even stride, the straw hat, wide grin, and thick dark hair. We waited and then we waited some more as a line of excited passengers filed down the gangplank, but no Edward. Suddenly Madeleine, standing next to me, caught her breath and said softly, "Oh, Dad." For a moment I was confused;

I didn't see him. Then I realized with a start that the elderly man being brought off the ship in a wheelchair was he. At the bottom of the gangplank he motioned for the steward to stop, then he carefully stood and waited for us to make our way to him.

The sight of him was a blow. Though he was only ten years older than I—seventy-two to my sixty-two—he looked far older, the result of a harder life. As he embraced his children and grandchildren, he leaned heavily on a cane, and I saw how frail he was. He was several inches shorter than I instead of taller, his blue eyes were clouded by cataracts, and his body was stooped, his hair thin and white.

But when the family made space for me and our eyes met and we embraced and exchanged a holy kiss, the younger man seemed to reappear. I saw the same zeal I'd seen in him when we met in Oklahoma, and I clasped his hand in mine, amazed he was really there. "Edward, my old friend!"

His eyes brightened and he smiled broadly. "Kung P'ei Te," he said, and the sound of my Chinese name nearly undid me, *"Shao-chien shao-chien."* I have missed seeing you.

I did not hesitate. *"Pi-tz'u pi-tz'u."* The feeling is mutual.

The afternoon was indeed a celebration. Madeleine's home was decorated with balloons

and streamers, and the house was filled with the easy conversation of family and the laughter and shouting of five grandchildren who until that day had not met their grandfather. Twenty years had passed since Edward's last visit to the United States, and there was much for him to catch up on.

Late in the afternoon the children escaped to a nearby park, and when the adults withdrew to the kitchen to clean up from the meal, Edward and I were left alone. He was sitting in a yellow wing chair next to an arbor window and seemed fatigued but peaceful. I glanced at his plate and saw he had eaten less than half of what he had been served: turkey and gravy, mashed potatoes and green beans, fruit salad and a roll, probably three times as much as he was accustomed to eating at one meal. I knew Madeleine had put a great deal of thought into the day's menu; she had so wanted to please her father and had quizzed me several times about what sort of American food he liked. I did not tell her that while I knew her father well, there was no reason for me to know what he liked to eat in the United States and my suggestions had been guesses.

He motioned to his uneaten food and laughed softly. "I believe my appetite is still crossing the Pacific. We'll see how long it takes to catch up." Then he breathed in the fresh air from the open window and said, "It smells like China."

I nodded. "Someone has a fire in their fireplace."

He breathed in again. "The air always smelled of smoke in Ch'eng An Fu. When I was returning home from some village or faraway town, it told me I was getting close to the city again."

"Smoke meant home," I said.

"Exactly so, *mu shih*." He paused for a moment, then said, "May we continue in the standard language? My old mind is more comfortable there."

I was delighted. "Nothing could please me more," I said.

We fell easily into Mandarin. Edward talked of his time in the remote northwest of China and I of the church in Los Angeles, and when we finished with the present we began working backward, reminiscing about our early years in the Middle Kingdom. We talked of Katherine and Naomi and of Christmases we had spent together, of our successes and failures. We recalled the particulars of that time and place: the loud squeak of a cart's wheels on a rutted road, the clean scent of wheat fields after the rain, the sound of townspeople bargaining excitedly at the market, the taste of steaming noodles with vinegar and cayenne bought from a street vendor on a cold day. My dear China came to life, and I missed her deeply.

I thought Edward was feeling similarly, but

when I looked at him I saw not sadness in his expression but wonder. He said, "To love a *place*. To hold it so dearly that one aches at the memory of it. Are we not most fortunate?" Then his countenance darkened. "But my Lord's largesse troubles me at times; I am at a loss as to how to return His love. I have given Him my all, yet it seems I have done so little." He looked at me with tears in his eyes. "There was so much more yet to do."

I was at first shocked by his words; I knew of no one who had given himself more completely to God. I started to say this but found myself unable to speak, for I realized he had uncovered a secret I had not voiced to Katherine or anyone else: my regret in leaving so much unfinished in Kuang P'ing Ch'eng. I was suddenly overcome with losing China and Katherine and our work there, and I blurted out in English what I had never intended to. "Edward, I am in such pain," I said. "I am so angry, and this desolation seems to have no end."

I was immediately ashamed, but Edward nodded matter-of-factly. "This part of the journey is not so easy," he said quietly. "This forging ahead alone after the years together."

I stared hard at my hands. I could not meet his eyes and keep the little composure I had. "No," I said. "It is not easy."

Edward gazed through the window at the

orderly suburban street outside. "When Naomi passed, I asked God to take away the pain. I believed He could, and I pointed out to Him that doing so made sense. *Spare me this grief so I can get back to work,* I told Him. But He didn't; He saw me through the pain, but He didn't take it away." Edward turned to me. "He honors our sorrow by allowing us to experience it. How else to deepen us? How else to increase our trust? Instead of fighting the pain, He asks us to surrender to it. Only then can it begin to heal us." Edward looked at me then with great compassion. "Thank Him for the emptiness. He will fill it when He sees fit."

The adults started to drift back into the room then, and soon the children came spilling in, and the festivities began to draw to a close. Madeleine said she would drive me home if I was ready and I accepted; I was suddenly very weary.

Although I was tired, the afternoon had cheered me. I felt a comfort in Edward's presence that I'd not found anywhere since Katherine's death, and the prospect of seeing him regularly encouraged me. But when I said goodbye to Madeleine in front of my home and went inside and closed the door behind me, a despair unlike anything I had ever known descended upon me. Every other time I had traveled—in China, in Los Angeles, whenever I

left home—I had always returned to Katherine; she was always there to greet me. That afternoon I understood for the first time what her passing meant: I would not see her again on this earth. The enormity of that fact seemed to drop to the bottom of my soul, and after I had let myself into the house and walked from room to room for a while, I sat down at our small kitchen table. In my anguish I asked my absent wife, "Surely you cannot have deserted me?" The only answer was silence, and I voiced the heavier question in my heart: "Surely You cannot have deserted me?"

I sat in the late-afternoon quiet for some time, listening to the even sound of my own breathing, and my eyes fell upon Katherine's Bible. It had been a gift from her father before she left for China, and I had found her reading it most mornings of our lives together when I arose, whether in Kuang P'ing Ch'eng or in Los Angeles. Its spine and cover were worn, its pages thin. I took it from the kitchen shelf where Katherine had kept it with her medical books, and when I opened it, my eyes found a handwritten note on the inside back cover:

We often wait for God with hope. But sometimes we must wait for hope. We may feel nothing, but we do not rely on our feelings. When we don't feel hope, we wait for it, and it always comes.

The date next to these words was October 11, 1917—six months after our daughter's death.

I read these words several times, for they soothed me. The idea of waiting for hope was one I could grasp, and I began to see that I would not feel this way forever. I felt something give way inside, and despite the deep sadness there was also relief.

From that night on I yielded to my sadness. I began to speak to God more forthrightly than I ever had in my life before, unburdening myself to Him, confiding in Him, questioning Him, even railing against Him. Doing so often made me ill at ease; a part of me feared my outbursts might cause God to distance Himself. But I continued to reveal myself to Him, and His Presence became imbued with a fierceness I had never known, as though He were clinging to me as much as I was to Him. When the pain was great, I thanked Him for it. Not always sincerely, but I said the words and trusted that that was enough.

A month passed, and one night I slept for nearly twelve hours and woke feeling more rested than I had for a long time. I was in no hurry to get up, and as I lay there not really thinking of anything in particular I suddenly remembered Katherine so vividly that it was as if she were lying there beside me. All at once I could see her expression, hear her voice and her laugh, feel her hand on my shoulder, even smell

the soap she used. I realized I was not merely remembering her; she was somehow truly present, and though unseen, her presence was as real as anything else in my bedroom. It seemed I could feel the weight of her in the bed next to me, and I was as surprised and joyful as if I had met her unexpectedly on the street. She was as real as I was and I knew—*I knew*—she was there.

On my walk that morning, I breathed in the cool air that precedes rain, and at breakfast the strawberry jam on my wheat toast was sweet and good, and I thanked Him for it. In the afternoon a neighbor whose husband had recently passed on hailed me from her driveway. This woman liked to talk, and although I usually didn't enjoy hearing her detailed stories of their lives together in the Philippines—the stories alternated between too long and too intimate—I always listened anyway, for it seemed she needed to tell them to someone. But that day I listened to her in a way I hadn't before, and as she spoke of her husband and of places they'd traveled and lived, I heard how much she had loved him and how blessed she had felt when he was near, and I heard her grief and sorrow. Later, when I asked God to give her comfort and healing, I found I was the one who had been comforted.

That night as I knelt in prayer to give thanks for my day, something under the bed caught my

eye. When I investigated I was at first puzzled then amazed to find the silver hair clasp given to Katherine by Mo Yun in Kuang P'ing Ch'eng, the very thing I had hunted for like a madman after Katherine's death. I have no idea how it came to be there, or how I had missed it when I'd searched high and low after her death. I know only that it was there, and I clutched it gratefully throughout that night, fully convinced it was a tangible gift from my intangible Lord, evidence of His loving and unpredictable crazy-quilt ways.

A few weeks later I awoke with a feeling I had not had for some time: a sense of anticipation, of wondering what the day might hold and how I might be useful. My sturdy old heart began to beat faster at the idea that I might still be of service to my Lord and at the possibilities of what might yet lay ahead in this life. From that time on I began to heal, and to wind my way back to a good and joyful life.

Think and Want, Family and Home

1966

It has been twenty years since my wife's passing and, although there are days where I still miss her deeply, I have not felt the darkness and despair of that time again. I dream of her often, good dreams that are like brief visits with her, and I feel in some strange way that we are still married. I find myself wanting to be a good husband. I turn to her often in gladness, I speak to her as though she is beside me, and I give thanks for her; and when I do these things, I feel her near. Chung Hao once told me that the dead are sensitive to our thoughts and do not wish for us to be sorrowful; he said our grieving worries them and prevents them from living the new life they are to live. I have come to agree with this.

Though still the man my wife loved, I am old now, eighty-one last month. I continued as pastor of First Chinese Church for nine years after Katherine's death, good years that were filled with purpose and hard work and with frequent visits with Edward until his death in 1951. When I reached the age of seventy I felt it time to retire, less because I wanted to than because I believed the church would benefit from a younger pastor.

Also, around that time I began experiencing a few health problems of my own—occasional shortness of breath, increasing aches and pains—and because I did not want to worry my congregation or my nephew or niece, I chose to leave the house I had shared with Katherine and move into the retirement home where I now live. While it's true that I am assured of everything I need here, including the built-in companionship of other residents and hospital care if and when I require it, coming here has not been easy. It is odd to know that this is where I will most likely live out my days, and I do not think of it as home. But moving here seemed to be the right decision, and I have made peace with it.

Although I still do not understand the death of my daughter, I have made something approaching peace with that as well, and each year on the day of her birth I think of her with love and joy and I give thanks for her brief life. I have no idea why Lily was taken from us; perhaps each soul has its time. To search for a reason more than that seems futile. I have come to accept that at present I have only a partial view of reality; there are answers I will not be given until I leave this life. I know that my Lord is the God of wheat fields and oak trees, of mountains and valleys, and that His answers, like His works, often require time.

My days and nights are uncomplicated now. I

rise early and follow a schedule of prayer, for I believe that is how I am best able to serve at this time in my life. On Sunday mornings, Thomas and Rebecca Kung come for me and we attend the ten o'clock service at First Chinese Church, which now holds five services each Sunday, three in Mandarin and two in Cantonese. After church, the three of us walk to a nearby Chinese restaurant for lunch, where our conversation continues in Mandarin, and when I return here in the late afternoon, I feel nourished in every way. In the afternoons I read, although at this point in my life I have given most of my books away, for I realize that one of these days I will go to sleep and not wake again, and I do not want someone else to be burdened with the task of sorting through my belongings. The books I've kept have been part of my life: Katherine's journal and her worn copy of *The Home Physician*, which she was never without in China; her Bible; my Chinese Bible, which I could not read when Edward gave it to me in 1906 and which is now the only Bible I read. I also have some classics of Chinese philosophy—*The Analects*, *The Great Learning*, and *The Doctrine of the Mean* by Confucius, *The Works of Mencius*, and the *Tao Te Ching* by Lao Tzu—given to me when I arrived in China by Li Lao Shih, who said these books were found in nearly every Chinese home. They have become my respected and beloved old

friends. There is also the book about China that I checked out so frequently from the public library when we first returned to the United States. After borrowing it for ten years I saw my worn and dog-eared copy at the library book sale, so I own it now and have the luxury of reading it whenever I want.

My life is colored by unexpected moments of grace, small awarenesses of God's presence that speak to me of who He is as much as any mountaintop experience. The huge old red roses that bloom on the grounds here tell me of His deep and passionate love, and the heavy slate-gray storm clouds on a winter's day speak of His strength. The painstaking construction of a snail and its beautiful slow progress tell me of God's attention to the smallest details of my life, and the leaves falling crazily from the sycamore tree remind me that He is a Mystery I cannot fully comprehend. At night when I look up into the heavens and see the same stars I saw in China's skies so many years ago, it is as if they have been my companions all these years and witnesses to my life in China. They tell me of God's constancy and of a love that will not let me go.

A strange sort of arithmetic is at work in my life. While the calendar tells me that Katherine and I spent twenty-seven years in China, that thirty-three years have passed since we left, and

that I have been without her for nearly twenty years, these numbers do not ring true. I feel instead like a man who lived nearly all his life in China, with a few of his later years in America, and a few of those without his companion. Also, the longer I am away from Kuang P'ing Ch'eng, the more my mind dwells there. My room here is on the west side of the building, the one closest to China, something that perhaps sounds foolish but that nevertheless pleases me. Each morning when I begin my daily walk, I start out by heading west, toward China. At times my life there seems almost imagined; bandits and soldiers and magistrates, floods and droughts and famines and war, seem as distant as the moon. On other days it is the present that feels imagined and Kuang P'ing Ch'eng that seems more real than the poached egg and toast I eat for breakfast. Certain smells make China instantly real to me: anything cooked with garlic, freshly cut wood, antiseptic, the crispness of the air on the first autumn day. These scents stop me in my tracks.

I follow the news of what is happening in that country intently. Edward and Naomi's older son, Paul, was forced to leave mainland China in 1951 with many other missionaries, but he has his father's ardor and he continues to serve in Taiwan. I know that Kuang P'ing Ch'eng was occupied by the Japanese and fell to the

Communists in the late 1940s. I have read that mission compounds were looted and ransacked during these tumultuous years; one report described a worship hall being used as a gambling den. The establishment of the People's Republic in 1949 changed the Christian church in China permanently and dramatically, and while the new government allowed churches to meet under certain conditions, authorities soon took control of church property, and the church has suffered. These reports tear at my heart.

But if I were younger I would go back, for while I am thankful for the care I receive here, with Katherine gone this comfortable life is uncomfortable, and this continent feels more foreign every year. I believe I could still be of use, despite my age and decreasing stamina, and I envision the trip—the days at sea followed by the days overland—and imagine what I would take with me. I would not require much, only some bedding, a few pots and pans, a little cash. I would not take many clothes, for I would prefer Chinese clothes again. Then I remember how greatly changed everything must be. People travel to China by air now, not by sea, and the cities in the interior are linked to Peking and the port cities not by carts and wagons but by modern trains and planes. In Kuang P'ing Ch'eng, what once were footpaths must be wide paved roads, what once were fields are no doubt

factories, and what was my beloved old city must be a busy urban center. At present it is not even possible to go to mainland China. I know in my heart I will not return, and I do not nurture these thin hopes.

When I wake in the early morning, I get down on my stiff old knees to thank my Lord for another day. My mother taught me to place my shoes under the bed at night so that I would have to kneel in the morning to get them, for when we thus humble ourselves He cannot deny us. It is a habit I still practice, and with my head bowed, I give thanks for my sweet Katherine and for our Lily, and for my parents and Edward and Naomi. I pray for Paul and John and Madeleine and their children, for my congregation in Los Angeles, and for the people I loved in China: Chung Hao, Mo Yun, Hsiao Lao, the magistrate and his wife, and the members of our church. Then I pray for Kuang P'ing Ch'eng and the country itself, and I feel a familiar homesickness. The Mandarin word for homesick is *hsiang chia*. *Hsiang* is to think or want, and *chia* is family or home, and the combination of these words describes my feeling well: I think and want family and home. As I've aged, this feeling of longing has intensified and become my companion. I have come to see it as a gift; being homesick feels right, a reminder that this earth is not my home. My ties to this world become more tenuous with

each passing year, and the more deeply I feel this, the closer I feel to Christ.

Lastly I pray that throughout the day God's will, not mine, be done, whatever that may mean. When I was younger, I thought it meant traveling a road that was straight and confining and predictable, something to be done correctly, like finding my way through a maze where only one path is right. I thought following that path would always feel true and safe and virtuous and that it would give me a surefooted, foolproof sense about life. This narrow thinking was mine, not His; I no longer believe it. When I am in God's will, sometimes I do feel comfortable and at ease, but I just as often feel anxious and unsettled, for He often leads me into unfamiliar waters. I do not let these feelings guide me. Nor do I heed what the world must think of me, for I know that in its view my life would seem a failure. Some would look at me and see a childless widower, living alone, his life's work in question. But I think of myself as extraordinarily blessed, rich beyond measure, the unlikely recipient of the great honor of serving my Lord in a faraway land, and I am amazed at my great good fortune.

Over time I have come to believe that God's will is a mystery, fluid and surprising. Following it is like stepping out into something I cannot see, and I am frequently unsure about whether I

am doing God's will until after the fact. But I have learned that while I don't always know when I'm doing something right, I always know when I'm doing something wrong, and I rely on this as I go forward, trusting that He will use my mistakes as well as my triumphs and knowing that He does not ask me to be perfect, or even good. He simply asks me to be His, which to me is the heart of His Good News: that I am deeply and passionately loved exactly as I am, despite the faults that grieve me most, by a God who delights in me more than I can know—a God who created me so He could love me. With the gift of that renewed certainty when I awake each morning, I rise to meet the day and to praise my dear Lord, and to finish my course with joy.

ACKNOWLEDGMENTS

City of Tranquil Light is based on the lives of my maternal grandparents, Peter and Anna Schmidt Kiehn, who were Mennonite and later Nazarene missionaries in China and Taiwan from 1906 to 1961. Late in his life, my grandfather wrote a memoir, *The Legacy of Peter and Anna*, which was privately published, so that his grandchildren would know of his work. Those pages gave me a start for the novel; I then read the biographies of other missionaries who served in China. The characters of Naomi and Edward Geisler were based on my grandmother's older sister, Nellie, and her husband, Henry Bartel, who served in China for most of their lives; their biography, *This Mountain Is Mine* by Margaret Epp, was invaluable in terms of inspiration and information, as was the biography of their son, Paul, and his wife, Ina: *Giants Walked Among Us: The Story of Paul and Ina Bartel* by Anthony G. Bollback. The biographies of the following missionaries also moved me and added greatly to the novel: Edward Bliss Sr. (*Beyond the Stone Arches* by Edward Bliss Jr.), Gladys Aylward (*The Small Woman* by Alan Burgess), Thomas and Eva Moseley (*Moh Ta-Iu, Man of Great Plans* by Eva M. Moseley), and Reuben and Janet Torrey (*Ambassador to Three Cultures:*

The Life of R. A. Torrey Jr. by Clare Torrey Johnson). The autobiography of Ruth Hemenway (*A Memoir of Revolutionary China, 1924–1941* by Ruth V. Hemenway, M.D.), who served as a medical missionary, was also informative and inspiring.

A note on the romanization of Chinese names and phrases: I have used the Wade-Giles system, which was in use from the nineteenth century until 1958, when the People's Republic of China introduced pinyin, the current system of romanization.

I received many gifts during the writing of the novel. My mother, Hester Caldwell, gave me the idea for it by telling me for many years that the story of her parents' lives would make a wonderful book. She shared her memories about her childhood in China and about my grandparents, and she gave me photographs from their years in China. She also read the novel in several versions over several years and cheered me on, as she always has.

For their steady encouragement and emotional support, I'm grateful to Nita Willis and Bill Riney. I'm indebted to my longtime friend Tony Lee for his help with Chinese culture and traditions, and to my brother, Dan Caldwell, for his valuable contributions to my research in the form of old files, rare books, and tapes of

interviews he recorded with our grandfather a few years before his death. My aunt, Helen DeSimone, patiently answered my questions, generously shared memories of her childhood in China, and read early drafts of the novel. I'm also grateful to other early readers: Heather Washam; Fr. Tenny Wright, S.J.; and Paul Capobianco. My agent, Paul Cirone of The Friedrich Agency, encouraged me greatly and offered astute comments on the novel's early drafts, and my editor, Helen Atsma at Henry Holt, pared the manuscript down and worked wonders in the way of polishing and focusing. For its financial support early on, I'm grateful to the National Endowment for the Arts.

From my husband, Ron Hansen, always my first reader, I received all these gifts and more. He paid the bills, read and reread chapters, listened to my woes, and offered wise criticism, calm perspective, and hope.

Thank you, all. I'm grateful to you, and thankful for you.

ABOUT THE AUTHOR

BO CALDWELL grew up in Los Angeles and attended Stanford University, where she also held a Wallace Stegner Fellowship in Creative Writing and a Jones Lectureship in Creative Writing. She has received a fellowship in literature from the National Endowment for the Arts and the Joseph Henry Jackson Award from the San Francisco Foundation, among other awards. Her personal essays have appeared in *O: The Oprah Magazine*, the *Washington Post Magazine*, and *America Magazine*, and her short stories have been included in *Story*, *Ploughshares*, *Epoch*, and other literary journals. Her first novel, *The Distant Land of My Father*, was a national bestseller. She lives in northern California with her husband, novelist Ron Hansen.

Center Point Publishing
600 Brooks Road ● PO Box 1
Thorndike ME 04986-0001 USA

(207) 568-3717

US & Canada:
1 800 929-9108
www.centerpointlargeprint.com

East Smithfield Public Library
3 2895 00116 8892